DECLAN REEDE: THE UNTOLD STORY
(BOOK 4)

MICHELLE IRWIN

COPYRIGHT

DEDICATION:

To you, dear reader, for sticking with Declan (and me) through it all.

DECLAN REEDE: THE UNTOLD STORY

Decide (Book #0.5)

Decline (Book #1)

Deceive (Book #2)

Decipher (Book #3)

Declare (Book #4)

CONTENTS:

GLOSSARY:

Note: This book is set in Australia, as such it uses Australian/UK spelling and some Australian slang. Although you should be able to understand the novel without a glossary, there is always fun to be had in learning new words. Temperatures are in Celsius, weight is in kilograms, and distance is (generally) in kilometres (although we still have some slang which uses miles).

Arse: Ass.
AVO: Apprehended Violence Order.
Bedhead: Headboard.
Bench: Counter.
Bitumen: Asphalt.
Bonnet: Hood.
Boot: Trunk.
Bottle-o: Bottle shop/liquor store.
Buggery: Multiple meanings. Technically bugger/buggery is sodomy/anal sex, but in Australia, the use is more varied. Bugger is a common expression of disbelief/disapproval.
Came down in the last shower (Do you think I): Born yesterday
CAMS: Confederation of Australian Motor Sport.
Cherry (Drag racing): Red light indicating that you "red-lighted"/jumped the start.
Cock-ups: Fuck-ups/mistakes.
Dagwood Dogs: Corndogs
Diamante: Rhinestone.
Dipper: See S Bends below.
Do (Charity Do): Function/event.
Dob: Tell on.
Doona: Blanket/comforter.
Fairy-Floss: Cotton candy.
Fillies: Girls.
Footpath: Sidewalk.
Formal: Prom.
Fours: Cars with a four-cylinder engine.

HANS: Head And Neck Support.

Loo: Toilet.

Message bank: Voicemail.

Mirena: An IUD that contains and releases a small amount of a progesterone hormone directly into the uterus.

Mozzies: Mosquitoes.

Necked: Drank from.

Newsagency: A shop which sells newspapers/magazines/lotto tickets. Similar to a convenience store, but without the food.

Off my face: Drunk/under the influence (including of drugs).

Pap: Paparazzi.

Panadol/Paracetamol: Active ingredient in pain-relievers like Tylenol and Panadol.

Pavlova: Meringue-based desert, usually served covered with fresh cream and seasonal fruits (aka: sugar heaven).

Phone/Mobile Phone/Mobile Number: Cell/cell phone/cell number.

Prep (school): Preparation year.

Privateer: Someone who finances their own races.

Real Estate: All-inclusive term meaning real estate agency/property management firm.

Rego: Registration (general); cost of vehicle licence.

Ricer: Someone who drives a hotted up four-cylinder (usually imported) car, and makes modifications to make it (and make it look) faster.

Rugby League: One of the codes of football played in Australia.

S bends (and into the Dipper): Part of the racetrack shaped into an S shape. On Bathurst track, the Dipper is the biggest of the S bends, so called because there used to be a dip in the road there before track resurfacing made it safer.

Sandwich with the lot: Sandwich with the works.

Schoolies: Week-long (or more) celebration for year twelves graduating school. Similar to spring break. The Gold Coast is a popular destination for school leavers from all around the country, and they usually have a number of organised events, including alcohol-free events as a percentage of school leavers are usually under eighteen (the legal drinking age in Australia).

Scrag: Whore/slut.

Scrutineering: Process of going over the car and rules to ensure there is no corruption or mistakes.

Shout (referring to drinks or food): Buy for someone. "Get the tab."

Silly Season: Off season in sports. Primarily where most of the trades happen (e.g. driver's moving teams, sponsorship changes etc).

Skerrick: Scrap.

Slicks: A special type of racing tyre with no tread. They're designed to get the maximum amount of surface on the road at all times. Wet weather tyres have chunky tread to displace the water from the track.

Skulled: (can also be spelled sculled and skolled) Chugged/Drank everything in the bottle/glass.

Soft Drinks: Soda/pop.

Stiff Shit: Tough shit/too bad.

Sunnies: Sunglasses.

TAFE: (Technical And Further Education) Trade school

Tassie: Tasmania (in the same way Aussie = Australia)

Taxi: Cab.

Thrummed: Hummed/vibrated.

Tossers: Pricks/assholes/jerks.

Tyres: Tires.

Year Twelve: Senior.

Wag: Ditch school.

Wank: Masturbate

Wankers: Tossers/Jerk-offs.

Weet-Bix: Breakfast cereal brand.

Whinge: Whine/complain.

Uni: University/college.

CHAPTER ONE

MOVING ON

I PULLED MY car into the cemetery car park and cut off the engine.

With it off, the silence in the car was stifling. I didn't even need to look at Alyssa to know that her expression would probably match my own.

Sombre.

Today was the day. The day Alyssa and I would move forward with the rest of our life. First though, we had to look to the past.

"Are you ready?" I asked, grasping her hand to ground myself and show her that I was there for her. Neither of us desired to be the first from the car. Even though the keen agony of regret sliced through me, Alyssa's pain was greater than mine. She'd suffered through the heartbreak firsthand, and I'd only learned of it years later, when it was too late to mourn with her.

Alyssa turned to me, her honey-gold eyes filled with tears, and shook her head. She ran her free hand through the fringe of her mahogany hair. "I don't even know how to do this, Dec. I—I already said goodbye to him once, I don't know how to do it again."

How could we say goodbye knowing it could be months,

maybe even as long as a year, before we could come back to visit again?

I held her hand in mine and gave it a gentle squeeze, trying to offer her some strength even though I had none left to give. Part of me wondered whether it was harder for her having me there. Whether my presence was a sharp reminder of the fact that I wasn't there when she'd needed me.

Eventually, with a small sigh that echoed her heartbreak, Alyssa turned to me and nodded once.

I climbed from the car. By the time I'd reached the front, she still hadn't moved.

Realising she needed a figurative push, I opened her door and offered her my hand to help her out of the high vehicle. She practically fell into my arms, so I wrapped them around her as fast as I could. I wondered whether her mind was solely on the cemetery in front of us, or whether part of it was still thinking back over the events of the night before. In the harsh light of day, facing our last visit to our son, I thought back to how stupid I'd been. I'd risked losing Alyssa, risked my happiness and the happiness of my family, for what? Revenge? I was such a fucking tool.

After a moment, Alyssa pulled away from my hold and reached for my hand. The sun beamed brightly in the sky as we weaved our way through the plots to the back, to my family plot and the little angel we sought. Halfway through the cemetery, Alyssa and I dropped each other's hands. Maybe it was because this goodbye was one we had to face alone, or maybe neither of us had anything left to give.

My feet were on autopilot, remembering the way from my last visit such a short time ago. As it had then, the first thing that captured my eye was the cold white marble cherub. He sat with his head buried in his hands while his white wings extended out from his shoulders. My gaze fell to the horses on the tombstone, the symbol of Castor and Pollux.

Of Gemini.

Of the Twins.

I could almost feel the horses tattooed onto my back come alive, as if granted some magical power from the proximity to their inspiration. I didn't need to read the inscription on the stone; it had been burned onto my heart the first time I'd seen the grave.

A name: *Emmanuel Pollux Reede Dawson.*

Two dates: *11th June* and *14th June.*

And an epitaph: *An angel opened the book of life and wrote down my baby's birth. Then she whispered as she closed the book, "Too beautiful for earth."*

As if she was reciting them again, Alyssa's words when she'd first told me the story of Castor and Pollux came to mind. Then something she'd admitted to me later—that Emmanuel had been a replica of me. I wondered whether he'd have grown to have my turquoise eyes, like Phoebe, or if they would have darkened to Alyssa's honey-gold. Would his hair have been the same auburn as mine, or the richer brown of his mother?

I sensed rather than felt Alyssa by my side. The distance between us was gaping, but I wasn't ready to attempt to bridge it yet. Neither of us were, it seemed. We both needed time alone to process, to think. It occurred to me that at least this visit wouldn't be like my last.

Then, I'd felt nothing but desolation and destruction, tearing at me from inside and with no way to return from the agony. Just like then, an apology was seared across my soul and an agony keener than any other in my life twisted through my body. This time, though, I had something I didn't have before. Hope and love tangled with the pain, protecting me from the worst sting of the barbs.

Alyssa's hand curled against mine. She clutched me so tightly her knuckles turned white. I traced my thumb along the back of her hand in response. She took a deep breath and swallowed around the lump in her throat. When I glanced at her, I could see her lips moving. She was talking silently to our son. When I saw her mouth form the word, "Daddy," I closed my eyes as my tears pooled in them.

We stood hand in hand for at least an hour before the wind shifted and it grew cold. I wrapped my arm around her shoulders, but neither of us was willing to move. It was as if there was a cosmic signal we were waiting for, something to tell us the time was right to say goodbye, even though we knew it would never be the right time.

"I'm sorry I wasn't there for you," I whispered. Even I wasn't sure whether the words were intended for Alyssa or Emmanuel. Possibly they were meant for both of them.

Alyssa nodded as fresh tears slipped down her cheeks. She stepped forward out of my grasp and dropped to her knees in front of the cherub. Reaching out her hand, she placed something against the marble base. I hadn't even realised she'd brought anything with her.

Once she'd left her gift, she stood and slipped her hand over one of the cherub's hands, cupping his face. Then, without another word, she walked back to my side. I couldn't see past her to see what she had left, but even if I could have, I didn't want to look. I didn't want to invade the moment she'd shared as she said goodbye. She turned when she reached me, grabbing my hand and wordlessly leading me from the graveside.

I followed her, allowing her to guide me away, because I wasn't sure my feet would trail the path away from our son without her help. I resisted glancing backward for as long as I could, but finally, I couldn't help myself. I flicked my head around and saw a small toy car resting in front of the little angel. I almost choked at the image of Sinclair Racing's colours. It was a promotional item from last year—a die-cast model of my car.

"I wanted to leave something of each of us with him, so he knew we weren't abandoning him," Alyssa said softly when I turned back toward her.

I nodded, embarrassed that she'd caught me looking. I wondered what she had left of herself, and of Phoebe, but couldn't ask. What I had seen was already an intrusion of what I was certain was supposed to be a private goodbye.

We remained silent as we headed back to the car. For me, I was partly lost back at Emmanuel's grave and partly preparing myself for the journey ahead.

"Do you think we should have brought Phoebe?" I asked as I opened the car door. It hadn't occurred to me to ask until that moment. As far as I knew, she was still working on the assumption that we would be able to take Emmanuel with us somehow.

Alyssa shook her head. "I needed that. Mum brought her down yesterday and told her what was happening."

I swallowed down the emotions that threatened to overwhelm me. Part of me wanted to celebrate the fact that we were just hours away from being on the road to the rest of our lives, but the rest was still at Emmanuel's graveside.

Alyssa gave my hand a gentle squeeze of encouragement. "Let's go get Phoebe and load up the trailer."

As I started the car, I nodded. It was the reminder that as hard as the goodbye had been, it wasn't the only one we needed to face in the next few hours.

By the time I pulled up in front of Alyssa's parents' house, my stomach was in knots. She'd want to spend as long as she could saying goodbye. I just wanted to grab the last of her shit and go. Her dad, Curtis, was still not my biggest fan. He'd seemed to begrudgingly accept that we were together, and that Alyssa wanted to marry me, but it hadn't made him any less cold toward me. I had no hope that we'd ever get back to the relationship we'd once shared.

Alyssa went into the house while I hitched up the trailer. While I was debating whether I could maybe just wait in the car, Phoebe came to their screen door and waved at me. An easy smile lifted my lips at the sight as I walked straight to her.

"Hey, princess," I said after I'd opened the door and scooped her into my arms. "Are you ready to move into your castle?"

She nodded before snuggling against my chest.

I took a moment to draw her into a hug. "It might take a couple of days to get there, we'll have to see."

"Nana said. No planes."

I chuckled. "Nope. No planes. Not this time."

"We're in the kitchen, Dec," Alyssa called to me.

Drawing in a bracing breath, I followed the sound. Alyssa sat at

17

the table. Her mother, Ruth, sat next to her, but Curtis stood at the bench, shooting daggers at me with his eyes.

"I made some food," Ruth said, waving to Curtis in a clear instruction to give her what he had. With a sigh, I sat on Alyssa's other side. Curtis dropped the platter of fruit and cheese on the table before sitting down at the table with his arms crossed.

It was clear the two women had obviously planned this awkwardness masquerading as a goodbye in advance, no doubt trying to make things better between us, but it was never going to work so long as Curtis had the bee in his bonnet about me.

To break the silence, Ruth asked Alyssa something about Josh and Ruby, and my heart plummeted. I twisted my mouth into the best smile I could offer, which wasn't much, and hissed through my teeth at Alyssa, "Don't tell me Josh's coming too?" That would be just what I needed.

She shook her head and I sighed with relief. Then she ruined the moment. "We've got to drop in and say goodbye to them on our way out."

Even though I turned to argue with her, one look at her earnest, pleading expression left me unable to. How could I deny her the opportunity to say goodbye to her brother before tearing her from his life? I closed my eyes and asked a question I knew I was sure to regret later: "Did you want to go to Flynn's too?"

Her eyes flicked up to meet mine and, with the ghost of a smile on her lips, she nodded. "Only if you don't mind."

I bit back on the jealousy and the accompanying bile that rose in my throat, reminding myself of all the reasons I shouldn't be jealous. That Alyssa and I had lodged the forms to amend the birth certificates already, and had received confirmation the new certificates were on their way. He'd soon have no claim on my daughter. I reminded myself that he was gay and not interested in Alyssa as anything more than a friend. Finally, I forced myself to recall the generous offer he'd made on Alyssa's little four-cylinder car.

Covering the swell of emotions with a widened—but fake—smile, I shook my head to let her know I didn't mind. Having to deal with Curtis and Josh had already put a damper on the day, so it would be easier to get all the fucked-up shit over with at once. If that meant fake-smiling my way through a shitload of awkward meetings for Alyssa's and Phoebe's sakes, so be it.

Ruth seemed to sense the unease around the table and rose to her feet. "Declan, I want a quick word with you please . . . alone?"

With a nod, I stood. Once I had, I dipped to press a few small kisses onto Alyssa's cheek, partly because I wanted to remind her that I loved her, but mostly to rub Curtis's face in the fact that she'd chosen me.

I followed Ruth into the room we'd been staying in. Everything we'd been using temporarily was packed into the back of the Prado, so it was back to looking like Alyssa's old bedroom—except without the personality of her photos and mementos. After glancing around the room, I looked down at Ruth and saw the tears on her face.

"Hey, now, what's up?" I asked, as softly as I could. I reminded myself that regardless of how Curtis reacted to me and Alyssa being together, Ruth had been in my corner. She at least was happy about my reunion with Alyssa.

"It's just sinking in that she's really going. I won't be able to just pop in to see her anymore."

"Sydney's not that far away, and there's always Skype, and phone calls," I said, trying to cheer her up a little. "And emails."

"You'll look after them, won't you?" She looked at me pleadingly.

"With my life." Every word was sincere. I wouldn't let anything hurt either of my girls. I'd made enough mistakes where both of them were concerned.

She nodded. "Thank you."

She pulled me down to her, wrapping her arms tightly around me. In that moment, she was a mother saying goodbye to her son. For me, it was the goodbye I hadn't been able to say to my own mother.

"Ruth?" I asked, my voice soft and filled with the emotions roiling inside me.

"What is it, sweetie?" she asked.

"When Mum comes back, can you make sure that she's not alone?" I couldn't bear the thought of Mum returning to her old life since she'd been freed from my cheating fucking bastard of a father. I didn't want to think of her going back to him, or worse sitting around an empty house consumed by her loneliness.

"Of course," she said before pulling me into one final embrace.

We walked back into the kitchen to find Alyssa and Curtis in a tight embrace of their own. Phoebe was on the floor, switching between their legs.

Alyssa's eyes were closed, but it was easy to see she'd been crying. "I'm going to miss you too, Daddy," she whispered.

In that instant, I had a moment of crystal-clear clarity. Despite the fact that I'd only been in her life for a short time, I couldn't imagine losing Phoebe. Even if she was an adult, it'd be hard to say goodbye. It would be impossible knowing I couldn't see her whenever I wanted. When Curtis and Alyssa finally broke apart, I walked over to him and offered him my hand as a peace offering.

He stared at it for a beat before shaking it with his own.

"Don't worry, sir. I'll be there for them both."

Out of the corner of my eye, I saw Alyssa smile before darting off to give Ruth a hug goodbye.

"You'd better be, son," Curtis whispered venomously the moment she was out of earshot. "Or you'll have me to deal with. I won't have you hurt her again."

His hand tightened around my own. Before he could hurt me though, I responded in kind. We shook hands for a few seconds longer than was strictly necessary, both tightening our grip as much as we could. I was certain his hand would be aching as much as mine when we finally let go. I vowed to myself that I would make him trust me and when I had, I'd make him eat his words.

The visit with Josh and Ruby had gone much the same way. Truthfully, I would have been happier to have avoided it altogether, but I sucked it up for Alyssa. Instead of tempting fate, I stayed outside in the car. The temperature was well over forty, and hotter still inside the car, but it was better than the icy reception waiting inside. Not that it mattered when the goodbyes spilled out onto the front lawn and Josh shot pointed gazes and a shouted warning at me from his front door. It took everything I had not to shout at him in response, but I did flip him the bird when no one else was watching.

"Daddy, why was Unca Joshie mad at you?"

"It's a long story, sweetheart," Alyssa said, saving me from having to explain. "Granddad and Uncle Josh just take a while to let go of the past."

Phoebe nodded as if that were all the explanation she'd ever need. Maybe it would be.

When we pulled up at Flynn's, I expected the same harsh words and cold stares I'd borne the brunt of the last time I'd seen him—the same ones that were the only thing both Curtis and Josh were willing to offer me before I left—but he was actually polite, even if he barely spent any focus on me as he ensured Phoebe was fed and had gone to the loo before our drive.

As Alyssa was loading Phoebe into the car, after she and Flynn had shared a long, teary goodbye, he called me over to him. Before I could think of a few smart-arse responses to the cutting remarks I was certain he'd make, he pulled me into a hug. Shocked by the movement, I stiffened in his hold.

"I was wrong about you," he said as I pulled away.

I narrowed my eyes at him. "What are you talking about?"

"Not long after you got here, when Alyssa was telling me all about the things that you were doing, I was so sure I knew the sort of person you were. When you came crashing back into her life, like a drunken arsehole, I thought that's all there was to you."

My jaw ached with the pressure I was exerting to stop myself from telling him to fuck off while I waited for him to get to his point.

"But I was wrong. I'd have to be an idiot not to see the smile on Lys's face when you're around." He looked over to the car. "She loves you. But the thing that changed my mind the most is that you've got the same smitten look on your face whenever you don't think anyone is watching. You try to hide it, but you can't. You should let your guard down more often, Declan. You might be surprised by how people respond."

I cleared my throat, uncomfortable with the intensity of the conversation.

"I'd tell you to look after them both, but somehow I think it'd be a moot point."

Nodding once to acknowledge his words, I moved toward my car. After taking one step, I swung back around. "Thank you," I said. The words were genuine, but they tasted funny on my tongue. I was sure my face indicated my discomfort in issuing them. "For being there for her when I wasn't."

He ran his hands through his hair and nodded, his mouth twisting downward into a frown. "Let me guess, that's a thanks, but now you're back in her life, so I can just get fucked?" He looked like he had a number of arguments against it ready on his tongue.

"Actually, no." The words were out before I'd thought about them, and they surprised even me. "As hard as it was to accept it at first, it's actually nice knowing she has someone else she can rely on if anything was to happen to me. Or if she's so pissed at me that she can't see straight." I chuckled. "Just do me a favour when that happens and remind her of what you told me today."

There was no point saying if, because I was certain there would be days I'd piss her off, just like there'd be days she'd get on my last nerve. Just like the night before at the New Year's Eve party. But those moments would only be temporary, fleeting, and then we'd find our way back to the happy. I understood that now better than I ever had before.

He laughed. "Sure thing, Declan."

I shook his hand. "Just call me Dec."

"Don't let her be a stranger, will you?" he asked. For an instant, his heartache flashed across his face. He may not have wanted her as a lover, but it was clear he loved her in his own way.

"Never."

"And thank you, for, you know, not telling her the truth about the value of the car."

I laughed. "Who am I to interfere with a private transaction?"

He nodded and I waved as I walked away.

"Oh, and Dec?" Flynn called from behind me. "Keep your nose clean so that you're back on the track soon, yeah? I miss seeing your fine arse on TV."

I choked on my spit as he burst out laughing. With a shake of my head, a smile on my lips, and heat in my cheeks, I waved him goodbye.

As I walked back to the car, Alyssa gave me a questioning look. "What was that about?" she asked as I pulled my car door open.

"You," I said before laughing at the expression on her face.

"Are you good?" she asked.

"Baby, I'm better than good. All of my dreams are coming true."

The trip home ended up being slower than any I'd ever taken before. Between the toddler in the backseat, and the trailer behind us, the stops were more frequent, the car slower, and the trip more tiring. In the end, just like I'd warned Phoebe we might have to, we stayed at Coffs Harbour for the night so we didn't have to drive through the night with a cranky arse in the car — and that was just me.

In the morning, we stopped briefly at the Big Banana and did the obligatory family photo before driving the rest of the way to Sydney — to the rest of our lives.

We were a little over an hour out of Sydney when Eden, the team strategist for Sinclair Racing and one of my few friends, called. She let us know that everything was arranged for our arrival — they'd flown back on the first. Even though I'd given the key to my house to Morgan, he obviously didn't want to risk calling when I might have him on speaker.

"Thank you for all of your help, Eden," I said after she had given us the information about where she'd left the key.

Alyssa offered her thanks too.

"Anytime," Eden said. "That goes for Morgan too . . . when you forgive him."

Alyssa groaned and I stifled a chuckle. Morgan and Alyssa's first meeting hadn't been anywhere near as smooth as her introduction to Eden, and his assistance with my little New Year's plot hadn't helped his case.

"I know you love him, Eden," Alyssa said. "But I still can't face him yet."

I wasn't sure if she didn't want to see him yet because of the email, or because she was embarrassed by how she had reacted.

"I know," Eden said. "I'm sure you will one day."

"Maybe," Alyssa replied.

"And you, mister," Eden added, "don't forget tomorrow's the big day."

I groaned. How could I possibly forget that I was returning to Sinclair Racing the next day? It was the day I had been looking forward to, and equally dreading, ever since I'd accepted Danny's offer to return. It was the day the life Alyssa and I hoped to create in Sydney would start—the real life of work and routine, of day care and dinnertimes. It scared the absolute fuck out of me even while I looked forward to every minute.

"It'll be fun," Eden said. "You'll learn new things, and you know Danny will look after you. In fact, he has a surprise for you when you get in tomorrow."

I swallowed around the lump that had taken up residence in my throat. "What is it?" I croaked.

Eden let out a titter. "If I told you, it wouldn't be a surprise, would it?"

Alyssa chuckled. "She has you there."

I narrowed my eyes at her. "Don't you start on me too," I said.

Alyssa pouted. I moved quickly, grabbing her hand and pulling it to my lips. "Don't tease me," I whispered threateningly.

"Or what?" she asked, licking her lips.

"Or I just might have to punish you." I grinned.

"That's enough about that. I'll see you guys later," Eden chirped.

I chuckled. I'd all but forgotten that Eden was still on the phone, or that Phoebe was in the back seat for that matter. God, I couldn't wait to get Alyssa home.

Home.

Never had I heard a more beautiful fucking word.

And with home came Danny's surprise. I could barely wait to find out what it might be. Especially when Eden's teasing reminded me of Danny's words from the New Year's party just days earlier. Something told me there was a lot more in store in the next chapter of my life.

Bring on the new season.

CHAPTER TWO

MINI MOMENTS

THE ALARM BLARED loudly, interrupting my peace. There had to be something wrong, because there was no fucking way in hell I needed to get up when it was still dark outside. Especially not when I'd been up unpacking the car until late the night before; the aches in my body were testament to the work.

I lifted my head off the pillow and growled at my phone, trying to intimidate it into silent submission. When that didn't work, I unwrapped one arm from Alyssa and reached for my phone, sliding to snooze the alarm and ending the horrid sound. I groaned, dropped my head back onto the pillow, and prepared to go back to sleep.

"Come on," Alyssa murmured beside me, nudging my shoulder. "You have to get up."

"Don't wanna," I muttered as I moved closer to her side. I wanted nothing more than to pull the blanket over my head, curl around Alyssa, and forget about the rest of the world.

Alyssa broke that desire by pulling away from me, sitting up, and pushing the blanket off us both.

"Fucking hell," I murmured. "It's too early to be up."

She chuckled beside me before leaning over and kissing my cheek. "You've just gone soft with all the sleeping in that you've been doing lately."

"Fuck off!" I said. "I'm as hard as ever."

I grabbed her hand and pressed it against my morning wood, just to prove my point.

Alyssa surprised me by tightening her hand around my length and giving it a gentle rub.

"Oh, baby, that feels good," I moaned.

She giggled before letting go of me and climbing out of bed, tugging the blanket back up over her side of the bed. As she moved, her short baby-doll nightie pulled up, revealing her boy-leg panties. The sight of her perfect, pert arse covered by the black cotton made my mouth water.

Once her side of the bed was made, she leaned forward, giving me a glimpse down her top at the creamy skin of her breasts.

"I'm going to have a shower," she said as she headed for the door to the en suite. She turned back around to look at me and ripped off her little dress. Her nipples were already standing to attention, begging to be licked. "You know," she continued, "it seems a shame to waste all that room under there. That huge shower really is far too big for just one person."

I was out of the bed and across the room in less than a second, all fatigue gone with the promise of shower sex with my personal goddess. I clasped her thighs in my hands and wrapped her legs around my waist as my mouth found hers. It was exactly the reason the alarm was set so early, so that I had a few moments to spend with Alyssa and Phoebe before I had to go to work.

Alyssa wasn't due to start her new job for another week, when Pembletons, the firm she'd be working with, opened again after their Christmas closure.

Holding her tight, I carried her into the en suite, pressing her roughly against the wall in my desperation to taste her. Once I had her pinned securely, I took one of her breasts into my mouth and tasted her skin—she was sweetness and honey, just like always.

Releasing her from my hold, I slid her underwear down her legs, slowly following them to the floor. I paused along the way to kiss her breasts, then her stomach and one of her thighs before pulling her panties off completely. Once she was naked, I ran my tongue over her thigh.

"Oh, God," she panted as my mouth trailed from her thigh to her pussy. She reached for my hair and guided me closer. When she shifted slightly, widening her stance, I slipped a finger into the mix. Even though I had her panting for more, she sighed and gently pushed me away.

I growled and gripped her hips tighter, refusing to let her out of my hold.

"Shower first." She laughed as she pulled away from me. With a teasing wiggle in her hips, she walked past me and turned her back to me to turn on the shower.

Standing with another growl, I followed her under the now-running water. Without giving her the chance to spin, I dragged my fingers up the length of her thigh before cupping her arse. I couldn't help myself; I pulled my hand back and gave her a quick, gentle slap. "That's for teasing me," I whispered against her neck.

My morning wood had turned into a full, raging boner, and I needed her. I made short work of my now-wet boxers. In the time it took to strip them off, she turned around and grinned at me. In two steps, I had her in my arms then claimed her under the water. I pulled her up and slid my cock into her ready pussy.

"Fuck, baby," I whispered into her neck.

With my lips on hers, I pushed her against the tiles in the shower. A small squeal left her and her nipples hardened even further as the cold pressed into her back. I took one into my mouth and bit down gently. Alyssa gave a small cry of pained pleasure. Pinning her in place with a kiss, I pressed harder against her, slamming my cock into her and pushing her body flush against the wall. The sounds of our bodies slapping together under the water filled the room like a fucking symphony. Dipping my head, I ran my tongue up between her breasts, sucking in some of the water as it cascaded down.

I wanted to enjoy Alyssa some more—the pace my body was setting was much too fast—so I sank to the ledge in the shower, pulling her down with me. She climbed on top of me and slid over my cock. Her hips rose and fell in a slow, steady rhythm. I used the extra freedom to explore her body more thoroughly with my hands. My fingers found her nipples and they danced there for a moment, pulling, rolling, and gently twisting them.

She gave a delicious groan when my thumb brushed against her clit.

I ran my hands around to cup her arse before pushing her hips down harder on me while pushing up with my own. I brushed her clit again, and she brought her eyes to mine. The love and passion I saw there filled me with confidence. It was exactly the boost I needed to face the day ahead—my first day back at Sinclair Racing.

The day was going to go well, but I would miss the hell out of her. My time in Brisbane had spoiled me with late nights, sleep-ins, and lots of uninterrupted time with both of my girls. Getting back to reality was going to be tough.

Wanting to enjoy the precious moments we had before real life came crashing into my day, I moved my thumb against her clit softly, no longer caring for my own needs or desires. I wanted to make her feel good. I wanted to show her how much I fucking loved her. While she moved her hips in a delicate pattern, I continued gently thrusting. My other hand cupped her face and guided her mouth to mine. I pushed my tongue forward to meet hers and closed my eyes, relishing her body's response to my touch.

Her hips swivelled against my hand and dick as she found her way to her climax. I kissed her long and hard until she was unable to contain her orgasm any longer, and she dropped her head back to moan softly into the water. When that happened, I simply moved my attention from her mouth to her breasts. Her hands clenched around my shoulders, and her nails dug into my skin. My tongue flicked across her nipple as my thumb grazed her clit one final time before she found her release around me.

"Fuck, baby, you're so beautiful when you come."

She dropped her head to my shoulder as she came back down to earth. Once her breathing was almost back to normal, I stood, pulling her up with me. I kissed the tip of her nose and smiled at her. I turned to grab the shampoo, but when I turned back with a dollop in my hand, Alyssa grabbed hold of my dick and began to stroke lightly. All thoughts of actually getting clean in the shower flew out the window as I got lost in her touch. I closed my eyes and leaned my head back against the glass of the shower wall.

The next instant, I felt her warm mouth close around me, and I whimpered with pleasure. I felt my balls tighten almost immediately. My fingers found her hair, running back and forth through her wet locks as she sucked my length in and out, and my knees grew weak as the sensation overwhelmed me. The intensity was too much for me to bear, and I soon grunted as I found my own release, collapsing back against the wall.

"Wow!" I panted. "Good morning."

"Good morning to you too," Alyssa said, a huge grin on her face.

"So, do I get a wake-up like that every morning for work?"

She swiped at my shoulder with her hand playfully before answering, "Maybe not *every* morning."

It was the best start to the day I could have asked for. I was feeling so blissed out that nothing could bring me down. We finished our shared shower and got dressed before waking Phoebe up. She was starting at her day care in preparation for Alyssa's return to work the following week. The reasoning was that it was better to have Phoebe get used to full days while Alyssa was available to pick her up early if it was absolutely needed.

Thankfully, Phoebe had been excited about her new "school" when we told her about it. So excited, in fact, that she'd picked out her outfit while I was unpacking the car. Apparently, she'd pulled one outfit out of her suitcase. Then another. And another. Finally, she had worn herself out so much that she couldn't make any more choices and had fallen asleep. That was where Alyssa had found her the night before.

After we woke Phoebe, she picked a new outfit. Then, an hour and three more last-minute clothing changes later, we finally had her wrangled and in the car.

She chatted animatedly while I drove, and Alyssa held my hand in the passenger seat.

Truly, life couldn't get any better.

We arrived at the day care earlier than we had planned, which turned out to be a good thing as Phoebe sobbed into Alyssa, refusing to let her go. All of the previous night's excitement had fizzled away and only fear remained. Finally, one of the caregivers had to simply pull Phoebe away and try to distract her with some toys, while I tugged Alyssa away.

Once we were back in the car, Alyssa sat staring at her hands. "I shouldn't have left her there. She's going to hate it. They're not going to look after her properly. They . . ."

"Alyssa, baby, shhh," I whispered, trying to infuse my voice with as much calm as I could. "She'll be fine. We looked at the options, remember, and Eden checked it out for us. We picked this one because they had the best caregivers."

"But—"

"No buts. She'll be fine."

She gave a little nod before turning to me. "Okay. I'm all right now. Thank you."

We drove on to Sinclair Racing headquarters. As soon as we pulled into the car park, I was the one who needed to be calmed. The building loomed into view and my hands began to shake.

Pull yourself together, fucktard.

My thoughts did shit all to calm me. I let out an uneven breath as Alyssa and I climbed from the car after I had parked it. With my hand shaking, I dropped my car keys into her hand.

"You'll be fine," Alyssa whispered, kissing my cheek.

"Of course I will," I lied.

"I'll be back later to pick you up."

I nodded. "Promise me you won't go pick Phoebe up early," I said.

She looked at me innocently. Too fucking innocently.

"Promise?"

She narrowed her eyes at me, but nodded. "I promise."

I pulled her to me and kissed her tenderly. I filled my mind with her scent and the feel of her touch so I could get through the day without her by my side. This was us, living in the real world. I walked up to the glass doors, pausing briefly to take a deep breath. I reached for my security card to gain access, but then I remembered I didn't have it anymore. Danny had destroyed the old one and had refused to give me a new one until I actually started back at work.

After sucking down one more breath, I pressed the buzzer and waited for security to come to the door. It was the height of fucking embarrassment, waiting for someone to escort me in. I swore that if anyone even so much as smirked at me, I was going to beat their fucking arses.

Luckily, the security guard was quick and didn't seem to find my situation amusing in the least.

"Declan," he greeted me with a nod. He led me straight into his little security office, snapping a photo of me for my new pass. Within minutes, he'd printed the card.

When he handed it to me, I cast my eyes over it quickly. After a moment, I looked again, because there was something unexpected on the pass. "Wait . . . there's a mistake here," I said.

Under Employment, it had, *Mechanic/Driver*.

The guard cast his eye over the page in front of him, and then looked at his computer. "Nope, that's what I got."

Maybe it was a practical joke, but there wasn't an ounce of amusement in his voice.

"But it says driver," I said, my voice pitching slightly higher than normal. I tried desperately to shake the hope that maybe, just maybe, Danny had already changed his mind and was letting me back behind the wheel of a ProV8.

"Yep, that's what I was told," the guard said. "If there's a problem, you'll have to take it up with the boss man. I've got instructions to take you straight to him anyway."

After giving a small nod to let him know I'd heard, I stared at the card in front of me. The word "driver" was printed in letters so small they may have seemed insignificant, but they leapt off the card and danced in front of my eyes with such promise that I couldn't help but grin.

As I followed the security guard to Danny's office, I clutched my security pass tightly. I slipped my hand, pass and all, into the pocket of my jeans. I silently dared anyone to try to take that little piece of plastic from me.

Driver. I could still see the word emblazoned in front of my eyes; six little black letters that meant so much.

The guard left me at the door to Danny's office, and I knocked to get permission to come in.

"Enter," Danny called from his desk.

I walked into the room with a newfound purpose. *Driver*.

"Declan Reede," Danny started, a small but welcoming smile crossing his features. "I trust everyone is settled in at home."

I nodded. "Yes, sir."

Danny raised an eyebrow at me. I wondered if he could sense my excitement and my willingness to toe the company line if it meant I could be back in the hot seat. Or maybe he was just relieved that there hadn't been any new scandals despite my plans for New Year's.

"Liam is very excited to have you on board," Danny said. "Although, I have to say you are the oldest first-year apprentice we've ever had."

I nodded, afraid that talking would break whatever magical spell or good mood Danny was in.

"I also have some news, Declan, concerning your position here."

"Yes?" I forced out around my nerves and building excitement.

"I've decided to run another car this year."

My mouth involuntarily crept into a grin. Another car. Three V8s—three drivers. I swallowed down the huge bubble of excitement building in my middle. With thoughts of being back in the car again racing through my head, I had to remind myself to breathe.

Already, I could smell the rubber and hot bitumen. Could feel the vibration of the car on the track. Sense the heat in the cabin. It was all so familiar and I wanted it all so desperately. Danny continued to talk, but I was lost. My mind filled with the track, with the music of the machine, and with the hum of the crowds trackside at an event. It pulsed through my veins and hummed in my ears. Perfect.

". . . of course, your pit duties will take precedence on race day," he finished.

"Huh?" I asked, confused because I hadn't listened to the first part of his conversation. My mind raced over the possibilities of how I could be in the pits and on the track at the same time. It didn't make sense.

"I don't want you losing that unique touch that makes you such a skilled driver," he said. "But I also think the time with Liam will serve you well. Understanding how the cars tick can only help in the long run."

I nodded, wishing I could ask him to repeat himself, but knowing that admitting I hadn't been paying attention wouldn't be the best move right now. Not within the first hour of being back on board.

"So?" Danny asked. "Do you want to see your new car?"

I grinned. "Fuck yes!"

"I have to say, Declan, you're really surprising me," he said as he pointed me out of the office toward the garages. "I wasn't sure how you would take this. I was a bit worried, in fact, but you seem to be very understanding."

"I get to drive again," I said. "That's all that matters."

"I'm glad you feel that way. That sort of mature attitude is going to take you far."

As soon as we reached the shed, Liam came over. His palms were greasy, but he stuck it out for me to shake regardless. It was clearly a test, so I met his eye and shook his hand anyway. I had worked on my karts when I used to race them, and serviced my own cars at home, so I wasn't exactly afraid of a bit of grease.

"Welcome aboard, kid." He chuckled, slapping me on my back.

"Thanks, Spanners," I said, using the nickname his crew had given him. Drivers and the team management almost never used the nickname, but I figured if I was going to be working alongside him, I should get used to it. After all, it would seem like I was brownnosing to use his real name. It would be easier to be accepted if I acted like I belonged in the pits. More than anything, I had to be one of the boys if I wanted to find my feet there—not that I'd need them for long if I was going to be back in the driver seat.

"That reminds me," he said. "We'll have to think of a nickname for you too, kid."

"Try squirt," Morgan called as he made his way over to us. "It always worked for me."

"Fuck off," I hissed at him. That nickname had been nothing but trouble for me over the years.

"Aww, is ickle squirt angwy about his nickname?" Morgan asked in a mock-baby voice. He slapped me on the back. "Seriously though, dude, welcome back."

"Fuck you very much," I replied through gritted teeth.

"Well, I don't think you'll have too much trouble fitting in with the boys down here with that attitude," Liam said. "I never really doubted that too much anyway, or else I never would have agreed to Danny's suggestion. I wouldn't want to put a cat among the pigeons."

I nodded, but was largely ignoring him because I saw Danny pull out his key card to get into the end shed. The new car was obviously in there. I wondered whether it was a brand-new VFII Commodore or one of the old VFs rebuilt. Not that I minded either way; I was just happy to be back.

I stood anxiously behind Danny as he pushed open the door. The car was red and almost bare, with only a handful of sponsor stickers. Based on the placement, I guessed they were the series sponsors stickers and nothing to do with the team. But worse, so much worse, was that it was *not* the car I was expecting.

Not even close.

"You've got to be kidding me!" I shouted as I took in the car. To say it wasn't what I expected was a goddamned understatement. To say the sight of it pissed me the fuck off would be, too. "What the fuck is *that*?"

Danny turned to me, surprised. "That's the new car. We're trialling the series this year, as a privateer for now. If it's successful, we'll run it again next year with sponsors."

"But," I said incredulously, "it's a fucking Mini!"

"You'd be surprised how much the crowds are getting behind these cars," Danny said. He shot a pointed glance at Liam, who left the room without saying another word. In fact, Liam looked almost relieved for the opportunity to escape.

Oh, fuck.

Danny shut the door and locked it so that we were completely alone before he turned back to me.

"Why didn't you give me this reaction up in my office?" he asked with a voice of ice and steel.

Fuck. I'd fucked up again.

"That's why I met you up there first." He pinched the bridge of his nose. "Are you *deliberately* trying to embarrass me in front of everyone? Because I guarantee you, Declan, that will *not* work out well for you. Not as far as a position here goes at least."

"Shit, no, fuck," I said, trying to backpedal as fast as I could. "I just, uh, well, I-just-thought-it-would-be-a-V8." The words tumbled from my mouth as one jumbled mess.

"A V8?" He was incredulous and his eyes flashed with something akin to disbelief.

I swallowed down the rising tide of *oh fucks* and *holy shits* that bubbled to my tongue.

"After everything I told you about sponsors and racing when we discussed you coming back, you seriously thought I'd put you back into a V8 already? Do you have any idea how much those things cost to run? To fix? I can't do that without sponsors, and no one is willing to put their name anywhere near your reputation at the moment."

"So, who's paying for this car then?" I asked, confused.

"I am." Danny's voice was still cold. Hard.

Fuck!

"I thought you'd appreciate the fact that I was trying to ensure you still had some time on the track and would be able to keep your skills honed, even if it isn't in the car you wanted. But if you're satisfied with wielding a goddamned wrench for the rest of your life, then suit yourself."

I needed to do some serious backpedalling, and a shitload of grovelling. "No, fuck, I mean thanks. I get it. I was just . . . surprised." I looked at the Mini again and winced.

Why a Mini? Why couldn't I just go back to a fucking production car or some shit? Even as the thought struck me, I knew the answer. It was also a test. My life until I got back behind the wheel properly was no doubt going to be a series of fucking tests to see if I had the mettle and maturity to be driving again. Until I'd proven it without a doubt, Danny wouldn't let me near anything more expensive.

Well, if that was what they wanted to do, I would just have to man the fuck up and deal. At least I would be back racing competitively again.

Even if it was in a fucking Mini.

THE REST of my first day back at Sinclair Racing passed relatively smoothly. Most of the mechanics seemed to be willing to accept me—even if they did choose the nickname Spark Plug for me because I was replaced so easily when the spark went out of my career. *Fuckers.*

The only dark patch on my day, besides the fucking drama with the Mini, was Hunter Blake, the fucking psycho who'd replaced me in the driver seat and seemed to have made it his objective to give me hell. And not in a "find me a left-handed screwdriver" way, like the boys in the sheds.

Instead, he found my weak spots and rode them hard all day. He asked about Alyssa, insisting she was too far out of my league, and that he would show her what a real man was like the first chance he had. He said things to me which, had they come from Morgan, would usually have warranted a fuck-you and a laugh before we'd have moved on. But because they came from Hunter, his words stuck in my craw and scratched until I was irritated and aching.

By the end of the day, I was dirty, tired, and sick to fucking death of the lunatic. It had been a long time since I'd had a day quite that hard. Usually, my hours at Sinclair were filled with meetings, strategy, and just general fucking around.

I rang Alyssa to ask her to bring my 4WD to pick me up rather than the Monaro, and to put a garbage bag over the seat as well. There was no fucking way I was going anywhere near my Monaro covered in as much grease as I was. I made a mental note to remember how dirty I would get in the future, even though I nearly cried thinking it. Driving my Monaro home to be with my girls should have been the highlight of my day every day, but now it would be reserved for special occasions. I needed to know I was able to drive at least one V8 and not live in a world full of fucking Minis and Micro-series cars.

Eden found me just before I left for the end of the day. Her excitement bubbled onto her face when she bounced up to me.

"Welcome back!" She threw her arms around my neck even though I was covered in shit.

"Thanks, Edie. It's good to be back."

She leaned against the toolbox. "Did you like your surprise?"

"You could have given me a little more warning," I said before telling her about the incident with the Mini.

As my story went on, she was all but doubled over with laughter. "Only you could manage that," she responded when I finished.

"Fuck you, Edie," I said, but my laughter told her I wasn't serious.

"I heard a rumour on the grapevine today too. I thought you might be interested."

She was better connected than most team owners. "Yeah?"

"Yeah, apparently after your first no, Paige started working to get Anderson on her team."

"Okay. And?"

"And she pulled out of negotiations when she thought she had another driver stitched up. A driver who fell through on New Year's."

I chuckled. "Well, sucks to be her, doesn't it?"

"Yeah, now she's scrambling to get another driver. Any other driver. She'll probably have to bump Jenkins from production cars, and you know he's not ready."

"If she puts him up now, what's she going to do for a second driver in the enduros?"

"That's the question, isn't it?"

"You know what? It couldn't have happened to a more deserving person."

She chuckled. "I thought the same thing. I saw Alyssa drop you off this morning. Is she picking you up too?"

"Yeah. In fact, she'll be due any minute."

Eden linked her arm with mine and led me to the door. "Well, let's not keep her waiting. I want to say hi."

I shouted out a "see ya" to everyone else left in the workshop as I followed Eden out.

Alyssa was already waiting when we reached the car park. She'd picked Phoebe up on the way over to my work, which was probably a good thing, because I was just anxious to get home, have a shower, and crawl into bed. I was ready to wash away the filth of my first day and hope for better ones to come.

Five minutes down the road, I started to tell Alyssa about my day. "Danny's running a new car this year. In a new series."

"Okay?" It was clear she had no idea where my conversation was going.

"He wants me to drive it," I finished.

A broad smile stretched across Alyssa's face. "Really? That's awesome."

"No, you don't get it, Lys." I buried my face in my hands. How could I admit that I was going to be driving that car? "It's a fucking Mini!"

"Language," she said, nodding toward the back of the car. "Little ears are always listening."

"What are little ears, Mummy?" Phoebe asked.

Alyssa raised her eyebrows as if to say, "I told you so." "Your ears are little, baby," she said aloud.

Phoebe thought for a moment, and nodded.

"Now, what were you saying?"

"Danny wants me to drive a fu—a Mini."

"But he wants you to race again. Isn't it a good thing?"

"No. I mean, yes, I guess it is, but God, it's a Mini! What're people going to think?"

Alyssa looked like she was trying to hold back laughter. "You're not worried it will somehow make you less manly, are you?" she teased.

Even though she might have hit close to the mark, I wasn't about to admit the truth. "Please, Lys, be serious. This is a big deal."

"I agree. Just a few days ago, Mr. Sinclair—"

"Danny," I interrupted.

She waved her hand to dismiss my correction. "He indicated that you wouldn't be driving for Sinclair Racing for a while. He's really showing his support by giving you this chance."

"I guess."

"You guess? It's a huge deal. You'll be driving professionally again. How many people get that chance once, let alone twice?"

Of course she'd try to make me see the positive in the situation. I crossed my arms over my chest.

"How was your day otherwise?" Alyssa asked, still trying to draw me from my funk.

I shrugged. "It was okay, I guess. I've had worse."

My words were the reminder that I'd had a lot of shitty days lately. Both the best and worst days of my life had all happened in just the last few months. It was enough to force me to relax my position, moving one hand to Alyssa's thigh for comfort.

"Things will only get better from here," she said, putting her hand on my knee.

Thinking how right she was, I nodded and rubbed my palm lightly against her jeans.

CHAPTER THREE

HOME

AFTER JUST A few days of having Phoebe and Alyssa in my life—
in my house—so much had changed. Toys littered almost every
room. The shelves under my entertainment unit housed a dozen or
so new DVDs, from the Wiggles to Disney. Each time I saw a new
addition, it reminded me of Morgan's comments about being pussy-
whipped and wrapped around little fingers. The odd thing was that
I didn't care. Sure, many people might have thought of me as the
eternal bachelor—for a long time I had nurtured that image—but I
actually liked seeing the little signs of my girls around the house.

Even with them in my life, I still had the occasional night where
things weren't perfect. Where I would wake in fucking cold sweats
as nightmares ripped through my mind. I had a new method for
coping though. One that didn't involve letting my insomnia take
over or force me to turn to tablets and booze.

The few times I'd woken in the middle of the night, I had
padded down the hall to Phoebe's room and found solace in the
knowledge that she was there and safe. While I stood guard in her

doorway, I would watch as her chest rose and fell softly in time with her light snores. As it had so many times since learning the truth, my mind turned to her brother, the child I would never know but who would always hold a place in my heart.

Once more, the loss that our small family had been forced to endure rocked me to the core, but I took comfort in the thought that maybe he was somewhere out there watching over us. That he would guard his baby sister from trouble and look after her from afar.

"What are you thinking about?" Alyssa asked, pulling me from my thoughts.

I shrugged. "About life. About where we were versus where we are now."

She wrapped her arms tightly around my waist, and I turned to press my lips to the top of her head. "We've got each other," she said. "That's half the battle won before we even start."

"I know." I wanted to leave it at that, but the worries that had woken me still raced through my mind. "But what are we going to do? Even with the higher wages Danny is giving me, we're barely going to make ends meet." The money had pushed us over a tax threshold, cutting the amount of child care help we would get, and the day care centre had put their fees up for the new year. Between those two things and the extra tax, the slightly higher wage of the driver mantle had been more than offset.

It was more than just that though. Money concerns were something I'd never had to consider before. When I'd been given the contract for Sinclair Racing at seventeen, I'd seen the money I would earn and thought I'd be set for life. I hadn't counted on losing the contract just four years later. Or having a family to support when I did.

"We'll manage," Alyssa said against my chest. It was what she said every time I voiced the concern.

Regardless of her assurance, I felt like a failure. I wouldn't be able to provide for my family the way that I should have—the way I wanted to. Even though I'd been back at Sinclair Racing for a week, I still had to face each day treading the road from high-flying driver to pit-dwelling grease monkey. Because Danny's offer of driving the Mini was being kept under wraps except for a few key people, I couldn't even tell anyone that I'd be back on the track when the season started.

The divide that Eden had mentioned, between those who wanted me back and those who were glad I was gone, seemed to have festered and split wider with my return. How could I have expected anything else? I'd gone from the top of the heap to the very bottom.

Eden was on my side, I was certain of that, and her position as strategist would see her residing in the pits alongside me on race days. Those were the days I dreaded most of all. Those would be the days where the ache in my chest would fester as I thought of that psycho, Hunter Blake, driving onto the track in the car that should have been mine.

That still could be mine, I reminded myself.

I just had to let the controversy and stress of the last few months blow over. Becoming someone the family-friendly sponsors would support was my top priority, and then the money would come, allowing me to support my family. It was easier to deal with stepping into the apprentice position when I was able to remind myself that it might only be for a short term.

After the initial shock of seeing the Mini had worn off, I was able to see it for what it was: a peace offering and a chance to prove that I still had what it took to be out there, running the curves and kicking arse. Spend the next twelve months in a car—even if it was a fucking Mini—rather than purely trackside. I would still have to work hard to prove I was willing to do the apprenticeship, but that was the part that actually excited me. It was nice to know that I was working toward a goal, even if that goal wasn't my initial dream.

The rest of my first week back at Sinclair Racing passed in much the same fashion as my first day. I settled in quickly, so much so that I'd learned more about my fellow mechanics than I had in my previous four years there. I wasn't sure whether the new knowledge was because of the forced proximity, and becoming one of the boys, or simply because I'd previously had my head so far up my own arse that I hadn't given a shit about them or their lives. Regardless, I was enjoying their company more than I ever would have thought.

In fact, I'd struck up a quick and easy friendship with a few of the other mechs. We were allocated into two crews, with each team assigned to a car. My little gang consisted of Johnno, Calem, Sam, Ryan, and Mia. I hadn't really known any of them except Mia.

I knew her because she'd been with Sinclair Racing longer than I had, and I'd learned very early on not to question why she got into the trade. If you were on her good side, and didn't ask stupid questions about her sexuality, she was a ripper chick. If, however, you crossed her or implied she was a dyke, well, that was it. You were on her bad side, and that was neither a nice place to be nor easy to recover from. I knew that *very* well from when I'd first arrived in Sydney as a rookie driver.

Two of the boys, Calem and Ryan, were a couple of years younger than I was, but they were second-year apprentices and therefore technically outranked me in the pits. I was the lowest of the low, but my crew didn't treat me that way. To them, I was just another apprentice. A not altogether hopeless one, at that. I suspected some of them thought I might have been useless, so it was probably a relief for them.

My crew had tried all the usual tricks on me, even requesting that I go to spares and ask for a *long weight*. I told them to fuck off because there was no way in hell I was *waiting* for anyone. I was not falling for that shit. My retort probably helped me to gain at least a little respect because they could see I wasn't a complete moron.

On the Friday of my first week, Danny posted the new racing season schedule on all the notice boards as well as sending around an invitation to the preseason launch party. My eyes quickly scanned the dates, and I sighed with relief when I saw the wedding date gamble Alyssa and I had taken had paid off perfectly. The Townsville race was being run over the weekend before our wedding, and then there was nothing else until the first of the enduro races in September. It gave us a few weeks to have a proper break, depending on what holidays Alyssa was able to wrangle off work.

After the initial elation, I studied the schedule in more detail and my heart sank. It was different to the previous year.

Very different.

In the previous season, the Bahrain race had been run near the end of the year. In the new calendar, they'd added a race in Abu Dhabi and moved the two offshore races to February.

I wanted to scream and shout or kick something as I read the dates again. The first race was the same weekend as Alyssa's university graduation.

I'd promised her we would fly together to Brisbane so she could attend the ceremony and collect her diploma in person. I'd planned on sitting proudly in the audience and watching her march in her graduation gown. Even though I hadn't been there for her during her time at uni, I knew she'd worked her arse off. It was clear in the fact that she'd graduated with high distinctions on top of single-handedly raising our daughter and working in the shop to pay the bills. I would never be able to tell her how much I admired her for that—attending the ceremony was a way to start showing her.

Only now, I couldn't do it. I'd be halfway around the world, once again choosing my career over her.

I dreaded going home and having to tell her the news. For the first time since she'd moved in, going home wasn't going to be the highlight of my day.

Even though it would have been easier to get the pain over with as fast as possible, I decided to wait until Phoebe went to bed before I raised the issue. If Alyssa wanted to get "drag 'em out, shoot 'em down" over it all—and I wouldn't blame her if she did, considering our past—at least Phoebe wouldn't have to witness it.

"Lys, can we talk?" I winced, knowing I had to tell Alyssa some good and some very bad news.

Her face paled as she looked at me. "What's wrong? I haven't seen you this nervous since . . ." She trailed off, but fiddled with the ring on her finger, showing me the direction of her thoughts. At least then my nerves had been about something good.

"Danny posted the race schedule."

"Okay?"

"The break in the season is between the middle of July and sometime in September. The seventeenth is free."

I could see Alyssa practically bounce with excitement over the fact that our wedding date was free. She knew I would be there regardless, but she'd been worried about Eden not being able to attend.

"But I'm going to Bahrain and Abu Dhabi in February."

She nodded, but then her features turned downward as she no doubt put together my concern and the news I was giving her. "Do you mean that you won't be able to make it to my graduation?"

"I can ask for the time off, but it probably won't go down well. I want to do everything I can to ensure I'm in that car at the end of the year." As soon as I'd said it, I wanted to reel it back in. Fuck, I sounded like an arse. Once again, I was picking my career over her. "Fuck it. I'll tell Danny I can't go."

She shook her head. "You can't do that."

"I won't pick my career over you. Never again."

"It's not picking if I tell you to go and give you my support to do whatever you need to do."

"Baby—" I started, but was cut off.

"No. Don't *baby* me. You're going. I'll have Mum and Dad there, and I'll have Phoebe. I'll have them get lots of photos for you." Her tone left no room for arguments. Her foot was decidedly down.

It was the conversation about my weekend away for the last race of the previous season all over again. Just like then, I was certain she would win. I couldn't say no to her, but that didn't stop me from trying to argue. "I really want to go to your graduation."

"I know you do, and that alone means the world to me," she said, smiling softly as she moved to straddle my lap.

I reached for her, wrapping my arms around her and resting my head against her chest. "And *you* mean the world to me," I replied.

She leaned forward so her cheek rested against my hair.

"You're still going. We have our wedding date free. That was the important one."

Nodding in agreement, I decided that maybe a change in topic was needed. "Are you ready for Monday?"

Her wary smile belied her worry even as she shrugged and assured me she was.

"This is what you've been working for, Lys. Years of study for this. Just remember that. And the fact that they wanted you out of everyone who applied."

"Yeah, I know, Dec. It just marks the start of so much. There's so much more I need to do before I can practise law on my own, and it's still a little overwhelming sometimes."

"You'll do it the same way you've done everything else so far. With one added bonus."

"What's that?"

"You'll have me too."

"And that's a bonus?"

"Well, the bone part is right." I thrusted my hips forward to emphasise my words.

A peal of laughter left her lips as she leaned back in my hold. "That could be a hindrance to my career, you know?"

"How do you figure?"

"Well, you and your *bone* are much more distracting than anything I've ever had to contend with before."

Shifting her in my lap so she could feel said bone, I thrust my hips up toward her. "It is a pretty damn good distraction though, if you ask me."

She cupped her hands around my face and drew my lips to hers. "No arguments here."

Within minutes, I'd been swept away with the need to touch her and taste her, and all thoughts of anything that didn't involve having her naked disappeared.

IT WAS a good thing in the end that I'd had the week to gather my bearings, because things changed when Alyssa started her new job at Pembletons the following Monday.

Technically, it made no difference to my day or schedule, and yet somehow it made all the difference in the world.

Rather than waking to foreplay and shower sex, like I had almost every day for a week, I found a raging monster tearing through the bedroom. She hissed at me to pack Phoebe's bag while she ironed her blouse.

Then she decided that the blouse was all wrong for her first day, put it back in the wardrobe, and proceeded to iron another. It was in that moment that I saw precisely where Phoebe had inherited her indecisive wardrobe gene.

We had raced out the door with barely a minute to spare. Alyssa had all but thrown Phoebe out of the car at the day care. Maybe that was a slight exaggeration, but we definitely didn't have the luxury of time to settle her in that we'd had the previous week. As we'd planned, I'd dropped Alyssa off at her job in the city then driven myself to Sinclair Racing.

That afternoon, I ran the same race in reverse; I collected Alyssa in the city before speeding to the day care to pick up Phoebe before they closed at six. We arrived home in an exhausted heap.

I was desperate to have a shower to get the grease and shit from the day off me. Before I'd even hit the first step to go to our en suite, Alyssa declared she would organise dinner, and directed me to please bathe Phoebe while I was upstairs.

The notion terrified me, because I'd only ever helped Alyssa out with the bathing arrangements a few times. I'd never been left alone to handle that shit. It was all still a little new and a lot scary. I had managed eventually though, even if Phoebe's pyjamas had ended up buttoned through the wrong holes, and Alyssa had needed to fix them all before serving the food.

Finally, after wrangling with Phoebe and getting things organised for the next day, Alyssa and I had collapsed into bed, drained and exhausted. I rolled over, pulling her into my arms. Needing her touch, I kissed her forehead once before trailing my attention along her cheek. I captured her mouth with mine.

She kissed me back for less than a second then pulled away from me. She smiled slightly at me before uttering eight little words that ruined my entire evening, "Not tonight, honey. It's been a long day."

Fuck me.

The whole week followed the same pattern, except instead of organising things in the morning, we arranged it all the previous night, using those few precious minutes in the morning to sleep in.

All and all, it was a successful week, except for the serious case of blue balls I'd developed. Lack of sex was definitely a form of torture, especially when it was coupled with sleeping next to Alyssa every night.

CHAPTER FOUR

THREE'S A PARTY

"SQUIRT!" MORGAN SHOUTED from the other side of the almost Olympic-sized swimming pool before diving in.

I gave him a wave before leading Phoebe and Alyssa further into the party. Danny and Hazel had given up their backyard for the preseason launch party, just as they did every year. It was great, because the house was enormous, had ample parking on the street and in the drive, a huge swimming pool, a large patio close to the house, and a gazebo near the pool. Why a couple in their early forties with no kids needed that much in their backyard, especially a pool that size, was beyond me, but it did make for a good entertainment venue.

Eden appeared out of thin air and pulled Alyssa and Phoebe off in another direction. I watched as Alyssa walked away, heading toward a group of WAGs. I took a second to admire the outline of her hips, visible through the almost-but-not-quite see-through material of the sarong she was wearing over the top of her black swimmers. I squirmed a little in my boardies because the sight of her arse wiggling was turning me on, and because things had been lacking on that front, I wanted her so fucking badly. I was entranced by her when Sam sidled past me.

He whistled. "Nice legs."

"Hey, fucker, that's my girl!" I said.

He laughed. "Who said I was talking about the girl?" he asked before winking at me.

I made a mental note to introduce him to Flynn if the opportunity arose.

Morgan rose out of the water, hoisted himself out of the pool, and walked over to me. When he got close enough, he shook his ridiculous mane of hair over me like a fucking dog, drenching my shirt and boardies.

"Hey, shithead," he said. "Where'd the little woman go?"

"Your woman bundled her and Pheebs off to chick central." I nodded in the direction of the girls. The sound of cooing and all the other noises women make when confronted with babies and little children issued from the pack. I shuddered, glad to be able to head off in the opposite direction.

We walked over to the almost car-boot-sized esky, and he bent over into it.

"You want a Pure Blonde?" he asked.

I chuckled. "You offering, beautiful?" I made kissing sounds. "Then again, I wouldn't say there was anything pure about you."

"Fuck off!" he exclaimed as he stood. "And just for that, you get a XXXX."

I wrinkled my nose in disgust, but accepted the beer he threw at me.

"Man, I've barely had time to talk to you at work," he said, cracking open his own. He didn't mention the fact that we never hung out outside of work, mostly because Alyssa hated him. "What's this shit about you driving a Mini?"

"You heard about that, huh?" I asked.

Danny had kept the Mini under wraps for as long as he could, because he didn't want anyone to think I was getting *preferential* treatment—as if being shoved in a four-cylinder tin can was something to crow about.

Like any good secret though, news had spread like wildfire. Especially once the update hit the official website to include the Micro Series logo underneath the ProV8 and Production Series ones. It served as a reminder of the pecking order—as if I didn't already know that the fucking Mini was going to be putting me at the bottom of the heap, racing wise.

At least I was in a car; that's what both Alyssa and Dr. Henrikson, my psychiatrist, said I had to keep telling myself.

"Everyone's heard about it by now," he said.

"And let me guess, I'm the fucking laughingstock."

"Nah, man. In fact, I think you've even started to win over some of your biggest detractors."

I scoffed before taking another big swig of my beer. I hadn't had anything to drink in such a long time it felt like saying hello to an old friend.

"Seriously, man, most everyone I've spoken to has agreed that they think it's gonna be great seeing you back on track. There wasn't anyone who wanted to see the shit hit the fan like it did."

I could imagine exactly who the main exception to the "most everyone" was. I could guarantee his name started with a H, and he was a psycho who'd stolen so much that was important to me. I chugged the last of my beer before grabbing another one.

Morgan continued to talk shop, telling me the goss from upstairs, where the drivers, publicists, strategists, and other "important" people worked. I couldn't believe how long I'd held the same belief, but in my short time with the mechs, I had grown to realise that the people on inflated salaries were no more important than the lowest apprentice. After all, the promoters signed the sponsors, and without the money there would be no car, but without a decent driver and a well-maintained car, the sponsors wouldn't get their required track time.

It was the circle of life, baby—or at least the circle of racing.

The afternoon passed quickly in a haze of swimming, sun, and booze. I gazed in the direction of Alyssa and the girls regularly to make sure she and Phoebe were having a good time.

Eventually, Morgan and I became surrounded by my crew. Ryan and Calem had clearly decided that knowing me gave them an "in" with Morgan, a reason to shoot the shit with him—something that would generally never happen—and they used it to their full advantage. Although it could have been seen to be opportunistic and maybe should have pissed me off, it didn't. It made me feel somewhat important to be the bridge between the two worlds.

By the time the sun was starting to set, I figured it had been a while since I'd last seen Alyssa and decided to go look for her. As I stood, my head spun a little from the alcohol and sun. I hadn't realised quite how much I'd had to drink. It made me a little unsteady on my feet as I staggered off toward the last place I'd seen her.

I hunted around the party for a little while. Most of the couples had come back together and paired off, so I couldn't understand where she could be. Eventually, I spotted her sitting in one of the banana lounges a distance away from everyone else.

She was shaded by the darkness, but it was clear she'd been in the water because the moonlight shone off her wet skin. She'd tied her sarong loosely around her hips, revealing one of her perfect legs right up to her thigh. I licked my lips, longing for a taste of the creamy skin there. I was getting ready to go over to her when I heard her laughter ring out and realised she was talking with someone. I squinted through the darkness to see her companion, expecting to see Eden, or possibly even Hazel, but was instead greeted by the image of Hunter's dark hair and beady black eyes.

Without thought, I raced over to her.

"What the fuck is going on?" I asked, looking between them for a second before closing my eyes. I tried to do my creative visualisation shit that Dr. Henrikson had been teaching me, but it was doing jack shit when faced with the sight of Alyssa and Hunter having a cosy little chat, face-to-face alone in the fucking dark.

"Declan?" Alyssa asked, sounding surprised.

"Who else would it be, Lys?" I couldn't stop the anger that infused my voice.

"I'll leave you two *lovebirds* alone, shall I?" Hunter said, not even attempting to mask his sarcasm. He touched Alyssa's shoulder, and whispered, "I'll talk to *you* later." The innuendo he managed to squeeze into those five words stuck in my craw.

I growled at him, conveying that Alyssa was mine and I was not to be fucked with. I didn't care what the hell Danny said about being a team and my neck being on the line; if Hunter laid even one finger on Alyssa again, I would break it off. Fucking gladly.

She stood quickly and skipped over to me. "What's the mat—" She cut herself off. "God, Dec, how much have you had to drink?"

I shook my head. "Doesn't matter. What matters is you going off into a fucking secluded area with a man who wants nothing more than to devour you."

"Please," Alyssa snapped, the sarcastic tone in her voice clear and undisguised. "We were talking, that's all."

"Don't be so fucking naive, Lys."

"Naive?" She raised her eyebrow. "You think I'm naive?"

"Yeah, I do. Especially if you think Hunter wanted to do anything other than to corner you in a dark place and fuck you stupid."

She stepped back from me. "How stupid do you think I am, Dec?" she spat before turning away.

I reached out for her arm just before she disappeared, grabbing hold so she didn't walk away. I didn't want a repeat of New Year's. "Alyssa, wait!"

"Why?"

"Because . . . I'm sorry, I shouldn't have reacted like that."

She stopped.

"But I do know that he just wanted to bend you over and screw you."

"Oh, you read minds, do you?" The bitter tone in her voice was hard to ignore, and ignited its counterpart in me.

"No, of course not," I snapped back. "But I know the look in his eye and the tone in his voice. He's scum, Lys."

"And how would you know that, Dec?" she asked.

"Because I used to have the same look in my eye and the same tone in my voice. I used to be scum, until I found you again."

She huffed but didn't say anything else.

"Lys," I said, trying to fill my voice with a calm that I didn't feel. I still wanted to go track Hunter down and give him a blow-by-blow on what would happen should he come near Alyssa again, but I needed to fix things first. "I'm sorry. This is supposed to be a party. Can we just forget it and have a good time?" Thinking of having fun reminded me of the missing person in our little party of three. "Where's Phoebe?" I asked, knowing Alyssa wouldn't have just left her alone or with anyone she didn't know.

Alyssa gave a heavy sigh, turned on the spot, and walked off without another word. The set of her jaw and her heavy breathing were like a neon warning sign that I'd overstepped the mark and made her mad.

No, she was more than mad; she was fucking pissed off.

She grabbed something off a small plastic table beside the banana lounge and began to stalk off. I followed her instinctively.

"Alyssa? What the fuck is wrong?" I demanded when she refused to acknowledge me behind her as she walked toward the house.

She whirled on me. "I really shouldn't have to explain it to you!"

I laughed disbelievingly. "Didn't we just fucking work out that I'm not actually able to read minds?"

She sighed. "It's nothing." She turned and started walking again.

"No, fuck that." I reached for her arm. "I know it's not nothing. So spit it out."

When she turned back to me, tears filled her eyes. The sight left me instantly disarmed.

"I came here to support you today, because I wanted to show everyone that we're a family. That we're strong. A united front."

"Yeah, and I appreciate that," I whispered, pulling her in to me.

She let loose a sob. "I've barely seen you all day. I don't know anyone else here. At Hazel's insistence, I put Phoebe to bed in the main house, and then I was alone. I couldn't see you in the throng of people who surrounded you. Then when you finally bother to try to find me, the first thing you do is accuse me of trying to run off or something with the one person who actually made the effort to come over and talk to me while the rest of you boys were doing whatever the fuck it was you were doing."

"What do you want from me?" I asked.

"A little support and some trust."

I had to make her see that I trusted her—it was the snake in the grass, Hunter, I didn't trust. "Baby, do you know that when I was . . ." I didn't think bringing up a reminder of my past would be the wisest thing at that moment. "Well, *before*, I didn't give a shit who someone came to a party with? Only who they left with."

Which was usually me.

"What's your point?" she asked, growing angry again.

I knew I had to be careful stepping around the minefield she was slowly laying out. If I didn't catch shit for the Hunter thing, then it would be for leaving her alone. If I managed to sidestep that devastation, it would be my past that would blow up in my face. But I could see those things coming—what would really set me on my arse were the bombs I didn't expect.

"I love you and you're mine."

"Yours?" she repeated, rolling the word around on her tongue. "Like a piece of furniture? To be paraded around as needed and then dumped when it suits you?" She pushed away from me.

Damn! "You know I don't think of you like that," I growled. "You and Phoebe are everything to me."

"Whatever," she muttered, turning away again.

Fuck! "No, not whatever!" I exclaimed. I grabbed her arm and pulled her roughly against me. To silence her argument, and show her the truth, I kissed her. Hard. Without giving her a chance to resist, I pushed my tongue against her lips and demanded entry. She stiffened at first, her hands pressing against my chest to push me off, but after a beat she responded as I'd hoped she would. She relaxed into me, and her own tongue snaked forward to meet mine.

We moaned with desire in unison. It had been too long. Far too long. My hair trigger was back in force, and my dick was pressing hard against her thigh, with only the material of my board shorts separating us. She hitched one leg around my waist, and I supported her weight with my hands. With her in my arms, I staggered forward until we hit the house. Pressed hard against her, my head swum from the heady combination of Alyssa and alcohol.

She hummed against my mouth before kissing my neck. Even without her touching me, I was just about ready to drop my load.

"Fuck, I want you . . . so badly," I whispered to her.

"Me too," she said, her voice little more than a sigh. "It's usually right about now that Phoebe interrupts us. Or one of us falls asleep."

I grinned wickedly. "Good thing she's inside the house fast asleep and we're out here wide awake, right?" I winked at her.

She smiled slyly. "Good thing," she agreed.

Running her fingers into my hair, she brought my lips back to hers. Then she dropped her hand down to gently rub the tip of my cock through my shorts.

I grunted at the feel of her touch. *Fuck me.*

Someone came up behind me, but I was willing to ignore them.

"Well, I guess it isn't a Sinclair Racing party unless Declan Reede is grinding into someone pinned against the house," one of the promoters said with a laugh on his way past.

Fuck me! I thought. That fucking prick! And just when I'd managed to get Alyssa back onside. I turned back toward her, but she was blushing bright red, and I knew it was over. She untangled herself from me and then set about adjusting her sarong to cover herself back up. *Fuck me!*

"I'm going to check on Phoebe," she whispered before running for the door.

I growled to the empty night. I was alone, pissed off, and had a raging boner to contend with.

Fuck my life.

After a moment, I sucked down a breath and followed Alyssa into the house. Even if I had no chance of getting lucky, at least I could apologise so I didn't spend the rest of the week in the doghouse. Sometimes being a grown-up wasn't much fun.

CHAPTER FIVE

WHAT'S IN A DATE

OVER THE NEXT few weeks, we both became time poor and exhausted from the combination of both working full-time and childrearing, making the well dry up even more. I was nearly at the end of my rope most nights, and most mornings I had to service myself in the shower just to get through the day.

Two afternoons a week, I left work early. On Danny's insistence—and because he was picking up the tab—I started back with private weekly sessions with Dr. Henrikson. In addition, I went with Alyssa one afternoon a week for couples' counselling. It had actually been her suggestion. Rather than simply enjoying our post-setting-a-date high, she'd pushed for the appointments. Even though I wanted nothing more than to tell her to fuck off when she made the suggestion, she'd quickly backed it up by saying that she wanted to make sure everything was on the table before we took the final plunge so we could enter married life unencumbered by the shit of our past.

I couldn't say I blamed her for wanting that.

Maybe it was too early to judge, but the sessions we'd been to so far seemed like a waste of time to me. We never talked about the future during our joint sessions, and despite the reason Alyssa wanted to start them, we rarely talked about the past, either. It was only when something was said that hit one of our "hot buttons" that we would discuss anything other than our day-to-day lives.

All we seemed to do was rehash what had happened during the week between our visits, talking about our high points and our low points. Alyssa had blushed scarlet when I'd listed her giving me a midnight blow job as a high point in one session, but Dr. Henrikson hadn't even blinked. I often spent the sessions wondering why we were paying to see someone to do what we could do at home for free. After all, it wasn't like he was helping us through issues the way he did with me privately.

At one of my private sessions, the irritation became too much and it all boiled over.

"Declan, you are the one who requested additional meetings," Dr. Henrikson responded calmly. "I just want to ensure that you have the space and tools to discuss your lives and any issues which may arise in a calm and rational manner. That will be the key to a successful, long-term marriage. If you wish to stop our sessions, just say the word."

"Alyssa wouldn't like that," I grumbled.

"Have you asked her?"

I stared at him blankly.

"Have you asked her how she feels about the sessions? Whether they are a benefit to her? Whether she feels they are a benefit to you both?"

I shook my head and crossed my arms.

"Talk to her about it."

"What's the point?" I said. "She's the one who wanted to do weekly fucking sessions."

"The point is to communicate," he replied.

I harrumphed and crossed my arms tighter. He correctly interpreted it as a desire to change the subject.

"How's the Mini coming along?" he asked, almost conversationally.

I groaned and buried my head in my hands, thinking of the disastrous attempt at testing a few days earlier.

The car had fit me like a pair of boxers two sizes too small. With all the gizmos, gauges, and gadgets squeezed into the cabin with me, there was barely room to move. In fact, everything was so cramped and tiny, I could practically taste my balls. Worse, I'd barely had ten minutes on the test track before my time was cut short when Hunter decided he needed to urgently test some adjustments made to his car.

The call in my ear telling me to "bring 'er in" so Hunter could do his thing was proof of the pecking order—the reminder I didn't need that I was bottom of the heap. Lowest of the fucking low.

"Seriously, Doc, why would you even bring that shit up?" I asked.

"Because I don't know if you see it as the positive that it is yet. I think one day you will see that it *is* a step in the right direction."

I shook my head.

"I know you don't believe me. But will you at least trust me?"

"It's a tin can on wheels," I snapped. "There are no positives in that. And before you say it—I know, I know 'at least I'm racing again'." I mimicked his accent and made a mocking face at him.

He chuckled. "You know, Declan, if nothing else, you bring me amusement."

I covered my face with my hands. "If nothing else I bring you a pile of money, you mean." Once I'd lost the more lucrative paycheque of being a driver, he'd dropped his billing rate and bulk billed as many sessions as he could to ensure I could continue to get the help I needed. But now that it was back on Danny's dime, he was earning a small fortune every week.

He was silent for a while, and I peeked out from between my fingers. He was smiling when I glanced at him.

"There's that too," he said with a laugh.

I chuckled and shook my head.

We moved swiftly onto other topics. I had to hand it to the doc; no matter how unorthodox he might have been, he could read my moods and respond accordingly. Overall, I did actually feel better after each session.

Between the counselling sessions and having Alyssa and Phoebe living their lives with me, things seemed to get better day by day. Even work was pretty decent. The only stain on my first weeks as an apprentice grease monkey was the same as my first day: Hunter.

Fucking Hunter.

Somehow, our team drew the short straw, and we ended up being allocated as the primary crew for Hunter's car. No one else on my crew seemed to mind too much, but I hated that jumped-up fucking prick and his bullshit ideas. Memories of the way he'd disrespected his pit crew at Wood Racing were stuck in my head at every turn.

Not to mention the fact that his head was so far up his arse he'd need a map and a flashlight to ever find his way back out again. Although, he would probably refuse the torch considering he thought the sun shone from there anyway.

It seemed as if his day wasn't quite complete until he had found me and given me shit about something. At first, it was about my apparent inability to drive, even though I had driven circles around him when we were both on the racetrack the previous few years.

The article in *Woman's Idea* was also a source of fun for him, with him quoting my own words about Phoebe and Alyssa back at me with a voice filled with derision. He'd also taken to asking me about my "gold-digging" girlfriend. It got to the point at one stage where I stalked up to Danny's office near the end of January and barged in, not even waiting for an answer after knocking on the door.

"You have to get rid of that lunatic," I said, waving my arms as if Hunter-the-fucker was right behind me.

Danny looked up at me and sighed. "What is the problem now, Declan?"

"It's that psycho, Hunter!"

"Hunter is a valued driver with this team, Declan," Danny said, his tone patient even if that patience seemed to be wearing thin.

"No, he's a fucking disaster. He's arrogant. He doesn't have any regard for what anyone else thinks. He's hit on or slept with every female in a hundred-mile radius of this building—"

Danny cut me off with a quiet chuckle.

"What?" I demanded.

"You could be describing someone who is standing not very far from me right now, you know."

I realised he meant me. "I am *nothing* like that fucker."

"Maybe not now," Danny answered diplomatically. "But it wasn't that long ago that almost those exact words were used in complaint about you."

To say I was fucking stunned was an understatement. "Who by?"

He shook his head. "I never betray the confidence of a source, but I will tell you what I told them. Your comments have been noted, and I will take them on board, but as long as he keeps his nose clean, stays away from bad press, and gets around the racetrack cleanly and quickly, I have no reason to let him go."

"You've got to be fucking kidding me!"

"Declan, of anyone's neck around here, yours is the one I would worry about."

"What?" I asked, shocked. I'd been working my arse off to learn the trade. I'd done everything asked of me and, in my opinion, I'd kept my nose clean.

"Don't get me wrong," Danny said. "I've heard good things about you from Liam and, as I've proven to you, I believe in giving you this second chance. But at the end of the day, this is a team and all members need to get along with each other. If you can't make the effort to get along with Hunter, we might have problems."

I gaped at Danny for a second before murmuring, "Fine, *I'll* make an effort." I turned away. "But I guarantee he won't." I stalked from his office without another word.

Danny no doubt thought I was just mad that Hunter had stolen my position on the team, but that wasn't the only thing that pissed me off. He was the epitome of arrogance. He propositioned every girl in sight, harassing them until they finally submitted, and then spread rumours about how easy they'd been to bed.

At least I hadn't heard any whispers about spiked drinks yet, and I was listening pretty hard. The smallest shred of evidence and I would have been up in Danny's office over and over to demand action.

Even though it seemed impossible, I did as Danny asked. I tried to make nice with Hunter, at least as much as I could, but I found it far easier to avoid him completely.

I WAS at the end of my fucking rope when Liam sought me out. It was a typical Tuesday early in February, except for the fact that prep for the overseas races was in full swing and had left all of the crew up to their eyeballs with shit to do. I was tired, dirty, covered in grease, and had just narrowly escaped another encounter with Hunter.

"Sparky, you need to speak to Danny," Liam said when he caught me.

"Hi to you too," I muttered.

He rolled his eyes. "Just get your arse up to Danny's office, would you?"

"Fine. Whatever." I really wasn't in the mood to argue. All I could do was hope that Danny wasn't going to pile more shit on me; I was already at my limit for the day. Especially when I was due to fly out for Bahrain in just a few days, and while I was preparing for that, Alyssa was getting ready for her graduation. A huge event in her life that I was going to miss just because of a fucking car race.

I trudged myself up to Danny's office, wondering whether he'd be upset if I asked to be excused from the Bahrain race. Maybe I could make it to Alyssa's graduation—and be left jobless in one fell swoop.

With a sigh, I gave up the thought. I knocked on his door and waited.

A quick rustling of papers sounded from within before his voice called out, "Enter."

I walked in and sat without waiting for further invitation. It was hard to forget the last few times I'd been in his office—the good and the bad. It was hard to know whether to be anticipating or worrying about what was going to happen next. "You wanted to see me?"

"Indeed." He met my eye as he leaned back against his chair. "A little while ago, I was given some information about the new race season, and I've been wondering what to do with it."

I nodded, thinking he was trying to tell me they weren't going to race the Mini after all. Even though I'd expected to be relieved, I actually didn't. Instead, I felt . . . disappointed almost.

"It seems that ProV8 officials have changed the rules for the endurance races. All championship drivers have to race in their own cars." He paused and regarded me.

I nodded to show I was listening—intently this time, not like when he told me about the Mini in the first place.

"It means, of course, that we can't pair up two lead drivers like we have in previous years."

"Why?" I asked, surprising myself at my outburst.

"Something about helping to even up the odds and trying to increase the number of cars in the field. A whole pile of reasons really, but regardless of why, it's happening and will be formally announced just before the Bahrain race."

"Okay." My fingers bounced against my leg as I considered the possible reasons he could be telling me this.

"Now I'm left with something of a quandary. I need to find another driver for each of the cars I'm running in the races."

I tried to beat back the bubble of hope building rapidly in my chest. I really didn't want another disappointment like the one with the Mini. And yet, it expanded until I could barely breathe and swallowing became impossible.

"I was wondering whether you—"

I was nodding my agreement before he'd finished the sentence. *Yes, dammit, yes!*

"—know anyone who knows how to handle a ProV8 car?"

"What?" I asked, slumping back down in my chair as the

bubble burst, leaving a cold emptiness in its wake. I couldn't believe he would ask me that. Did he want me to go on a fucking recruitment drive on his fucking behalf or something?

He chuckled. "So you don't know anyone who would want to drive a V8 again, and who knows how to get around a track?"

"You mean other than me, right?" I snapped, pinching the bridge of my nose to try to calm myself.

"I never said that."

I sat bolt upright in my seat, my eyes wide, barely daring to hope that I was hearing him right. "Are you asking me?" I asked. "To drive?"

"I'm asking whether you would be interested in the potential for the opportunity to drive."

"You're shitting me?!" I couldn't stop the shit-eating grin that spread across my lips.

"I most certainly am not shitting you," Danny said with a chuckle. "I'm saying that there just might be an opportunity for you to hop back in a car for a few races at the end of the year—"

I cut him off. "What's the catch?"

He shrugged. "The usual. Keep your nose clean. Keep yourself together. Do what we need you to do. Any questions?"

"Just one," I said.

He raised his eyebrow at me.

"Can I drive with Morgan?"

His returning smile was enigmatic. "I wouldn't dream of putting you in a car with Hunter."

I breathed a sigh of relief. "Well, thank fuck for that."

I practically skipped out of Danny's office once we were finished. I spent the day working hard, knowing I needed to finish early to make my couples' appointment with Alyssa and Dr. Henrikson.

"SKIPPING OFF early again, huh, Reede?"

I rolled my eyes when I heard Hunter's voice behind me as I was packing away the last of my tools. I didn't respond to him though.

"I heard a rumour that you leave early often so you can go

home and have a bit of afternoon delight with that chick of yours."

With a deep breath, I clenched my fist but said nothing as I continued to pack up. He leaned against the wall that my toolbox rested against, and I could see him in my periphery.

"Of course, I don't blame you. God, if I had a chance I'd be all up in that again and again. I'd have her screaming my name so loudly. In fact, I would make sure I ruined her for all other men."

I dropped a spanner roughly into the box. I couldn't react. I knew I couldn't react. I needed to be Zen. I took a deep breath and returned to my stance of trying my damnedest to ignore him.

"I can just imagine what her tight pussy would feel like," he said, groaning softly. "Wait, it is tight, isn't it?"

A low growl escaped my chest—so much for my "ignore him" policy.

"It's not all stretched from childbirth, is it? I just thought . . . Well, she looks like she's too posh to push."

"Shut. Up," I warned.

"Of course," he continued, dropping his voice lower. "If her pussy *was* too loose, I could always fuck her mouth. Her sweet little mouth . . . I bet she'd like me fucking it hard while I pull her hair tight."

I spun toward him, my hand clenched into a tight fist. He anticipated my move and ducked out of the way seconds before I contacted. My fist slammed into the wall behind him. I cried out as it impacted.

"Uh-uh, Reede," he said, as he wiggled his finger in front of my face. "Careful now, you wouldn't want to tarnish your reputation, would you?"

"Fuck you," I spat at him, shaking my hand in an attempt to relieve the pain.

"Temper, temper."

"You talk about Alyssa ever again, I'll show you a fucking temper," I warned. "If you talk *to* her, I'll fucking kill you."

He smirked.

"You wipe that smile off your face, or I'll fucking wipe it off for you," I threatened.

He held his hands up in surrender. "I just came to congratulate you on your engagement, man. I don't understand why you hate me so much."

I scrunched my eyebrows in confusion. What the hell was his game? "Just stay the fuck away from me and from Alyssa."

I turned to leave and almost ran straight into Danny. One look at his face told me he'd seen the end of the conversation, but not the beginning.

Fuck my life.

"Declan, can I have a word before you go?" His clipped tone told me it wasn't really a question.

"Mmm-hmmm." I forced the sound out through clenched teeth. I couldn't trust myself to say anything more than that. Not now. My mouth was liable to get me in even more trouble.

Once I was tucked away in his office, I listened silently to Danny's rant about how he was disappointed that I didn't keep up the improved attitude I'd demonstrated so far. I nodded and said I'd try harder in all the right places. Of course, what I really wanted to say was that he needed to get rid of Hunter because he was a troublemaker, but I held my tongue.

At least until I got to my appointment with Alyssa and Dr. Henrikson.

"That fucker!" I fumed as I slammed open the door and entered the room. "That motherfucking son of a bitch."

"Dec, what is it?" Alyssa asked, leaping up to rush over to me.

I sighed. Holding her in my arms helped to lessen some of my anger. "It's nothing," I said. I sighed again and looked into her eyes, softly brushing my thumb along her cheek.

"No, Declan," Dr. Henrikson interrupted our moment. "It's not nothing. Something was clearly upsetting you, and you should take this opportunity to share it with Alyssa."

I huffed. "It's really nothing," I said. "Just that motherfucker, Hunter." I felt Alyssa stiffen in my arms. Even though she'd apologised a hundred times, she still felt guilty over the preseason party incident. We'd discussed it a few times during our sessions, so I knew she didn't know who he was at the time and hadn't meant to be so crazy. I just hoped she understood now that he wasn't as clean-cut and wholesome as he'd appeared then.

"What happened?" Dr. Henrikson knew all about my past with Hunter, and everything that had happened since his start at Sinclair Racing.

"He said some not very complimentary things about Alyssa," I said. "The fucker," I murmured under my breath. "And he might have cost me my chance to get back into a V8."

Alyssa pulled back from me. "You might be back in a V8?"

I smiled slightly at her. "If I keep my nose clean."

"Wow, that's awesome news." She smiled.

"That bastard makes it awfully hard though," I said. "I just want to take his face and smash it into my toolbox sometimes." I saw the doc open his mouth, but I cut him off by raising my hand. "I know, I know, I need to work on my temper. That's what I pay you for though, right?"

Alyssa giggled. The sound of it was like angels fucking singing or some shit—it was enough to soothe the beast that wanted to make an impression in someone's face with my knuckles.

"That's exactly what I needed to hear," I told her. "That makes my shitty-arse day that much better." I leant in and touched a gentle kiss to her lips.

We sat on the couch and I listened as Alyssa spilled about her day. Apparently, some new chick had started in her office. Some bird named Lily or something. Alyssa listed it as the low of her week, saying she'd met the girl on her trip to London, and they didn't exactly hit it off. As she spoke, she leaned further and further away from me. She cast odd looks in my direction whenever she looked up from her hands, which wasn't often as she'd been staring at them for most of the conversation.

"What is it?" I asked.

I saw Dr. Henrikson nodding out of the corner of my eye. I could see this was what he was trying to get us to do—ask questions and communicate with one another.

"It's just that, well, you know her," Alyssa muttered into her hands.

71

I shook my head. "I didn't meet anyone you worked with there—"

She cut me off. "At the bar."

I couldn't understand what she meant at first, but then I remembered. After almost a week of waiting for Alyssa to call, I'd been ready to give up the search. Then, she'd called but hung up before I could speak to her. With the new hope and information the call had left me with, I'd waited in front of her hotel for nearly an entire day.

Then, I had given up well and truly and decided I needed to get my own needs serviced. I'd dressed up, gone to a bar—an Australian-themed one recommended by the cabbie—and . . .

"Fuck, baby, I'm sorry. I didn't know you worked with her. I didn't even know her name." The words tasted poisonous, and worse, they weren't even a lie.

A tear dropped from Alyssa's eyes, closely followed by another. "That's worse," she whispered. "You would have screwed her, wouldn't you? I mean, if I hadn't been there."

I ducked my head so I wouldn't have to meet her gaze if she looked up at me. She knew the answer as well as I did. After all, she knew my past. She knew everything about me. I'd thought she'd accepted it, but obviously being faced with such a sharp reminder of it must have bought the pain back.

"Yeah," I whispered, refusing to lie to her even though the truth was a barbed pill. "I would have."

Out of the corner of my eye, I saw her nod once as her mouth mashed into an unhappy line.

"I'm sorry," I said, turning to her and grabbing her hand softly. "I was an arse. A fucking jerk. I know I'll never be able to apologise enough for what I did when we weren't together, for the way I treated you and, well, fuck, everyone really, but I hope one day you'll be able to forgive me completely."

"I have," she murmured. "At least I thought I had. Seeing Lily today just sent my mind back to the place I was in while in London. I was so scared, and so angry, and I just didn't know what I wanted. I couldn't believe your reaction to Phoebe was so strong—or so negative."

I bobbed my head in shame, still unwilling to meet her gaze. "It was just a shock. I should never have acted like that."

"No," she whispered. "You shouldn't have."

Those four words, and the pain that echoed in them, hurt me more deeply than almost anything else she had ever said. I bit my lip. I knew apologising again wouldn't do anything.

"But you shouldn't have found out like that, either. I should have found the courage to tell you on the plane. Or when you were in hospital after Bathurst."

Instead of focusing on the what-ifs and the regret, I decided to turn my mind to what we had.

"That doesn't matter now. What matters is this . . ." I held her hands in mine, tracing my thumb over the line of her engagement ring. It was the reminder of what I needed to say to her. "Thank you. For raising our daughter into the wonderful child she is now, despite all the odds you faced."

Her shoulder lifted into a half-hearted shrug. "I did what I had to."

I finally looked up to meet her eyes.

"No, you didn't," I disagreed. "You went so far above 'what you had to.' You could have sat around on the single-parent pension and not got a job, but you didn't. You showed our daughter the value of hard work. You could have given up on your dreams and not gone to uni, God knows it would have been the easier path, but you didn't. You're the strongest person I know. When we were apart, I took the easy road. I turned to drugs, alcohol, and loose chicks to try to satisfy what was missing. You were so much stronger than I ever could have been. And not only did you not give up on yourself the way I did, you raised another person. And you did it all without becoming bitter or twisted. Without telling Phoebe what an absolute shithead I was." I reached out for her hand and pulled it gently to my mouth. I kissed each finger softly. "I am in awe of you."

She gasped as I finished. Dr. Henrikson applauded lightly. At the sound, I turned to look at him. I'd completely forgotten his

73

presence.

"Declan, you were asking what the point is behind these meetings."

Alyssa glared at me, and I gave her my best "I'm innocent" look.

"This is the point," he declared. "You have taken the mundane, the everyday struggles, and used it to raise and discuss a bigger issue from your past without shouting and arguments. When you argue and fight, you need to try to find the reason behind the argument, because it is rarely what you are actually fighting about."

We talked a little bit more, with Dr. Henrikson chipping in occasionally as needed. It was probably our best couple session ever, and I couldn't help the not-so-small amount of pride I felt, knowing that we got to that point ourselves. I had to hand it to him—the doc was a fucking genius.

CHAPTER SIX

EVERYTHING

I STARED USELESSLY at the ceiling, just as I had for the past four hours, willing myself to sleep, but failing miserably. Despite the progress Alyssa and I had made at Dr. Henrikson's earlier, I couldn't shake the remorse I felt over what had almost happened with Lily right in front of Alyssa's eyes—the guilt that Alyssa had to deal with the fallout every day—or the anger I felt toward Hunter. I shivered as dark memories of the night he'd shown me the depths he'd go to in order to get what he wanted invaded all of my senses.

The scariest thing for me was that his darkness was only a few steps away from the way I'd lived my life. True, I'd never gone so far as to drug someone, and I hoped I never would have no matter how bad things got, but it was still a fine fucking line I'd been toeing.

I'd honestly fooled myself into thinking that had been the ideal lifestyle. I'd been so certain that nothing in the world could satisfy me more than a quick screw with a complete stranger. I had been so utterly and completely wrong. Despite going days without sex due to our day-to-day life, the moments I shared with Alyssa still satisfied me more than anything else ever had or could.

Even as I recalled the blonde and brunette I'd saved from Hunter's clutches that night, I knew it was too late to share my knowledge with anyone else regardless of what he did to me at work. Too much time had passed. Too much of everything had passed. It would just look like sour grapes if I brought it up with Danny. It was why I had kept it hidden for so long; nothing could come from sharing what I knew—nothing but more retribution and heartache.

I could take comfort in knowing that if it was still happening, Danny would not allow Hunter to stay on the team. Above everything else, Danny had a prevailing sense of justice. It was a cold comfort though, and one I hated myself over for trying to find.

As dark memories swirled, threatening to choke me, I shivered in the night. There was no way I could ever let myself fall back into those habits, or let anyone subject Phoebe to that sort of treatment.

"Cold?" Alyssa mumbled sleepily before sighing and cuddling into me.

I hummed in response, not wanting to wake her further.

She curled herself onto my chest with half her hair splayed out over my arm and the other half curled around under her chin.

I shifted my gaze from the ceiling and onto her angelic face. My heart expanded looking down over her. She and Phoebe looked so similar when they slept. Both held my heart hostage, and I never wanted that to change.

Alyssa's fingers twirled through her hair as if she weren't able to kick the nervous habit, not even in her sleep. I captured her left hand with my right and interlocked our fingers. I still couldn't believe the joy I felt every time I touched the warm metal band and diamonds of her ring. It was a small reminder that she'd agreed to spend her life at my side. The thought made me smile and shoved the darkness aside for a moment. I pulled her tighter into me, kissing her forehead while silently reaffirming everything I'd previously promised her aloud.

I would never hurt her again.

I could never leave her again.

I couldn't imagine my life without her.

It was the reason I had to keep her as far away from Hunter as humanly possible.

With that thought came the sickening reality that he could seriously hurt me now. After all, I had something that I hadn't had during our previous encounters.

I had something—*everything*—to lose.

And in the morning, I was getting on a plane and leaving everything important to me for two weeks. I tightened my hold on Alyssa, not wanting to let her go until I absolutely had to.

WITH MY eyes closed, I tried everything I could to ignore the turbulence rocking my seat. Every time I thought it might finally be over, the plane would dip or bounce. My nails were practically embedded in the armrest and my mind overran with thoughts that I'd seen Alyssa for the last time. That I'd kissed Phoebe goodbye forever, not just for the trip.

The plane was going to go plummeting into the ocean; I was certain of it.

The turbulence on the way to London had been a fuckload easier to contend with because I'd had someone to distract me. To soothe me and talk to me—even if we had spent half the flight fighting. A smile crossed my lips just thinking about that eventful trip. God, it was crazy how pussy-whipped I'd become, but the truth was there'd been an Alyssa-shaped hole in my life for a damn long time before then.

A ding indicated that the seatbelt lights were off, but fuck if I was going to chance opening my eyes just to see the plane lunge downward again.

"What are you smiling about, fuckhead?"

The decent mood that had been slowly gathering over me, that might have been enough to wipe away the terror I'd felt over the crazed leaps and falls the plane was making, dissipated the instant I heard Hunter's voice.

The space beside me, that had been occupied by Morgan until about fifteen minutes earlier when Eden stole him away—no doubt for some mile-high action—was now filled with Hunter.

I huffed out a breath and ignored him as best as I could.

"Are you picturing that fine arse you left at home? I'd be smiling too."

Even though I pretended to be completely unaffected, my breath grew harsh and my fingers were curled into fists, so it was impossible for Hunter not to see that his words were hitting their target.

"You know, if I'd had just a few more minutes alone with that woman, she wouldn't have been yours. She would've been screaming my name while I stripped that little black bikini off her body."

A low growl reverberated in my chest. I needed to shut him up. My fingered curled and uncurled as I formed fists over and over. "Shut up."

"Aww, what's the matter, *squirt*, can't take a little ribbing?"

His use of Morgan's nickname on top of everything he said forced my eyes open. "Fuck. Off."

"Do you really think that she won't have guys sniffing all over her while you're gone? How long do you think she'll resist before falling to her knees and sucking their cocks?"

With one hand, I pinched the bridge of my nose. The other curled around the end of the armrest so it didn't fly at his face.

"I can see her now with those fuckable lips of hers wrapped around cock after cock. Can't you just picture it?"

"I said shut the fuck up!" The words burst from me without thought, filling the whole cabin.

Two cabin crew turned to look at me, each wearing a frown. Fuck. If I kept it up, I'd probably end up tied up in the back of the plane—or at the very least booted back to economy.

"Touchy," Hunter said, his lips curling into a smile that was almost a sneer. A second later, he moved away back toward his seat.

A couple of minutes later, Morgan slid back beside me with an I-just-had-sex grin on his face. Fuck. Between Hunter's fucking mouth and Morgan and Eden having it on as if to remind me what I was missing, the trip was going to be hell.

It was going to be a fucked-up couple of weeks before I could finally go home.

CHAPTER SEVEN

YAS, DEAR

I ROLLED OVER, trying to let sleep claim me. As if she were there, and aware how badly I needed to rest, Alyssa's voice called to me from the void, tempting me into the darkness to join her.

"Hey, you," her words carried to me, and I turned to greet her. It'd been too long since I'd looked at her face, too many days I'd spent away from her.

My eyes practically bugged out of my head at the sight that met me. She stood beside a car, which barely earned a second glance despite how hot it was. From my cursory inspection, I could tell it was a red 1969 Chevelle with full chrome accessories, but that didn't matter. It was a shit-hot car, but had nothing on the chick in front of it.

The saliva left my mouth as I watched her move. A vivid purple halter-neck bikini top held her breasts front and centre. The round curve of her cleavage was on display, begging me for attention. She twisted her hips slightly and the micro-mini skirt she wore rode up just a little, revealing the bottom of her arse cheeks and the lace of the boy-leg shorts wrapped around them. A pair of black thigh-high come-fuck-me boots encased her feet and most of her legs, hinting at the shapely calves within. A messy bun on the top of her head and aviator sunnies completed the look.

She was hot.

Fucking hot.

Melt my dick before I got it anywhere near her hot.

It was all I could do to root myself to the spot so that I didn't bend her over the hood of the car and fuck her stupid. I grew painfully hard at the sight of her. The slightest touch would have been more than enough to set me off.

I grinned goofily at her. "Hey, yourself."

She hitched her leg up onto the car's chrome bumper. Usually, I would have freaked at a car being disrespected in such a way, but I was too distracted by the way the lace of her boy-leg panties hugged her thigh. I licked my lips hungrily as I imagined my hand trailing under the lace.

"You wanna ride?" she asked, her voice dripping with innuendo as her fingers traced along her thigh.

I nodded silently.

"Well, come inside then," she said, dancing her fingers over the material that covered her pussy before moving her deft fingers lower to the top of her boot, causing her waist to bend and more of her arse to be revealed.

I gulped and stepped closer to her. I took my time in examining the small patch of skin showing at the top of her legs. It may have been small, but it hinted at things that sent my body racing. I shivered with pleasure as I slid my hand along the outside of her thigh and pushed it up under her skirt. I hooked my finger into her panties and slowly peeled them off without removing any other item of clothing. I hoped she understood that, given the chance, I would fuck her all night long with those sexy-arse boots on. I pushed her forward over the bonnet of the car, her micro-mini unable to cover her arse or pussy any longer. I ran my fingers over the curve of her cheeks and lightly slapped one, earning a soft moan in response.

Alyssa stayed in the position I had placed her in while I stepped back to admire the view. The combination of fuck-hot car and even hotter chick had my boner raging and begging for attention. I closed my eyes and slid the zipper of my pants down. I wrapped my hands around my cock and pulled it free before pushing my hips forward. I ran my hand along my length, anxious to drive it into her.

I squirmed in the seat in anticipation.

A frown crossed my brow. *Seat? What the fuck?*

Something was wrong.

Panic rose in me, choking me until all thoughts of Alyssa were gone as I clawed at my throat to shake loose the lump that stopped me from breathing. Gulping down on oxygen, I tried to work out what happened. I was sitting, but I'd been standing seconds before. The movement wasn't possible, and yet it had happened. I opened my eyes and they met Alyssa's.

She was staring at me through the windshield of the car with a smile on her lips. A low moan escaped her as I met her gaze. Seconds later, her eyes rolled up in pleasure and she grunted as her pelvis pushed against the car, causing the whole thing to shake.

"More," she whispered. "Oh, God, yes."

I was almost unable to turn away from the look of pleasure on her face, but when I did I saw Hunter snarling at me from behind her as he rocked to the rhythm of her body. His hands clutched her hips tightly as he pounded into her relentlessly.

"No!" I screamed.

"Yes!" Alyssa cried in unison.

I tried to get out of the car, but I couldn't. I tugged on the door handle repeatedly. My heart beat like a drum, louder and louder. As it sped up, so did the rocking of the car. I clawed at the lock to break free, but it wouldn't budge.

"Right there, oh, baby," Alyssa moaned. "Oh, fuck, yes. Oh, God."

I pulled at the door lock urgently. "No, Alyssa, don't . . ." I cried, body-slamming the door in a vain effort to get free.

"Alyssa!" I cried, sitting bolt upright.

Holy shit. I panted as the efforts of my nightmare left me breathless. I sighed and collapsed back onto the bed, relieved that it had just been a dream. When I rolled over to pull Alyssa in to me, to remind myself that she was mine, she wasn't there. My heart pounded faster again as I rolled to the other side of the bed, wondering where she was.

When I was unable to find her or even a trace of her existence, I couldn't breathe. I patted her side of the bed, but it was cold. Her smell didn't linger on the pillow the way I had come to expect.

Was everything that had happened just a dream? Would I find myself back in the arms of a different woman each night, seeking solace that I would never find? Nightmares and dreams were an ever-present part of my life back then, but I'd mostly escaped them since being with Alyssa; although I didn't know that my insomnia would ever fully abate.

Oh, God, had I even been with her? I silently begged God, or whoever would listen, to not let it all be a dream. I needed her. I couldn't live in a world where I didn't have her.

Stumbling out of the bed, I hip-checked an unfamiliar dresser. A loud clinking sound disturbed me. God, was I in some stranger's house even now? I shook my head to try to clear the fatigue, and struggled to remember where I was. There were two empty Jack bottles resting on top of the dresser. Things weren't looking good for me. Two bottles was pushing the limit—even for me. Although part of me reasoned that my head wasn't aching as badly as it would have had I drunk that much on my own.

I fumbled along the wall to find a light switch. As soon as my fingers touched the smooth panel, I flicked the lights on. The room burst into sudden brightness. The generic, un-lived-in feel startled me at first. Then I sighed as memories of where I was came flooding back.

Sagging with relief, I walked over to the window and looked out at the Yas nightscape. Fuck, I missed Alyssa. I'd only been in Abu Dhabi for a couple of days, but it was too long. I remembered that my crew, as well as Morgan and Eden, had come to my room last night to attack our duty-free supplies for a post first-race celebratory drink.

We'd only had a few each in the end. Enough to leave me buzzed and disorientated, but not enough to warrant an apology to Alyssa.

I sat on the end of the bed, trying to calculate the time difference. It was early Sunday morning in Abu Dhabi, so I guessed it would be sometime during the day on Sunday in Brisbane. The exact time didn't really matter though; what mattered was that I was an arse. Because Saturday was Alyssa's graduation. Which meant I'd been in a foreign country, most likely drinking with my work buddies, while my future wife had walked across the stage to get her diploma. I sucked. I'd failed as a husband before I even became one.

Needing to talk to her, I picked up the phone to dial her mother's number in Brisbane. I knew there was a risk I'd get Curtis or Josh, but I didn't really care. I just needed to talk to Alyssa — especially after the nightmare I'd had. If they didn't help me do that, they could go fuck themselves.

"Hello?"

I breathed a sigh of relief when she was the one to answer.

"Hi," I said sheepishly. I wasn't sure if she'd be upset with me now that she'd actually gone through her graduation ceremony without me.

"Declan!" I could hear the genuine smile in her voice and it helped calm some of the worry I had felt.

"How'd it go?" I asked.

"Congratulations," she said at the same time.

We both chuckled nervously.

"You first," I said.

"It was good. I think Phoebe got a little bored though. Mum ended up taking her out of the room to get her to quiet down."

My guilt ratcheted up another half-dozen notches. I should have been there for her. I should have been the one trying to calm Phoebe down. I couldn't help the thought that if I'd been there I would have miraculously settled Phoebe, and we both could have watched as the most important person in our lives crossed the stage.

"I'm so—"

"Don't apologise, Dec, I understand. And from the looks of it, you kicked some butt out there."

I smiled at her attempt to cheer me up. "Anyone else could have done it."

"Your team placed first and fourth. That's great by anyone's standard."

I shrugged. It had been worth celebrating the night before, but faced with what I'd missed, it seemed irrelevant. "First, second would have been better. Besides, it's not like I had any real control over it."

She sighed. "Isn't it a team effort? If you hadn't completed the pit stops as quickly as you did, Hunter would never have won."

"Well, isn't that fantastic," I muttered. "I can change a fucking wheel faster than anyone else. Yay, me."

She laughed. "Are you going to be this moody after every race?"

"Probably," I contended. "But more at the moment, because I feel like a jackass for missing your graduation just so I could change a few fucking tyres."

"We've been over that, and you know that I understand. Besides, from what I've been told, there's plenty of video of it. You'll be able to watch me falling flat on my face again and again."

I couldn't help chuckling before I bit my lip to stop myself. "You didn't."

She laughed loudly. "Oh, I most certainly did. Much to Flynn's amusement. I didn't hear the end of it all night."

"Flynn was there?" I don't know why, but that piece of information surprised me and pissed me off just a little too. Even though things had been on decent terms when we'd left Brisbane, the fact that Alyssa hadn't mentioned anything to me made me wonder whether I had cause for concern. Had she confided in him the disappointment that she didn't feel she could show me?

"Of course. You didn't think he was going to miss it after spending so much time studying, did you?"

My gut twisted tightly on itself. Once a-fucking-gain, Flynn had been there when I couldn't. I just growled something noncommittal in response.

She stifled a laugh. "Are you jealous?"

"No!" I snapped too quickly.

"Dec, it was his graduation too, you dill. Even though he started before me, he studied part-time for a while, so he ended up finishing the same time as I did."

"Really?"

"Yes. God, you worry about the strangest things sometimes." She laughed for a second, but then her voice turned serious. "I miss you."

I clutched the phone as I stood and leaned against the window, looking at the sky. Somewhere, many kilometres away, Alyssa was under the same sky. The thought comforted me a little. "I miss you too. So fucking much."

"There's only a little over a week left now. It won't be too bad," Alyssa said, but she sounded about as convinced about it as I was.

Due to there being only five days between the Abu Dhabi and Bahrain races, Danny had decided it was better for the team to stay overseas. He had booked out some workshop space and had shipped over more than enough materials and equipment to make all the necessary repairs to rebuild before Bahrain. Unfortunately, it meant that I would be away from home for at least another eight days—despite the way Alyssa had tried to spin it to sound like it was shorter than that. It also meant that I had to be in close quarters with Hunter not only for our usual working hours, but practically 24/7.

Fuck. My. Life.

"It's fucking torture," I admitted. "I've barely been sleeping."

As if my words reminded her of the time difference, she asked, "What time is it there?"

"Fuck knows," I said. I didn't want to admit the actual time, because I knew she'd kick me off the phone and back into bed.

"Should you still be asleep?" she asked.

"Probably," I admitted. "But I can't sleep. I need you."

"You've managed without me before."

"Barely," I whispered. If only she knew just how hard I had to work to keep her out of my mind, to get through even one day without her. I couldn't expect her to ever really understand though. It was only after I'd stopped trying to do it that *I* had realised it.

"So, what's on the agenda for you for today?" she asked, clearly trying to change direction.

I sighed. "Just the usual shit. I have to be at the track in a few hours to help prep the car."

"You should probably get back to bed then," she murmured.

"I probably should," I agreed. "But I really don't want to. I'd rather keep talking to you."

"I know. Me too. But I'd feel guilty if your performance suffered because you were up at all hours talking to me."

"I don't give a shit."

"You will if Danny sees the bill and realises what you were doing."

She was right, which was the only reason I relented. That didn't make it any easier to actually disconnect the call though. In the end, she did it and I was left alone again.

Fucking hell.

CHAPTER EIGHT

PREDICTABLE PATH

AFTER I'D HUNG up the phone, I kept my fingers pressed against it, wishing I could drag Alyssa through it to be with me. I stared at the bed for a few minutes but realised it was useless—I wasn't going to be getting any more sleep anyway.

I flicked on the TV and scrolled through the channels, but nothing held my interest. Only one thing interested me—and she was thousands of kilometres away. I ended up turning the TV off and heading out of my room. I didn't know what to do with myself. Usually when my insomnia hit, I would go to Phoebe's room and watch her sleep, but I couldn't do that.

Instead, I paced the hallway.

After fifteen minutes or so, Eden's room door cracked open a little. "Is the carpet too thick?"

"Huh?"

"Well, you seem to be content to wear it down." She smiled.

I shrugged.

"Can't sleep?"

I shook my head. I paced the length of the corridor once more under Eden's watchful eye. Then I turned to her and blurted out everything about the nightmare I'd had earlier.

"You don't actually think Alyssa would cheat on you though, do you?" She laughed as if the idea was preposterous.

"Course not," I muttered. "I don't know why the fuck I feel like this. All I know is I've been having the same sort of fucking nightmares for four years. Practically every night I have had to sleep without her beside me I've woken to similar dreams. Or worse. They went away for a while, but now they're back with a vengeance."

"I'm sorry, I didn't realise it was so bad," she whispered.

"How could you?" I snapped. "I never told anyone."

Eden nodded. "It'll get better. Everything will. You'll see."

"Is that one of Eden Bishop's infamous predictions?" I asked, strangely feeling better as the words hung in the air.

"Damn straight." She laughed.

"I'll hold you to it then."

"Why don't you come in, considering you're keeping me awake with all your wanderings anyway?"

I smiled. "Sure. Thanks."

We talked until the sun began to rise. Finally, about an hour before I was due to leave to go back to the track, I snuck back into my own room for breakfast and a shower.

I arrived at the Marina Circuit as fresh as could be expected after only having a few hours' sleep. Of course, fucking Hunter was there to brighten my fucking day. Just the sight of him brought back visions of my nightmare—of Alyssa licking her lips while he fucked her from behind. I could recall every detail with almost perfect clarity, the pitch of every note in her cries of ecstasy. My skin crawled every time I looked in his direction—more so than usual. I gritted my teeth and did what I needed to do to get the job done.

Thankfully, Morgan won both the second and third races, with Hunter coming in third and ninth. At least that meant I didn't have to put up with the insufferable prat crowing about how good a driver he was on top of everything else.

BY THE third day in Bahrain, I was going out of my mind. Even though I knew I was being an irritable bastard, I couldn't find it in myself to care. I snapped at anyone and everyone—even Danny at least twice. He was the only one I apologised to.

Hunter had picked up on my obvious discomfort and used it to taunt me.

"Don't worry," he declared loudly, making the whole workshop pause. He held his hands up in the air as if to gain everyone's attention. "Dec's just got a case of blue balls. I know just the remedy—a couple of blondes. Maybe I should order him some room service tonight."

He winked at me as everyone turned back to their tasks.

"Fuck off," I muttered under my breath.

"Aw, what's the matter, *squirt.*" Once again, he used the nickname Morgan had given me, as if he had any right to it. "Don't you know the time zone rule?"

I didn't ask what the time zone rule was—I could imagine, and I wasn't interested in instigating it. In the end, my interest in the conversation wasn't required because he continued regardless.

"You know the one—it's not cheating if you aren't in the same time zone. I'm sure your girl is taking full advantage."

I turned on him, pinning him quickly against my toolbox.

"I don't give a shit if Alyssa is on another planet, it's not happening."

"Pussy," he growled.

I gave him one last shove before releasing him. "Stay out of my way."

He smirked at me. "I'm the one in the fucking car. You stay out of my way. It wouldn't take much for me to accidentally turn the wheel at the last minute."

"You wouldn't dare. Danny would have your arse and you know it."

"Out of the two of us, I think Danny would be more inclined to think it was your fuck-up in the pits than anything I did." He shrugged and walked away, leaving his threat hanging in the air.

I growled at his retreating form. His comment pushed me past my limit, and it was all I could do to stop myself from charging after him. Between the late nights we were pulling to get the cars ready in time and my inability to sleep without nightmares, I was a fucking mess.

The months I'd spent with Alyssa had spoiled me with mostly restful nights, and even when I hadn't been able to sleep, at least I could find peace knowing my girls were safe and well. But it wasn't like that now. Being away from Alyssa was hurting like hell. The stolen minutes on the phone when the time zones aligned just weren't enough to cut it for me. Worse, for over twenty-four hours, she hadn't answered on any line and no one would tell me where the fuck she was.

On the Friday of the race meeting, I was awake far too early once again. Even though it was the first day of qualifying, and I needed to have my head in the game, a series of nightmares had woken me up once again just like they had the rest of the week.

Knowing there was little to do at the hotel, I went to the track early, eager to just throw myself into the day and my work. The more I did that, the faster time would go and the sooner I'd be back home.

I'd been there for a little over an hour, just messing around in the pits, when noises started to fill the space around me. Something small barrelled into my legs. After buckling forward with the weight, I looked down, startled. When I did, I thought maybe I'd gone crazy because what I saw looking back at me was a mini-Alyssa. A near-perfect replica, but with sparkling turquoise eyes.

"Daddy!" the vision in a pink sundress squealed.

Bending down, I picked her up, hoping for the life of me that my mind hadn't snapped and that I wasn't accosting some poor stranger's child.

I looked up in the direction that she'd hit me from and saw Alyssa standing back, watching me. It looked like she was itching to run to me too, but was holding back for some reason. She wasn't dressed as provocatively as in my dreams and nightmares, but fuck if she wasn't shit-hot. I smiled at her, still uncertain that it wasn't just a dream. That seemed to break whatever bond was holding her back and she sprung at me.

I held Phoebe securely on one hip while I pulled Alyssa close to me, breathing in her scent. It was heaven. Absolute fucking heaven. I spent a few minutes just setting the moment in my memory.

"What are you doing here?" I asked when I had finally convinced myself it wasn't a dream.

"Danny flew us over. He even pulled some strings with Pembletons to have me here on official business so that I didn't need to take the time off unpaid. Apparently, *someone* has been a little disruptive. For some reason, he thought I'd be a calming influence on the team. Any idea why?" She pulled back and raised her eyebrow at me.

My lips curled upward and I chuckled. "None at all."

Phoebe wrapped her arms tighter around my neck and squeezed. It was fucking awesome. I grabbed Alyssa's hand and the three of us did a walkthrough of my "office" in pit lane. When we got to my station, I placed Phoebe on the ground and showed her some of the tools I used before promising to let her sit in one of the cars later. As the rest of the crew began to gather, I pulled Alyssa aside and thanked her for coming. I reacquainted myself with my fiancée while we watched our daughter dance around in excitement. With the two of them so close, the pain and heartbreak of the previous week became nothing more than a bad memory.

Not even Hunter could ruin my good mood.

At least as long as I could keep Alyssa and Phoebe away from him.

Easy.

Within half an hour, Hazel had come by to whisk Alyssa and Phoebe away again. It didn't matter too much though, because just the knowledge that they were nearby was enough to force everything else into focus. They were all the good reasons I was in the pits, after all.

The rest of the trip was uneventful, and Hazel's impromptu adoption of Alyssa meant I didn't need to have half of my thoughts on whether Hunter could be going near them. I could just relax and enjoy the last of my overseas adventure.

CHAPTER NINE

PRACTISE RUN

I WAS SUITED up and ready . . . almost.

Regardless, I climbed into the car and prepared mentally for the run. I tried not to think of how quickly the days were disappearing or about the fact that it was only Thursday, which marked the halfway point between leaving Alyssa and Phoebe and when I'd be able to see them again.

Being away from home once more was harder than I'd imagined. I hadn't anticipated how much time I would spend away during the season. It hadn't even occurred to me before how much I'd travelled for my job. It never mattered to me whether or not I was in Sydney. I was either in Sydney with a random girl or at a hotel with another; it ultimately made no difference. But since Alyssa returned to my life, and introduced me to the joy of a family—to Phoebe—every minute I spent away from the house was a noticeable ache.

It had nearly driven me insane while I was overseas, or at least it had until they were back in my arms. Then when we'd arrived back in Australia, I wasn't even home for a week—a crazy week with long hours in the sheds at Sinclair Racing, rebuilding the cars—before it was time to head off for Adelaide for the meet.

Rather than an empty house, takeaway food, and random fucking in-between race meets, it was filled with games, laughter, and healthy food. How the fuck had I not realised what I was missing? At least until I'd had to leave them—again. Packing up and leaving them alone every couple of weeks was already getting fucking old and the season had only just started.

It was an important race for so many reasons. Not only was it the first Australian leg of the ProV8 calendar, it was the first round of the Micro Challenge. Which meant it was the first official round where I was racing again.

I can do this.

My hands shook as I thought about what happened next. It was fucking ridiculous how nervous I was. It wasn't like I was rolling out in a beast of a machine that had to be wrestled under control. And it wasn't like I hadn't driven the red Mini before—after all, I'd had a couple of practise laps while Liam and the boys tuned it. But somehow getting ready to lead it out onto the racetrack, even if it was just for the practise session, made it all different.

It's easy. Just a matter of accelerate, brake, and turn the wheel.

It's not hard . . . I've done it a million times before.

Yeah, but not in a Mini, a snarky part of my brain countered. I tried to tell it to fuck off, but it had already instilled doubt—the self-hatred bubbled through my body and threatened to derail my ability to drive a fucking car. It was as though downsizing the car had also downsized my confidence. I may as well have been back in karts for all the power the Mini would deliver.

I edged the car down through the paddock and lined up with the other racers. Moments later, the gates were opened, and we all took to the track for the first of the practise sessions. As I drove through the turns, I tried desperately to get comfortable in the car; its compact size took some getting used to every time I jumped in. Not that I'd had the luxury of space in the V8 even with its larger cabin, but the Mini had almost as many gadgets with only half the room.

Drawing down a breath, and adjusting myself in the seat, I tried to keep my mind on the positives as I drove.

One, I was back in a car.

Two, I was racing professionally again.

Three, if the worst happened, and I wrecked the car, it wouldn't break the bank—or more to the point, Danny's pocket. The whole thing could probably be replaced for less than the cost of a single panel or component on the ProV8.

During the first few laps, I prepared myself mentally for being back on the track, and that I would soon be under race conditions. This time it was only a twenty-minute practise session. Over the next few days, it would progress into qualifying before finally entering into the first three races of my new life.

As I got a few laps under my belt, I began to picture Alyssa and Phoebe in my mind. Instead of fighting off the images like I had done the last time I was in a car, I embraced them. I wrapped my girls tightly in my thoughts and used it to spur me on to greater things. I pictured Alyssa smiling by my side as I climbed the podium. I imagined the greeting I would get when she arrived with Phoebe on Saturday if I qualified in pole position, hoping it would involve some positioning of my pole in our hotel room after Phoebe was asleep.

I made my way cleanly around the laps and began to get a better feel for the car. I knew the technical aspects because, over the past few months, I had stripped the engine down and learned everything I could about it. On top of that, I'd absorbed all the information I could from the various fact sheets about the series, but focused more on the specific car that Danny had put me in. I knew that despite its smaller size and engine, the Mini was only a couple of hundred kilograms lighter than the V8s I was used to handling. It was capable of producing just shy of one-sixty kilowatts of power, which seemed like nothing compared to the four-fifty the V8 could get. It was also shorter and had a higher centre of gravity than the V8, which made it easier to roll and harder to corner.

But all the theoretical knowledge in the world couldn't tell me that the Mini was a little more skittish around the corners or that I wouldn't need to brake as early or as hard. In fact, some corners I barely needed to brush the brakes. I had to adjust my driving style, but it was nothing I couldn't respond to quickly. I was made to drive, and ultimately it didn't matter what fucking vehicle someone wanted to shove me in. I was nothing if not adaptable.

Fifteen minutes into the session, I actually found myself disappointed by the fact that there were only five more minutes of practise left. Despite all of my fear and concern over the Mini, driving it around the track was actually fun. The pressure for a win wasn't as great as in the ProV8, especially considering there were no corporate sponsors for my car.

Although I still would have killed to be behind the wheel of the bigger cars, in the Mini I could just drive for the enjoyment of driving. And it was fucking enjoyable.

To make matters even better, the ProV8 division didn't begin practise or qualifying until the following day. Technically, it meant the drivers weren't required at the track, which meant no Hunter.

Morgan was unique though, and came in regardless. He always liked to be there with his crew to help set up the pits and, of course, he wanted to be there to give me shit about the Mini.

I pulled the car off the track and followed the procession of cars into the pits. Our pits were located toward the back of the paddock, in one single tent way behind the ProV8s, reflecting our lower status on the race circuit. But I didn't care. Nothing could bring me down from the high I felt after taking control of the Mini so effectively.

There was one more practise session later in the afternoon to get the feel of the car down, and then qualifying started the following day. I was determined to nail the techniques in the next session, and I'd be damned if I wasn't going to be in pole position at the end of it.

That was my goal for the weekend. Well, that and winning the round, of course. I fucking knew I could do it. It felt fucking fantastic being back on the track, and nothing could stop me. It was like gasoline had replaced the blood that pumped through my body.

"Man, you owned that car!" Morgan enthused, slapping me on the back as I unzipped my race suit.

Once I had air circulating, I removed my helmet and balaclava and ran my fingers though my hair to shake out a little of the sweat. I'd been having so much fun out in the car that I hadn't even realised just how hot it was inside the cabin. I grabbed the cold, wet towel Morgan held out for me and wiped my brow down, ran the towel over my hair, and then wrapped it around my neck so the water could drip down into my fire suit.

"You think?" I asked as I reached for the water bottle and drank deeply. I hadn't looked at my times; I hadn't been concentrating on racing per se, just on getting a feel for the car and the track. Excitement over the weekend bubbled inside me, and a smile naturally radiated onto my face.

Morgan watched me for a moment, and then chuckled before shaking his head. "Man, you don't even realise how fucking much you've changed, do you?"

I stood stoic for a second before answering. "Actually, man, I think I do."

Morgan nodded briefly. A second of silence passed before we got over the girly shit and started discussing the car again. "Watching you shake the shit out of this thing around the corners really had me wishing I was out there with you. It looked like a hell of a lot of fun."

"It *was* a hell of a lot of fun." I grinned widely. "In fact, I'm sure I could talk Danny into putting you in one too. Maybe the team can ditch the V8s altogether," I teased.

He laughed. "It *looked* like fun, but not enough that I'd give up my V8."

I punched his arm. "I fucking hear you, bro. I know which car I'd rather be in."

"Oh, that has to be the Mini, right?" He laughed.

I laughed with him. "Definitely. It's the Mini all the way."

"Sparky," Calem called to me from the back of the pits. He and Ryan had volunteered to be my pit crew under Mia's watchful eye.

It knocked a few extra hours off their apprenticeships while also giving them the opportunity to work with another type of car and a different engine.

"Yeah?" I replied.

"The boss man is looking for you. He came by while you were on the track and said to send you to the trailer when you were done here."

I nodded. "Thanks, man."

I stripped off the top half of my race suit, securing it around my waist before pulling off my undershirt. The cool air and warm sun felt good against my bare skin. I took a moment to enjoy the feeling while I had a little more water to rehydrate myself. Eventually, I felt refreshed enough to face Danny. I quickly ducked into the back of the pits, grabbed a t-shirt, and slipped it on. I spent half a minute trying to tame my hair before giving up and allowing it to stick up in long wet spikes as I walked off to see Danny.

I wandered over to the trailer, trying not to stress about the call-up. I knew from experience that Danny would just be interested in finding out what I thought about the car. He regularly saw drivers after their races, especially the first few times in a new car.

I knocked on the door of his room in the trailer. He called out his permission for me to enter and I stepped into his home away from home at race events. He treated the room as his office, so much so that at any given moment during a meet, he would either be in the trailer or in the pits. One wall was lined with monitors. Some showed the racetrack from various angles, others were continually updated with the in-car telemetry during a race. The last one in the bank was permanently tuned to the weather channel. He liked to keep his finger on the pulse of the team, and the information provided by those screens allowed him to do it and make all the necessary calls on the fly.

"So?" he asked, turning to face me before leaning forward on his desk to steeple his fingers over his mouth.

"So?" I queried back, raising an eyebrow at him. I was being a smart-arse, forcing him to ask the question, but I couldn't help it. I was still on a high from being back on the track and the fun of hurtling the Mini around the corners at reckless speeds.

"How was that session?"

"It doesn't have the boogie of a ProV8," I said seriously, my face set into a frown. "It corners like a freight train."

He raised his eyebrow at me and waited.

"And the cabin is too small."

My statement was met with a stoic glare.

I decided to end the joke and grinned at him. "It was a fuckload of fun."

"So I presume by that reaction that you aren't taking this seriously?" he asked, his face impassive and his voice cold.

My heart fell a little as my body stiffened with fear. I'd been having a little fun with him, the way we used to, but maybe it was too soon. Maybe he would never be that carefree with me again. Had I fucked up with my little attempt at a joke?

Just as my thoughts began to descend into a full-blown panic, he laughed.

"Don't try to bullshit a bullshitter, Declan," he joked. "I'm glad you had fun out there. Just remember that this is still ultimately about winning the races."

Relief flooded me and I slumped into a more relaxed position. "Absolutely. Truth be told, I can't wait to get out there and kick some arse."

He smiled. "Good. That's exactly what I wanted to talk to you about."

"Really?" I smirked.

"I just wanted to give you a little added . . . incentive," he said.

"Yeah?"

"Yeah. I'd like to offer you a sweetener." He watched me carefully to ensure I was paying attention.

"Go on," I murmured, eager to find out what he was going to offer.

"I'm going to give you a bonus each time you place." He slid across a piece of paper with the details on it.

I nodded. It wasn't anything new really. There had always been a bonus system in place for winning a V8 race. Of course, the bonuses he was offering now looked paltry in comparison to those, but I understood that. The Micro Challenge wasn't as big a drawcard as the ProV8s—to the crowds or the sponsors—so the money didn't flow as freely. Especially considering the lack of formal sponsors on my car.

"And if you claim pole twice between now and Townsville, I'll give you three flights and access to my unit in London for your honeymoon. If you want it, of course."

I thought about earning the opportunity to take Alyssa back to the unit and fucking her in the bedroom again . . . or on the cold steel of the counter in the kitchen. I was thankful that the knot of my race suit was low enough to hide the fact that I was straining against the zipper.

Just thinking about the intoxicating taste of the whiskey-and-Alyssa cocktail that I'd enjoyed there made me hard, and my mouth watered. I was certain Alyssa would love a do-over of our time in London. A chance to make right all the things we'd done wrong, and to repeat all the things we'd done right. I quickly calculated my chance of success. There were four rounds before our wedding. Two poles from four starts. I was certain I could do it, which was why I grinned at Danny and offered him my hand. "You've got yourself a deal."

"Great." He nodded and shook my hand. Just before he let it go, he spoke again, his voice low and solemn. "Seriously though, great work out there today, Declan."

I grinned widely.

"It's exactly the sort of behaviour I need to see from you going forward."

I couldn't miss the barb in his final words, but decided to ignore it. Nothing was going to put a damper on my day. My life would have been perfect were it not for the blight of having to work in the pits for Hunter over the weekend.

I decided to hunt down Eden to tell her the good news, and eventually located her in the pits, setting everything up for the coming event. While she buzzed around organising her workstation, I sat my arse down in one of the chairs and watched. I would have offered to help, but I valued both my balls and knew her well enough to know she would rip one off if I set anything up wrong.

She chuckled as I told her about the offer for London and finished with Danny's parting words.

"He really does like you, you know," she murmured.

"Sure," I said, dragging out the word to show my scepticism. "He has a funny way of showing it."

"Don't you see? It's *because* he likes you that he expects so much from you."

Her twisted logic made me laugh. "That makes absolutely no sense."

"It makes perfect sense when you think about it." She had her wiser-than-thou sage-like voice on, the one that didn't leave room for argument. "If you had no potential, he would've just fired you long ago, and you would've been nothing more than a blip on the radar of ProV8 history. Not even a footnote. But he didn't. He stuck with you through the drugs." She stuck her finger at me. "He offered you a second chance after realising that he'd made a mistake in firing you rashly, and he's giving you another opportunity to drive despite it all. And don't give me any of that 'but it's a Mini' crap. You know he'll have you in a V8 as soon as he works out the best way to handle the press and sponsors. I think you remind him of himself when he was younger. Except the whole leaving the love of your life and love-child behind thing, of course."

I rolled my eyes as she finished her speech. Even though she was arguing why he apparently liked me, it was clear she was defending his actions just as much. She could be weirdly protective of him sometimes.

"Anyway," she said brightly as she turned to me with a smile to show she'd finished. "On to another unrelated topic—we need to organise a date for you and Morgan to get your suits fitted."

Fuck. I hadn't wanted to think about anything wedding-related over the weekend because wedding-related was Alyssa-related, which made the hole in my chest swell to swallow my lungs as well as my heart.

103

"Isn't it the bride's job to hassle me about that sort of thing?" I laughed in an attempt to cover up the ache. "Or at the very least the matron of honour's?"

"Oh, that's nice," Eden said. "Rub that one in again." She winked at me to let me know there were no hard feelings.

Alyssa and Eden had come to an understanding that although Ruby was going to be the matron of honour and help with all the Brisbane arrangements, Eden was Alyssa's on-the-ground assistant in Sydney—and in charge of keeping Morgan in line when it came to the stag party arrangements.

"Well, how about the weekend before Townsville?" I asked.

She shook her head. "That's no good. I'm going to be in Brisbane that weekend."

I tilted my head in confusion and she giggled.

"The hen night, remember?"

"Fuck, that's right. I forgot."

Alyssa had already marked the weekend off her calendar, telling me that someone else was going to arrange the event. I hadn't pushed her for any more details yet; I wasn't sure I wanted to know.

"Forgot, or forced it out of your mind?"

I groaned. "The latter."

"Don't worry, squirt, it's just a night out with a couple of strippers."

"Strippers, Edie?" I asked, an ill feeling spreading through me. "Really?"

"What do you expect?" she asked as she shrugged. "It *is* a hen night after all. You don't expect her to celebrate her last night of freedom without looking at semi-naked men, do you?"

"Why the hell would Alyssa want *strippers*?" I spat the word out in disgust.

"Surely you're having strippers?" Eden asked.

"You'd have to ask your boyfriend about that. I haven't arranged a thing."

"Declan, I know you well enough to know you'd be happy as a pig in shit to be surrounded by boobs and half-naked women. Why deny Alyssa the same privilege?"

"Alyssa's going to be surrounded by boobs and half-naked women?" I asked with a snicker. "Now that's a party I could probably get behind."

In fact *that* would be preferable to having skanky strippers hanging around me at my bachelor party. The part of my life where I enjoyed that was over. It was over from the moment I decided that I wanted Alyssa in my life.

Eden rolled her eyes at me. "You know what I mean. If that's what Alyssa wants . . ."

"*Is* that what Alyssa wants?" I asked, feeling sick at the thought. Had she expressed some desire to get down and dirty with a mob of G-string-wearing Hercules wannabes?

"I don't know. I told you already, I haven't organised anything."

I felt like I was pulling teeth. "Okay, so who *is* organising it?"

Eden shook her head as if I were stupid. "The matron of honour, of course."

"Ruby," I muttered under my breath.

"Yeah, she's arranged a night out at the Ball Pit."

"The Ball Pit? You've got to be fucking kidding me."

Eden shrugged. "Dunno what to tell you, it is what it sounds like."

"Fucking strippers. The fucking Ball Pit. Fuck, I have to talk to Ruby."

Eden was practically doubled over with laughter when I left her to make a phone call to Brisbane. I hoped Danny wouldn't mind me abandoning the pits for a moment. In fact, I was sure he would understand. It was life or death, after all.

I yanked out my mobile and scrolled to Ruby's number, which Alyssa had programmed into my phone, together with a few others, so I would always be able to contact her family in case of an emergency.

"Hi, Declan," Ruby answered cheerfully. Apparently, Alyssa had given her my number as well, because I sure as shit had never called her before. "To what do I owe this pleasure?"

"Strippers, Ruby?" I asked, my voice dripping with incredulity. "Seriously?"

"So, you heard about the plans for Alyssa's last hurrah?"

"Yeah, I fucking heard about it. And all I can say is what in the actual fuck?"

"What's good for the goose and all that," she answered, her voice still too fucking cheerful considering she was talking about my future wife ogling other men's junk.

"Don't give me that shit," I growled. "I don't like it."

"Oh, I get it. Me, Declan. You, Alyssa." She made some ridiculous fucking monkey sounds before laughing.

"What the fuck?"

"You're a caveman!" she exclaimed. "You'll happily go look at strippers, but the mere suggestion that Alyssa is going to and you freak."

"If I have to go see strippers, it won't be happily."

"Whatever. I'm not going to deprive my baby sister of the opportunity to make a final comparison before settling down."

I growled, beyond words. The thought of Alyssa being around half-naked men made my skin crawl. But just as bad was the thought of having half-naked strangers pawing all over me. I'd been there before, and I didn't want it again.

"What if I don't have strippers?" I asked.

She laughed loudly. "I know you are turning over a new leaf and all that, but somehow I find that hard to believe."

I pulled the phone away from my ear and flipped her the bird. I didn't care if she couldn't see me—I fucking knew I was doing it and it felt good. I lifted my mobile back up again and said, "Watch me."

She laughed. "Well, I do believe you are stubborn enough to not do it if you're dared. But really, you should be able to enjoy your night. So should Alyssa."

"And enjoying the night entails looking at half-naked men? Is that what you're saying?"

She laughed harder. "I had no idea that was your idea of enjoyment, Declan. I'm sure Flynn would love to hear that. Are you sure you're marrying the right person?"

"Fuck off, Ruby."

She pretended to gasp between her hysterical laughing fits. "Such language! And to a mother-to-be at that."

She wasn't going to be of any further assistance, but I decided to try one last time. "So, nothing will change your mind?"

"Not that I can think of."

"Fine," I seethed. "Bye, Ruby."

I didn't want to hassle Alyssa about it. Especially considering it would mean calling her in Sydney during a work day. Besides, she had enough on her plate, between worrying about me and the stresses of the graduate program at her job. I decided maybe Ruby had a point. If it *was* genuinely what Alyssa wanted for her last hurrah, who was I to deny her? If only I could be sure the boys— and the other hens, for that matter—would behave.

A stroke of inspiration hit me, and I headed off to hunt down Morgan.

I had no doubt he would be a more-than-willing accomplice.

CHAPTER TEN

GOOD VIBRATIONS

THE SECOND PRACTISE session of the day went exactly the same as the first. With each lap, I learned a little more about the car and how to treat it around the Adelaide circuit. I took time to dance from one side of the track to the other and pushed the car harder into the corners to try to find its limit.

Somewhat surprisingly, I was able to put all thoughts of male strippers out of my head and just focus on my driving. By the time the session was finished, I felt the fastest I ever had . . . at least the fastest I had *in the Mini*. I pulled the car into the shed at the end of the last practise lap, leaving it ready for early qualifying the next day.

After debriefing Danny and Liam on how I felt about the session, I packed up the little I had and said goodbye to the few people who were still around. By the time I left the track, I was practically jubilant.

I climbed into a cab and gave him my hotel address and Visa card. For a brief moment, I debated going out to celebrate. Only I didn't know where to go or what to do. In the end, I decided to head straight back to the room to call my girls instead.

A phone call home and room service for dinner were on the agenda. Except for the phone call home, it was how I'd spent my evenings before a big race. At least until the last six months of my former career, when I'd ramped up the efforts to get the images of Alyssa out of my head by trying to score before the races. Even though everything about my life was different, I figured I should stick to my pre-race routine as best as I was able.

My post-race routine—celebrating and relieving my tension with a random screw—could go and get fucked completely. There was only one girl I wanted to celebrate and release my tension with. And I only had to wait one more day until she was with me again.

When I arrived back at the hotel, I realised it was still a little too early to call Alyssa, so I jumped in the shower, ordered my dinner, and then surfed the TV channels for a few minutes.

I tried to work out what would be the best time to catch both Alyssa and Phoebe. I was in the middle of that internal debate when room service arrived. While I ate, I surfed the channels again, without finding anything that grabbed my attention, and waited as another hour passed—albeit slowly—before I was sure things would be more organised back home. It was close to seven when I grabbed the hotel phone and dialled home.

Alyssa picked it up on the first ring.

I laughed at her enthusiasm. "Anyone would think you were waiting for a call."

"I knew you'd call." I could hear her wide smile. "So, yeah, I've been waiting for you."

"Of course I'd call. What can I say? I'm under the thumb," I joked.

"You're in a better mood than I was expecting," she mused.

"I had a better day than I was expecting."

"Well, that makes one of us," she murmured.

The sadness in her voice stopped me cold.

"Talk to me about it," I offered, feeling immensely proud of myself for noticing the tone in her voice and acting upon it. Dr.

Henrikson would have been pleased.

She quickly ran through her day, how it started with her spilling coffee on her white blouse on the way to work and ended with having a run-in with one of the other graduates—whose father just happened to be a partner of the firm. Apparently, after leaving the office, Alyssa had broken down in tears as soon as she reached the car.

I was proud of her for not giving them the satisfaction of breaking down in front of them. The bastards didn't deserve that victory.

"I'm sorry to hear it was fucked-up," I whispered. "If I was there, I would kiss and hug"—and fuck—"you until it was all better."

She giggled lightly down the line. "It's better already just hearing your voice. Thank you."

I grinned. Since we'd reunited, she'd often had to be my oasis in this shitty-arsed world, so I was glad I could do the same for her at least once. We chatted a little more about her day, and mine, before being interrupted by a ruckus on her end. I could hear Phoebe asking something, but I couldn't make out all the words. I wondered if Alyssa had her hand on the mouthpiece.

"Would you like to talk to Phoebe?" she asked when I had her attention again.

"Hell yeah," I said, perhaps a little too enthusiastically, but I'd been missing my little girl just as much as my bigger one.

I heard Alyssa chuckling as she passed the phone on.

"Hi, Daddy!"

It was amazing how those two little words made my whole fucking day even better. "Hi, baby, how was your day?"

"Good. I did some painting and played in the sandpit today." She barely took a breath before telling me all the other details of her day. "Netty said she's my best friend, and Miss Mary read us lots of stories and taught us a new song." She launched straight into it, singing down the line about a town that was upside down or something.

I smiled as I listened to her. It was actually a little frightening each time I spoke to her because it forced me to see just how grown-up she was. Talking to her over the phone made me appreciate how well she could converse. After she finished her song, I told her how good I thought it was, and in return she made sure I knew all the words before we were allowed to move on to the next topic.

"Did you win today, Daddy?" she asked.

I snickered, but then decided it was easier to tell her I had won rather than try to explain the differences between practise sessions, qualifying, and races just yet. That could be a conversation for another day when she was older. Besides, I did feel like I'd won. The Mini was never going to be my dream car, but being back on the track was indescribable. "Yes, I won today."

I heard her squeal, and then she was off and talking to Alyssa rather than into the phone. I chuckled when Alyssa came back on. "I think I'm going to hear about your *win* for a while. Everyone at her day care will know about it in the morning. I'd better go get her into bed. I'll see you tomorrow night."

I felt suddenly bereft. An overwhelming pang of homesickness and loss washed over me at the thought of ending the call so soon. Even though it would only be a little over twenty-four hours before they'd be in Adelaide with me, it wasn't soon enough.

"Can you call me back after Phoebe is in bed?" I asked Alyssa with a desperation I'd never thought I'd feel coursing through me. I needed more of her. I needed *all* of her.

I heard delight colour Alyssa's voice as she agreed. She took down the hotel number and promised she would call back the moment Phoebe was asleep.

I WAITED impatiently for Alyssa's phone call. I tried to distract myself any way I could, but nothing worked. Nothing could occupy my mind for more than a few seconds. I gave up on distractions and paced across the room, missing my family more with every step.

Finally, the phone rang and I raced to answer it. I reached it by the third ring.

"You took your time," Alyssa joked.

I laughed. "Give me some credit. I was on the other side of the room."

"Here I thought you *wanted* to talk to me?" I could hear the laughter in her voice. "I can always go if you'd prefer?"

"Don't you fucking dare," I growled playfully.

"I won't," she murmured. "I couldn't." She sighed. "I miss you."

I sighed as well. "Me too, baby, me too."

"This bed's so cold and lonely without you in it to warm it."

I pictured her sprawled out on our bed—alone and waiting. My mouth grew dry.

"Are you in bed at the moment?" I asked.

"Yeah, I thought it was the best place to call you from. Less distractions."

"I'm in bed too," I told her.

My mind offered up an experience that I'd never had, but now wanted more than anything. Or at least, more than anything else I could have while she was in a different state. It was something I could share with Alyssa, and only Alyssa.

"What are you wearing?" I asked my voice dropping lower and quieter.

"Just my pyjamas, why?" she asked, but then a startled "Oh" came down the line as she understood the intent behind my question.

"I want you, Alyssa," I whispered. "I wish you were here with me already."

"Me too." She sighed.

"But since you're not with me, you'll have to be my hands."

"Dec, I don't know if—"

I cut her off. "Please, Lys, for me." I paused, desperate for her to understand exactly what I wanted and why I needed it. "I need you."

I heard her almost muted acceptance down the line. As soon as the little "okay" reached me, I was assailed by images of her pleasing herself. Forefront in my mind was the vision I'd had a lifetime ago in London, after I'd seen the vibrator in her luggage. Even though I'd found out later that Ruby had put it there as a joke, I could still readily retrieve the mental image I'd had of Alyssa using it on herself while she panted my name.

"You've still got the *toy* that you had in London, right?" I asked.

Her voice was shaky when she replied. "I . . . umm . . . yes." The last word was almost silent.

"I want you to use it," I instructed. I could tell that the same thing that was driving me into a frenzy, and causing me to be utterly and completely erect, was also causing her more than a few nerves. By being assertive, I hoped I could give her more courage. I didn't want her to be embarrassed or anxious about what I wanted—*needed*—in that moment. With the amount of travelling I'd be doing during the season every year, I could only hope a good outcome would mean many repeat performances.

"Please, Lys," I cooed after getting no response. "You would not believe how hard I am just thinking about it."

That seemed to be the motivation she needed. She breathed heavily into the phone.

"Okay," she squeaked.

I heard her standing up before moving to rifle through the drawers. My heart pounded as I heard her footsteps as she walked back to the bed. I closed my eyes and pictured her lying on my pillow.

"Put the phone on speaker and place it beside you on the pillow," I directed.

"Why?" she asked. Her voice quivered, but I wasn't sure if it was with need or fear.

"I want you to use both hands," I explained.

An instant later, I heard the slight echo of the speakerphone.

"That's a good girl," I murmured. I was so fucking hard it hurt. "Now, turn on the toy and have it near you ready to go."

I heard the click and then a soft buzz echo down the line. I was getting harder by the second at just how readily she was following my instructions.

"I'm going to unzip myself now," I whispered, pulling the zipper on my jeans down as I said the words.

I heard her gasp, but then her breathing grew heavier. When she spoke again, her voice was husky. I could tell she was starting to get into it.

"What are you doing?" she asked seductively.

"I'm rubbing my hand along my stomach, picturing your hands. Oh, fuck. They're so smooth, and light, and warm." I growled. "I love it when you touch me."

She moaned softly.

"What would you want me to do to you?" I asked. I was already palming myself lightly, trying to ease some of the pressure without blowing my load too soon. I wanted to prolong the experience as desperately as I wanted to just jerk off and release the pent-up energy humming through my body.

"I like it when you kiss my neck," she whispered.

"Close your eyes. Now, picture me kissing your neck. I'd start just below your ear before running my lips and tongue over your jaw. I would swirl my tongue to get more of a taste of that delicious skin of yours." I closed my eyes too and imagined my mouth tracing the path I was talking about.

"Then what?" Her voice almost sounded like a plea.

I moaned in response to the lust I heard. "I would kiss into the collar of whatever blouse you were wearing . . ."

"I'm not wearing a blouse," she murmured.

"Are you wearing a bra?" I hoped not.

"Not at the moment."

I growled again and my palming grew a little more frantic. I didn't know how long I would take to release, but I was damn well going to take Alyssa with me when I did. "Then I would suck on your breasts one at a time. I'd take the nipples between my lips and stroke them with my tongue. My fingers would play with the other, rolling it between my fingertips until you arch your back and beg me for more."

"Oh, God," she exclaimed. "That feels—" Her voice broke off breathily and I could picture her hands tracing the imaginary path I was describing.

"While I still have my mouth on your fucking fantastic breasts, I would run one of my hands along your stomach and dip my fingers down into your panties." I slid my fingers frantically up and down my shaft, groaning as I imagined my fingers slipping into her slickness.

She moaned and she panted. "Then what?"

"Then, I'd move my mouth down to join my fingers. I'd taste you and lick you until you begged for me to fuck you."

She grunted. "Oh, God, Dec, I want you. Tell me . . . tell me what you would do next."

"Then, baby . . . then, I would worship every inch of you. I would kiss my way back up to your mouth and position myself at your entrance." I hoped she realised this was where her little toy came into play. I heard the vibrations move further away from the phone. "I would touch your silky skin as I slid into your warmth. We would find our rhythm together, baby, the way that only we can. My cock would fill your tight pussy over and over and my lips would find yours."

My voice was straining. It was thick with desire, and I was sure she would be able to hear the sounds my hands were making as I pictured my words. I was so close it wouldn't take much to push me over the edge, especially not with the little moans and mews she made as the sound of humming undulated as she moved the vibrator rhythmically within her.

"Tell me how that feels." I groaned. "Tell me how it feels when I fuck you."

"It . . . it feels so good. I want you, Declan, I want you so badly. What . . . what now?"

"As I move inside you, my mouth would find your nipples again, and I would take my time playing with each one. I would suck them until you came, hard, squeezing tightly around me while I was still buried deep inside you."

The undulating sound of the vibrator dipping in and out of her body buzzed through my ears. Her ragged breathing indicated she was just as close as I was.

"I'd make you come so fucking hard, baby," I said. "Can you feel my fingers on you? My lips against yours?"

"Yes, Dec. Oh, God yes."

"Fuck baby," I cried out as I heard the sounds of her moans signalling her release a moment later. I groaned as I came over my hand and stomach. "Oh, fuck."

We panted to each other for a few minutes before she giggled nervously.

"Well, that was different," she said.

"Good different? Or bad different?"

"Good different." She laughed then sighed. "Definitely good different."

I was glad that she'd enjoyed it, because it meant that we would be able to do it again . . . and again . . . whenever I was away. After all, not all locations were close enough that she could fly out for the weekend.

We chatted for a few more minutes before we both needed to go. We both had early starts and huge days ahead of us. She had work and then negotiating a flight with Phoebe. I needed to be at the track by seven to prepare for my qualifying round, and then I had a full afternoon of racing and working the pits.

Between talking to Alyssa and our little adventure, I felt almost relaxed and ready to sleep. I flicked on the TV to distract me long enough to settle completely. The next day couldn't come soon enough.

CHAPTER ELEVEN

RIPPLE EFFECT

I WHIPPED THE car around the track, faster and faster each lap. A euphoria spread through my body as I poured my energy into the accelerator. The connection between me and the car was flawless. It responded to my touch the same way Alyssa's body did.

I was on track for the perfect race.

The engine of another car roared behind me. A much bigger car, one I had no chance of outrunning, filled my rear-view mirror seconds later. I should have tried to get out of the way, but I was on track for such a good lap that I couldn't.

Glancing up at my rear-view mirror, I saw the new Sinclair Racing ProV8. Hunter's number, sixty-six, was printed on the windscreen. The car drifted closer and closer. I was surprised to see that Hunter wasn't wearing any safety gear; not even a race suit. He snarled at me in the mirror before his car dropped away just as quickly as it had appeared.

The roar of his engine sounded again and then he was on me.

I heard the impact before I felt it.

The keening of metal on metal reverberated through my ears as I was pushed toward the cement barrier. As his car shunted mine roughly, I noticed a flash of colour out of the corner of my eye. Something was on the passenger seat of my car. I couldn't turn to see what it was, because at that moment, my car collided roughly with the concrete barrier of the track and my forehead smashed against the steering wheel. I was tossed like a rag doll as the car barrel-rolled back onto the track.

After the car finally came to a rest back on all fours, I flicked my head around to see what had caused the flash I'd seen. Alyssa was curled on the seat beside me. She was completely still and her head slumped forward to her chest, causing her long hair to form curtains around her face. I couldn't tell whether she was sleeping or something else; I couldn't even tell if she was breathing. I reached my hand over to touch her lightly.

She didn't respond to my attempt to rouse her, so I shook her gently.

Still no response.

I grabbed her chin gently and turned her face toward me. The instant I saw her face, I gasped and choked with horror. Her lips were blue, her skin even paler than normal—grey and chalky—and her eyes looked through me, unfocused and unseeing. My heart stopped as the reality of it all struck me.

I was seeing the face of death.

My Alyssa was dead.

"NO!" I shouted the word into the empty hotel room as I jolted back to consciousness.

Tremors of shock ran through my body, each of my muscles quivering in response to the images that were still on replay in my head. Without thinking, I picked up the phone and dialled home. I waited as the phone rang; each extra ring caused the certainty that something had happened to her to grow and my panic to rise.

"Hello?" Alyssa's sleepy, confused, and groggy voice was on

the line.

Tears of relief sprung to my eyes. "Lys. Thank fuck," I whispered.

"Dec?" she asked. I could tell she was still trying to shake off her slumber.

"Yeah, it's me. I'm sorry for ringing so late, or early, I don't fucking know."

"Why are you calling? Is something wrong?" I could detect the panic rising within her.

"No," I murmured. "I just had a . . ." I couldn't finish, unable to admit that I had practically torn from the bed to call her just because of a nightmare. That would make me sound like a monumental pussy. I squeezed my eyes shut, but each time I did, all I saw were the images of her grey pallor and lifeless eyes. "Fuck, Lys, I can't lose you." My hand found my hair and I pulled hard at it, trying to force the images out of my mind.

"Declan? What is it?"

I sighed. I needed to get my shit under control. The dream was obviously a reaction to having to deal with Hunter at the track over the weekend, and a manifestation of the danger he posed to me and to Alyssa, but it had felt so real. Even now, fully awake and conscious, the images of her death were right behind my eyelids. "I love you," I told her. "Never forget that. No matter what happens, you can't forget that."

"What do you mean?" she asked. "You're scaring me."

"I'm sorry, baby. I am so, so sorry. I really don't mean to scare you." I couldn't keep my voice level or my thoughts sane. I just kept picturing her face as I'd held it in my hands before I'd awakened. "I just don't want anything to happen to me" —*or you*— "without you knowing just how much you mean to me."

She gave a little sigh, but there wasn't any frustration in the sound—more relief. I wondered if she had climbed back into bed while we were talking. "Don't worry, I know."

"Lys?" I asked. My voice still clung to my vocal cords as anxiety squeezed my throat.

"Mmm," she hummed sleepily.

"I'm sorry for calling you so late. I just needed to know that you were okay."

"I'm okay," she whispered. She sounded incredibly tired, and I felt fresh guilt over waking her about something as silly as a dream, even if I could still see her hollow eyes staring past me.

For a few minutes, I sat on the bed quietly, holding the phone in my hand, and listened to Alyssa's steady breathing. I was sure she was falling back to sleep. I waited the length of a few more peaceful breaths before I finally, begrudgingly, said goodbye and let her get back to sleep. I felt a little calmer, but there was no way I could risk going back to bed myself. It was easier to sneak down to the hotel gym and get a little bit of exercise in before it was time to head to the track.

When I reached the gym, I jumped on the treadmill and ran like a man possessed. It was as if I were trying to outrun all my demons, even though I knew it was impossible. I used the time to try to get my head together and concentrate on what I needed to do on the track and in the pits. The last thing I needed to do was start crashing out of races again.

Surely that wouldn't happen now . . .

Would it?

I tried not to think about Hunter, or my mind would invariably wander back to his face in my dream, which would lead me back to Alyssa . . .

When it was a reasonable enough hour to head to the track, I packed up and left the hotel. It would be easier to put my nightmare out of my mind when I was surrounded by other people. Morgan and Eden met me at the track early. They weren't required until much later in the day, but they were keen to watch my qualifying session and support me as much as they could from the sidelines. The other boys from my pit team were already in the garage when I arrived.

"It'll be good crewing for a driver who's head isn't utterly up his arse," Calem said as he did a final run over the car—even though nothing had changed since my previous session.

I laughed. "You do realise there isn't any *actual* crewing

involved, don't you?" The races were too short for more fuel or extra tyres so the only reason I'd be in the pits at all would be if there was an accident, and usually there wasn't time to get the car repaired and back out again in time to finish the race.

He shrugged. "We might not be in the pits like we would if you were in a V8, but we'll be with you on the track in spirit. Our blood, sweat, and tears have gone into that car just as much as yours."

"I know, man," I said, slapping one hand on his shoulder and the other on Ryan's. "And I can't thank either of you enough."

"You wanna thank us? Then get out there and kick arse!" Ryan enthused, handing me my helmet.

I stopped, my dream coming back to me full force as I looked over the car. Taking a deep breath, I pushed the nightmare out of my mind.

I climbed into my seat and glanced at the passenger side in my periphery—I was relieved, but not surprised, to see that no one was there. When I was satisfied that the circumstances of the dream were impossible, I drove out to meet my destiny.

CHAPTER TWELVE

LONG WEEKEND

I PULLED OFF my helmet and balaclava before shaking out my hair. Running my fingers through the sweaty tendrils, I brushed them back off my forehead while trying to force them into some kind of shape. Then I pulled down the zipper of my race suit, waited for the final confirmation of my results, and prepared for scrutineering to begin.

When I'd pulled the car back into the holding area, I was certain I'd had a good lap in my qualifying. I felt fast . . . or at least fast*ish*. It wasn't nearly as speedy as the V8, but I'd felt the fun in the laps. More than that, I felt the joy of racing again. Something I hadn't really experienced in such a long time; certainly not since I'd seen Alyssa with Flynn at Queensland Raceway, and perhaps not even for quite some time before then. Even if I hadn't really realised at the time how much better it could be.

I could barely wait for my first race later in the afternoon. There was just my stint in the pits for Hunter to contend with first.

After the officials did the weigh-in and looked over my car, I was told that I'd qualified in second place. I couldn't help the small disappointment I felt over the fact that I didn't make it into first—especially with the London offer on the table for poling twice—but I was still fucking happy with the result. Especially when I hadn't raced in so long, and never in a Mini. If I could translate it into success on the track in the afternoon, I would be over the moon.

After parking the Mini in the pits, I had very little to do for the day, so I spent as much of my time as possible in hiding. I retreated to the very back of the small garage and tinkered away on the car. I knew I would get more peace and quiet there than in the Sinclair Racing trailer or pits. I made appearances as needed at both the pit crew briefing and Danny's little pre-practice pep-up that he always did. The second they were over, I hid away again.

The result was a slightly boring day—there wasn't much to look at in the garage—but it also meant that I didn't have a single run-in with Hunter. At least, not until it was time to pit for him.

Hunter's practise laps didn't go nearly as smoothly as he might have liked. Liam decided the first session was a good time to make a few adjustments to the car on the fly. My team did everything exactly as specified as Hunter ended up back in pit lane again and again. He began to curse us out each time Liam called him back in for another slight adjustment. I could almost understand his frustration at not being able to get a solid run on the track, but the changes were being made for his benefit. There was no need for him to be such an arse about it.

Once time was called on the practise, and I could be free of the pits, I ran straight for my garage. I only had a matter of minutes to get in my car and into the marshalling area for my first race. My stomach was full of butterflies at the thought of being back under proper race conditions again. I had eight laps—a little less than twenty minutes—to prove to the world, and myself, that I wasn't a failure and that I could get around the track cleanly under full race conditions.

I felt the pressure bearing down on me, and it was almost enough to make my knees buckle. Bile rose in my throat as I started the car and put it in gear.

My heartbeat thumping in my ears was louder than the drone

of the engine.

Fuck. Fuckity fuck fuck!

Would an image of Alyssa haunt me now? I'd exorcised my demons, but would they return to attack while I was most susceptible? Would I see her face from my dream?

My fingers clenched around the steering wheel and I had to take some deep breaths to stop myself from hyperventilating. There was so much riding on this first race, it seemed impossible to overcome the pressure. And with the way my heart raced, I was going to have a fucking heart attack or something.

I wished that Alyssa were alongside me, but that thought brought back images from my horrendous dream in force. Squeezing my eyes shut for half a second, I took another deep breath and imagined instead that Alyssa was in the stands waiting patiently for me. I pictured her mouth turning up into a smile as I lined up on the grid. Instead of haunting me, it slowed my heart and let me breathe a little easier. It was just the inspiration I needed to put the car into gear and drive onto the track.

While I sat on the grid waiting for the green light, I focused only on the pedals at my feet, the gearstick to my left, and my hands firmly planted on the wheel. I closed my eyes in my usual pre-race ritual, allowing myself one second of solitude. I pressed my foot deep onto the floor, listening to the far too quiet buzz that issued from the Mini's tiny engine. It didn't block out the thoughts quite the way the V8 had during the same routine. I took a deep breath, then my eyes snapped open and it was time to go.

Ride on instinct.

Don't think.

Don't overthink.

I threw the Mini into gear, floored the accelerator, and mentally willed the car to go as fast as possible. I watched as the car beside me—driven by Randall Wilkins, the championship winner the previous year and the one touted as the one to watch this season—dropped away slightly.

At corner one, I had the inside line. If I could just make a clean dive for it, I would be in the best position possible for the rest of the lap. And the rest of the race.

This style of racing was completely different to the ProV8 series. In the bigger cars, there was so much strategy at play. Pit windows and mandatory stops. So much was outside of the driver's control and everything could change in a heartbeat. In the Mini, it all came down to the skill of the driver, and getting to the front of the pack as quickly as possible really could be the difference between winning and losing.

I threw the car hard into the corner, braking as late as I could — using the knowledge I'd gained in my practise and qualifying sessions to my benefit. I edged Wilkins out and drove in hard across his nose. I knew I needed to leg it to turn two or he would have the line there. I scraped it in.

He rode my tail tightly as I charged through turns two and three. By turn four, I was just starting to put some distance between us.

I flicked the car around the hard right before banking straight across for the hard left to block anyone who could have dived around me on the inside. I hit the straight and gunned it. I pushed as hard as I could, wishing that I could find an extra kilometre or two per hour—just that little edge over my competitors—even though I knew the cars were all equal.

My car swept around the soft curve of turn eight, hitting the racing line perfectly. Then I braked hard and cut sharply inwards to get around the tight bend. My eyes flicked up to the overpass that extended over the track and I imagined Alyssa up there, watching and waving as I sped by. It gave me the boost I needed.

I passed the V8 paddock, refusing to give into the little niggle that started at the back of my head. *You could have been in one of those if things had gone differently.*

If things *had* gone differently, I might not have had Alyssa back in my life. I would rather drive a Mini in every race until the end of eternity than give her up again.

I steadied the car, enjoying the freedom of my half-second buffer, and drove it hard around the last few turns, to finish the first lap in first place. When I did, I let out the breath I'd held tightly in my chest for the last quarter of the lap. I was one-eighth of the way to the end of the race. I was in first with a bit of a lead, and I didn't have to worry about my concentration being invaded by guilt over leaving Alyssa or stress over her finding comfort with another.

Despite that, the next seven laps were not exactly a walk in the park. With the Minis being so evenly matched, one bump in the road or one misjudged corner and the game completely shifted. My buffer was reduced, and then eroded completely.

Before long, I was staring at the arse of another car. I began to panic about being unable to finish on podium. I needed a solid finish so badly for so many reasons. To reward Danny's gamble, to silence the critics, but most of all, to earn Alyssa's pride. She would love me no matter the outcome, but I wanted her to be proud of what I'd achieved. I wanted there to be a genuine reason for her coming to Adelaide to support me.

By the start of the eighth lap, I was door to door with Wilkins. He was taking the aggressive lines as often as he could, neither of us willing to give up our track position to the other. We drove side by side through turns eight, nine, and ten. Despite the tight grip I had on the wheel, the set of my teeth as I clenched them tightly, and my absolute focus on the track, I was actually having a lot of fun.

I knew turn fourteen was critical. Gaining control over that corner at that stage of the race would place me in either the winner's or the loser's seat, so I wanted to be out front when we hit it. I dropped back a little, pushing the car hard to the left side of the track. I took a deep breath—and a huge risk—drove in hard, broke late, and cut across the nose of Wilkins's Mini just as he was entering the turn. I whipped my car around and exited the corner on the far right-hand side of the track. I didn't even pause to breathe again as I moved my foot from brake to accelerator and smashed it to the ground. One hand steadied the wheel as my other snapped through the gears.

A smile graced my lips when I saw the gamble had paid off. I was ahead. By a few fucking whiskers, but that didn't matter. Wilkins made a last-minute push for the line, but he was too late. The smile stretched into a mile-fucking-wide grin.

I was back.

I'd finished a race.

More than that, I'd won, and fuck if it didn't feel fan-fucking-tastic.

Although I just wanted to celebrate, I didn't have time to revel in the afterglow of my win. By the time I'd finished in scrutineering and parked the car back in the garage, I had less than a minute to sprint to the pits for Hunter's second practise session. I was panting as I took my position, thankful that Ryan and Calem had covered my arse by having everything I needed ready and waiting.

I rolled my eyes as I heard Hunter's complaints about his crew not being ready, knowing full well he was referring to my close-to-being-late arrival, but it wasn't like he'd been delayed at all. The car was more than ready when he rolled out onto the track right on time.

Once Hunter had disappeared around the first corner and we knew we weren't likely to see him again—it was Morgan's turn for the bulk of the fine-tuning—I said a quiet thank-you to my boys. They in turn congratulated me on a job well done in the Mini.

"That looked like so much fun," Calem said. "I wonder if I could convince Danny to put me in one next year."

I grinned. "It was a fuckload of fun."

Hunter only came into pit once during the thirty-minute practise and then only because he wanted to practise on the new soft-control tyre.

I was out of the pits the moment I was able to leave, retreating into the Mini garage once again. Not that I had anything to do there. Sure, I was being a coward, but at least I was a coward who was keeping my arse out of trouble, which was why I was so surprised when Mia dropped by and told me I needed to get up to the Sinclair Racing trailer to see Danny immediately.

At first, I thought maybe Danny wanted to congratulate me on the race, but his main priority for the rest of the day and into the evening was the V8s, so it didn't really make sense.

My race was little more than a blip on the radar in the grand scheme of the weekend. I knew his schedule well enough from when I was in the V8. He would go over all the statistics, have a brief discussion about tactics with Liam, and then he would meet with the drivers and go over the plan for the qualifying run in the morning. At the same time, he would be meeting with sponsors, arranging grid girls, and organising meet-and-greets.

In other words, he was far too busy to be seeing me over something as trivial as my win.

As it turned out, it wasn't Danny who wanted me at all. Hunter had decided to pull an impromptu meeting to discuss "tactics" of his own for the race. I openly objected to some of the suggestions he was making; some of what he was planning was sabotage thinly veiled as strategy. But even I had to admit that at least some of his requests were valid.

I tried to be the first to leave when he finished the meeting, but unfortunately he called my name. Ryan and Calem hung back a little when they realised I would be alone with him, but I waved them forward. If he wanted a confrontation, I'd give him one.

"I know your game," he said, smiling his stupid smirk. "You think that by being the good boy of the team, you'll get your shot in my car again. You're wrong though. Danny wouldn't let you touch the controls of a V8 with a ten-foot pole. But I don't care what you think may or may not happen; you just better fucking watch yourself and your smart mouth when you pit for me tomorrow. If I lose, it'll be on your head."

I scoffed. "If you lose, it'll be because your head is so far up your own arse that you can't see the track."

I turned and left the room as quickly as I could, taking just one brief second to enjoy the look on his face at my words. He obviously hadn't expected me to fight back. As I pushed out of the room, my mobile rang. I smiled when I read Alyssa's name on the screen.

I answered it, knowing that hearing her voice would be the icing on the cake for the pretty fantastic day I'd had. Especially when I suspected she was calling to let me know she was about to board the plane. "Hey, baby."

Instead of her voice though, I heard a choked sob.

All traces of good mood were wiped away in an instant.

Had something happened?

Was something wrong with Phoebe?

"Alyssa?" I asked, beginning to panic. "What is it? What's wrong?"

"It's—It's Ruby—" She managed to squeeze out the words between sobs. Then a stack of words fell out in a jumble. I could only pick out random ones, but they were enough to make the cold grip of fear clench tightly around my heart.

Hospital . . . baby . . . danger . . . Brisbane.

"What is it? What's happening?" I felt inadequate, utterly unable to deal with whatever it was. But most of all, I felt isolated. I was in another state when Alyssa needed me. I may not have known all the details, but I knew that much.

Alyssa took a couple of deep breaths and managed to calm herself enough to speak. "It's—It's Ruby, she's been rushed to hospital. Oh, God, Declan, they think she might lose the baby. It's all just too—" She cut off as her voice was stolen by a series of chest-wracking sobs.

I could easily imagine what was causing Alyssa's pain. It was all too similar to what happened with the emergency with the twins. With her own experience of birth.

"I need to go to her. I need to be there for her . . . like she was for me." Alyssa's voice was little more than a whisper.

"Go," I told her. It broke my heart to say it, but it wasn't the time for being selfish. As much as I wanted her beside me, as much as I needed her in my arms again, I couldn't demand that she come to Adelaide rather than go to Brisbane.

"I'm so—so—sorr—sorry." She sobbed.

"It's not your fault," I murmured. "I know you'd be here if you could, but if Ruby needs you, you need to go."

I leaned against the side of the trailer, feeling the blood draining from my face even as I said the words. I couldn't help but wonder how Alyssa would feel being back at the hospital. Would it bring back too many painful memories for her? Would she have to relive all of them with me in another state and unable to help?

I longed to be able to rush to her and support her in all the ways I didn't before. But I couldn't see how that was possible, at least not without pissing off Danny. It was career suicide to do that.

Alyssa sobbed again, and I decided I didn't care. Danny could go fuck himself if he didn't realise how important this was.

"Alyssa, you organise your ticket. Use the emergency money and just fly home. Let me know your flight details when you can." I hoped my tone was such that it wouldn't allow for argument.

"Okay," Alyssa said softly, then, "Are you sure about this?"

"One hundred percent. Go."

"Thank you."

"And Alyssa," I added.

"Yeah?" Her voice was still muffled, and she was sniffling.

"I love you."

After I had hung up the phone, I headed straight for Danny's offices. I knew he would be busy, and I was certain my course of action would result in me upsetting the apple cart, but I couldn't find it in myself to care. Alyssa needed me, and that was all that mattered.

When I reached my destination, I saw Danny facing away from the small window, but Eden was facing toward it. Toward me. I waved to get her attention and signalled for her to leave the strategy meeting before quickly explaining what had happened and what I needed to do.

"I'll get you a meeting with Danny as soon as possible," she said before rushing off to join the meeting again. She walked straight up to Danny and whispered in his ear. His eyes darted quickly to me before he held up his hand to stop the meeting. Moments later, he came out and nodded for me to follow him into his office.

Because I hadn't expected Eden's "as soon as possible" to be instantaneous, I wasn't entirely prepared. I swallowed nervously as I walked behind him. Would he understand why I needed to leave? Would he be okay with it? Or would it jeopardise the effort I had been putting in?

Did it matter if it did?

I trailed about three steps back as he walked wordlessly into his office. He headed straight for his desk drawer and pulled out his mobile. Without a word to me, he scrolled though his contacts before putting the phone to his ear.

"Ashley, it's Danny Sinclair. I need to book a seat on the next flight from Adelaide to Brisbane."

I felt my jaw drop as I listened to him book a return flight for me. After he'd ended his call he finally turned to me. "I booked the return flight just in case you can make it back. But family comes first in situations like this."

My eyes burned as he handed me a sheet of paper with the details on it and wrote down Ashley's number so I could reschedule the flexible return flight if necessary. He told me that he'd get Ryan and Calem to prep my car for the morning, just in case.

I thanked him profusely before pulling out my phone to ring Alyssa to tell her the good news. As soon as she answered, she launched into the details of her flight. I realised as she ran through the details that my own flight would arrive about fifteen minutes before hers.

In that moment, I decided to make my own dash to Brisbane a secret.

CHAPTER THIRTEEN

EMERGENCY DASH

ONCE MY FLIGHT had landed, and I'd fought my way off the plane, I ran through the domestic terminal to get to the gate that Alyssa would be coming through. Every one of my spare fifteen minutes was needed to ensure that I was there before she disembarked. When I arrived, I waited anxiously, watching the gate carefully for her arrival.

I stood by the door, my eyes taking in every person as they passed by. Finally, she emerged. She was almost the last one off, carrying her overnight bag over one shoulder and Phoebe on the opposite hip as she walked.

Her body was bent and weary. It was as if a hundred years had wreaked havoc on her since I'd last seen her just a few short days ago. Her eyes were red and puffy, showing that she'd clearly been crying on the plane. I hated that I wasn't able to do anything more for her earlier, but silently vowed to do everything I could for her now.

Phoebe was the first to see me.

"Daddy!" she called as soon as her eyes locked with mine.

I gave her a small smile as Alyssa hushed her quietly, telling her that Daddy wasn't there.

Phoebe shook her head and laughed. "Silly! He's right there, Mummy!" she exclaimed, pointing at me.

Alyssa raised her head a little as her eyes followed Phoebe's finger to find me, widening as they traced over my body.

I smiled, walking over to her as quickly as I was able and wrapping my arms around the pair of them. Phoebe curled her arms around my neck before giving me a quick peck on the cheek. I felt Alyssa surrender herself to my embrace almost instantly. Clearly, it was sheer perseverance and determination that had carried her onto the plane and then through the terminal.

"You came," she whispered against my chest as she descended into tears again. "I can't believe you're actually here."

"Here for you," I murmured into her hair. "For as long as you need me."

"But your race? Your pit obligations?"

"If I can get back to Adelaide before the meet is over, then I will. Otherwise . . ." I trailed off, letting her know through touch instead that I would remain by her side for as long as she needed.

She leaned heavily against me as I moved her away from the gate.

"Did you have any luggage?" I asked.

She shook her head and indicated her small overnight bag. I reached out and slid it from her shoulder before pulling Phoebe into my arms. I needed to take as much of the physical load from Alyssa as I could. Unfortunately, there was nothing more I could do for her emotional one.

"Have you heard anything more?"

Alyssa shook her head. "Nothing. All I know is that Ruby was rushed to the RBH earlier. Josh was beside himself when he called."

"It'll be all right," I assured her, hoping like hell I wouldn't be proven wrong when we arrived at the hospital.

After we'd found our way up to the right floor, we looked for Alyssa's family.

Ruth saw us first and rushed over to our side, surprise at our arrival evident in her features. She thanked us for coming and took Phoebe from my arms. I sank back behind Alyssa, using her as a shield between myself and her family. Not that I really thought I needed it. Even Curtis wouldn't be so heartless as to attack me at such a time.

I placed my hand lightly on the small of Alyssa's back, wordlessly letting her know I was there for her.

"What's happening?" Alyssa asked. "How is she?"

"She's okay," Ruth said as she embraced Phoebe tightly. "She gave us all a major scare though, passing out the way she did. She's just come back from a round of scans. The doctors were most concerned about the bleeding. They're not saying much at the moment, but they are taking extra precautions because of her high-risk pregnancy. Josh is in there with her now."

Alyssa sighed in relief and leaned back into me. I wrapped my arms around her and rested my hands on her stomach. I ducked my head to rest my cheek against the crook of her neck. I was thankful it was nothing too serious. I wasn't sure how Alyssa would have coped if anything had happened to Ruby or the baby.

"Can I see her?" Alyssa asked finally.

Ruth nodded. "But she's only allowed two guests at a time, so you'll have to go in alone." She eyed me apologetically.

I brushed my lips along Alyssa's neck. "Go. I'll be waiting here when you come back out. I'm sure she'll be happy to know you're here for her."

Alyssa turned and gave me a questioning look that was filled with concern, no doubt trying to seek out the lie in my words, but I nodded to indicate she should go. That I'd be okay. After all, it was what she'd come to Brisbane for.

Once she'd moved off, I sat in the corner of the waiting room, trying to blend into the walls so no one noticed me. I felt like an interloper on a private family time.

After a short time with Ruth, Phoebe came and planted herself on my lap and gave me a hug. "I missed you, Daddy," she whispered.

"I missed you too, baby." I hugged her closer. "I hope you were good for Mummy?"

She nodded and smiled. I could tell she was getting bored and restless, so I grabbed a small pile of magazines from under the waiting room table—the most recent one was from Christmas the previous year—and began to make up little stories about the people in them.

"Look, Daddy! It's you!" she squealed as she recognised me on one of the covers.

In the fraction of a second it took for me to look at the magazine, I hoped like hell it was the issue of *Woman's Idea* from when Alyssa and I had gone for our joint interview.

Instead, I found myself staring at the cover of *Gossip Weekly* and the photo of me sandwiched between Tillie and Talia—the two bitches who'd had a big hand in securing my public fall from grace.

I shoved the magazine to the bottom of the pile and tried to distract Phoebe with other stories. I resorted to looking at the Christmas edition of *Woman's Idea*; at least Christmas held positive memories for me. After all, it was when Alyssa had agreed to marry me.

Finally, Alyssa reappeared in the waiting room, looking like the world had been lifted from her shoulders. She gave me a small smile as she found her way over and sat on the chair beside me. "I'm sorry I dragged you away from your race meeting for nothing."

I put my hand up to silence her. "It wasn't nothing." I wanted to say it could have easily gone the other way, but I didn't want to be the reason the stress returned. "I wanted to be here." *For you.* "How is she?"

She rested her head against my shoulder. "She's fine. They are keeping her in for a while just to be on the safe side, but the baby seems to be fine too."

"That's good," I murmured, knowing Alyssa would have been close to inconsolable if Ruby had lost her baby.

"Mum's asked if we want to stay at their house," she whispered, knowing that under normal circumstances I would've preferred a hotel.

But I was well aware we weren't in Brisbane under normal circumstances. I nodded, knowing that accepting would mean that our accommodation would be one less thing for everyone to worry about.

Over the next few hours, Curtis drove home to get their spare child seat and then drove the three of us home. Then we had the news that Ruby was being released from the hospital, and Ruth refused to let Ruby go home alone, despite the fact that Josh wouldn't leave her side.

In the end, Alyssa and I went to Josh and Ruby's house while everyone else stayed with Curtis and Ruth. Because neither Alyssa nor I had eaten since before our flights, we grabbed takeout on the way to our temporary accommodation.

We were all so exhausted that we crashed into bed almost the instant we had finished eating. Alyssa fell asleep quickly in my arms, drained from the stressful day she'd had. As I watched her sleeping, I rested my hand on her stomach, trying to imagine what it had been like for her when she had been pregnant with the twins.

After experiencing her grief firsthand over the course of the day, I was even more disappointed with myself than ever that I hadn't been there for her during that time. I vowed to never let that happen again.

I woke early the next day and caught a cab back to the airport, leaving Alyssa to spend some more time with her family. I arrived back at the track just in time to jump in my Mini for the second race of the meeting. It was a reverse grid race, so I had to fight my way through the pack. I came in third, but somehow I couldn't find the same enthusiasm that I'd enjoyed the previous day.

Instead, my mind was filled with concern for Alyssa.

On Saturday night, I rang Alyssa at her parents' house and got all the latest news on Ruby. The doctors said that she was still high risk and that she needed to relax, putting her fainting spell down to a combination of heat, exhaustion, and being pregnant.

On Sunday, I woke early and dragged my arse to the track. My final race of the meeting was over before 9:00 a.m., and I'd managed to wrestle another first place in that one.

It meant that I was already in first place on the Micro Challenge leader board. I was able to muster a little more enthusiasm now that I had the knowledge that Ruby—and therefore Alyssa—was all right. But I still missed Alyssa and Phoebe terribly and wanted to be with them. It was almost a relief when the weekend was finally over and it was time to go home.

CHAPTER FOURTEEN

THREE DAY BREAK

BEFORE I KNEW it, March was almost over—passing in a flash of repairs, race meets, and a lot less time with the family than I would have liked. The Grand Prix had raced past just like the rest of the month. Luckily for me, and for my honeymoon plans, I had taken pole position at the Melbourne meet. It meant I only needed one more pole out of my next two races to secure our getaway.

The end of March saw the arrival of Easter coming at me fast. During the lead-up, it dawned on me that it was going to be a year of firsts for me. It was my first Easter as a father, and I'd be damned if I was going to screw it up.

The Thursday before we broke for the long weekend was a particularly difficult one.

It was the first of April—April Fools. Around the workshop, there were countless opportunities for April Fools pranks, and I had to stay on my toes the entire time. There was glue on seats and phones, thumbtacks in tool boxes, and fake spiders on toilet seats, to name just a few. The muffins Alyssa and I had made the previous night—baked with salt instead of sugar—went over a real treat in the staff kitchen at morning tea. I found myself still chuckling about the look on everyone's face as I packed up for the day.

Even though Alyssa and I usually carpooled, I'd driven myself in to work that day so I could hit the shops on the way home in preparation for my first Easter Bunny gig. I had the whole scenario planned out in my head, and I hoped it would work exactly as I imagined.

By the time I left the shop, I had four huge bags containing more chocolate than Phoebe could probably eat in a year, but I didn't care. I was going to make sure my little girl had an Easter to remember—screw the cost . . . and the consequences. As soon as I got home, I hid the bags at the top of the pantry.

The long weekend was going to be exactly the break I needed from my hectic schedule. It was the break we *all* needed.

On Good Friday, we all woke early and had hot cross buns for breakfast. Then the three of us headed to pick out one of the classic cars buried deep in my back shed. I decided on the '67 Chevy Impala—black, of course.

Alyssa almost gagged when she saw the size of it.

"That's huge!" she exclaimed loudly. "I'd ask if it were compensating for something, except I know it's not. How does it even fit through that gap though?" she asked, pointing at the door to the garage.

"It's a tight squeeze, but the opening is more accommodating than it looks," I said as seriously as I could, even though my mind had gone to dirty places. "You just have to pay extra attention as you slide it in." I couldn't stop the small chuckle that escaped me.

Alyssa looked at me quizzically, and I burst out laughing.

"What?" she asked.

I shook my head and tried to stop the laughter. Phoebe looked at me with confusion all over her face but giggled at my laughter.

Alyssa must have run through her words because just as my laughter died down, she giggled and shook her head. "You and your dirty mind!"

"You were the one who said it, baby."

"I was *talking* about the car." She was scarlet as she quickly explained herself.

I stepped up to her, kissed her forehead, and whispered, so

quietly that only she would hear, "I know, but I'd be up for more practise fitting other big things into small spaces later if you like."

She slapped my chest lightly. "Let's just go."

I nodded and shifted the car seat from my Monaro to the Impala. Then I left Alyssa to load Phoebe into the car as I opened the roller door.

"This is a big car, Daddy," Phoebe told me as I eased it out of the shed.

"It's a fast car too," I told her. "I'll show you later." I grinned at her in the rear-view mirror.

"No, you won't," Alyssa insisted.

I pouted. "I'll take it on the highway. I'll make sure she's safe."

I eyed Alyssa out of the corner of my eye.

"Please?"

She sighed.

"I wouldn't do anything to hurt either of you, but you gotta have a little fun, right?" I added a shrug and tried to throw her a smouldering look—anything to tilt the argument my way. It'd been too long since I'd driven any of my collection, and I really wanted to stretch the legs of the Impala.

"We'll see." The way she said it was so final, I doubted she'd say okay.

Even though the conversation was closed, I couldn't help spinning the tyres as I left the driveway. A grin was planted firmly on my face as I did. I hadn't had much of an opportunity to drive my other cars between my responsibilities at work and home, the study I had to do at TAFE for my apprenticeship, and trying to assist in the planning of the wedding as much as I could—especially with Ruby on enforced bedrest for most of the day.

Now that the opportunity to put my foot down just a smidge had presented itself, I was going to take full advantage.

I stopped to fill the tank up—I tried to leave all my cars with minimal fuel so it wouldn't go bad in the tank—and then we drove to the beach. I intentionally drove around the long way, ensuring I got to spend as much quality time as I could with my big, black beauty of a beast.

143

When we arrived at the beach, we claimed a small patch of sand for ourselves. I spent the morning making sandcastles with Phoebe before she knocked them over or poured water on them, leaving them twisted and destroyed. Each time she busted one, I would pretend to chase her, and she would run away giggling. Alyssa sat on a blanket beside us, reading a book, catching some sun, and occasionally giving suggestions for a better design for my castles.

Once Phoebe started to complain that she was hungry, we walked across the road to grab fish and chips for lunch. We sat watching the passers-by as we ate, talking about everything and nothing, just reconnecting in ways that we hadn't had the chance to during our usually hectic work weeks.

After we'd all finished eating, and waited the appropriate time according to Alyssa, we returned to the beach for a splash in the waves. We spent the better part of a few hours in the sand and surf. The best part of the day was listening to Phoebe's squeals as she darted into the retreating water before running from it as the next wave came.

By five, we'd had enough sun, sand, and waves, so we headed back to the car. I made sure everyone brushed the sand off before climbing in. Before we hit the road, we scouted for a restaurant for dinner. We picked a family-friendly place that had an all-you-can-eat buffet so Phoebe could be as fussy as she liked but still get fed.

On the way home, I took the highways so I had plenty of time to give Phoebe a small taste of just how fast the car could be. She giggled as the momentum pressed her into the seat each time I nailed it. Before long though, her laughter had died off as she fell asleep in the back seat. Once that happened, I just cruised in the car with Alyssa at my side, my hand in her lap.

When we got home, I slid the car into the shed then negotiated a sleeping Phoebe out of her car seat. As I carried her to bed, I realised it had been the best day I'd had in a long time. But more than that, I found myself regretting again that I'd missed so many of the early days of Phoebe's life.

For the first time, I felt a pang of something else, something I couldn't quite put my finger on. A little niggle in the pit of my stomach that had made my eye follow the path of the expectant mothers during the day.

I was certain it was just lingering concern for Ruby—even though she was fine.

Once Phoebe was bathed and settled in bed, I followed the sound of the shower to find Alyssa in our en suite. I stripped quietly before climbing into the shower and wrapping my arm around her. She squealed and jumped at my touch before spinning around in my arms.

"Sorry," she murmured. "You startled me."

"I didn't mean to." I pulled her against me.

"I was just distracted, I guess."

I glanced down at her naked chest before kissing the base of her neck. "I don't blame you," I whispered. "You're all wet after all. I find I get very easily distracted when you're all wet." I growled the last word against her skin. I had only joined her in order to rinse off, but I was quickly getting new ideas.

Alyssa mewed softly, and I took it as an encouragement to continue. I licked and sucked along her clavicle before kissing her neck softly. I traced a path up to the soft skin just underneath her ear, kissing it softly, and then murmured, "Very distracted, in fact."

I ran my tongue along the shell of her ear before breathing softly on her skin, and relished the way she shivered against my body.

"But I don't find my wetness to be a distraction," she teased.

I ran my hands along the sides of her body, pushing against her and pinning her to the tiles. "Do you find my wetness distracting?"

She grinned wickedly then shook her head.

I rested my lips against her ear and ran one hand down her body, cupping my hand against her pussy. "How about when I make *you* wet, is that distracting?"

I slid my hand down to her arousal, slipping two fingers inside and curling them around to rub gently within her. I pulled my face back from her delectable skin to ensure that she was satisfied. The look on her face was one of such ecstasy that it was clear I was more than welcome to continue. I trailed my free hand over her sides and across her breasts before running it down onto her stomach. Without removing my fingers or slowing their pace, I kissed my way down her body before finding myself almost eye to eye with the small scar on her stomach—the tiny reminder of her pregnancy. I traced a finger across it lightly before kissing along her hip and touching my mouth to the apex of her thighs. I enjoyed the sensation of kissing her deeply while she raked her fingernails across my scalp. She was making such delectable sounds— amplified by the enclosed space of our en suite—that I was painfully hard long before I was done satisfying her.

I removed my fingers and trailed my way back up her body with my mouth. As I stood, I lifted her legs one at a time, wrapping them around my waist and positioning myself to plunge deep into her. She wrapped her arms around my shoulders, and I pushed her upper body harder against the tiles; her shoulders rested flush against the wall and her hips angled out perfectly toward me. I thrust into her hard and fast, my need for her driven by a desire for intimacy that I couldn't explain. I needed to be near her—and in her. I needed her to surround me completely. I just needed *her*.

I clutched her hips tightly, shifting her ever closer to me, until she came undone in my arms and fell against me, spent and exhausted. Then I carried her to the bed and made love to her again.

CHAPTER FIFTEEN

BUNNY DAY

SATURDAY, WE SPENT the day around the house. I tinkered with a few of my cars because I'd been champing at the bit to apply some of what I had learned since starting my apprenticeship. Phoebe trailed around behind me, wearing a set of little overalls with her hair in pigtails and my tools in her pockets.

She looked up at me, pleased as punch with herself for being like Daddy.

"There's something missing," I said, staring at her thoughtfully.

Her gaze trailed over her outfit. "Nah-uh."

"Yah-huh," I said. I ran my finger over the carburettor I was working on, and then ran a small trail of grease over her cheek.

She squealed with laughter before declaring I was missing it too. Obliging her, I ran my finger over my cheek as well.

I really enjoyed showing Phoebe a little bit more of that side of myself and was surprised about how proud I felt about the smallest things she did that demonstrated she was paying attention to me. Like when she explained to Alyssa what the rattle gun was for minutes after I had given a demonstration. I joked with her that she would be able to start an apprenticeship under me one day. The earnest look of pure excitement she gave me in response was enough to melt my heart.

ON SUNDAY morning, I set my alarm super early and woke to do the Easter Bunny thing. I littered a course of Easter eggs around the house. It started with a trail of tiny eggs and powdered "rabbit tracks" from her bedroom door, leading to slightly bigger eggs down the staircase, and finally to a collection of large eggs and a rabbit in the living room.

I padded quietly back to the bedroom and waited for Phoebe to wake up. I knew the instant that she realised what was waiting outside her door—I think the whole neighbourhood did. She squealed excitedly then ran into our room at top speed and skidded to a halt in front of our bed. She already had chocolate smeared across her mouth and a wide grin on her face.

"The Easter Bunny camed!" she shouted excitedly. "He left me lots of chocolates! Dey're everywhere! Come see!" She grabbed one of my hands and one of Alyssa's and pulled us from the bed. I wrapped my arms around Alyssa and walked in step with her. I was grinning widely because she had yet to see my handiwork.

"Oh, my . . ." Alyssa gasped as we came to the staircase and she saw the trail of eggs running down the stairs.

I suppressed a chuckle and released her in order to chase after Phoebe who was halfway down the stairs and babbling about the rest of the eggs she got. She stopped on each stair, picked up the egg, and put it with the ever-growing pile that she was gathering in a makeshift basket she made with the front of her nightgown.

Alyssa covered her face with her hands when she saw the contents of the living room. She spun toward me quickly, staring at me with one eyebrow cocked. "The Easter Bunny really went over the top this year, didn't he?"

I shrugged.

"It's mores than I got last year!" Phoebe exclaimed, picking up one of the giant rabbits that sat on the couch.

"How about you go and find them all and take them into the kitchen?" Alyssa said to Phoebe.

I turned to help, but Alyssa stopped me. "Daddy and I need to have a little talk."

I gulped as I spun back to Alyssa. She had her arms crossed and a "what the hell were you thinking" look on her face. I shrugged again and gave her an "I'm new to this and wanted to make it memorable, really . . . I'm innocent" look.

We were certainly getting the non-verbal communication thing down pat.

I stepped closer to her. "I acknowledge that I may have gone a little bit over the top," I murmured as I wrapped my arms around her waist. I wasn't above using tools that Dr. Henrikson had given us to show her I was serious. "I couldn't help it though, I got a little excited." I ducked my head to meet her eye.

Alyssa looked up at me, and I could see the shock and anger had melted away a little in the face of my admission. "She would have been happy with one or two eggs and then to just spend the day with you," she said exasperatedly.

I nodded. "I'm sorry. I promise I won't go quite so over the top next year." I drew a little cross over my heart.

"I'll hold you to it." She smiled, and I knew I was out of the doghouse.

Thank Christ.

We managed to convince Phoebe to put the chocolate down long enough to eat a healthy breakfast and get changed to ready ourselves for the arrival of our lunch guests.

Morgan and Eden arrived first. Phoebe practically threw herself into Eden's arms and wished her a happy Easter. Soon after, the rest of my motley crew—Calem, Sam, Ryan, Mia, and Johnno—turned up. A couple of girls from Alyssa's work were the last ones to show. Apparently, Alyssa had invited the one girl she was friendly with, who had in turn invited the other girls in the office. I immediately recognised one of them as the girl from the bar in London. I felt Alyssa bristle beside me as I said hello, but Lily seemed as willing as I was to put the incident behind us and not mention it at all.

I stoked up the BBQ and passed around a few beers. Before I knew it, there was a party in full swing.

I made sure I didn't leave all the hosting duties to Alyssa; instead, I mingled and served drinks. I entertained Phoebe and got her to help me out a little—just simple things like grabbing food from the kitchen and drinks from the eskies. I noticed Alyssa approach Morgan and Eden and strike up a tentative conversation. I knew that Alyssa and Morgan would never be best friends, but at least they were being civil and trying to put their differences behind them, which meant the world to me.

At one point during the afternoon, I had Alyssa under one arm and the other around Phoebe. As I watched over our friends mingling with one another, I couldn't believe how shockingly and absolutely *domestic* my life had become. As much as I would have been loath to admit it a few months earlier, I was in my fucking element and blissed the fuck out. Aside from a few special days with Alyssa and Phoebe, I couldn't think of a day when I'd had a better time.

When evening started to close in on our little party, most of the people started to leave; although Eden and Morgan stayed for the clean-up, which was greatly appreciated. After the paper plates were discarded and the dishwasher was running, Alyssa, Eden, and Phoebe raced upstairs for some girly shit to do with the wedding, so Morgan and I sat to have a beer.

"Man, can you believe how different your life is now?" he asked.

I laughed. "I was just thinking that earlier. Last Easter . . ." I trailed off with a shudder as I recalled my adventures of the previous Easter. Sure I'd thought it was fun at the time, but it just couldn't compare now.

"I'm thinking about doing it." Morgan choked. His face was earnest, but his wide eyes and tight lips made him look dreadfully afraid.

"Doing what exactly?" I had a suspicion, but I wanted to make him suffer.

"Asking Edie." He made the strange choking sound again. "To marry me, I mean." His voice squeaked as the last few words escaped past his lips.

I grinned. "I guarantee it'll be the best question you ever ask."

He sat bolt upright and choked a little more—I was beginning to wonder if I needed to take the big-boy drinks off him. "Holy fuck! When did my little squirt grow up so much? I mean, sure you're getting married and all, but fuck, to hear you talk about marriage as if it's the best thing in the world . . . and you aren't even married yet!"

I shrugged. "Man, marriage, kids, all that stuff. It's scary as fuck, but it's the biggest thing you will ever do with your life. More important than any fucking championship."

He laughed. "Seriously, who are you and what the fuck have you done with Declan Reede?"

I sat grinning like the cat that got the cream. "The Declan Reede you knew . . . Well, he's gone. I am the new and improved version." I sat back and stretched out along the sofa.

"Well, new maybe." He pretended to size me up. "Not sure about improved."

"Fuck you!" I punched his arm.

He laughed. "Fuck you!" He punched me back.

We fell into our old dynamic and had a mock-wrestle in the living room before the girls came down to break us up. As we said goodbye, Morgan turned to me. "I'll talk to you later for some more advice . . . about that thing."

Alyssa and Eden looked between us, puzzled, but I just nodded. "Anytime, dude."

Alyssa quizzed me after he'd left, but I didn't spill his secret. Over the years, he'd protected so many details about my life. I figured I at least owed him the same courtesy.

ON MONDAY, Alyssa and I took Phoebe to Luna Park. We had a great time—thanks in no small part to far too much fairy floss, dagwood dogs, and soft drinks. It was interesting to watch Phoebe on all the kiddie rides, but even more interesting to watch her sizing herself up against the adult rides and come away upset when she wasn't quite tall enough for them.

In order to give her some thrills, I took her on the Tumble Bug and then on the Rotor. Her giggles and excited screams were all the reward I needed.

Both Alyssa and Phoebe laughed as I wrestled against the forces sticking us to the wall to try to get sideways. Phoebe begged to go on it again, but she was already looking decidedly green so we opted for the Ferris wheel instead.

After the Ferris wheel and the carousel, we went on to the bumper cars. The first time, I took Phoebe in the car with me and avoided the worst of the carnage. The second time, she was with Alyssa. Freed from the responsibility of making sure she didn't get hurt on my watch, I took great joy in ramming into the other cars, especially any that came too close to my girls.

Overall, the weekend was fan-fucking-tastic. I was glad for the respite and the breathing space with my family, because a little over a week after Easter, I was heading to New Zealand for the Hamilton 400. It would be an excruciating torture for me for three reasons.

One, I would be away from my family.

Two, I would have to pit for Hunter.

And three, I wouldn't even have the luxury of the Mini to escape from his fuckery.

CHAPTER SIXTEEN

FAMILIAR FEELING

THE HAMILTON 400 was every bit as horrid as I'd thought it would be.

Hunter rode my arse the whole time, never letting the opportunity to insult me, or Alyssa, pass. When we were around others, it always sounded mischievous and light-hearted, like when Morgan and I bantered, but as soon as we were alone—even momentarily—it took a darker turn. It took every ounce of my patience to not smack his smart-talking mouth.

It was hard, but somehow I managed to continue my resistance against assaulting him physically. I realised I had to fight him my own way—a way that wouldn't get me in trouble with the Sinclair Racing brass—so I started tailing him to the nightclubs in town and cock-blocking him at every possible opportunity.

After all, what we did in our own spare time had nothing to do with the team, so I had the opportunity to get a bit of vengeance without repercussions—from the team at least. It didn't even affect my family moments because of the two-hour time difference between New Zealand and Sydney. I was able to call home before I hit the town and again when I returned to the hotel.

He was so tense by the end of the weekend, it was fucking hilarious. Especially so, because I knew he was heading home to a lonely and empty house. I was going home to a lovely house, a beautiful daughter, and a highly fuckable fiancée who had missed me terribly. In fact, she'd demonstrated just how much during our late-night phone calls. We'd been practising our aural technique regularly and were at the point where it was almost as good as the real thing. Well, at least as good as I could expect without any skin-to-skin contact.

On top of avoiding Hunter at the track, and chasing him through the clubs, I spent the weekend trying to stay out of Morgan's way. He was wound tighter than a tin soldier over some special plans he had for the trip. He'd arranged to stay a couple of days longer with Eden, but he wouldn't tell me exactly what was happening. I knew they were heading to the Waitomo Glowworm Caves and figured that meant that somewhere beneath the dark earth, by the tiny light of thousands of glowworms, he was going to ask her a question that could change the course of both of their lives.

If that was the case, I couldn't be happier for them.

My suspicions were confirmed a few days after arriving home when Eden called and squealed down the phone. She demanded I put Alyssa on, and the two of them squealed to each other again. I rolled my eyes at Phoebe, who giggled and reached out for me.

All I got in actual confirmation from Morgan was a text message. *I did it. Best Man?*

I laughed and texted back. *Definitely.*

APRIL HAD headed toward May much too quickly. As it did, Alyssa and I seemed to spend most of our time passing each other like ships in the night. I was putting in crazy hours at the office, and whenever I was lucky enough to be home at a reasonable hour, she was always on the phone with either Eden or Ruby. My own phone had been going crazy with phone calls from one Brisbane number. Although I didn't know the number at first, the corresponding voicemail that arrived told me all I needed to know. Dad was trying to reach me, but I wasn't ready to talk to him again. I wasn't sure I ever would be.

Things started to look up a little when Alyssa booked flights to go to Brisbane for the weekend I was racing at Ipswich—at Queensland Raceway—for the first time since I'd begun crashing out. The thought that she'd be supporting me there, where I'd need it the most, left me ecstatic.

My excitement over her travelling to Brisbane with Phoebe was short-lived when I realised that she was going primarily to arrange some more of the finer details of the wedding—the things that were impossible to arrange over the phone.

She and Ruby had already lined up back-to-back meetings with the photographer to select the shots and locations for the photos, the bakery to choose the type of cake we would serve—I voted mud cake rather than that horrid fruit stuff—and with the decorators to pin down the colour for the bows for the fucking chairs or something.

It all boiled down to one simple truth: I wouldn't get any quality time with her despite being on our old home turf. I would have to relive so many memories while at the track—of crashing for the first time ever, of the date I'd arranged for her after my return to Brisbane, of many visits during my youth—and I would have to do it all alone.

Fuck my life.

The team truck left for Ipswich on the last Wednesday in April with Danny in tow. The rest of the crew were flying up on Thursday morning to meet up at the track. I got permission to drive up on Wednesday night rather than leaving with the rest of them. It was a hard decision, because it meant an extra day away from Alyssa and driving would take a little longer. But it meant I would have my own car, which hopefully would leave me free to come and go from the track as I pleased to see my family at least a little.

The drive was long and lonely. I tried putting the radio on, but it did little to distract me from my thoughts. An uneasy feeling settled into me. I found myself stopping at every service station along the highway. I didn't want to be on the darkened road anymore; it was making me mad. Something began to eat away at my sanity, but for the life of me I had no idea what that "something" was.

As I drove, I longed for some kind of peace. I longed to see Alyssa by my side and Phoebe giggling at me from the rear seat. Instead, the car was empty and silent. I drank more coffee and ate more shitty servo food than was probably healthy in a twelve-hour period. If I tried to think about my race, I inevitably became more wound up and would need to stop again.

When I arrived at the track on Thursday morning, I helped everyone with the set-up before heading to the hotel to sleep and prepare for my early start. I was due at the track for my first practise session at eight the following morning.

IT WAS hard to put the memories of my first DNF out of my head as I drove around the all-too-familiar track of Queensland Raceway. I'd learned the cause of it I was now able to deal with; Alyssa was back by my side, Flynn wasn't the love rival I'd thought he was, and I had mostly come to terms with the stupid decisions I had made to get Alyssa and me to that point. But knowing the *reasons* for my crash didn't help when I drove that section of the track. The crash itself played over and over in my head. Back then, if I'd been killed in an accident, I probably would have welcomed death, but now I had too much to lose.

Instead of focusing on that first DNF, I tried to think of other times I had driven the track, like on my date with Alyssa, but it was no good. At the time, I'd had her presence in the car to distract me while I was driving.

I didn't have that anymore.

There was nothing to distract me in my Mini. There was nothing except my own mind and the squawking of the radio to offer me companionship—and my mind wasn't good company away from Alyssa.

I stumbled from the car once I got it off the track, feeling much worse for wear. My chest was tight, and I was beginning to feel the familiar constriction that had always pre-empted my panic attacks. I'd thought being on my home ground, so to speak, would help me. I'd thought Queensland Raceway would be the easiest track to conquer, but instead it was overpowering me. Even though I'd hoped to get the opportunity to prove myself on the track that was the most familiar to me of them all, it proved to have too many lingering ghosts.

After practise, I parked my Mini and walked away from it for a while, knowing I only had a few hours to get my head back in the game before my next practise session. This race meeting was going to be an extra-long one for me with four races in total—on top of the practises, qualifying, and my usual pit crew duties.

The next practise was just a little bit more calming. God knows how, but I managed to get around smoothly and without too much hassle. I found a groove on the track that I'd missed during the first session, but I still felt wildly off task. I should have been able to push it faster, but I just couldn't. I wasn't able to get my head into the game properly. Images of my first DNF, along with the sounds of the car hitting the wall, flooded my mind, and I felt like a failure.

Those memories melded into the vision from my recurring nightmare of Alyssa being in the seat beside me. I couldn't get my head clear. I needed something, some kind of inner peace that I'd managed to feign at other meets, but that had been impossible to even imagine since my horror drive up from Sydney.

I went back to the hotel disappointed. Alyssa wasn't arriving in Brisbane until sometime on Saturday, so I rang home. Even that didn't help. It was a quick conversation with both my girls before I was cast off the phone so they could have some sleep in preparation for their early flight.

The next day, I just went through the motions. I survived the qualifying session and was not at all surprised when told I had qualified fifth. I could see the London dream slipping away. I had to get pole in Townsville or I was fucked.

I walked around like a fucking zombie the rest of the morning, doing what was required of me and nothing more. I didn't have the energy to try, and I just couldn't shake the dreadful feeling in the pit of my stomach.

Finally, it was time for my first race. I had no idea how I was going to make it through. My stomach was wound up in knots, and I was a few short breaths away from a full-blown panic attack. Everything in my body told me not to get in the car, but I needed to buck up and move past my demons if I was ever going to be successful at Queensland Raceway again.

I couldn't ever expect to get back into a V8 if a simple racetrack could beat me.

Lined up on the grid, I took a few deep breaths, running through my usual routine while the light was red. When the light turned green, I planted my foot and flicked through the gears. As the race wore on, I managed to get into the swing of things a little. I was actually jostling for third at turn six on the final lap when everything turned to shit.

The driver beside me took a line that was too aggressive and raced through the corner with far too much speed. I felt his car nudge mine roughly and saw his tyre mount my wheel arch. I closed my eyes for a moment, knowing this was what I'd been dreading the whole time, but thankfully when I opened them again a split-second later, my car was still on the track and still pointed in the right direction.

I looked back to see what had become of my competitor, but he wasn't there. My eyes flicked back to the track, and I watched in horror as his car completed a roll before beginning to cartwheel toward the safety barrier.

My heart stopped as his Mini missed the barrier completely and sailed over the top of the fence that separated the crowd from the track. His car settled roughly in the middle of a scattering crowd. My heart raced and all I could think was that Alyssa could have easily been standing there. She would be in Brisbane by now, and if she hadn't been off doing her wedding stuff, she could've been standing in the path of that deadly weapon.

I managed to keep my wits about me enough to execute the final turns and finish the lap as the stewards cancelled the rest of the race. My hands shook wickedly as I climbed out of the car. I raced to the fence separating the scrutineering field from the Paddock to find Eden—I knew she'd be all across the incident.

"How many people were—" I couldn't finish the sentence.

"I don't know, Declan." She held out a mobile phone for me. "But I've got someone on the phone for you."

I grabbed the phone, knowing who it would be.

"I just heard about an accident or something there. Are you all right?"

I sighed in relief as Alyssa's voice washed over me. "Yeah, baby, I'm fine. I wasn't involved." I didn't think I needed to clarify that I'd been only seconds away from being involved.

"Oh, thank goodness." I could hear her physically slumping in relief over the phone. "Do you need me to come there?"

I debated being selfish for a moment and saying yes, but decided against it. "No, I'll be fine."

Eden looked at me sympathetically. She knew I wasn't *fine*, but she also wouldn't argue with me or worry Alyssa unnecessarily.

"How did you hear about it so quickly?" I asked.

"I was actually on the phone with Eden about something else when she started swearing and shouting about a Mini that'd crashed. God, I was so worried . . ."

I was too, I thought, but I didn't want to add to her concern.

"Actually, I needed to talk to you about something else too."

I knew from her tone of voice that now that she knew I was okay, she was back to business—wedding business.

"I finally got a call back from Miss Wendy, the dressmaker. She said she can fit me in this weekend, but it's got to be tonight. Is it okay if I meet you later on? Around eleven? Mum'll come with me to look after Phoebe. But if you need me to be there for you when you get back to the hotel, I'll tell her no."

I sighed and shook my head. "No, go. You should do this while we're here anyway. It'll be easier in the long run. I'll see you later

159

tonight."

"Thanks, Dec."

Even though she couldn't see me, I plastered a smile on my face and wondered if it looked as fake as it felt. "No problems."

My second race was an unqualified disaster; I was too afraid to go near another car for fear of being involved in another incident and breaking the car. I couldn't stand the humiliation if I was thrown out of the Micro Series on top of everything else. I took the pussy-line on every corner, braking early and accelerating late. I hated myself for being unable to get past the worry, but I just couldn't find the thing that was missing. Missing to the tune of third last at the end of the race.

After I finished at the track, and the Mini was wrapped up safely for the night, I headed toward Browns Plains. I had no idea where exactly I wanted to end up, but I felt the need to drive my old streets. I drove aimlessly until I pulled up in front of the Browns Plains cemetery.

Once there, I knew my purpose. I knew why I'd been unable to find peace, why my heart had been clenched ever since my drive to Brisbane.

The last time I'd driven to Brisbane on my own, I was in the middle of a crisis. It had been a crisis of my own making, and one that I'd only gone part of the way toward fixing. I was certain I would be able to find peace where I always found it — with family. I climbed from the car and followed the familiar path toward the tiny cherub in the back rows.

Unlike previous visits, this wasn't one filled with sadness or a need to make amends. I was purely visiting my son to spend time with him. I ran my fingers along the little headstone and stood beside his grave for a few moments. Resting on the marble of the headstone, right in front of the tiny cherub, were a few items that I assumed were the gifts Alyssa had left with Emmanuel before we'd moved to Sydney.

Except the car she'd left to represent me was gone.

Once upon a time, I probably would have taken that as an omen. Instead, I decided to see if it had simply fallen into the grass.

As I bent to look around the base, I briefly examined the other items that had been left. A purple plastic ring—the kind you get out of a gumball machine. Despite it being faded by the sun, I recognised it as the gift I'd given Alyssa the day after our first kiss. I felt my chest clench to know that she had kept it through everything I had put her through and that she'd given it to Emmanuel as a keepsake. There was a tiny hospital band looped through it, but the weather had wrought a bit of damage on the paper inside so I couldn't tell whose it was. I could only assume it was Phoebe's.

I brushed a small pile of leaves off the corner of the marble at the base of his headstone, and my hand brushed across something solid and metal. I picked it up and turned it over in my hands. The little Commodore was decked out in red with a flaming car along both sides—the traditional Sinclair Racing design. The paint on the toy car was patchy, faded to a soft pink in a number of places.

Looking at the car, I felt something stir inside of me. I'd never been afraid when I drove its likeness.

At least, not before my last race at Queensland Raceway.

I turned it over in my hands again and again as I wrestled with the best thing to say. I settled for, "Hi."

I sighed and sat down on the grass where I had lain in agony less than six months earlier. I stared at the little car in my hands. "I'm sorry I haven't been back to see you much lately. I hope you understand why we had to move to Sydney. Both Mummy's and Daddy's jobs needed us down there, but we haven't forgotten you. Not a day goes by when you aren't in our hearts. I just wanted you to know that."

I rested the car back in its rightful place and looked up at the cherub.

"You know, I really regret never getting the chance to meet you and that you never got the chance to live your life. I know I would've been so proud of you. You would've been my little man. But I worry sometimes. I worry that you wouldn't have been proud of me." I stopped to inhale deeply.

"I worry that I can't be everything I need to be . . . for your mummy and for Phoebe. Don't get me wrong, I love them both so much, and I'm never going to leave them again, but what if I fail them? What if I don't get a chance to be back in a ProV8? Or worse, what if I get kicked off the team entirely one day? What if Hunter does something that I can't fight?"

Closing my eyes, the images from my dream assaulted me again, now with the vision of the Mini crashing into the crowd edited into the mix. I continued in a pained whisper, "What if something happens to your mummy because of me? I don't know if I could live with myself."

I wrung my hands together and took another deep breath before pausing to look around. The trees at the back of the cemetery rustled slightly with a soft breeze. It was such a peaceful place, which was strange because it was the worst place in the world in so many people's minds, and yet I found it calming.

As I listened to the utter peace in the darkening cemetery, a realisation struck me, as if it had been whispered through the night. A revelation that untangled the knot in my chest in a heartbeat carried in on the breeze.

"You wouldn't actually care if I was kicked off the team . . . would you? You'd be proud of me anyway." I felt a bubble of hope. "Phoebe and your mummy would be too, wouldn't they? They wouldn't care if I was a mechanic at a country servo earning squat for the rest of my life, would they? As long as I was with them, and being the best father and husband I could be, they would be proud of me. Because that's what family is about."

I stood as my epiphany settled over me. I felt an inner peace unlike any I had ever experienced before. It didn't matter to my family if I won or lost. It didn't matter to them if I ever drove a ProV8 again. They supported my efforts because they wanted me to do it, for myself. I smiled widely at the little cherub.

"I *can* do this." I didn't know what *this* meant—marriage, fatherhood, racing—but it didn't matter because I had realised that I *could* do it. All of it.

And if I did fail, my family would be there to help me through.

As I stood beside Emmanuel's grave, I couldn't help but think of my own father. He'd been making an effort to reach out to me, and I'd been steadfastly ignoring his calls. I'd done that to someone once before and, as I'd since discovered, it had had disastrous consequences.

I said farewell and thank you to Emmanuel before walking back to my car. When I got there, I pulled out my mobile and rang a number I had been pretending didn't exist.

"Dad? It's me. I was wondering if you wanted to meet up for a drink?"

CHAPTER SEVENTEEN

UNEXPECTED

THE CALM I had found at Emmanuel's side faded quickly as I edged closer to the city. I was going to see the man I'd once admired and looked up to, but whom I had lost all respect for in one fell swoop.

I didn't know if we would ever mend the bridge between us, but I had to try. I had to be the bigger man, especially after my epiphany that family was what mattered in the world. It might be what I needed to push the demons from the track out of my mind for good.

After parking my car, I walked to our agreed-upon meeting place—an Irish pub on a busy corner in town. I think we secretly hoped that the loud music and busy atmosphere would help us to avoid having an in-depth conversation—at least that was certainly *my* hope.

As I approached the bar and saw his familiar figure waiting for me, I breathed deeply. I began to wonder whether I was making the right choice, and was about to turn to leave before he had a chance to spot me. As if he'd sensed me behind him, or maybe because he was watching in the mirror behind the bar, he turned before I could make my escape.

"Thank you. For, well, for agreeing to, uh, meet with me," he stammered. He offered me his hand for a handshake before deciding against it and leaning in for an awkward hug instead.

I stepped back quickly and held my hands up to him, palms facing out. Just seeing his face brought all my anger back to the surface. I might have been willing to try and be the better man, but I wasn't going to blindly ignore everything he'd done.

He'd cheated on Mum, he'd barged in on Alyssa when she was in the shower—accidental or not—and he'd allowed his whore of a girlfriend to sell me—his own son—out with a story that was utter bullshit. I wasn't about to *hug* him in greeting as if all of that hadn't happened.

"I may have suggested a meeting, but I'm not completely ready to jump back onto the father/son bandwagon," I told him.

"Then how do you see this playing out?" he asked.

I sighed. "I don't know. Maybe I made a mistake. I should go."

His hand reached out and grabbed my arm. "Don't. I need to talk to you about something. Please, just let me buy you a beer."

Against my better judgement, I agreed. I slid onto the bar stool beside him and ordered a Pure Blonde; if it was going on his tab it was going to be something better than a local beer.

He asked about my race meeting, and I waved him off with an, "I really don't want to talk about it."

"I heard about the big crash today. Someone died, didn't they?"

I shook my head in exasperation. Did he always have to fucking exaggerate? "No, two spectators had minor injuries, and the driver was taken to hospital to be safe."

Even as I started to explain the truth, his eyes wandered around the bar; he was clearly disinterested in everything I had to say. I followed his line of sight to a group of women in the corner. I couldn't believe I'd ever looked up to him, or worse, that I'd actually been like him.

He tried again to make some small talk, but I found that I just couldn't keep it up. It was too exhausting, because I had nothing I wanted to say to him.

"So, how are things at home for you?" His question surprised me.

"Terrific. Alyssa is the absolute best. I couldn't even imagine being with anyone else again." I answered sincerely but with a touch of venom in my voice. I honestly meant it, but I also wanted to let him know that *he* was the one who'd stuffed up by cheating on his wife.

He'd made his own damn bed.

"So, you're not sick of being trapped?" He laughed, sickening me.

I clenched my fist. "I'm not *trapped.*"

"Okay, so you're happy." He held his hand up in apology. "Then again, that little woman of yours certainly has a long list of assets." His smile appeared more like a leer in my mind.

A wave of red washed over me as the image of him watching her in the bathroom when she was pregnant grew in my mind. I slammed my hand down against the bar. "Don't you *dare* talk about Alyssa," I said with a tone that left no room for argument.

He sighed. "Just sit and stay calm, will you please? I will not have you making another scene like the one at the café."

"*I* made a scene?" I scoffed. "*You* were the one who was all over a two-bit whore, who, by the way, is fucking *younger than me!*" I was shaking with rage and trying very hard to calm down. The last time I lost my temper with Dad was when he'd made up his mind to sell me out—or at least when he'd justified it to himself. I shook my head and turned away. "This was a fucking mistake."

"Declan, wait!" he cried desperately as I pushed away from the bar. "I need a favour."

I shook my head without looking back at him.

"I need you to sign a statutory declaration stating that your mother stole the funds in our joint account."

I was livid. I turned back to him in shock, my rage mixed equally with disbelief. "What?"

"I have nothing, son. *Nothing.* I can't even get a job. All I want is my half of what was in that account."

I laughed. "You are fucking pathetic. You really want me to

dob on Mum? You really think I would *ever* sell her out like that? Anything you got out of this, you deserve. I hope she spends every fucking cent."

"Please? I think Hayley is thinking about leaving me, especially now that my account is running low." His voice was pure desperation. "I can't let that happen."

I wasn't surprised by the fact that he had all but admitted having a hidden account; I wouldn't have been surprised if he had a handful of them. However, the fact that he honestly thought he had some claim over the money Mum took—money that I had no doubt he rightfully owed Mum, probably with interest—blew me away. To try to use me to steal half of it, and set Mum up as some kind of criminal, just pissed me off. "Not in a million fucking years. And if that gold-digging whore leaves you, then, well, I think you should consider yourself pretty damn lucky."

"How dare you!" he roared. "I don't care what you say about me, but you *will* stop calling Hayley such horrid names."

Half the bar was watching us, but I didn't care.

"You had a perfectly good, loving, beautiful woman waiting at home for you every night, but you treated her like shit and fucked scum like Hayley fucking Bliss. That's how dare I! How could you even think I would *ever* turn my back on Mum in support of you and that little slut?"

I turned and stalked from the bar before I could do something that I would really regret; something that might give Danny a reason for kicking me off the team.

Without looking back, or stopping at his shouts to come back, I raced to my car as quickly as I could. I practically ripped the door off in my attempt to get inside. I slid onto the seat before slamming the door shut with a growl on my lips.

Where in the hell does he get off?

I should've known better than to try to see my scumbag father. There was an old saying I'd heard a hundred times, "Let sleeping dogs lie." The meeting had made me understand the exact meaning behind it.

I sat in the car and waited, trying to calm down. The hood light clicked off after a few minutes, but I was still livid and breathing heavily. Definitely not in any fit state to drive.

After the shitty start to the weekend, I'd finally managed to find calm and was ready to race after my visit with Emmanuel. Yet, a few seconds spent in Dad's presence, and it had all been completely erased.

My thoughts turned to Alyssa, and how she had been encouraging me to take the step toward forgiving Dad. She'd argued that I needed to look at Phoebe and decide if I would want her to forgive me if I fucked up badly. I already had and hoped that she would in the long run. But there was one key difference—I actually wanted to do better.

I didn't know if I could tell Alyssa about my failed attempt. I would have to admit just how big a piece of scum I came from. How could I be certain that no more of his shittiness rubbed off on me? I didn't need to make a choice just yet. I wasn't sure what time Alyssa was due back from her fitting, and I wasn't even sure she'd bother coming all the way to Ipswich if she finished up too late. She might just crash at her mum's.

I took another couple of deep breaths to try to calm down a little more before finally putting the car in gear and heading back to my empty hotel room.

It's times like these I could use a drink, I thought to myself, even while knowing I could never go back to using alcohol to dull my anger.

"DEC?" A hushed whisper echoed through my dreams. A giggle followed.

I mumbled something incoherent, not completely awake.

There was a bang then another giggle.

"Alyssa?" I tried to see through the thick night. "Is that you?"

A third giggle burst from the dark shadow in the middle of the room.

I was about to climb from bed when the shadow ran toward me

at full steam.

She leapt onto the bed at the last moment. When she landed, she knelt on top of the covers of the bed, pinning me beneath them.

"Hi." Alyssa giggled.

I chuckled in response. I'd missed her so much and after the fucked-up evening I'd had, her silliness was welcome, even if it was a little unexpected.

She leaned her face in to mine, and I was treated with the sweet scent of champagne.

"I bumped into something before." She giggled again.

Because of her proximity, her hair fell into my eyes and across my face. I tucked it gently behind her ear and cupped her cheek. She crinkled her nose and grinned at me.

"Lys? Are you drunk?" I asked, unable to hide the amusement in my voice.

She shook her head, taking my hand with her. "Nah'm not drunk, I'm just really happy to see you, baby!" She wiggled her hips over mine.

I bit my lip to stop myself from laughing at her again. I gently placed my free hand on her other cheek, guiding her face back toward mine in an attempt to refocus her attention on me. "Lys, baby, where's Phoebe?"

She stared at me with confusion in her eyes before turning her head to the door.

"Mum!" she exclaimed suddenly, turning back to me. "Mum's got her. I was worried about you when they were squeezing me into my dress, so they gave me some wine." She closed her eyes and licked her lips. "It was really yummy," she whispered, as if it was a secret. "Then Mum took Phoebe to her house. And Eden took me here."

"Did you have fun?" I asked.

She shook her head. "I was worried about you." She brushed her face along my neck and her tongue pressed forward to run a sloppy trail over my throat.

"I know. I was worried about you too."

"I wish I coulda been there today."

"No!" I exclaimed, startling her. She sat up and gave a small cry of surprise. I wrapped her up in my arms again. "Sorry, just the thought of you being anywhere near that out-of-control Mini . . ." I held her tightly as I trailed off.

"I'm safe. I'm here."

"I know," I whispered against her hair. "I can't tell you how glad I am about that."

She obviously sensed I needed a change in the conversation, or maybe she was upset about losing her buzz, because she shifted her body so her hips were flush with mine. She turned her head so her hair fell around both our faces, enclosing us in our own private world.

"How are you?" she asked.

Flashes of the disastrous meeting with my father crossed my mind. "Don't ask."

She frowned.

"I'll tell you about it later."

I could see she was going to ask more, so I cupped her face gently and guided her lips to mine. I kissed her passionately, and she moaned loudly in response.

She laughed as she pulled away. "You don't want to tell me."

I grinned. "I didn't think I was making it that obvious."

She giggled before leaning back in to kiss me again before pulling away. "That's not the only thin' you're making obvious." She wiggled her hips, rubbing herself against the boner that was growing steadily.

"Well, can you blame me when a drunk, sexy woman just crashed into my bedroom and climbed on top of me?"

"Told you, I'm not drunk."

"Ah, maybe not completely, but you *are* sexy."

She smiled. "You think I'm sexy?" She sat up and ran her hands across her breasts and down her body.

"Fuck yeah, I do."

She leaned into me again. "I think you're sexy too."

I smirked. "I know."

She smacked my chest lightly but left her hand where it landed.

171

Her fingers splayed on my naked chest. She looked down at me in deep concentration.

I lifted my hand and clasped her fingers. "Something on your mind?"

"I'm just wondering how far down this skin goes."

I chuckled. "All the way to my toes."

"I meant without being covered."

I grinned. "All the way to my toes."

She gasped. "You're naked under there?" She wrinkled her nose.

I laughed. "I will be by the time *you* get under the covers."

She laughed loudly and kissed me again. As she was focused on the kiss, I grabbed her shoulders and flipped her so she was beneath me. In one movement, I pushed my satin boxers down to my ankles and knelt in front of her, my hard-on reaching out for her through the night.

"See," I said, waving my hand over my body.

She blushed lightly—something I would never tire of—and kissed my thumb.

I groaned at the sensation. "Don't tease me like that."

She gazed up at me and licked her lips. "Like what?" She turned her head and took my thumb into her mouth.

I closed my eyes and moaned as she sucked my thumb in and out of her mouth. "Like that," I groaned.

"Who said I'm teasing?"

I growled as she pushed me off her and scooted up the bed a little, resting against the bedhead. Then her hands reached forward to grasp my hips and guide me toward her mouth. I clasped the wood behind her as she sucked my length into her mouth. I passed control of my hips over to her, closing my eyes and relishing the sensation as her hands gripped my hips tighter.

She hummed around me, and I groaned in response. She certainly knew the right way to get my mind off shitty evenings. I kept one hand tightly gripping the bedhead while the other gently traced through her hair. I tried to express how fucking good it felt, but was largely past words.

Alyssa giggled again and pushed me away from her a little. She licked and sucked her way up my body before reaching my mouth and kissing me deeply. My hands travelled to the hemline of the dress she was wearing, and I pulled it over her head in one tug. My fingers made light work of her bra, and I tossed it across the hotel room. I tasted her greedily, needing to take every part of her in.

I pulled off her panties and helped her gently back onto the bed, laying my body gingerly over hers.

She looked up at me and laughed. "You're just taking advantage of me 'cause I'm drunk."

I shook my head. "But you're not drunk."

She smiled and kissed my cheek.

I turned my face and traced my nose gently along her jawline before kissing her softly. My hands and lips began to roam her skin possessively, claiming every inch of her as mine. I wanted to ensure she understood just how much I adored her as I slid myself into her.

She moaned as I filled her completely and then again as we moved in rhythm together. We loved each other absolutely, harmonizing together and rolling from side to side in a battle for dominance.

We both burst out laughing when we rolled off the bed. Not that it stopped us from our perfect game of parry and thrust.

After we'd both taken each other to satisfaction, I slid down her body and rested my head on her chest—both still panting and laughing. A few moments later, once our breathing had calmed and our laughter had died down, we began to talk about our days. I told her about my fears on the racetrack, and she told me about the photographers and wedding cake.

I told her about my visit to Emmanuel's grave, and she seemed genuinely touched that I would even consider visiting on my own. I still couldn't tell her about meeting my father, at least not just yet.

"How's Ruby?" I asked, both out of curiosity and to turn the subject away from my evening.

Alyssa chuckled. "She's doing great. She's getting really fat now. It's so funny to see Josh doting on her at every turn. Not that he didn't always dote on her, but somehow it's just different now."

I touched the scar on her stomach lightly. "Will it be different for us when we have more kids?"

Her body jumped lightly before stiffening.

I pushed up onto my elbows to look at her face. Concern and stress were evident across all of her features. All the happiness and light-heartedness was wiped away. Her eyes sought mine out, fear and desperation dwelling in their depths.

"What is it?" I asked.

"I never thought I'd hear those words come out of your mouth," she whispered.

I shrugged. "A lot has changed for me over the past few months. Now, I—well, I guess I'm more than open to the idea." I trailed a few kisses over her stomach.

"Oh, God," she muttered.

"Alyssa, what is it?" Her body was so tense, and her eyes so afraid, that she was starting to scare me. I quickly scrambled up her body to touch her face. I cupped one of her cheeks delicately.

"Nothing's changed for me." Her voice was quiet and her words broken.

"What do you mean?"

"I don't want another baby, Dec." She sounded like she was close to tears.

"What?" I was absolutely confused. "But you always wanted a big family. We broke up because you wanted kids . . . and I didn't." *And because I was a fucking fool.*

"That was before . . ." She closed her eyes and scrunched her face in pain. "After . . . *the twins* . . ." She stopped and took a deep breath before opening her eyes again. As her eyes found mine, she whispered. "I just don't know if I can go through that again."

I pulled myself up into a sitting position and helped Alyssa to sit beside me. I wrapped my arm around her, and we leaned against the side of the bed.

"But you wouldn't be going through it alone," I murmured. I couldn't explain the feeling of loss that had settled over me at the thought that we might not have any more kids.

At some point, having to speedily adjust to Phoebe's presence in my life had become a genuine desire to have kids—lots of kids. I hadn't realised just how badly—or how soon—I wanted it to happen until the instant Alyssa had said she didn't feel the same way.

Was that how she'd felt when I'd been so insistent years ago?

"I'm sorry, Declan, I just ... I thought you knew ..." She sobbed lightly against me. "I didn't think you wanted any more either."

"I guess I just never thought—" I cut myself off, mentally pounding my head against the wall for being so stupid and tactless when raising the issue. I'd just assumed that nothing had changed for her since high school. But she was a different person now. We both were.

She went to apologise again, but I cut her off. "We don't need to talk about it anymore tonight."

She sobbed a little more, until I picked her up off the floor and carried her into the bathroom where I ran a warm bath in the built-in spa. I helped her in then climbed in behind her. I didn't say anything as I gently massaged her back, trying to bring us back to where we were before I had shot off my damn stupid fucking mouth.

After we'd climbed out, we wrapped ourselves up in the huge fluffy hotel bathrobes and fell asleep in a tangle of limbs and terry-towelling.

I LEFT Alyssa asleep in the hotel room to head to the track early on Sunday.

Somewhat surprisingly, given the fucked-up night I'd had, I successfully managed to put the negatives from the previous evening behind me and clung tightly to the positives.

Dad, kids, everything else could wait for another day. I was determined to prove to myself that I could win at Queensland Raceway again. My epiphany stood, reminding me that it didn't matter to Alyssa or Phoebe how I went, which somehow spurred me on more.

I wanted nothing less than first.

Not because they wanted me to get it, but because I wanted to get it for them. It made all the difference to my on-track performance, and I got my desire, claiming victory in the third race.

The fourth race managed to rattle me a little when another car speared off the track.

Worse, it happened at the same corner that the Mini from race one had lost control. Luckily, the driver hadn't leapt the guardrail like the previous incident, and no one was hurt. I held on to my sanity and finished in second.

I ended the weekend just a handful of points behind Wilkins in the Micro Challenge leadership table, with four rounds left to race. I had one last chance to claim pole to be able to take Alyssa to London for our honeymoon, but unfortunately I had to get through Tasmania and Darwin first. No Mini, no family, just me alone with Hunter and the rest of the Sinclair Racing team.

Then there was the birthday party Alyssa was planning for Phoebe. A gaggle of twenty or so four-year-olds running around my former bachelor pad.

I honestly wasn't sure which of the events would be worse.

CHAPTER EIGHTEEN

LIFE'S A PARTY

"SO, DID YOU get the information we needed?"

Morgan chuckled down the phone. "Oh, I got it all right. Eden is surprisingly talkative when plied with some alcohol and some of my particular brand of torture."

I smiled to myself as squeals of glee echoed from the backyard, reminding me of the party in full swing—the party I was taking a quick breather from. Watching through the window, I saw Alyssa herd the screaming mass of children around the jumping castle, trampoline, and bubble machine. As if she could feel me watching, Alyssa's head tilted up to glance at the window. I gave her a smile and a small wave, and though she smiled back at me, it was obvious she was exhausted.

Knowing I had to finish up so I could relieve her before long, I tried to concentrate on the call because Morgan was talking again, running through some of the details about timing and shit for Alyssa's hen night that he'd been able to find out from Eden.

Once he'd given me the information, and we confirmed our own plans for the night, it didn't take very long for the conversation to steer off onto complaining about Hunter, who was snapping at Morgan's heels in the championship. I was torn between wanting Sinclair Racing to win the team trophy—which meant both Morgan and Hunter needed to rank as high as they could—and wanting Hunter to come dead last in the series. Of course, I had no real control over the situation, so I just had to grin and bear it either way.

Morgan and I finished our little anti-Hunter rant and said our goodbyes. After all, there was no reason for a drawn-out conversation, as I'd be seeing him later that evening. He probably could have come around sooner, but had volunteered to stay away from Phoebe's party so as not to put extra stress on Alyssa. Secretly, I suspected it was more that he wanted to stay as far away from the horde of screaming children as possible. Instead, he would be coming around after the kids left—for my part of the birthday celebrations.

Before heading back to the party, I made another call—to Danny. It was that call, the one Alyssa had begged me to make, which was the real reason I'd been allowed a moment away from my party hosting duties, but I'd wanted to take the opportunity to call Morgan first while Alyssa had been otherwise occupied.

When I dialled Danny's number, I launched straight into an explanation of what I wanted—or more specifically, the request Alyssa had asked me to make. She wanted to give someone the chance of a lifetime with a visit to see the inner workings of a race team. Not surprisingly, Danny had listed out a series of rules and requirements that would need to be met for it to be possible. I agreed readily, knowing the reason behind them instinctively. Once we'd set everything up, I said thank you and goodbye to Danny before heading back down to rescue Alyssa from the rampaging horde, collecting a few stragglers lost in the house on my way.

Eden—who was in the kitchen helping out our latest arrival, Flynn—called out as I passed to let me know that it was time for cake. I had to laugh when I saw Flynn fanboying over Eden. His obsession with all things Sinclair Racing had been off the chain since he arrived in Sydney, and I hadn't seen Eden anywhere this morning without him glued to her side.

Initially, I'd been a little surprised when Alyssa had told me that Flynn was coming down for Phoebe's birthday. She'd sprung it on me just after my time in Tasmania—time that would have been nicer if I'd spent it in Hell.

After letting me know that Flynn was coming down, she'd explained that he hadn't missed one yet and really didn't want to miss this one either. He'd offered to stay in a hotel, but Alyssa and I had agreed that he should stay with us. After all, I really did owe the life I had to him. If he hadn't left Phoebe's birth certificate on my doorstep, I might have never found the courage to fight for Alyssa. I owed a lot to him; it just took me a while to realise it. That was why I had agreed to help Alyssa make his dream come true.

I found Alyssa near the back door, taking a quiet breather herself.

"So?" she asked, wrapping her arm around me. "Is it all arranged?"

I nodded. "There are a few rules, but nothing too outrageous."

She smiled. "Thank you." She kissed my cheek as I hugged her gently.

"No problems." I grinned. "It might even be fun. But for now . . ." I headed in Phoebe's direction before turning back to Alyssa briefly. "I have a birthday girl to catch."

I ran off and scooped Phoebe up in my arms. She squealed with laughter as I tickled her stomach before lifting her onto my shoulders.

"You ready for cake, princess?" I asked.

She screamed, "Yes!"

I grabbed her stomach and flipped her until her feet were back on the ground. "Go gather everyone up then."

She raced off and gathered up her friends. The rest of the afternoon was filled with cake, games, and lollies, resulting in about twenty hyperactive kids.

I put in my share of face time with the other parents, encountering every reaction from awe to indifference. I think in general most were surprised that I was Phoebe's father. We hadn't really made much of a deal about it at the day care, and were usually in and out before more of the parents arrived. Plus, for the time being, Phoebe was still a Dawson. After the wedding, both she and Alyssa would be Reedes.

By the time the parents took their children home, the sugar high was wearing off, and I had no doubt most of the kids would fall asleep during their ride home.

For us though, the evening was just starting. Since I was going to be in Darwin for my actual birthday, we were having an early bash for me. It had just made sense to get it all over with on the one day. Flynn had offered to get Phoebe settled so Alyssa and I could just relax and enjoy the night.

We'd settled on having an intimate dinner with just a few friends around—my pit crew mates, plus Eden and Morgan. It was quiet and low key, but the drinks flowed readily and I had a good time. Once Phoebe was settled and Flynn joined the table, I thought he was going to have a heart attack; he was so fucking excited. The only moment that caused concern was when Alyssa asked whether Flynn was coming to my bachelor party. Unable to answer, mostly because I couldn't admit what my bachelor party was going to consist of, I'd shifted the conversation onto another path. It wasn't that I didn't want Flynn there, per se, just that he would make my plans a whole lot more difficult.

After a great night, people started heading home. Each of them wished me a happy birthday as they left, even though the majority of them would be with me for my actual birthday.

Once everyone was gone, and everything was cleaned up, Alyssa and I headed up to bed. When we got there, Alyssa dragged a box out of the cupboard. It was a surprise because I hadn't expected her to get me anything, let alone give me something before my actual birthday.

"What's this?"

"It's a present, silly."

"Well, duh, but I mean why now? Why don't I take it to Darwin?"

"It might be a bit big for your carry-on. Besides, I want you to open it now." She was right; the box, wrapped in gold wrapping paper, was rather sizable.

"If you're sure?"

"Yeah. I was going to give it to you earlier, but I didn't want to in front of everyone else," Alyssa said, twisting the end of her hair around her finger. "Just in case . . ."

I furrowed my brow. "In case of what exactly?"

"In case you don't like it," she whispered, looking at me with such vulnerability, I almost wanted to throw the box aside and take *her* as my present instead.

"Why wouldn't I like it?" I put the box on the bed beside me and pulled Alyssa onto my lap.

She shrugged and rested her head against my chest. "Why don't you just open it and see?" she murmured.

I was starting to get worried about what she might have bought me, so I turned our bodies so I could reach around Alyssa to unwrap her gift. With my arms wrapped around her, I pulled the paper off slowly. The box was blank and gave away nothing about its contents.

With my curiosity well and truly piqued, I gently opened the box. Inside was a genuine race spec helmet. It was the same brand that we used at Sinclair Racing, but so different to anything I'd seen before. It wasn't the style or even the shape that was different though. Instead, it was the decoration.

The helmet was completely black, rather than the usual red, and instead of the Sinclair and sponsors' logos, I could see the top of two horses airbrushed onto the back.

My arms were still wrapped around Alyssa as I eased the helmet out of the box and turned it from one side to the other to inspect it. One of the horses was airbrushed in pinks and purples of varying shades, all blending together seamlessly. The other was painted almost identically, but in greens and blues. The thing that struck me the most, though, was that it was an almost perfect duplicate of my tattoo. I brushed my fingers over the horses one at a time, surprised by how seamlessly they'd been integrated into the helmet. Alyssa stiffened under my silent appraisal of her gift. I needed to put her out of her misery, but I couldn't find a way to speak.

"Baby—" I couldn't continue as my voice chose that moment to give out. I swallowed the emotion that was blocking my throat. "It's beautiful."

"I thought of it after you told me about your visit to Emmie's grave. I thought it would be a good reminder of why you *want* to get in the car each meet. But I wasn't sure if you would want it or not though."

"I do. I would be honoured to wear this . . . if I am allowed." I wasn't sure whether Danny would agree to me wearing something that wasn't team colours.

"Danny will let you," Alyssa whispered. "He actually really liked the idea when I suggested it." She looked a little sheepish. "I'm sorry I went behind your back to ask him, but I just wanted to make sure the helmet was the right one, just in case you did like it."

"Like it? Baby, I love it." I held the helmet in one hand and used the other to pull her tighter into me. "Thank you."

I felt her sigh of relief and stifled a laugh. She had given me something so personal, so perfect, how could I *not* love it?

CHAPTER NINETEEN

WORK ON IT

FLYNN SAT IN the car beside me grinning from ear to ear. I had never seen a grown man so excited. I was certain if I looked at his crotch—which was *not* going to happen—he would be sporting a massive hard-on.

Even though Alyssa had begged me to give him this experience, and told me again and again just how badly he'd wanted it, I hadn't really believed just how desperately until that moment. It might have started with a desire to grant a request from Alyssa—something she'd suggested and something I'd been more than willing to give him—but I hadn't understood how much it meant to him. Now that I did, I was almost humbled that I could be the one to offer it.

"Now remember," I said, trying to break the silence, "no cameras and no recording equipment of any kind."

Flynn nodded and smiled stupidly back at me.

"You'll need to surrender your mobile phone until it's over."

He nodded again.

"And you'll have to sign a non-disclosure agreement."

His grin stretched wider. "I can't believe this is really happening!"

I couldn't help grinning back. "It's really not that big a deal."

"Are you kidding me? It's a huge fucking deal!"

"It's nothing," I murmured again, suddenly embarrassed about how excited he was. I acted like it was nothing because, to me, it wasn't that big a deal. It was something I did every day, and now I saw that perhaps I'd become a little too blasé about it.

I pulled into the parking lot at work. "Okay, are you ready to do this?"

His eyes widened as he looked through the windscreen as if he was looking at the gates to Heaven. "I was born ready."

I thought he might wet himself as we walked through the doors and I directed him to security. Once he had the temporary pass, I led him to Danny's office. He spent the whole time glancing one way and another as quick as he could. It was almost like his head was on a stick, swivelling from one side to another. The grin on his lips didn't falter at all.

Danny ran through the formalities, getting Flynn to sign off on the NDA, and then they started talking about some new development that was installed on the ProV8 at the beginning of the year. I knew a thing or two about cars, and since my apprenticeship, a lot more about motors, but I had no idea about what the two of them were discussing.

They spent about ten minutes talking about aerodynamics and downforce before Danny said, "You've got some great ideas, you know. Have you ever thought about relocating to Sydney?"

Flynn grinned widely. "Once or twice."

"Well, if you do, send your résumé to this address"—Danny slid across a business card— "and we'll see if we have something open in R&D."

When that happened, I saw they were finishing up their conversation, and I joined back in as Danny welcomed Flynn again and dismissed us from the office.

"Oh, and Declan?" Danny called as my hand was on the doorknob.

"Yeah?" I turned back to him.

"Flynn knows your crew, right?"

I nodded. "They met over the weekend."

"Well, get him settled in with them and then come back up to see me. I have something I want to discuss with you in private."

I nodded again. As soon as my back was to Danny though, I swallowed heavily. I had no idea what he wanted to discuss, but "in private" didn't sound promising. Very few good things had followed his uttering those words.

Still, I did as Danny asked and took Flynn to get him settled with my crew before returning to the office. I didn't even get the chance to ask what he wanted before he waved his hand at a seat.

"Sit."

It was an instruction, not a request, so I complied without argument.

"I have some news for you."

I wanted to ask him to elaborate. At the very least, I needed to know if it was good news or bad news. I nodded in an attempt to get him to keep talking.

"I've had a couple of sponsors call up recently, a couple of whom are very interested in getting behind you."

My heart stopped beating for a second or two as the implications of what he was telling me sunk in. His words from when he offered me the apprenticeship came back into my mind. "I can't have you race for my team, Declan. Your latest series of stunts, whether true or not, have generated too much bad press. The sponsors that bring in the most amount of money are the family-friendly ones. You just don't have anything to offer in that department."

"Who?" I asked timidly.

He rattled them off quickly and I had to stifle my grin. One of them was a company that had backed me before everything had turned to shit. If they were willing to get behind me again, well, it boded very well for me. But I tried not to get my hopes up too much; it didn't necessarily mean anything yet.

"Starting at Townsville, your Micro Challenge vehicle will have corporate support."

I grinned. It may have been a small step, but it was a step in the right direction. It meant that I was getting attention again, positive attention, and that put me closer to the driver seat of a ProV8.

Danny's surprises weren't finished yet. He slid a small pile of paperwork over to me.

I picked it up curiously. "What's this?" The question had fallen from my lips before I ever had a chance to think it through or read the first page.

"It's a temporary driver contract. By signing that, you are agreeing to drive one of our ProV8s during the endurance races."

"Holy fuck!" We'd discussed the possibility of me being the second driver in Morgan's car, but seeing it printed in black and white made it real.

"Take it home and read it over. If you're amenable to all the terms, you're in."

I practically jumped for joy. "I'm in?" I couldn't believe how fucking happy those two words made me.

Danny chuckled. "Indeed. And I can imagine there is now a phone call you want to make, so you're excused."

I nodded and thanked him for giving me the chance to prove myself. I took the contract—I was going to hold that sucker tight until it was signed and returned to Danny—and ran off to ring Alyssa and give her the good news.

FLYNN WAS almost as thrilled as Alyssa had been when I told him my news in the car. I had debated glossing over the subject, but then I decided if I was going to make a legitimate effort to be friends with him, I needed to be genuine. I needed to be open and honest, and that meant allowing him to both celebrate and commiserate with me.

After I'd told him that, he asked me about the bachelor party. "I get it if you don't want me to come, man, but if it's 'cause you think I'll be uncomfortable in a strip club then don't be. Just 'cause I like dick doesn't mean I can't appreciate the occasional fine female form."

Oh, God, how to explain it to him? He was still Alyssa's friend after all. "It's not that, seriously it's not. I'm just, well, I'm not actually having a bachelor party. I haven't told Alyssa 'cause I don't want to make her feel uncomfortable that she's having a hen night."

He gave me a disbelieving look, but after a moment, his eyes widened and he laughed. "Oh, my God, *the* Declan Reede, eternal bachelor and ladies' man, isn't going to have a last hurrah before walking down the aisle?"

I shrugged. "I had my last hurrah long ago, before I asked Alyssa to move in with me. I haven't been interested in being the 'eternal bachelor' since then."

His nose wrinkled and I could have sworn he was about to say something along the lines of *that's so sweet,* but I shot him a look to shut him up.

"Fair enough," he said diplomatically, as if he didn't really understand it but wasn't going to press the issue. "Thanks for today though. It was great."

"Are you going to send in your résumé?"

He shrugged. "Maybe. Would you mind if I moved to Sydney?"

"It's your life. You need to seize any opportunity you want." I took a deep breath and pushed the small niggle of jealousy I felt out of my mind. "I know the girls would love to have you closer."

He smiled. "You really have changed, you know?"

Even though he didn't really know the me I'd been, outside of the gossip rags at least, I appreciated the sentiment.

"I'll think about it, just don't tell Alyssa yet, hey? I wouldn't want to get her hopes up if I decide not to."

"Sure thing, just so long as you don't tell her about the no-bachelor-party thing."

He laughed. "You are probably the only bloke I know who is worried about being caught out *not* wanting to see strippers."

I chuckled. Put that way, it did sound crazy. But I had my reasons, and I didn't want to tip Alyssa off early.

DESPITE HOW good my birthday bash had been, and how much fun we'd had in the lead-up to leaving for Darwin, my actual birthday weekend was fucking shit. It was stinking hot on the track all weekend, with the afternoon temperatures in excess of thirty degrees Celsius in the shade—in the pits, it was closer to forty. It was fucking June, for fuck's sake. It was supposed to be winter.

Hunter had given me shit from the moment I'd arrived in Darwin. I tried to put him out of my mind as best as I was able, but it was difficult because he qualified in pole position.

Then he'd gone on to win the first race, which put him in the championship lead.

My Saturday couldn't have been worse, but at least it ended on a positive note. Eden, Morgan, and I had dinner together in my hotel room. I told Morgan in no uncertain terms that beating Hunter on my birthday would be the best present he could possibly give me.

He'd laughed and told me that it was one birthday wish he was more than happy to grant. We had a few quiet drinks before I told them to get the fuck out of my room, because it was time to call Alyssa.

She and I spoke for an hour before our call slowly became hotter and heavier. I palmed myself anxiously as she talked me through what she was doing to herself. Needless to say, I wanted a live-action replay when I got home.

Hunter came into the pits early on Sunday morning with some dirty skank. He'd announced loudly that she was my birthday present and that he'd warmed her up for me all night long. The worst part was the chick actually thought he was serious and all but threw herself at me. I told her to get the fuck off me, but not before she'd managed to grope me with her fucking quick hands.

Hunter thought it was fucking hilarious and had his phone in hand taking a series of photos as I tried to get the bitch to back the fuck up. A few months earlier, I might have been worried about Alyssa seeing the photos, but with her knowledge of Hunter's sneaky tricks and the, no doubt, disgusted look on my face, I wasn't overly anxious. She'd shown trust in me for much more incriminating things—like with Eden where there was a genuine care, even if there was no attraction. I was more concerned with the fact that Hunter wouldn't just leave me alone to do my fucking job. It was going to cause me trouble in the long run, I was sure of it.

Thankfully, Morgan had won on Sunday. His win, and Hunter's fourth position, meant Morgan had wrestled back control of the championship.

I could only see a handful of positives coming from the weekend. It was my last race meeting without my Mini until after the wedding. Morgan had retained the championship lead, and my stag night was just two weeks away—even though I wasn't actually having one.

CHAPTER TWENTY

SHE RIDES

MY LEG BOUNCED nervously as I waited for my turn in Hell.

I couldn't think about what I was wearing or I would die of embarrassment. The lights from the stage alternated randomly from red to blue to yellow—a never-ending rainbow of illumination. The colours twisted sickeningly as they reflected off Morgan's outfit, which gave me another reason not to look at him.

As if I *needed* another reason.

As if his outfit alone wasn't enough to ensure that I didn't even glance in his direction.

I was still amazed at how easy it had been to get Morgan onside when I'd told him my idea. All I'd had to do was remind him what Eden would be doing at Alyssa's bachelorette party, and he'd jumped right on board. But he'd surprised me when he'd suggested that he go alongside me—or more precisely, *before* me.

Eden was a little bit more difficult to get onside, but she was the key to everything. I knew that unless I could win her over, I didn't really stand a chance of pulling off my planned gatecrash. While finalising arrangements with Morgan, it became clear that she could give me an in, and would be more likely to accommodate me than Ruby would ever be. I hadn't approached her until the Darwin races.

When she was on a high about Morgan's win, I struck. I'd sworn her to secrecy before I even told her what I was planning. But once I'd spilled the beans about what I wanted to do, she'd laughed. Then I told her that if I didn't do this, Morgan would probably organise me a proper bachelor party . . . and who knew what would happen then?

I wasn't sure whether it was the thought of Morgan's participation or my humiliation that caused her to agree in the end. Maybe it was both. I didn't really care, because I got my wish. Although, I was seriously fucking regretting making the decision, but it was way too late to back out.

I just hoped the plan didn't end in a disaster like the last time I'd made plans behind Alyssa's back—on New Year's Eve. This time was different though; this time, the few confidants I'd told thought the plan wasn't terrible. Even Dr. Henrikson had chuckled, questioned how I think Alyssa might react, and then given his support. Of course, I'd told him during the same session where I'd been worked into knots about the fact that Alyssa didn't want to have another baby, so he might have been a little more concerned about that.

The music started, and I rolled my eyes at Morgan's choice. How fucking predictable. He'd turned his surfer-boy looks into a country-boy thing that he was going to use to his advantage. If the guy wasn't a fucking great driver, he probably could have turned a dollar or two doing what he was about to go out and do for free.

As he stood he leaned over to me. "You owe me for this. Big time."

I turned my gaze away so he couldn't see me biting my lip to stop from laughing at his outfit. I was also turning away so I didn't have to look at said outfit. Under no circumstances should shiny silver chaps ever be allowed to be worn by a man.

Not ever.

Especially not shiny silver chaps with fucking tassels down the sides and nothing but a G-string underneath.

Then there was the matching silver-glitter cowboy hat. Why he'd picked that costume was far beyond me. Maybe it had always been a deep-seated desire of his to be a fucking shiny wannabe cowboy. I just hoped the silver mask around his eyes would stop Alyssa from recognising him long enough for me to get out there for my turn.

As the first chorus of Morgan's song started, I heard what sounded like every fucking woman in the house clap their hands and sing the words. I rolled my eyes. I guess Big & Rich got something right—some girls loved to ride the cowboys.

Morgan's song neared the end far too quickly.

By the time the final chorus came over the speakers, my nerves were practically eating me alive as I pulled on the gloves that matched my outfit. Fucking red vinyl. It was fucking tight, but at least it wasn't shiny. It looked like a very tight, very red version of my racing suit, but unlike my normal suit, it wasn't a one-piece. There were at least four pieces to the outfit, each of them able to be removed separately.

And in a flash.

My leg wouldn't stop bouncing as Morgan's song drew to a close. I wasn't sure whether the appreciative catcalls he was getting made me feel better or worse. All I could focus on was that his moment in the spotlight was ending and mine was about to begin.

Why the fuck did I think this would be a good idea?

I slid my helmet on. It was a lightweight costume one so it wouldn't hinder my moves, but at least it would hide my identity.

Seconds later, Morgan raced back off the stage. He held his hat clutched to his groin and wasn't wearing a skerrick of clothing, at least none that I could see and definitely not enough for me to be comfortable in his presence. I couldn't be certain whether he'd taken everything off himself, or if he'd been attacked. I wasn't sure that I wanted to know, but I sure as hell didn't want to ask.

"Man, those girls are nuts!" he exclaimed, grinning goofily. "Good luck out there."

He scuttled off, no doubt in search of some pants. Then again, maybe he was meeting Eden for a private encore.

Again, I really didn't want to know.

"Who likes a man who knows how to handle curves?" I heard the emcee start the introduction. "I know there's one little lady here who has the hots for things that go *fast*. I give you our red-hot racer!"

The first few bars of my song came on, the steady drumbeat, and I put all thoughts of embarrassment out of my mind. The wailing guitar had started by the time I reached the stage.

I was doing this for Alyssa, even if she didn't know it was me.

Better her hands explored my semi-naked, G-string-clad arse than some random stripper dude's. Before I knew it, the girls were hollering for me to "take it off," and I was bumping and grinding my way toward the only woman I had eyes for.

I took my time crossing the small stage to where Alyssa sat front and centre. The lyrics still hadn't kicked in, but I was gyrating my hips to the beat of "She Rides" like nobody's business.

When I was close enough to see all the details, I took a moment to regard Alyssa's outfit. The black dress she was wearing was wickedly short, but only because of the way she was leaning back on her seat, her face hidden behind her hands while she cringed at the stage.

The veil that Ruby had no doubt made her wear was red-and-black netting with little pink charms dangled intermittently along the edges. When I looked closer, I realised that the little "charms" were in fact small plastic penises. I had to stop myself from bursting out laughing at the ridiculousness of the situation.

I was three-quarters of the way to Alyssa when I reached out and ripped off the top of my outfit. I saw her eyes gaze appreciatively across my exposed chest and abdomen. All that was left on my top half was a loose vest that rose high enough to cover the tattoo on my back so Alyssa wouldn't recognise me too readily. I danced my way a little closer, close enough to touch her. I gently grabbed her hand and ran it along my stomach. She flinched and looked away.

Good. At least she wasn't enjoying the show. Even if it was me beneath everything, it wasn't like she knew that yet.

I pulled her other hand away from her face and trailed them both down my stomach, allowing her fingers to hit the muscles of my six-pack. I was sure she must have known it was me by the way my skin danced beneath her touch. No one else's fingers had ever done to me what hers could, and I was certain it was the same for her. She had to feel the connection, even if she didn't recognise the feel of my muscles beneath her fingertips.

She was mesmerized by the waistband of the bottom half of the suit, so I pressed her hands gently underneath the material. The girls around her were squealing and hollering, but a sly grin crossed her face, and she looked up at me. I could see the recognition in her eyes, but obviously she'd decided to play along.

Her hands bunched into fists, holding the material tightly.

"Pull," I whispered, and she did.

The entire bottom half of my outfit ripped away, leaving me standing in nothing but red gloves, the small red vest, a red helmet and a red G-string. I couldn't help the fact that I was incredibly turned on with Alyssa right in front of me, oh so close to all the areas I wanted her to lavish attention on. I grabbed her hands and ran them along my thighs. She shocked the hell out of me by leaning in and kissing my stomach. Unconsciously, I thrust my hips against her.

Her hands circled around the backs of my thighs and pulled my body closer still as I gyrated and danced in front of her. I groaned as she peppered small kisses along my stomach.

"Alyssa!" Ruby exclaimed, calling my attention back to the fact that we were not alone. "Watching is one thing! Declan would flip if he knew you were *handling* the strippers."

Alyssa laughed. "Oh, I don't know. I think Dec would be okay with this."

I reached down with one gloved hand and stroked her cheek tenderly. Then I busted out my best stripper moves and ground against the bride-to-be. My dick was straining to be released, but that could wait until I had Alyssa back in the privacy of our hotel room.

My body cried out knowing that wouldn't happen until at least the following night. But I understood this was Alyssa's hen night, and even though it was all I wanted to do, I wasn't about to steal her away from her friends.

As my song drew to a close, I jumped back up onto the stage and did a little dance for the benefit of the other girls. I knew they wanted me. Half of the girls in the club were practically leaping out of their seats like cartoon wolves with bugging-out eyes and thumping hearts in their chests. But none of them would ever see any more of me.

None of them would touch me.

None of them—save one.

I blew Alyssa a final kiss and gave a little bow before I exited the stage.

I was back in the dressing room getting dressed when the club manager came up to me.

"You two boys made a great impression tonight. If you ever want to consider doing this full-time, I'll be more than happy to take you on."

I laughed. "Thanks, but no thanks. It was a one-time affair."

He shrugged. "I have one more offer for you. One of the girls has asked for a private lap dance."

I shook my head. "Definitely not. Despite doing this, I am a one-woman man."

"She said you'd probably say that. She also asked me to tell you to reconsider. She gave me this and said to tell you this time, she would be the one doing the moves." He held out his hand and I saw one of the plastic penises that had been dangling from Alyssa's veil.

I'd never been happier to see a fucking penis in all my life.

CHAPTER TWENTY-ONE
CRIME AND PUNISHMENT

I SAT IN the small room . . . waiting.

I didn't want to think about how many other people had been given private lap dances in this particular room. My dick was entirely too ready for action to care. I hoped to God I had interpreted the tiny plastic penis correctly and it was Alyssa coming in to see me. If not—if I was wrong and some other random chick came in instead—I was going to chuck a fucking fit.

After almost ten minutes, the curtain pulled back and my jaw dropped. My eyes leapt out of my fucking skull and my mouth turned into the Sahara fucking Desert.

Alyssa sashayed into the space wearing a shiny black vinyl bodysuit. Spaghetti straps rested across the curve of her shoulders, her nipples were just barely covered with the sharp V shape of the bustier. Laced fastenings crossed her cleavage, leaving just the right amount of skin on show. Her legs were bare, pale white and silky smooth to contrast the dark colour of the vinyl. Six-inch heels and a black whip completed the ensemble. Just the sight of her made me anxious to drop to my knees and beg for her permission to touch.

"You were very naughty, crashing my hen night like that, weren't you?" she said in a downright husky and sexy-as-fuck voice.

I nodded. "So bad," I whispered, more than willing to call her bluff. "What are you going to do to me?"

Her eyes widened in surprise. "Um, wait. Do you actually want me to use this on you?" she asked, sounding just a little mortified as she looked down at the whip in her hand.

"Fuck no!" I assured her. I would do anything she wanted me to, if she genuinely wanted me to, but I'd never been spanked before and a Brisbane strip club wasn't exactly my ideal choice of location to start exploring being on the receiving end of some BDSM.

"Have you . . .," she started before trailing off.

I raised my eyebrow. "Do you really want to know?"

She hesitated and I opened my arms.

"Why don't we discuss it later? Right now, I'm waiting for the striptease I was promised." I winked at her.

She stepped closer to me. "I don't really know how to do it," she stammered.

"Baby, you don't have to. Just standing there, you are a thousand times sexier than any chick who has ever graced any stage."

She smiled. It ruined the overall Domme effect of her outfit, but it made her so much sexier in my eyes.

"Come here," I whispered, crooking my finger to call her closer to me.

She moved toward me, staggering a little in her ultra-high heels. I stood, reaching out to stop her from tumbling. I ran my fingers along the inside of her thigh and wrapped her legs around me one at a time before lifting her up and carrying her back with me to the sole chair in the room. As I walked, I trailed kisses along her throat. I slid down onto the seat, ensuring Alyssa's feet rested on the floor as I loosely held her hips.

"So, did you want to learn how to do this?" I asked.

She bit her lip, but I could see the excitement in her eyes at the idea.

"Stand back just a little." I pushed her off my lap. I made sure she had her legs under her and then sat back to enjoy. I spread my legs to accommodate my cock, which was so hard it almost hurt.

She watched me adjust myself, taking obvious pride in my raging erection.

I smiled encouragingly. "Just do what comes naturally."

She began to swivel her hips slightly to the music that filtered into the room from the main stage. Although muffled, we could hear that it was a slow, tantalizing beat overlaid by breathy female vocals. She closed her eyes, her half-naked arse beginning to sway gently back and forth as she moved in a tantalisingly slow circle.

"Oh, fuck, Alyssa!" I exclaimed as she dropped down and ran her hands along her own leg, sticking her arse squarely in front of my face in the process.

As her circle completed, she closed the small distance between us and leant her knee onto the chair between my legs. I felt the slightest pressure from her knee resting against my balls, and fuck, it felt good. I moaned and shifted lower in the chair to be closer to her.

She twisted suddenly, raising one leg over mine so she was facing away from me and her thighs were grazing along mine. The loss of contact between her body and my balls almost hurt. I raised my hands, grasping loosely on to her hips. She continued to sway from side to side while my fingers ran along the bottom edges of the outfit. I was trying to calculate exactly how difficult it would be to fuck Alyssa without having to remove the whole thing, because it seemed like such a shame to waste something so fuck-hot.

As if she sensed what I was thinking, she murmured, "It releases at the back." Her fingers twisted around to show me the fasteners.

Oh, fuck me! It has an access panel!

I wanted to thank whoever had dreamt up the design as I made short work of releasing her pussy and then turned her around. I pulled her onto my lap, slipping two fingers down between us.

"Oh, fuck!" Her hot breath blew across my ear as I massaged my fingers into her. "That feels so—" Her sentence ended in a long, throaty groan.

I licked a trail along her chest, running from the opening of the suit to her collarbone.

"I . . . I need you . . .," she stammered as I pushed her closer to the edge.

All thoughts of stripteases and seduction were lost in the rampant desire coursing through us both. She lifted herself off my lap long enough for me to push my pants down to my knees. I pulled her straight onto me, relishing the warm wetness that surrounded my aching cock.

"Holy fucking Christ," I cried out as I thrust into her. I began to work the lacing that crisscrossed her breasts, longing to release them into my touch. I needed them under my fingers and in my mouth. I needed *her*. Finally, I managed to free them and brought my mouth to meet her nipples.

The same slow swaying motion she had used to tease me was now bringing me to ecstasy. I clenched her arse tightly with my fingers as I came in her, the slow burn igniting into a flash fire.

"Holy hell, that was hot," Alyssa panted against my neck.

I wasn't finished with her yet. I took the flesh of her throat into my mouth before ravishing her breasts again. As I kissed her, she began to giggle.

"I have to get back soon," she murmured.

I shook my head, all my previous thoughts about not wanting to spoil her hen night gone. I didn't want to let her go; in fact, I wasn't sure that I could.

She pulled away from me. "We can continue this tomorrow, if you'd like."

I nodded against her skin before a thought hit me. "Wait . . . where did this come from?" I ran my hands up the sides of her outfit.

"Eden." Alyssa chuckled. "She gave it to me as a gift tonight. Said she thought it might come in handy sooner or later."

"That cheeky minx," I whispered. "She wasn't supposed to give it away."

"Don't worry, she didn't. Trust me, I was surprised." Alyssa laughed loudly. "But not as surprised as Ruby. I'm still not sure she knows it was you."

I joined in her laughter. "I guess you should put her out of her misery."

"Yeah, maybe." Alyssa giggled. "Or I could let her squirm for a little while longer."

I guided her lips toward mine. "Wait a minute. That means this outfit can have an encore?"

She grinned at me. "Oh, it's definitely getting an encore."

"I love you," I said after we'd shared a sweet kiss.

She rested her forehead on mine. "I love you too. I can't believe we're actually getting married in a few short weeks."

"Believe it, baby. There is nothing I am looking forward to more."

CHAPTER TWENTY-TWO

THE PITS

I WAS HAVING a shitty day.

No, I was having a shitty weekend, and it was only Saturday.

And it'd looked so promising at the start.

With the wedding just one week away, Mum had arrived back in Australia and wanted to spend some time with her granddaughter. Even though Alyssa was anxious about leaving Phoebe in Sydney, Mum had convinced Alyssa to fly up to Townsville with me and the team. I'd been a little worried about taking her to a race meeting after the accident at Queensland Raceway, but I knew I had to get over that insecurity if I wanted to spend time with my girls, doing what I loved.

My Friday had sucked. I'd failed miserably in my bid to get two pole positions.

Four races, two poles. It wasn't a tough task, and yet, I had failed.

I'd qualified in third position, which wasn't bad, but wasn't good enough either. I'd failed Alyssa; I wasn't going to be able to provide her with the honeymoon we'd planned on.

To suffer that blow just one week out from the wedding was the worst.

And earlier that morning, my helmet had gone missing. I'd taken it with me to the event as my good luck charm, not that it had worked on Friday. But on Saturday morning, when I went to find it just before my second race, it wasn't where I'd left it.

I searched all around the Mini garage and just couldn't find it anywhere. Luckily though, Alyssa was in the Sinclair Racing trailer, and I'd decided there was no need to tell her just yet that it was missing. I pulled out my spare helmet and used it to go racing. I'd have a better look around once I was finished.

As I pushed the car around the track, I thought about Alyssa watching from the sidelines. It gave me a little boost. I finished in second and decided that even if I hadn't won the right to return to London, it wasn't that bad a result for the meeting, and overall my season had been pretty decent. I was first in the championship after all, and that was something worth celebrating.

I pulled up into scrutineering, ready to meet Alyssa like we'd agreed, but she wasn't there. A niggle built in the pit of my stomach, but I tried to push it aside. No doubt she was just caught up on the phone with Ruby or in the trailer with Eden. It was nothing to worry about, I was sure of it, but that didn't stop me from stressing.

After the officials were finished, I took my car back to the sheds, but Alyssa wasn't there either. I tried her mobile, but there was no answer. With each failed attempt to find her, the suffocating fear I felt gained more traction. I'd completed at least three laps of the pits, but she wasn't anywhere.

I raced to the Sinclair Racing truck, thinking that maybe she was in the office there with Eden. When I saw she wasn't there either, full-blown panic set in.

For the first time in a long time, my chest swelled and my breath shortened. I struggled to get enough oxygen into my system. Something was wrong. I just knew it.

There was no way Alyssa wouldn't be waiting for me. Not without trying to contact me in some way.

Every inch of my body was on edge. Alyssa was in trouble, and I had no idea where she was, or how to find her. The weight of it was staggering. I fell to my knees as a strangled sob ripped from my lips.

I tried to think logically, but I couldn't. All I could think of was my desperate need to find Alyssa and my hopelessness over not knowing where to start. I buried my head in my hands and leant back onto my heels. I knew I had to get up and start searching, but the task seemed insurmountable.

Knowing that if I let the panic overwhelm me, I would never find Alyssa, I staggered to my feet and did one more lap of the pits. I couldn't see or hear clearly through the mist that had invaded my head, but I made my way around as best as I could, certain that seeing Alyssa would clear my mind instantly.

After a moment, I grew aware of someone walking over and talking to me, but I couldn't make out the words or the face. Hands pulled me aside and pushed me against a wall.

"Are you all right, man?"

I blinked, trying to clear the fog in my head.

"Sparky?" a different voice added.

I swung my head back and forth between the two voices who kept talking to each other and to me. Then I was jostled inside a trailer. I was aware of being shaken slightly. I wanted to be sick. My stomach twisted and my chest heaved with each breath I tried to take.

"Alyssa," I croaked. I didn't care what happened to me, which seemed to be what the two boys were concerned about. I didn't care about exposure, or photos, or fans, or any of the other shit they were saying. I just cared about Alyssa. "Where is she?"

"I haven't seen her," one of the voices—which I finally realised belonged to Calem—said.

"Me either, but Hunter was asking about her earlier. He was over near the carrier trucks."

"Hunter!" His name burst out of me like a curse and suddenly, I could see clearly. I took a deep breath, needing every ounce of strength I could muster. If he'd laid even one finger on Alyssa . . .

I yelled a "thanks" behind me as I scrambled from the trailer and ran toward the freight area. If Hunter was talking to Alyssa, I knew what he wanted. He'd been trying to find a way to get to me for the longest time. I growled at the memory of his taunts at work. I knew exactly where he would have led her, if given the opportunity. The one place at the track that was always deserted once everything was set up.

The trucks that brought all the support equipment were lined up in a car park on the far outskirts of the track. I raced there as quickly as my legs, and the hot race suit I was wearing, would allow. I'd barely reached the gate when Alyssa slammed into me. She was running as fast as she could, looking behind her anxiously.

Relief flooded through me. She was safe and back with me, where she belonged. I wrapped my arms tightly around her. She screamed at first as I held her, but then she realised who I was and relaxed into me.

"What happened?" I asked. "Where were you?"

She pressed herself hard against me. "Hunter."

I set my jaw, furious. I couldn't believe she would wander off with him. I'd warned her—repeatedly—how much of an arse he was. How fucking dangerous he could be. I'd even told her about the girls I'd rescued, even though it was a reminder of how things used to be for me. The things he'd whispered to me at work came racing back into my mind and my hands clenched into fists. I lifted Alyssa and turned around, leaving me positioned between her and the direction she had been running from. The direction where Hunter, the snake, was slithering in hiding.

I'd begun to head in that very direction when Alyssa grabbed my arm.

"Don't!" she cried, as tears pricked her eyes.

"Why not, Alyssa?" I asked.

"I don't want you to get hurt."

I scoffed. "You don't think it hurts that you would go off with him, knowing everything he's done to me?"

She looked up at me. I could see rage and sorrow battling behind her eyes, and the mix stole my voice. I wanted to apologise, immediately knowing that I was out of line.

"You . . . you mean the world to me," she forced out finally between sobs. "I went with him, because I thought it was you! He . . . he has your helmet . . ."

I stared at her, my mouth dry and my heart between my teeth. I heard the sound of a muffled cry and whipped my head toward it. I guessed it was coming from near where Alyssa had appeared from.

I took a step in that direction, but again Alyssa reached out to stop me. It was hard to understand why, when I was so much stronger than her, a light touch of her hand was enough to paralyse me.

"Please don't," she cried. "I couldn't stand it if you got hurt."

"You think *I'm* going to get hurt?" I asked. "That fucker, he's the one who's going to get hurt. I am going to make him pay for ever laying his eyes on you."

She flinched.

"Wait, that was all he laid on you, wasn't it?"

She dropped her eyes to the floor, and I thought I saw her shake her head slightly. I didn't wait to find out what else the fucking bastard had done. I was off and running in the direction that I'd heard the sound come from. As I drew closer, the sounds of muffled fighting grew louder. I rounded the corner and saw Hunter and Morgan locked in a tight embrace. Both of them were throwing punches wildly.

"You prick!" I screamed. "You rat-bastard fucking prick. How *dare* you go anywhere near *my* girl!"

Hunter and Morgan both paused at the sound of my voice. Morgan was quick to use the momentary break to his advantage. He wrapped his hands around Hunter's shoulders, pulling his arms back and exposing his stomach to me. I cracked my knuckles and sneered at Hunter.

"Now, you pay. Fucker."

I drew my fist back and slammed it hard into Hunter's side, listening to his pained holler with sick satisfaction. I went to strike again, aiming for his face this time, but before I could connect, I heard the absolute last voice I'd wanted to hear at that moment.

"What the hell is going on here?" Danny asked, low and venomously.

"They dragged me out here and attacked me," Hunter said, his voice pathetic and pitiful.

"Tell him the truth!" I demanded. "Tell him what you did!"

Hunter shook his head. "I didn't do anything," he pleaded to Danny. "I swear."

"Morgan?" Danny's eyes shot straight to the third party in the situation.

"Hunter was out here alone with Alyssa—" Morgan started before Danny cut him off.

"And that's justification for this?" Danny asked, his tone indicating that the correct answer was not yes. "Let him go!"

Danny's calm authority was clearly not to be messed with, and with a firm shove, Morgan released Hunter.

"Get back to the pits. I'll deal with this later. Declan, I'll see you in my office as soon as the next race is over. Alone."

Hunter turned back to me and smirked. He knew as well as I did that I was going to bear the brunt of this. I was the fuck-up. I was the one with the history of fighting. I was the one who'd complained bitterly about Hunter. I was the one Danny had overheard saying that I would do whatever it took to get rid of him. I was the one who was supposed to be racing with Morgan in the enduros after the break, but now that dream was drifting away into the fucking distance, despite the contract. All I could hope was between Alyssa, Morgan, and I, we would be able to convince Danny that Hunter wasn't as innocent as he claimed.

Hunter snickered and licked his lips as he passed me. "Mmmm, tastes good," he murmured, just loud enough for me to hear.

"You fucking bastard!" I cried and leapt at him again. Before I could do any serious damage, Morgan and Danny dragged me off him as I fought against them to try to finish the arsehole off. I noticed with satisfaction that Morgan used the opportunity to get another kick or two in.

"Hunter! With me!" Danny snapped. "Now!" He led Hunter off without a second glance.

"What the fuck happened, man?" I asked Morgan, scooping down to pick up my helmet that Hunter had obviously stolen and worn to lure Alyssa away from the crowds.

"I don't know exactly. I just saw some kid talking to Alyssa earlier. Then she walked off in this direction, or skipped off might be more appropriate. A little while later, someone said you were looking for her. I couldn't find you, so I went in search of her."

I closed my eyes, almost afraid to ask what he found.

"It wasn't good," he said, confirming my worst fears. "He had her pinned tightly against the trailer. She was trying to fight him off, but he wasn't listening to her."

I growled. "I'm going to kill him. I am going to fucking *kill* him."

"Man, I get it. I really do. But you need to back off for a bit. You're already in enough hot water with Old Man Sinclair as it is. Just leave it to me. I'll set Danny straight."

He smiled, and I felt like agreeing, but I knew I wouldn't be satisfied unless Hunter suffered because of me. Only when I heard the crunch of his bones under my fists would I feel vindicated. I wrung my hands together in anticipation at the thought of inflicting pain and suffering on him.

"Go to Alyssa," Morgan said, resting one hand on the custom-designed helmet she'd given me for my birthday.

Of course, he would remind me of the one thing more important than revenge.

With that thought in mind, I rang Alyssa's mobile. Eden answered it and let me know that they were back at the trailer. I ran the whole way there and straight into Alyssa's arms. I let her sob against me until I finally had to leave. It was time for me to do my proper job. It had been drilled into me thoroughly that my pit job was my first and foremost responsibility at these events.

When I arrived in the pits, Ryan sidled up to me. "I hope you don't mind that I got Danny before. I'd hoped he'd see the truth about Hunter."

I waved him off. "Of course not."

"What happened?" Calem asked.

Even though I was certain he was asking what I'd found, I answered the alternative interpretation of his question. "I'll find out after the race."

I couldn't help but smile at the knowledge that Hunter had committed the cardinal sin in racing—never fuck with anyone who has your safety in their hands. I wondered whether anyone would notice if I didn't completely tighten the nut on his wheel when he came into the pit. Although maybe it was safer for me to convince one of the other boys to do it, considering any fuck-up on my part would be assumed to be intentional.

The cars had one final check-over then rolled out onto the grid. Morgan and Hunter waited by their cars, with Eden and Liam darting between them, while the official proceedings started at the start/finish line.

Despite my prime position in pit lane, I couldn't hear anything that was said over the blood pumping loudly through my ears as I watched the slimy bastard posing for photos with the grid girls. I could see his hands wandering all over their bodies, and I couldn't help picturing his hands roaming over Alyssa while she struggled to fight him off. I snapped the pen I had been holding in half, drawing my attention back to the sheet in front of me. I tossed the broken pen and the clipboard to one side.

Pull yourself together.

Danny already wanted my arse because of what happened by the trailers. At least, I could only assume he was going to take it out on me. Regardless, I couldn't make it worse for myself. No matter what anyone told him, he would likely assume that I was at fault. Despite the progress we'd made, I had no doubt this would put us back to square one. I would be the baddy and there was jack shit I could do about it. I wondered if that would ever change. I even began to wonder whether it was even worth it.

I looked up in time to see Eden come running into pit lane.

"Look sharp, guys," she called. "It's time."

She nodded to me briefly. The look in her eyes confirmed that she knew precisely what had happened with Hunter. I tried to put it out of my mind and took my position with the rest of my crew, waiting for the first pit window to open.

We were all on tenterhooks as we waited for the call that our driver was hitting the pits. Every one of us knew that pit stops were where the races were really won or lost. I may have hated Hunter, I may have wanted him gone from the team, but I was still a Sinclair man through and through and wanted us up on the podium. The V8s roared past us at regular intervals and, although it was still early, everything looked on track for a Sinclair Racing one/two.

Finally, the call came in to ready the pits. Morgan was due to come in for his first pit stop in four laps. Two laps passed quickly and Morgan's crew got ready to meet him, rolling his wheels and tyres into the pit area.

The lap before he was due to come in, Hunter's voice squawked through the radio. "I'm coming in."

"Hunter, no, we're ready for Morgan—not you," Eden said.

"Well, *get* ready for me," Hunter snapped. "I'm coming in."

"Fuck!" Eden exclaimed. She pulled her mic away from her mouth. "Everyone scramble!" she shouted before spending the next precious few seconds arranging with Morgan to stay away from the pits for another few laps.

"My tyres are wearing out," Morgan growled. "I need to come in."

"Hunter's coming in this lap—give us two laps," Eden said, exasperated. "Please?"

"Fine!" Morgan snapped. "What the hell is his game?"

I was wondering the same thing myself as I joined the rest of my crew getting everything we needed for Hunter's car out onto pit lane, sidelining all of Morgan's equipment. Hunter was already in the pits and waiting long before we were ready. Precious seconds had already slipped away before we even started.

I finished changing his front wheel and raised my hand to let everyone know I was finished and clear. I looked down through the netting and saw Hunter was giving me the finger. With a surge of anger rushing through me, I leaned forward to slap the car. At the same time, Hunter got the all-clear to go. He took off, almost taking my arm with him.

"Fucker!" I screamed.

"Reede!"

I snarled at the back of the car before turning around to look at Liam.

"What have I told you?" he snapped. "A thousand times. When you raise your hand, it means you're clear. Once you're clear, stay away from the damned car!"

"Yes, sir," I said. I knew there was no point arguing, because I knew the safety rules well enough. No matter what happened once you'd given the all-clear, you stayed back. It was far too easy to lean back into the car and have your foot run over or your arm broken.

Or worse.

CHAPTER TWENTY-THREE

RECKLESS

I WAS FUMING by the time I walked back into the pit garage.

"Take it easy," Eden said, slapping me on the back. "Try to stay calm."

"Fucker tries to hurt Alyssa and then has the nerve—"

Eden cut me off with a motion of her hand. It wasn't the time or the place.

I cleared out of the way so she could direct Morgan in. Glancing past the pits, I watched as Hunter circled again. I didn't know what the fucker's plan was, but I knew he'd deliberately fucked Morgan over with the pit stop.

Morgan had ended up having to run at least three laps on old tyres, which would definitely have caused him some delays. Not to mention that it fucked with the whole race strategy Danny, Liam, and Eden would have worked out with Morgan before sending him out.

Thankfully, the race wore on without any further complication. Lap after lap the cars raced past, and just as I had every other race meet, I felt my fingers twitching with need and desire to be out there with them. I loved being in the pits and, through my experience, I understood how things worked better than I ever had before. But that didn't mean I didn't want to be out there.

The inner workings of the cars were no longer the mystery to me that they'd once been. I'd always known the theory of course, and I'd been more than able to service my own cars, but actually stripping an engine down and rebuilding it was a priceless experience. Still, nothing could ever compare to the thrill of chasing down a competitor or the ecstasy of being out there with six hundred horses at the mercy of my right foot.

Another pit stop for tyres and fuel came and went.

Once the dust had settled on the second pit window, Hunter and Morgan were first and second on the track, with Will Reid right behind them. Hunter was defending his position aggressively against Morgan, throwing his car around the track and driving hard into the corners.

I couldn't understand why he wasn't just using his lead to push himself further forward. That's what I would have done. Leave second and third to battle it out while relishing the additional speed granted by the clean air. Instead, he was allowing himself to get mixed into the battle and slowing himself down. It was just all-around bad race strategy.

The defensive driving techniques of Hunter allowed Morgan to sneak up on him and slingshot around him coming out of turn thirteen. They were neck and neck as they hit the straight, with Morgan edging slowly in front.

"Go, you good thing," I whispered. Similar sentiments were murmured all around me. Although everyone wanted a Sinclair Racing one/two combo, there wasn't a single person in the pits who wouldn't have preferred to see Morgan in front.

Just as they approached the small bend in the straight, Hunter twisted his wheel sharply, clipping the rear right-hand side of Morgan's car. To anyone else watching, it may have just looked like Hunter had oversteered for the corner, but I knew him, and the car, well enough to know that it wasn't an accident.

"Motherfucker," I cursed under my breath.

He'd managed to hit Morgan's car in exactly the right place to send him pirouetting down the straightaway at top speed. It left little doubt in my head that it was deliberate. Will slid past

Morgan's car harmlessly as soon as it started its fast spin. I heard Eden's horrified gasp when she realised what was going to happen, almost at the exact time that I did. There was only one way it could go. Unless Morgan pulled some kind of fucking miracle out of his arse and wrestled control of the car, he was heading straight for the wall.

I turned to Eden and saw the colour drain out of her face. She chewed on her lips briefly before bringing her fingers into her mouth. The stress in the pits was palpable, despite the fact that only seconds had passed since Hunter's deception. I wanted to shout out that it was all right and to explain that the cars were designed for safety—that it was rare for anyone to get seriously injured in them—but everyone around me knew that just as well as I did.

I, who had crashed so many times in the last six months of my career, had never experienced the level of fear that ran through the pits as they watched helplessly. Those who couldn't see the track from their current position had their eyes firmly glued to the monitors.

I watched in horror as the rear of Morgan's car barrelled into the concrete barrier. The force of the hit was so hard that a ripple ran down the fence all the way back to us in the pits. The car ricocheted back across the track before finally rolling to a stop in the middle of the track just around the loose bend. Everyone in the pits crowded around the monitors and held their breath as the car finally settled.

"He's in the blind," I whispered. I remembered the track from last year. It was a loose turn, you barely had to twist the steering wheel, but there was a small section of track that couldn't be seen until you were committed to the line. Morgan's car was currently resting in that exact spot.

"Fuck!" Liam cried. He jumped onto the radio with the track officials, quickly explaining the full situation with Morgan. We were monitoring his vitals, but he hadn't left the car yet. We weren't sure whether it was because of safety concerns or injury—he wasn't answering any radio calls. Eden was practically a statue with nerves. I could see the tears behind her eyes and her lips were moving quickly as she muttered something indecipherable. No doubt a prayer for his safety.

Less than a second passed before the cars in fourth and fifth shot out of the hairpin and down the straight.

"No!" Eden cried from nearby me, but I couldn't take my eyes off the monitor to see her new pain. "They're going too fast," she whispered. "They're going too fast!"

The officials brought out the yellow flags and both cars started to slow, but it was too late. There wasn't enough room for both of them to get around Morgan, especially when they didn't even know he was there and hadn't seen his car until the last second.

I closed my eyes as the sound of metal twisting against metal rent the air. The sound of the collision was bad enough; I didn't need to see it too. Eden's pained cry made my heart ache. I turned and watched as, for the first time since I'd known her, she went against every rule in the book. She ripped her headset off and ran down pit lane in the direction of the accident. I didn't have time to consider just how out of character it was, though, because I was running right behind her.

I CAUGHT up with Eden just at the exit of pit lane. We couldn't see the carnage, and without our headphones, there was no way of knowing what was happening. We did see the marshals change the flags from yellow—meaning caution on the track and advising that the safety car was in control—to red.

Red: the conditions were too unsafe to continue the session and all cars had to stop.

The impact ahead was bad.

I grabbed Eden seconds before she ran blindly onto the track. I snaked my arms around her waist and held on to her from behind. She pummelled my arms with her fists.

"Let me go!" she wailed. "I have to go to him."

"We will, Edie," I said to her as calmly as I could while pulling gently against her. "But there's no point in getting yourself killed in the process. Come up along the inside of the barriers. At least until we know the track is clear and the cars are stopped."

I tried not to look at the red flags waving ominously from the sides of the track as we jumped over the barrier and ran in the relatively safe zone to where Morgan's car had finally come to rest. Whenever the flickering red material did catch my eye, I tried to remind myself that red flags meant nothing more than a total track blockage. It didn't mean Morgan was injured or . . . *worse.*

I held Eden's hand as we rounded the corner, partly out of a desire to comfort her in some way but mostly to ensure that I had a good hold so she didn't go barrelling off again. She wasn't thinking straight. Hell, I was barely thinking straight.

The scene wasn't pretty. There were three cars stretched from one side of the track to the other; although, I wasn't sure Morgan's wreck would still classify as a car. It was upside down, no longer had four wheels, and the entire front end rested near the far boundary fence, having obviously been torn off by the impact with car number fifteen.

Eden froze. She shook her head in disbelief before closing her eyes.

"No," she sobbed softly. "No, this isn't happening."

I watched as the drivers of the other cars pulled roughly on Morgan's doors, trying to wrench them open.

"Stay here," I commanded Eden. The last thing the scene needed was a hysterical woman, and even the most stoic professional was bound to become a little hysterical when confronted with a car accident featuring her fiancé. Regardless, I needed to help.

Despite there being five men on the track already, Morgan's door still wasn't open. Worse, from the little I could see through the netting, he wasn't moving at all.

I started off for the track and felt Eden close by my side.

"Eden, please?" I begged. "Stay."

"No! If . . ." She trailed off.

I could see the blind panic in her eyes. She closed her eyes and swallowed roughly. When she opened them again, her face was calmer and she was slightly more in control, but I knew from my own experience that her control would be tenuous at best.

"If anything happens, I want to be there."

I looked over at the scene. More people were flooding in now — not just track officials and fire marshals, but TV and photo crews. Each one trying to get the perfect photo of Morgan's broken car, or even better — in their newsworthy, jaded eyes — his broken body.

"Fucking vultures," I muttered under my breath.

Just as we climbed over the barrier and back onto the track, the rescue crew finally wrestled Morgan's door open and pulled him from the wreckage. He was on a stretcher and into the onsite ambulance in next to no time. Even as he was loaded onto the stretcher, he remained motionless.

At the sight of Morgan's prostrate body, Eden collapsed. Luckily, I saw what was going to happen seconds before it did and was able to get my arms around her just as she fell.

Unable to control herself any longer, she sobbed against me as I held her tightly. I picked her up into my arms as gently as I was able and carried her back through the pits and toward the trailer. I knew Morgan would want her by his side as soon as possible, but for the moment I needed to take care of her for him. I would make sure she was there for him before he woke. And he *would* wake. I couldn't even bear to imagine any other possibility.

By the time I got back to the trailer, all of the crew were outside waiting for news. The sight of Eden in agony sent a shockwave through them. She'd always been the strong one in the team, the one to rally the troops and give them hope when something went wrong.

Everyone parted before me as I walked toward the trailer, giving me space to take her through to the control centre. Each of the monitors was a reminder of Morgan's current situation. His car's in-car telemetry was ominously still, all of the on-track cameras were trained on the accident scene, and the in-car camera was cracked and showing an upside-down image.

After helping Eden onto a chair, freeing up my hands, I turned off all the monitors. Neither of us needed the harsh reminder of what we'd just witnessed firsthand.

I sat on one of the spare chairs and pulled Eden onto my lap. I cradled her against my chest like a child and gave her the opportunity to cry it all out so she could be strong when she went to see Morgan in the hospital. If she went in her current condition, she would be of little help to him.

My boys seemed to understand what I was doing and set themselves up as bodyguards at the door. They didn't allow anyone to pass, except Alyssa. She was in tears as she burst into the small room. She pulled the other chair up to my side and held my hand as I supported Eden. The three of us sat in near silence, broken only by Eden's heartbreaking sobs and Alyssa's quick, whispered update. Apparently, Danny had left for the hospital, but nothing more was known.

I wanted to give Eden the time she needed to recover, but started to grow more anxious about the passing minutes. I had to ensure she was by Morgan's side as soon as possible. I knew I would have wanted Alyssa beside me immediately if the situation was reversed. After a few minutes, Eden's body stopped shaking as violently, and she climbed off my lap.

She took a few tentative steps as she wiped the remaining tears off her cheeks.

"I . . . I'm ready," she whispered. "Can you . . .?" Her voice gave out.

I nodded. "We'll take you to him."

As soon as we hit the stairs to exit the trailer, the flash bulbs started. Although Eden and Morgan had never really gone public with their relationship—at least outside of our admission on New Year's that had never made it to print—they had never hidden it either, so the speculation had always been rife in the media. Seeing her on-track reaction seemed to have confirmed many suspicions, so everyone wanted her take on the accident. As we stepped outside, I had Alyssa's hand tightly held in one of mine, and my other arm was wrapped protectively around Eden.

Through the throng of reporters, I spotted Hunter out of the corner of my eye. He was leaning casually against the trailer parked alongside Sinclair Racing's, looking smug as fuck. If my mind weren't so preoccupied with getting Eden to Morgan, I might have taken the opportunity to pummel the living shit out of him.

I felt Alyssa's hand squeeze mine a little tighter. She must have seen Hunter too and was trying to keep my focus on the task at hand. Or gain comfort for herself. I guided Eden through to the car park, and she handed me the keys to her rental car. She climbed into the passenger seat, curled herself into a ball, and squeezed her eyes tightly shut. Alyssa sat in the seat behind me and rested one hand on my shoulder in support the whole way.

It was a silent and anxious drive to the hospital. I could feel the tension rolling off Alyssa, but I could also sense something else. Relief. I knew she'd never admit it, but I could tell that beneath her worry and concern, she was glad it wasn't me on the track.

I wondered whether it would make things harder when it came time for me to get back into a V8 for the endurance races. Then I remembered that I still needed to talk to Danny, and that I might not be back for the enduros at all. Momentarily, I considered the possibility that Morgan might not even be back in a car before then, but I pushed it out of my mind.

He *would* be okay.

He had to be.

CHAPTER TWENTY-FOUR

WAITING

I SAT WITH Alyssa in the waiting room. Now that Eden was in with Morgan, I was able to stop trying to be strong for her, so I fell apart in Alyssa's arms. We had moved closer and closer during our short stay in the waiting room. At first, we'd sat side by side on the cheap suede couch, Alyssa's two hands surrounding one of mine, lending me some of her warmth, but somehow over the course of an hour, I had ended up with my top half curled in her lap as she gently stroked my hair.

"Thank you," I whispered to her for probably the fiftieth time. I glanced up at her face and took in her sad smile.

"I'm just glad that I'm here and that you didn't have to go through it alone."

I turned my face back to the wall. "Me too," I murmured so quietly I wasn't sure that she'd even heard me.

We weren't family or important enough to be kept up to date on progress, so we just had to wait patiently for either Danny or Eden to remember we were there. The small TV in the corner kept getting turned on and off intermittently as we hungered for more information.

We soon tired of seeing the same footage again and again:

Morgan's car coming to rest in the bend before being slammed by the other two cars; Morgan being loaded onto a stretcher and carried away in the ambulance; me helping Eden from the trailer, her eyes red-rimmed and bloodshot.

It was late evening, well past eight, when Eden finally emerged from Morgan's room. She looked like death warmed up. Pale skin; wide, bloodshot eyes; and pink, puffy cheeks where she'd rubbed her tears away. I reminded myself that as hard as the last four hours had been for Alyssa and me, they'd been even harder on Eden.

I sat up to give her space to sit and give us the prognosis.

"He's awake," she started before coughing lightly to clear her throat. "He's badly concussed though. He has a broken leg, two broken ribs, a punctured lung, a concussion, and a sprained wrist. They . . ." She stopped again, summoning strength from somewhere within—it was a wonder she had any left.

Alyssa's hand reached across my lap to hold Eden's.

"They can't say whether he'll be back on the track this season."

"But he will be back?" I asked softly. Even though there would be an opening if he was forced to leave the team, I didn't want my opportunity to come off the back of Morgan's tragedy.

"They won't know for sure until he's started physio. They— they're hopeful. But there's no guarantees."

I nodded.

"He wants to see you," she murmured. "There're just a couple of minutes left before visiting hours are over."

I swallowed and felt Alyssa squeeze my leg gently. I wasn't sure if I was ready to see him just yet, but I had no choice. He was asking for me, and what an injured man wanted, an injured man received. I stood before following Eden's directions to Morgan's room.

I knocked on the closed door and heard a soft, "Come in," coughed from the room.

I pushed the door open and took in my surroundings. The curtains were half-drawn around the sole bed.

Morgan rested heavily against the pale hospital sheets with the bed angled up slightly so he was sitting almost upright. He was awake, but he still looked a little grey. Various monitors made a cacophony of sound in the room, ensuring that it was never completely silent.

He smiled weakly up at me as I entered.

I sat in the seat beside his bed, at a complete loss for words.

"Did you see what happened?"

I nodded, but then paused. I wanted to see what he remembered. "A car turned sharply into you and you lost control. When it stopped, you were in the blind. Two cars came through behind you, but they didn't see you in time."

"Who won?"

I chuckled. Of course that would be one of his primary concerns. "I don't know," I answered honestly. "I'm sure Eden is finding out as we speak."

"Thanks, man," he said, breaking the tension that was starting to creep into the room. "For looking out for Eden for me."

"Of course," I muttered. "Anytime."

He reached out for my hand. "You are a good man, Declan Reede. You're my best buddy."

I smirked at him. "What brought that on?"

"I just love you man. I absolutely love you."

I bit my lip to stop from laughing harder. Clearly, he was on some serious painkillers. I decided to have a little fun with him, and find out a few truths. "I have to ask you a question, and I need your honest answer," I started.

He looked at me seriously, his face full of an earnest desire to please.

"What did you think of me when I first started?"

"You were like my little bro, bro."

I chuckled, deciding to see how far I could push it. "Have you and Eden ever done it at a track?"

I half expected him to laugh or tell me to fuck off, but instead he seemed to think hard about his answer. "Once or twice." He grinned. "Per meet."

I wasn't sure whether to grin or grimace. I knew for certain that I would be more suspicious whenever the two of them disappeared in the future. "How do you really feel about Hunter?"

"I wish it was you I was driving against. You—you gave me something to beat."

"What about Alyssa? What do you think of her?" It might be dangerous territory because of their tenuous relationship, but I wasn't going to give up the opportunity for complete honesty when it arose.

"Alyssa . . ." He grinned cheekily. "She's a good sort. She's good for you. And she's got a killer arse."

I immediately regretted asking him about Alyssa and decided to stick to safer topics. "Has Danny been in to see you?"

"Yep, he was here with Eden for a while."

"Has he said anything about the accident?"

Morgan shook his head. "No, but man, I'm glad for good family. Danny's paying for everything in the hospital. He's even getting me a transfer to Sydney. I can't fly with the hole here apparently." He was pointing to his chest, no doubt referring to his punctured lung.

I was a little taken aback by his statement about family, until I realised he had to mean it figuratively. I knew how he felt; I often thought of the Sinclair Racing crew as an extended family, especially lately. It was the reason I wanted back in so bad. Besides, if there was any actual family in the team, I was certain I would know about it. Eden would have told me; she knew all the goss.

I didn't get a chance to press him further because a nurse came in to shoo me out—apparently visiting hours were over for the night.

GOING TO the track the next day and pretending nothing had happened was almost impossible. The track was clear, the damaged cars completely repaired—the rest of the pit crews had spent a long night fixing them all—and the officials were preparing to start the new day of racing. But the scars were still evident in my team at least; one of our drivers was absent, everyone was exhausted, and we were all counting down the hours until the race meet ended.

The news slowly filtered through the ranks that Hunter—who'd gone on to win the race after the restart—had been investigated for being at the centre of a red flag event. Unfortunately, it was regarded as an accident and he'd gotten off scot-free.

Eden arrived late to the track with heavy purple bags under her eyes. She'd obviously had a very hard night. I felt bad that we hadn't hung around the hospital longer to support her because, by comparison, our night had been easier.

When we'd arrived back at the hotel, Alyssa had quickly called our house. It had been too late to speak to Phoebe, so she'd had a brief conversation with Mum instead. We assured her that we were okay, that it was just a long night, and that we'd see her the following evening. After that, Alyssa and I'd curled into one another in bed and held each other silently the whole night long. I don't think either of us had any sleep, but at least we had each other.

I hadn't been at the track for long before the meeting I knew was inevitable was called. Liam came to find me and told me that Danny wanted to see me in his office. I refused to leave Alyssa alone, so I hunted down my boys to ensure they would be stuck like glue to her side.

"I CAN'T believe either of you would do something so reckless!" Danny was pacing from side to side along his desk and wasn't looking at either Eden or me as we sat in his makeshift office.

To my surprise, we'd both been called in to face the music together. I assumed it was an act of mercy. He would have been within his rights to tear strips off us individually, which would have been infinitely harder for us to handle. Neither of us needed an explanation of what we'd done wrong, because we both knew that our run onto the track was not only stupid and reckless, but dangerous as well. Either or both of us could have been hit by a car, not to mention we had no doubt distracted the race officials at a time they should have been concentrating on other things.

"I'm sorry," I started, but Eden raised her hand to stop me.

"It's my fault, Danny. Declan was just chasing after me. I just— I lost my head. I would've been in more danger if he hadn't been there."

She was throwing herself on the fire for me, but I couldn't let her. I had taken off with exactly the same mindset she had. I'd wanted to help. I'd wanted to get to Morgan and ensure he was okay. Even if Eden hadn't made the dash, I probably would have done exactly the same thing. It was only when it became evident her needs were so much greater than my own that my intentions changed.

"Danny—" I tried to explain, but Eden again cut me off.

"Declan got me off the track. He stopped me from running blindly to Morgan. He was also the one who stopped me from falling onto the track when it got to be too much. Please, I know what he did was wrong, but he shouldn't be punished for *my* stupidity."

"No one is getting punished," Danny assured us. He'd migrated to his seat and sat slumped with his fingers bridged on his nose. "The tribunal agreed to accept the extenuating circumstances and have given you both suspended sentences. But they don't want to see either of you do anything so stupid again."

We both nodded.

"Eden, I'm relieving you of your duties. Liam is going to monitor the next race on his own. Go back to the hospital and be with Morgan. They've said he's able to be released later this afternoon, but he can't travel by air. A car will be around to pick you both up and start the journey home later this afternoon."

"Thank you," she said before standing and crossing to his side of the desk. She wrapped her arms around his neck and hugged him tightly for a second. He patted her arm gently in a loving, almost familial gesture.

She unwrapped her arms from his neck, and he nodded toward the door to indicate that she should go.

After she'd exited the room, he sat staring at me for a second or two. I wondered if he actually did have some punishment for me that he hadn't wanted to dish out with Eden in the room. She wasn't the fuck-up after all. That was all on me.

"You make it very hard for me to put you in a V8 sometimes," he murmured finally.

I'd blown my chance. I cursed my own stupidity for leaving Alyssa alone when I went on the track for the Mini race, for not telling her about misplacing my helmet, for allowing my temper to take over and giving that fuckhead Hunter a taste of what he deserved, for running onto the track after Morgan's accident. So many screw-ups in just one weekend. All I could hope was that I could get him to understand why I'd reacted to Hunter the way I had. The fucker had assaulted Alyssa, and he deserved to pay for it.

I wanted to beg him to reconsider taking my chance away from me. I opened my mouth to try to come up with a magical statement that would fix everything, but I couldn't think of one.

"Would you care to explain what happened yesterday before the race?"

I decided to go with the truth. "Hunter tricked Alyssa into thinking that I was waiting for her by the trucks. When she got there, he pinned her against the truck—" The rest of my statement was stuck in my throat. During the night, I'd managed to find out that he hadn't been able to do much more than stroke Alyssa's cheek and kiss her before Morgan had interrupted them, but it didn't matter. He'd intended more—and that was as bad as the actual act in my eyes. My anger was rising just mentioning the incident. Alyssa and I had discussed going to the police, but she knew how unlikely it would be that anything would come of it.

"And Morgan found them like that?"

I nodded. "I didn't see what had happened . . ." I trailed off. If I *had* seen Hunter with Alyssa, I would have fucking killed him. He was just lucky Danny had turned up when he did.

"Do you think Hunter had a grudge against Morgan as a result of that incident?"

I gaped at Danny. Was he really asking what I thought of

Hunter? Did he think Hunter had a more nefarious role in the accident? I swallowed down my hope before it could grow. "Yes. Without doubt, but not as big as his grudge against me."

Danny nodded. "Thank you for your honesty. I'm sure you understand that I take all actions and accusations very seriously."

I nodded.

"And I want you to know I will be keeping a very close eye on the situation while watching for hard evidence of wrongdoing."

Mine, or Hunter's? His words didn't make it clear, so I read between the lines.

"I will be speaking to Hunter about this as well, and making my thoughts clear on the matter."

Make the fucker pay! Even though the words were on the tip of my tongue, what came out was, "Thank you, sir. I appreciate it."

"Do you feel up to your race today?"

I wondered whether I could, but I knew my response would no doubt count toward Danny's mental tally of how hard it was to put me back into a V8. If I couldn't even race a Mini after witnessing the accident, how could I possibly be trusted with anything more?

I nodded. "Yeah, I think so."

"Okay. I'll take you off pit duties though. We only have one car after all. Just compete in your race and then you're free to go."

I nodded. "Thank you."

"Then I guess I'll see you in Brisbane for your big day."

I froze. In the madness, I'd completely forgotten that this weekend was the last time I would see the Sinclair Racing team before my wedding. I blinked and couldn't help smiling a little.

"Thank you," I said again, unnecessarily. I decided against giving him the same hug Eden had and settled on a handshake before leaving the office.

CHAPTER TWENTY-FIVE

IT IS YOU

I STOOD AT the end of the red carpet, a conspicuous gap to my left where Morgan was supposed to have been. He should have been beside me to celebrate the happiest fucking day of my life, but instead, due to the sick fuckery of Hunter, he was back at home in Sydney still recovering from the accident. Even if he'd been well enough to stand next to me, he was still unable to fly because of the hole in his lung.

Flynn had agreed to be Morgan's fill-in, but stood a small distance away out of respect for the man who couldn't be there. Even though I appreciated Flynn's help, it wasn't really the same.

I looked around the room, marvelling at the details that Ruth and Alyssa had put into the planning. It was simple but elegant. There were no extravagant floral arrangements, just a single lily at the end of each row of chairs. I was in awe of her choice to have our wedding at the Suncrest Hotel, a place that held so many good and bad memories for the two of us.

Virginities and innocence were lost there, fights and make ups, and promises had been made and kept.

Drawing in a deep breath, I tried to dispel some of the nervous energy racing through my body. When I blew the air out slowly, I shook my legs and brushed my hand through my hair.

It had been over twenty-four hours since I had seen Alyssa. Ruth insisted that they needed to have a girls' day before our wedding, and I'd relented, especially after my own mother turned traitor and insisted on it too.

Even as they fussed over Alyssa and Phoebe, it was clear to me that I would spend the whole day as one big jumble of raw nerves. I had no one to offer me the level of support Alyssa had been given leading up to the event. I'd wanted to spend some time with Ben, but despite our attempts at renewing the friendship we'd once had, I just didn't feel right dumping all my pre-wedding crap on him, so I'd avoided him.

The thought of baring my soul in front of our families and friends terrified me. I'd managed to speak to Dr. Henrikson on the phone that morning to settle my pre-wedding jitters—something he'd offered as he'd wished us luck after the final couples' counselling session he'd had with Alyssa and me a few days earlier. It was good to get a chance to talk through the last of my nerves, but as soon as I'd hung up the phone, the stress had come back in force.

I'd even considered spending a few hours in another futile attempt to reconnect with my estranged father, but realised that his continuous pleas to see me were made out of the same selfish desire as the first. He truly had no wish to be a part of my life outside of what he thought I could do for him.

Since leaving Alyssa at her parents', I'd barely slept, only catching an hour here and there between nightmares and insomnia. All in all, it was not the way I'd expected to spend the night before the big one. At least the following night would be significantly better.

Once morning had arrived, I'd dragged myself out of bed, shaved, and then dressed before heading in to the Suncrest Hotel to help out with the final arrangements. In reality, though, there wasn't much to do, because Alyssa had planned it down to the last place setting.

The hall was set up with a makeshift altar and aisle for the ceremony. After we'd said our vows, we would head out for photos at the Botanical Gardens and a few other locations around town, while our guests were ushered out into the ballroom lobby for drinks and canapés. The hotel staff would use that break to convert the ballroom into the reception. Our guests would then be invited back in and shown to their allocated seats to await our arrival.

Part of me was excited about the evening, but mostly I just wanted it all to be over. I wanted to be back at home living as man and wife. Being married didn't frighten me as much as getting married. I was ready to know that Alyssa was mine, just as I was hers, forever.

I looked over the crowd, worried that trying to single out any individual face would make me ill. A quiet murmur ran around the room, providing a constant noise that I tried in vain to tune out. Ever since taking my position at the front of the gathering, I'd been counting down the minutes left in my head. The countdown ended, and then before I knew it, I was down to negative ten, which didn't bode well for me, because it meant Alyssa was late. I closed my eyes and tried to convince myself that she was still coming. She wasn't standing me up; it was okay for a bride to be fashionably late.

How late is fashionable though?

My count increased by another five minutes before music burst into life through the loudspeakers hidden inconspicuously around the room. I blew out a relieved breath, knowing that it was finally time. A silence fell over the room as everyone turned in their seats to watch the bride's entrance. My own eyes fell to the door as I waited for my perfect woman to walk through. I couldn't concentrate on the lyrics or the music—just the door.

Finally, it opened just a crack and a vision with brown hair walked through it. Her turquoise eyes were accented perfectly by the baby-blue dress she wore. Her hair was set in loose ringlets that rested on her shoulders. The little clips we'd picked out together pulled her curls up off her face beautifully. On seeing me, her mouth broke into a huge grin.

"Daddy!" she squealed, dropping the basket of rose petals she was carrying and hurtling toward me at top speed. She launched herself into my arms as giggles and muffled laughter broke out randomly throughout the crowd.

I pulled her in to me and gave her a small embrace.

"Hey, sweetie," I whispered quietly.

"You should see Mummy," she whispered back. "She's beautiful."

"I don't doubt it," I murmured before placing my finger on my lips to indicate she should be quiet.

Ruby walked through the door just then, glowing in her soft pink bridesmaid's dress. It flowed gently over her now-sizable baby bump. She shot me a knowing smile—obviously a reaction to the wide-arse, shit-eating grin on my face.

The doors opened again and suddenly everything stopped.

The world existed in perfect clarity as the music changed and Alyssa stepped forward. I could see, hear, and feel *everything*.

Her white dress was tight at the top, flaring out just below her hips. It was shaped perfect to accentuate her hips and bust. I was glad that all eyes were on her because it gave me a second to drink it all in. Her veil covered her features, but was thin enough that I could still see her clearly. Half of her hair was pulled up away from her face, but the rest fell in loose curls around her shoulders. She took a deep breath in the doorway as the lyrics began.

I met her eyes and caught her chewing her lip before her mouth broke into a smile almost as wide as mine. The lyrics that timed Alyssa's slow march down the aisle were perfect. We'd found the song on a *Shrek* soundtrack of all things, but the words had never been more fitting.

"I love you," I mouthed to her, causing her smile to widen even further.

"See, Daddy!" Phoebe shouted. "I told you Mummy was beautiful!"

I agreed with her, laughing a little before setting her down onto the ground, readying my arms to accept the second most important person in my life. Ruby quickly called Phoebe over to her side.

Each second of the minute or two that it took Alyssa to walk toward me felt like it stretched on forever.

Finally, she reached my side and Curtis's rough hand passed

her soft one to me. He wrapped his hand around our joined ones. At any other wedding, the moment would have been the perfect opportunity for the father of the bride to whisper words of encouragement, or give his final blessing, but this was *our* wedding, so of course, Curtis whispered, so quietly only I could hear, "If you hurt either of them . . ."

I met his eye, refusing to let him ruin my perfect moment. "I won't."

That said, I turned back to Alyssa, the one person who deserved my attention the most in this almost-perfect moment. The guests, Curtis, everyone else could go to pot. As long as I had Phoebe and Alyssa close to me, everything would be perfect.

The song finished and I couldn't help but smile through the nerves that had built steadily again as the room quietened, but only because I didn't want to fuck anything up. I wanted the day to be perfect for Alyssa.

The celebrant began by welcoming our guests, and as he did, Alyssa blushed brightly. I wondered if it was the first time she'd even realised they were present. She glanced across everyone, tears springing to her eyes as they met back with mine.

I grabbed her other hand and held them both tightly, unwilling to let go now that I was so close to having my dreams fulfilled. Even then, with every eye in the place on us, it was impossible to completely quell the nerves. Oddly though, I wasn't nervous about what I was about to do. No, instead it was a desire to not fuck something up accidentally that made my hands shake. I barely paid attention to the celebrant as he said all the required bullshit.

Finally, it came time to say my vows. We had agreed—despite my unease with the idea—to write our own. Unfortunately, I had to read mine first. Begrudgingly, I released her hands and unfolded the piece of paper on which I had unleashed my heart. A better man may have been able to memorise the words, but I was more concerned with getting them right than knowing them by heart. My hand shook so much it was hard to read them.

"Alyssa." I had to stop as my voice quivered. I cleared my throat and tried again. "In my life, I have faced the unexpected and made many mistakes. Through my trials, I have learned that you are my safe place to land. You are my heart's keeper, and despite the pain it caused you, you treated it with care throughout our separation.

"From this day on, I choose you, my sweet Alyssa, to be my wife. To live with you and laugh with you; to stand by your side, and lie in your arms; to bring joy to your heart, and warmth to your soul; to bring out the best in you always, and, for you and our daughter, to always be the most that I can be."

As I spoke the words, the rest of the room disappeared. There was only Alyssa and me. I was making her an earnest promise, one I never wanted to break.

No, that I *wouldn't* break.

"I promise to laugh with you in good times, to struggle with you in bad; to console you when you're downhearted; to wipe away your tears with my hands; to comfort you with my body; to mirror you with my soul; to share with you all my riches and honours; to play with you as much as I can until we grow old and, still loving each other sweetly and gladly, our lives come to an end."

I folded the piece of paper back up and slid it into my tuxedo pocket. I clasped one of Alyssa's hands so she could feel the truth in my words. As it always did, her touch steadied my nerves, and I managed to give her a tender smile.

Alyssa took a deep breath then launched into her vows. She kept her hands steady and her eyes on me as she spoke.

I could feel my eyes burning with emotion as she recited her words.

"I choose you, Declan, as my best friend and my love for life. I promise you my deepest love, my fullest devotion, and my tenderest care. Through the pressures of the present and the uncertainties of the future, I promise to always be faithful to you.

"I promise to love you completely, to commit to you fully, and to support you absolutely. I pledge to respect your unique talents and abilities, and to lend you strength for all of your dreams.

"Today, I join my life with yours, not merely as your wife, but as your best friend, your lover, and your confidant. Let me always be the shoulder you lean on; the rock on which you rest; the companion of your life. From this day on, you shall not walk alone. My heart will be your shelter, and my arms will forever be your home. As I have given you my hand to hold, I give you my life to keep."

I squeezed her hand gently and she smiled as a tear ran down her cheek.

Refusing to relinquish my hold on her, I guided our joined hands up underneath her veil and swiped gently at her tear with my finger. The crowd watching us no longer existed. I was in my own perfect bubble with her. Time stretched on endlessly and I didn't want it to end. I vaguely heard the minister saying something, but I was no longer listening to him. It wasn't until I heard a titter from the crowd and felt Flynn nudging my back that I realised something else was needed.

With a flutter of nerves, I turned to Flynn. He was holding out Alyssa's wedding ring. I grabbed it off him carefully, not wanting to drop it and look like a tool in front of everyone. When I twisted back to Alyssa, she offered me her left hand. I repeated what the celebrant said as I slid the plain gold band onto her ring finger. "To marry the person you have set your heart upon is a joy unparalleled in human life. Alyssa Celeste Dawson, take this ring as a sign of my faith and my commitment to our love, and share this joy with me today."

Alyssa pushed a wedding band onto my finger as she repeated the same promise.

I turned back to Flynn and he passed me another piece of jewellery. I ducked down onto one knee and motioned for Phoebe to come back over. It was maybe a little unorthodox, but I wanted to show my commitment to her as well as Alyssa.

When she was in front of me, I looked her in the eye. "Phoebe, you are the light of my life. I promise to always be the best daddy in the world. I will do everything that I can to make you proud of me. I will protect you, cherish you, and support you in everything you choose to do in your life.

"No matter what happens from this day forward, I will always be your daddy, and I will always hold you high in my heart. You mean the world to me. I promise you that I will always love and honour your mummy, and I will always be there for both of you. I am proud to be your daddy." I grabbed her hand gently, wrapping the little gold bracelet around her wrist. "I love you, my baby girl."

She wrapped her arms around my neck and kissed my cheek before skipping off to show Aunt Ruby her new jewellery.

I stood back up, seeing tears flowing down Alyssa's cheek unchecked. With a smile on my lips, I wiped them away softly. She leaned against my hand and the moment was fucking perfect.

The next words of the celebrant were without doubt the best words I had ever heard.

"I now pronounce you husband and wife. You may kiss the bride."

I eagerly grabbed the corner of Alyssa's veil and lifted it off her face, resting it onto her back. I placed one hand on her nape, snaking the other around her waist. I pulled her in to me, twisting at the last second to dip her as my lips hit hers. I moaned against her as I realised this was the most important kiss of my life—our first kiss as a married couple.

I lifted her back up and set her on her feet, softly kissing her plumped-up lips once more.

Ruby and Flynn each took one of Phoebe's hands and led her back down the aisle. Alyssa and I followed close behind, accompanied by a chorus of cheers.

"Are you happy?" I asked Alyssa quietly. It was a ridiculous question considering the smile plastered widely across her features, but I had to be sure.

"Deliriously." She turned to me and her eyes were flooded with tears. "I never dreamed . . ." She trailed off but she didn't need to finish. I understood.

I refused to let go of Alyssa's hand as we met the photographer at the entrance. She shut the doors behind my wife so we could get some photos on the grand staircase and beneath the chandelier. Finally, we went through the doors to the waiting limo. It was only a short distance to the Botanical Gardens, but I didn't want anyone to get sweaty between the wedding and the reception.

Once we reached the gardens, the photographer arranged a series of photos. We spent almost two hours in various poses, smiling and laughing together. It was actually kind of fun, but I hated the fact that Morgan couldn't be there and that Flynn would be smiling out from our wedding photos instead. Because Eden had stayed back to look after Morgan, it felt as if our lives in Sydney had no representation at all.

As the sun started to set and the city lit up, we walked to the Goodwill Bridge and had a few more photos there against the backdrop of the river and Southbank.

After the photographer was satisfied that we had captured enough memories, we headed back to the limo and drove to the Suncrest Hotel. The photographer got a few more photos in front of the entrance before we all headed back upstairs to the ballroom. The room was closed off—all of our guests were already inside.

We waited as the photographer went ahead, closing the door behind her. Before I knew what was happening, I heard the MC announcing Ruby and Flynn. They walked in together to a round of polite applause.

Then the MC started our chosen song for our introduction. "And now," he said. "It gives me great pleasure to introduce to you, Declan and Alyssa Reede."

My stomach twisted and my heart leapt hearing her name alongside mine in such a fashion.

I tugged Alyssa forward into the room filled with our family and friends.

Without warning her what I was going to do, I dragged Alyssa into the centre of the room and spun her around gently. It was all I could do not to spin her right back out of the door and to our suite in the hotel.

After one more kiss in front of everyone, I led Alyssa over to the bridal table and pulled out her chair for her.

The MC took over proceedings, instructing the room that any time anyone clinked their glass with a spoon, Alyssa and I were supposed to kiss. This of course led to immediate glass clinking, especially from the boys in my pit crew team. I leaned over and kissed Alyssa's cheek. There was a general cry that I could do better than that, so I guided Alyssa's lips to mine and kissed her with every ounce of passion I could muster.

The MC then went on to explain the order of events before announcing the food was due to be served.

"Thank God," Alyssa murmured beside me.

It was barely a minute later that our meals were laid in front of us. Alyssa dug into her food almost the instant it was set in front of her.

"I haven't eaten since breakfast," she explained to me between mouthfuls that were neither ladylike nor matched her picture-perfect appearance. It only reaffirmed my desire for her. "I'm famished," she finished.

I cast my eyes around the room at our family and friends. I watched, smiling, as Ruth and Mum doted over Phoebe down one end of the table closest to the bridal table. I was dumbfounded to see my father sitting at the table farthest away from us. I didn't know who had invited him, but I was shocked as shit to see he had actually turned up. Although I didn't really want him there, I was thankful that at least his skank Hayley wasn't with him.

Overall, the dinner was great and the service was impeccable. The night was passing as fast as the wine was flowing. Before I knew it, it was time for the speeches. I glanced anxiously at Curtis, knowing he was first up to the plate. I also knew that there was no one to give a speech on my behalf.

Fuck. My. Life.

CHAPTER TWENTY-SIX

PROS AND CONS

AS THE MC introduced Curtis, Alyssa placed her hand over mine in a soothing gesture. She must have noticed the tension in my body, because she gave me a small knowing smile when I looked at her. She was a vision in white, and the reminder that she'd agreed to be mine forever just a few hours earlier helped to relieve a little of my anxiety. Nothing Curtis could say would take that away from me

Even that thought wasn't enough to force me to relax enough to keep from gritting my teeth as I watched Curtis take the wireless microphone though. He staggered a little as he reached for it.

"I can't believe my little girl got married today," Curtis started. It almost sounded like he was choking on his emotions or that he was drunk; I couldn't work out which. "But then, this is what she wanted. She has always been stubborn when it comes to getting what she wants. When she was little, she would dig her heels in about almost anything and once she'd chosen a path, it was all but impossible to stop her.

"The first day she saw Declan, her first day at Browns Plains Primary, she came home and told us about her hero. When we'd asked her what her hero had done, she responded that he picked her first for a sport. From that day on, Declan became a near-permanent inclusion in our family. If he wasn't at our place, she was at his. Back then, I always thought this day was a foregone conclusion. Everyone thought so. It was easy to see their devotion for one another. I thought nothing could ruin it.

"But then he left her."

His statement hung in the air like a bad smell, and he allowed it to fester. Ruth reached over to him, grabbing his jacket and whispering something, but he just dismissed her with a wave of his hand.

He took a sip of his drink and people were starting to wriggle in their seats uncomfortably by the time he started again. "I remember everything about the night he left. I can still see it all as clear as day. It was a Wednesday night. They'd fought the weekend before. Alyssa had called him regularly to try to talk it out. Everyone assumed it was only a matter of time before they were back together again. Like always. Every night that week, I heard her sobbing herself to sleep. I remember so clearly wishing I could comfort her but knowing I would never be able to."

He stopped, taking another swig of whatever he was drinking. Drunk was starting to beat out choked up with emotion in my mind. Why had anyone thought it was a good idea to let him give a speech?

"She went out that night, to meet Declan, and when she came back, she was different. She was hollow. The daughter I'd raised was gone, leaving a mere shadow in her place."

I could see the mortification on Alyssa's face, and I wanted to stand up to stop him from saying anything more, but I wasn't sure that it wouldn't make it worse.

"This isn't the speech Mum wrote for him," Alyssa muttered. "He promised he'd read that one."

Even as she spoke, Curtis continued, "The look on her face when she came home that night." He shivered. "I *never* want to see that look on anyone's face again for as long as I live. For weeks after that, she would barely even move. The first time she showed us any real emotion, anything solid to demonstrate that she was still alive, was when she told us about the baby. *Babies . . .*" he trailed off. Ruth tried once more to grab the microphone off him, but he pulled it away and continued talking. Because of the shifting microphone, his voice blared louder than ever as he said, "I blame Declan for everything she went through after that night. Everything she lost, he owes to her. I never want to see my baby girl shattered like that again. Now, I propose a toast: may Declan never again break her heart so utterly and completely again."

Utter silence followed his toast, but the emcee picked it up quickly.

"Join me in a toast to the bride and groom," he said as cheerfully as he could manage under the circumstances. "May their joys be as bright as the morning, and their sorrows but shadows that fade in the sunlight of love."

At his words, everyone stood and toasted.

The emcee looked almost afraid as he said, "And now we'll hear a few words from the groom."

I swallowed deeply and stood. The words I'd prepared were useless in the face of Curtis's speech, so I decided to speak directly from the heart. I took Alyssa's hand as I raised the microphone to my lips.

"Alyssa, I've made stupid choices over the years, but I'm not an idiot. I know I hurt you, and you know I will never forget how deeply.

"I will forever regret the pain I caused you, and I will always mourn with you what we both have lost.

"But through our separation, I have come to better understand the depth of my love for you. I understand what it is like to live apart from you, so I will *never* take you for granted. What I said in my wedding vows was 100 percent true. If I ever forget a single word of them, please remind me.

"You and Phoebe mean the world to me, and I will never hurt you. You are the keeper of my dreams and the guardian of my soul. You hold me safe from all the troubles which threaten to overtake my mind. I can never thank you enough for what you have done for me with the simple act of agreeing to be by my side for the rest of my life. I love you. I know my toast was supposed to be directed at my new family, but I can't toast to that." I pointed in Curtis's direction. "So instead, I propose a toast to *you*, Alyssa. You and Phoebe. You are my life, my love, and my family."

There were murmurs around the room after the toast.

I passed the mic down to Ruby who was being introduced by the emcee. I wasn't sure which way her speech was going to go. I just hoped the Declan bashing didn't continue. I didn't know how much more I could stand before I just shouted, "Fuck the lot of you," and whisked Alyssa off to our suite.

"I've known Declan and Alyssa since they were both around fifteen. I have seen them in their highs, and their lows." Ruby looked pointedly at Curtis. "When Declan arrived in Brisbane last November, I would never have expected to be on his side.

"But when I warned him not to break her heart, he did something to me that no one ever does. He answered back. I told him to back away from Alyssa so she wouldn't get hurt, and he fought for her. I knew right then that I'd encountered a changed man.

"Since that day, I have borne witness to his utter devotion to his girls. I know the path hasn't always been easy for either Alyssa or Declan, and I know that mistakes have been made by both of them along the way, but I can unequivocally say no one will ever love Alyssa the way Declan does.

"He has been unwavering in his course to get his life back on track with Alyssa, and I think he should be praised for the bravery and commitment he has shown along the way. Especially considering the bumps in the road, like magazine articles which anyone with half a brain could instantly see was nothing more than fabrication and lies." She glared at Danny, and I groaned into my hands. "I toast to the happy couple. May the best of your yesterdays be the worst of your tomorrows."

Most of the guests were stunned into silence and the rest were laughing raucously—not that I could see anything fucking funny about it. The speeches were supposed to be an opportunity to share insights and, to be honest, I'd been hoping for a bit of a love-in from them. Ruby's should have been filled with fun anecdotes about Alyssa. Little moments of insight into the times I'd missed. I may have been expecting a little too much, but I really had wanted something more than what we had: a pro- versus anti-Declan debate.

"It'll all be over soon," Alyssa whispered into my ear. "We'll be in our hotel room, and I'll show you how happy *I* am about all this then."

Swallowing down my surprise at her words, I grinned. She always knew the perfect fucking things to say.

I expected Ruby's toast to be the last, since it wasn't like Flynn knew enough about me to have much to say. But once Ruby was finished, the screen that had been set up to show photos of Alyssa and me at various stages of our lives on a constant slideshow suddenly went blank for a second before Morgan's ugly mug filled the screen.

"Squirt," he said, moving a little and wincing in pain before he spoke. "I'm sorry I couldn't be there for you in person. You know if the docs had given me clearance, I would have been there in a heartbeat."

I nodded stupidly, not knowing whether it was a two-way feed or not.

"I haven't known Declan for as long as some of the people gathered in that room, but I've known him long enough to see that Alyssa was made for him. I've seen him do some pretty crazy stuff." He laughed, no doubt remembering some fucked-up thing we'd done together. I rolled my eyes; as if the anti-Declan people gathered in the room needed more ammunition against me. "But since reuniting with Alyssa, I've seen a change come over him. He's softened in some ways, but he's so much stronger in others. On the track, he is more focused and determined than I think I have ever seen him—even if he *is* just driving a Mini."

He chuckled to himself.

"His strength and commitment to his family are second to none. Even though it's something I never expected to see, it is clear he is devoted to not only Alyssa but also to Phoebe.

"Alyssa, I know we didn't get off to the best start, and I have to apologise again for what I did. It was stupid, inconsiderate, and I can't even begin to try to justify it. All I can say is that I did it during a time when I didn't understand love properly. Before I knew how much hurt the one you love can inflict on you. Love can cut you so deeply that you think there is no way you will ever survive the injury, but it can also heal you. I know this because I have seen you heal Declan in ways that I never thought possible. In ways I hadn't even known he was broken.

"I'm sure he won't ever admit how broken he was; perhaps he doesn't even understand it himself. I never realised until you came back into his life. In fact, if you'd asked me a little over a year ago, before Queensland Raceway last year, I'd have said he was in complete control, unbroken and unbreakable. But in making him stronger, you have demonstrated just how vulnerable he was. I hope we can begin to mend the bridges I have broken, because you are important to the two most important people in my life.

"It says on this piece of paper that Eden gave me that I'm supposed to toast to the bridesmaid, Ruby. I can't see you, I had to prerecord this, but I'm looking at your picture in *Gossip Weekly*, and I have no doubt you are smoking in your dress. To Ruby, for being there for Alyssa now and always."

I stood and toasted Ruby, giving her an extra round of applause. The emcee grabbed control of the night again, and everyone else seemed as relieved as I was that the speeches were behind us.

Before long, Alyssa and I were called over to cut the cake. We waited for the photographer to take what felt like 101 photos. Then after the official photographer was finished, we had to pose for all the amateur photographers amongst our family and friends. Finally, it was time to cut the damn thing, but it almost seemed a shame to take a knife to the three-layer masterpiece covered in sugar flowers.

The cake was whisked off as soon as our hands left the knife. We had ordered mud cake so it could be served as dessert. While it was off being sliced, diced, and garnished with cream, we were directed to the dance floor. The night was flying by in a haze.

The emcee gathered the crowd before starting the music, lowering the lights and setting the spotlight on us. "Please welcome to the floor, Mr. and Mrs. Reede for their first dance as a married couple."

"Mrs. Reede," I said as I offered Alyssa my hand in invitation. Even though I had known what was coming, I was blown away by the emotions that coursed through me as I guided Alyssa in front of me to dance to "Ocean Wide" by The Afters. I was glad that the music was a decent speed, because it allowed me to lead Alyssa smoothly around the floor with what little rhythm I had. Every few seconds, I had to swallow down the emotions that threatened to burst from me.

Alyssa didn't know, but I'd listened to the song over and over in the car. I wanted to be able to sing the lyrics to her as she danced. There was a reason I'd selected the song after many hours of deliberation; it was *our* song. It told our story more succinctly than I ever could.

At first, I twisted Alyssa around and gently dipped her as I serenaded her. The song was an extension of my vows. Before long, the rest of the world fell away, and it was just Alyssa and me swaying gently in our own private bubble. I brought her hands to my chest, pressing them gently so her palms rested over my heart. I dipped my head down and infused every word I sang with all the meaning I could muster.

We swayed against each other through the chorus and continued even after the music had faded away.

"I love you so fucking much, Lys," I whispered to her, causing her to giggle. It broke the moment, but it had to; if the intensity weren't broken somehow I probably would have taken her right there in front of all of our guests. I figured that wasn't exactly the sort of "first dance" they wanted to see.

"Wow," the emcee enthused. "Feel that love! Let's keep the lovefest happening, with the daddy-daughter dance. And just in case you are wondering, there is a bit of a difference tonight because all the songs were specially requested by the groom."

I dropped Alyssa's hand, but didn't leave the dance floor. Alyssa looked uncertainly at me, but I just winked at her and indicated she should go to Curtis. I headed in my own direction as the song started. I'd picked the music for this dance too, and had stumbled onto a song named "Call me Papa." It was a nice slow song but with a surfer-style sound. I held out my arms in invitation for my own daughter, wrapping my arms around her and pulling her up to my height. I slotted her into place on my hip and headed around the dance floor with her in my arms.

Out of the corner of my eye, I saw Alyssa and Curtis dancing too; there seemed to be a little bit of tension between them. Alyssa's entire body seemed rigid, much more so than in our dance just a few minutes prior. For our part, Phoebe and I just danced and giggled until the song came to a close.

"Aw, how's that?" the emcee called. "Any sweeter and we'd all have cavities."

I flashed Alyssa a smile as the next song came on. The emcee invited everyone to dance and announced the cake would be served in fifteen minutes. The music switched up to some party starters. Some people took to the dance floor, while others returned to their seats. But almost everyone took at least a minute to come up to either Alyssa or me to congratulate us and wish us good luck.

I was so fucking happy. The formalities were largely over and done with, and Alyssa was officially mine. It was just time to let down our hair and party. We mingled and mixed, but found ourselves constantly drawn back to one another.

Inevitably, every time we came within a few metres of each other, someone would clink their glass and we would have to kiss. My only complaint in the whole deal was that my cock was getting harder and harder each time. I wanted her so fucking badly, but I knew I was still a few hours off claiming her to consummate our marriage. I considered asking if she would complain about running upstairs to the suite for a quickie, but I knew it was impossible because people would realise we were gone.

After the cake, Mum brought Phoebe over to say goodnight. We both kissed her and hugged her, wishing her happy dreams.

We'd already organised that she would stay in the hotel, but in a room with Mum. That way, she'd be close by if anything happened, but—barring an emergency—Alyssa and I would be uninterrupted.

All.

Fucking.

Night.

Long.

Alyssa raised her eyebrow when she noticed my smirk, but I just shrugged. She knew what I was fucking smiling about. In fact, she was thinking the same things. I could tell by her come-fuck-me eyes.

I circulated some more, spending a few minutes chatting with my teammates. Danny and Hazel came over and gave me their best wishes.

"I'm sorry that you didn't make the two poles needed to claim your honeymoon," Danny said. "I had hoped to be able to offer you a chance to get away."

I nodded. "Yeah. I'd been looking forward to going back to London too. It changed so much for me."

He sighed. "If only circumstances had been a little different. But it might be a good thing in the end. I'll need you at a few track days coming up if we're going to get things tuned properly."

I grinned, knowing it was his way of letting me know I was still in the V8 for the enduros. I wasn't sure exactly how he was going to manage it with Morgan off the track, but I was willing to go for a little trust. "Tell me when and I'll be there. What happened to Morgan is all kinds of fucked-up"—in ways I wasn't sure Danny was willing to acknowledge—"but we'll get through it."

He nodded and looked across the room. I followed his eyes and saw him regarding Alyssa. "She really is good for you. You two are made for one another, don't let anyone tell you any different."

"Don't worry, old man, I won't." I slapped his back gently.

"Less of the 'old man', thank you very much." Danny laughed. "I can still call everything off."

I shrugged. "Yeah, but who else could you get on such short notice?"

"Oh, you'd be surprised."

"Okay maybe, but would they have my mad skills?"

He laughed.

Alyssa came over and touched my arm lightly. "I think they want to do the bouquet toss now."

I nodded and clasped her hand. I never knew how much fucking organising went into this wedding shit. Even while I was supposed to be having fun and socialising with guests, I was being pulled from pillar to goddamned post.

The emcee gathered all the single girls around and lined them up. Alyssa turned her back to them and threw the bouquet into the air. Before it had even landed, the girls were clamouring for it, roughly pushing and pulling at it and each other. It wouldn't have surprised me if they'd started sinking their teeth into one another next.

Women were fucking scary sometimes.

After watching that ruckus, I was a little worried about the next part of the evening. Alyssa had no idea what Morgan and I had hatched up, but I had absolutely no doubt that she would not approve in the least. I was glad that Flynn had seen the humour in it and agreed to go along with it when I'd told him about it.

Finally, one of Alyssa's uni mates emerged victorious with the tattered bouquet held aloft. I shook my head at the lunacy of it.

Then my heart plummeted as I watched them bring out the chair and set everything up for the garter toss. Fuck. I was looking forward to having a little fun, but I hoped I'd still have a wife at the end of it.

CHAPTER TWENTY-SEVEN
NAUGHTY NASTY BOY

ALYSSA SAT ON the chair provided for her. It had a white cover over it that fell to the floor so no one could see what was hidden underneath. The emcee started the song for the removal of the garter, and I began performing my stripper moves for Alyssa, which brought a delicious shade of pink to her skin as she no doubt recalled our night out where we turned stripper for one another.

I glided my hand down Alyssa's dress then gently clasped her ankle. Making a little circle there with my thumb, I offered a subtle promise of things to come later. I slid my hand further up her leg under the cover of her dress and teasingly ran my fingers softly along her inner thigh.

"All right," the emcee started, "he's going in! Now remember, Declan, you want the garter. Just the garter—not the whole belt."

I lifted Alyssa's dress over my head and settled in to the wonderful little space with her barely covered legs.

Taking my time, I kissed Alyssa's thigh to distract her while I fished under the back of her dress and reached below the sheet for the box of goodies Flynn had left under the seat while the girls were fighting over the flowers.

I pulled a tiny, lacy G-string out of the box first. I continued to run my lips along Alyssa's thigh while I lifted my "prize" out from under her dress before shaking it a few times then pressing it into Flynn's hand to show the crowd.

"Not those, Declan!" the emcee exclaimed as the crowd giggled, and I lapped it up with a few waves of my hands. "Aim a little lower maybe?" he suggested, and I gave him a thumbs up in reply.

Never breaking the contact of my lips on Alyssa's skin, I reached back under her dress and into the box. I wondered if I would be able to push my lips higher. The thought of being covered by her dress kissing her pussy in front of everyone made me hard as a fucking rock. My lips inched a little higher and I snaked my tongue out and licked a patch of flesh that was showing just above her lace-topped stockings, enjoying it all the more when she squirmed slightly in her seat.

Knowing I had to keep focused on the gag or I'd never get through it all, I pulled the Yellow Pages out of the box and slid it along the floor between my legs and out into the open. The book had been hard to find, but totally worth it.

"Well," the emcee quipped, "we can see that he sure lets his fingers do the walking."

I reached back into the box, knowing the next lines of the song were about icing her cake. To match the music, I reached in and pulled out a novelty toy cake that sang "Happy Birthday" when it was switched on.

When I held it aloft, I heard the emcee chuckle into the microphone. "Are you giving her your special frosting, Declan?"

I nodded emphatically under the dress, feeling the material rise and fall rapidly against my back as I did.

Knowing I wouldn't be able to get away with the jokes too much longer, not if I still wanted Alyssa to like me at the end of the night, I reached in for the second to last item we'd placed in there. I clasped the toy cat and held it up as high as I could without relinquishing my hidey-hole before passing it to Alyssa.

I heard the emcee laughing hard before he gathered himself enough to speak. "Well, it's obvious *someone* knows how to handle her pussy."

Alyssa whacked the back of my head, and I shrugged against her. Sure, I felt a little guilty for her embarrassment, but I was making sure our wedding was one to be remembered. Besides, I was quite happy in my private tent. Just me, her legs, and her . . .

With one more kiss to her thigh, I pulled the remaining item, a black lace garter, free and held it aloft as I climbed out from beneath Alyssa's dress. I decided I would definitely have to revisit there later—hopefully not too much later. I turned back to wink at her, and I knew a goofy-arsed grin was probably plastered across my face, but I didn't care.

Her actual garter remained in-situ and I would remove it in private . . . preferably with my teeth. The garter I held in my hands was a spare I'd put into the box because there was no way in hell I was going to throw anything that had rested against her thigh into a pack of salivating wolves.

I flung the garter high into the air aiming at the loosely gathered men then pulled Alyssa into me.

"You're going to pay for that later," she threatened in a low whisper.

"I was counting on it," I whispered back before kissing and nibbling on her lobe. I was harder than fucking cement, and I didn't care who saw it.

"Come on, let's dance a while," she said, rolling her eyes and pulling me gently to the middle of the half-full dance floor.

I felt the weight of someone's stare on us as we moved, so I turned to look at the crowd. Curtis stood off to the side, unabashedly watching us as I twirled her around the room. One look at the snarl on his lips told me that the time was right for my other plan. My "get back at Curtis for being a wank during the speeches" plan. In truth, I'd arranged it long before then, but his performance during our special moment gave me all the ammunition I needed to follow it through.

With a wave and a nod, I let the emcee know I was ready for my next song request.

Less than a minute later, the song I'd selected began to play. I swept one hand slowly down Alyssa's spine before pushing against the small of her back to press her tightly against me. With the other hand, I brushed the hair off her neck and as the song started, I breathed the lyrics for "Let's Make it a Night to Remember" by Bryan Adams against her neck.

As we danced, and I whispered the lyrics to her, I rubbed my hands along her bare shoulders. Slowly, I traced my fingers from her nape to her wrists and back up again.

I twisted her around so her back pressed into my chest. With her moving against me, I wrapped my arm around her waist and ground my hips against her arse. When she dropped her head back to rest against my shoulder, I guided her hands behind her and onto my thighs as I continued to caress her stomach.

Alyssa was letting herself go, relishing in the sensation and the music.

She turned her head toward mine, closing her eyes and moaning softly. I kissed her cheek then made my way down her throat, breathing the words across her skin.

I turned my head to make sure Curtis was watching his daughter unravel in my arms. I knew what I did to her—it was the same thing she did to me. My hard-on was pressed firmly into her arse as I splayed one hand out across her throat and chest. The other pressed her stomach firmly, guiding her body ever closer to me and pinning her there. There wasn't even a centimetre of space between us. If I'd been able to, I would have held her in place right there as I fucked her silly.

"Fuck, I want you, baby," I whispered to her, pulling her closer still.

"Mmm," she agreed. "I need you."

"Soon, baby, soon," I promised as I pressed my lips against her collarbone.

I risked another glance over at Curtis. He was attempting to look distracted and keep his eyes anywhere but firmly planted on us. However, I could tell by his rigid stance and the way he kept clenching and unclenching his fists that he could see me. No doubt, he was disgusted with our display on the dance floor, but I couldn't care less.

The way Alyssa's body reacted to mine, and mine to hers, was a big part of the reason I wasn't afraid of forever with her. Not anymore. I'd come to cherish our magnetic draw, the one that had once scared the living shit out of me.

With a sigh on my lips, I ran my hand along her thigh on the outside of her dress. I brought my mouth back to her throat before turning her around to face me again. I kissed her hard, forcing my tongue into her mouth. She responded, returning every ounce of passion I gave her. It was almost surprising that we didn't rip our clothes off then and there. God, I wanted to.

After the song ended, Alyssa backed away, panting slightly. Her eyes held the promise of a long night to come.

I turned away from the crowd so I could adjust the now-painful lump in my pants.

In the two seconds I was turned around, Alyssa was whisked away by Jade and Ruby for something or other I didn't understand—although I was certain I had heard the words "Jager" and "bombs" used repeatedly in their conversation.

I turned around to mingle some more, and came face to face with Curtis.

"I know what you're trying to do," he said in a gravelly growl.

"I'm not trying to do anything." I shrugged innocently.

"It's bad enough to know that you two are married now, I don't need to be subjected to *displays* like that one."

I rolled my eyes at him. "Alyssa is my *wife*. I will touch her where I want, when I want, and how I want."

"Even against her will?" He had seized onto my words and bent them to his own requirements.

I scoffed. "If she'd asked me to stop, I would have. I mean, I don't know what you think you were watching, but that was hardly 'against her will'."

"I was watching you use my daughter as a pawn against me."

I grew angry. "Fuck, Curtis, not everything in this world is about you."

"Are you denying it?"

"I just wanted to fucking dance with my wife, is that all right

253

with you? Or do I need to get a signed permission slip even though she is a grown-arse woman?" I was beginning to shout. Obviously, it caught my father's attention from the corner of the room because he came barrelling up to us.

"Curtis, you need to lay off Declan!" he snapped.

"God, Dad, just leave it," I warned. I didn't need his lame-arse protective bullshit now, especially when I didn't even understand why he was at my wedding at all.

"Maybe if you'd set a better example of treating people with respect, we wouldn't be here right now," Curtis snapped back.

"How dare you! You know nothing about what I have taught Declan."

"I know enough police to be able to look at the evidence in question and make informed judgements."

"Please, guys." I forced myself between the two of them. "Knock it off, you're causing a scene."

"I'm just telling Curtis here that he should get over it." Dad crossed his arms.

"Get over it?" Curtis fumed. "You weren't the one who had to force-feed their child after their heart had been broken. Who had to wake at three in the morning to check on them and make sure they hadn't done something stupid. Who lay awake until all hours of the morning, every single day, listening to the utter heartbreak of their daughter who sobbed herself to sleep. Who had to help his grown daughter do the simplest things—like shower and change. You have no idea what Ruth, Josh, and I went through to look after Alyssa during those first few weeks after the breakup. You will *never* understand."

"So tell me," I whispered. Everyone had hinted at Alyssa's pain, but having Curtis spell out why he was so angry at me so plainly hit hard. Had I really left Alyssa in that much agony? And that was all before she'd found out about her pregnancy. "*Help me* understand."

"What?" he exclaimed in surprise.

"Tell me everything she went through. I want to know."

"Why?"

"Because I want to know. I want to know everything about Alyssa. I know you don't believe me, but I love her. I don't want to skip over the bad stuff. I want to know it all," I answered honestly. "And I want to never do it again."

"I don't . . ." Curtis sighed. "I don't know if I can go into all the details."

"I'm not going to force you to. I just want you to know that I'm not going to ignore what happened, I'm not trying to, and I don't expect you to just get over it."

I glared at my father; I couldn't believe the things that he'd said. I was furious that he was even trying to defend me when he didn't understand—when he was a big part of the reason that I'd run in the first place. I turned my back to him, facing Curtis. I heard Dad huff and ignored him as he stormed off.

"I understand why you are pissed off at me," I said to Curtis. "Really, I do. I get it. If someone fucked with Alyssa, or Phoebe . . ." I growled. "I would fucking rip them a new one."

Curtis chuckled before quickly stifling it, obviously not wanting to appear on my side.

"I'm not asking for you to forgive me for what I've done," I continued, rolling with the momentum of the small piece of goodwill I felt from him. "I'm just asking you to give me another shot—to try to make right what I fucked up. That's what Alyssa has done."

Curtis regarded me carefully.

"It doesn't fucking matter to me," I said. "I'm a big boy, and I can handle your hatred. Fuck, I've had worse, but don't you think it'd be easier on the girls—hell, on everyone—if we could just get along?"

He hummed but didn't say anything more.

Alyssa came back over to us, giggling her head off. Whatever Jade and Ruby had done with her had clearly pushed her over some edge and now she was drunk.

"You two aren't fighting again, are you?" she asked, pointing her finger between Curtis and me.

I stifled my grin at her playfulness and shook my head. "Us?

Fight? Never!"

Alyssa snorted. "You two hate each other."

"That's not true, love," I said. "I don't have a problem with Curtis . . . he has a problem with me."

"For good reason," Curtis added gruffly.

"For good reason," I agreed.

Our eyes met briefly, and I felt the chasm between us shrink — just a little.

"Just so you know . . . I want you in me all night long tonight," Alyssa murmured in my ear. Her intent may have been to whisper, but it came out more like a yell.

I tried not to grin at the look on Curtis's face as her words sunk in.

From then on, the night couldn't end fast enough for me.

CHAPTER TWENTY-EIGHT

FIRST NIGHT

ALYSSA SOBERED UP a bit as the night wore on. By the time it started to wind down, she was only a little tipsy.

We said our farewell to everyone in a unique twist on the receiving line. The emcee gathered all the guests into a large circle, and we had a few minutes one-on-one with everyone as we made our way around the circle, kissing one another when our paths intersected.

For our goodbyes, Alyssa and I had selected songs that would reflect the positivity we felt about our marriage. We hoped that it would help everyone realise we were happy and allow us to move on to the next phase of our lives without the baggage of their disapproval.

Each person had at least a few words of encouragement as I greeted them. Out of the corner of my eye, I could see Alyssa. Just before we intersected, the song changed and by the time we came to each other the lyrics were telling us not to be afraid. I wasn't now.

There was nothing I wanted more than to spend the rest of my days with Alyssa.

Finally, the party wound down and the last few guests left. Alyssa tried to find Ruby for a final farewell and thank-you, but was told she'd already left for the evening. The last of the stragglers were being led out by the hotel staff, so Alyssa and I were free to go whenever we wanted.

Grinning widely, I grabbed Alyssa's hand and led her to the elevators. I chuckled as I realised how eerily similar it was to the first time we'd stayed at the Suncrest Hotel together—right down to the room card burning a hole in my tuxedo pocket. Only this time, there were no nerves, only anticipation.

The elevator doors opened and, hand in hand, Alyssa and I stepped into our future.

Before the doors had even slid shut, we attacked each other. The short trip to our floor was almost torturous after the hours-long seduction we'd already experienced. However, it was long enough for Alyssa to undo my tie and rake her hands through my hair to pull my lips against hers.

When the elevator dinged at our floor and the doors opened, I swept Alyssa up into my arms and carried her down the hallway toward our room. I set her on the floor long enough to negotiate the door open then picked her up again to carry her across the threshold.

"Mrs. Reede," I whispered reverently. I couldn't comprehend or contain the love and excitement that threatened to burst from my chest at the mere utterance of those words.

Her lips crashed into mine, and she began tugging on the buttons of my shirt. I could see she was eager for more, for us to lie skin to skin, and I was willing to oblige. But I wanted one thing first.

"Stop," I whispered into her mouth before putting her back onto the ground again. I circled around her slowly, taking in the magnificence that was Alyssa in her wedding dress. I stopped when I stood directly in front of her, and reached out for her hand. She complied willingly, and followed my slow backwards steps. I silently led her to the couch and motioned for her to stop. I sat in front of her, taking another moment to drink her in with my eyes.

"There's something I want to do before we get undressed."

She tilted her head in question, but I was sure she'd catch on soon enough. We'd had hours of foreplay during the reception, so I was sure neither of us needed more. I raised my arm toward her slowly before trailing it down the length of her dress to the floor. The material was soft and smooth beneath my fingers, but I knew her skin would be softer and smoother still. I curled my hands underneath her dress before running my fingers back up along the length of her leg. My other hand made short work of the buttons on my tuxedo pants and I lifted my arse just high enough to push all the clothing off the lower half, down to my knees. I reached for Alyssa's panties and pulled them off swiftly, leaving her deliciously bare under her dress.

She took the lead then, planting one knee on the couch to the left side of me and guiding her hips over mine. My fingers traced small patterns on her arse as she lowered herself onto me. I closed my eyes and hissed at the feeling of relief that washed over me as I buried my cock deep within her.

We moved together slowly, alternating between staring at each other intently and kissing each other tenderly. It wasn't rushed; instead, I enjoyed every sensation. Even though I was desperate for her, I was certain we'd last for a long time. While we moved, I committed the image to my mind. I couldn't get over how fantastic she looked while fucking me in her wedding dress.

AFTER THE session on the couch, which was over much too quickly for either of our liking, Alyssa led me into the bedroom of the suite where I had stripped her slowly. The pace was more due to all of the buttons and fasteners on her dress and underwear than any desire on my part to go slow. I was more than ready for round two.

When I had Alyssa naked aside from her jewellery and garter, I peeled my own clothes away piece by piece. Alyssa watched me appreciatively while removing the diamonds and gold that seemed to be dripping from her, and put them all away in their proper cases. Then she held out her hand, complete with her new gold band, and led me into the bathroom.

I helped pull the metal from her hair—I still remembered the booby trap that had awaited my unsuspecting hands the night of our formal—before removing her garter in my special way and helping her into the shower.

We caressed each other under the cascade of water provided by the large, ceiling-mounted showerhead. The water caused Alyssa's make-up to run, so I grabbed the face cloth and gently wiped at her cheeks and mouth. She pouted her lips as I ran the cloth over them, and it was too much temptation for me. I dipped my head down to meet her mouth, hoping desperately to convey my passion with the right combination of lips and tongue. It was like a private code only we knew.

I stepped back from her and blew out a breath. She grinned wildly up at me, and I knew she was feeling all the same things I was. Effectively nothing had changed from a week before, and yet everything had. We would still be living together just as we had been. Only now it would be as man and wife.

I handed Alyssa the face cloth, and she swiped at her eyes a few times until all the black was gone.

"There's the woman I love," I murmured, touching one finger to her chin.

"Was my make-up that bad?" she joked.

"No, definitely not. But you don't need all that goop on your face to be beautiful."

She smiled at me before turning the water off.

We slipped into the large, fluffy white bathrobes provided by the hotel and stepped back into the bedroom, completing the few tasks that needed attending to before we could devour each other. As we moved around one another wordlessly, we watched each other hungrily—both eager for the moment we would begin our seduction anew.

Once the urgent tasks were seen to, it was like a siren went off to say that it was time to come together again. We raced at each other so quickly that it was almost as if a starter's gun had been fired. Bathrobes were discarded with reckless abandon, limbs tackled each other for dominance, and mouths moved steadily along skin.

No matter how much I had, I wanted more.

No matter how much skin I touched, it wasn't enough.

When we were done—not satisfied because being fully satisfied was impossible when it came to Alyssa—we fell asleep wrapped together.

I held Alyssa tightly under my arm as she murmured in her sleep, muttering repeats of all the things she'd said during the day. Our wedding day. I could hardly believe it had come and gone already, and now she really was mine.

I thought back over the event and realised I wouldn't change a thing. Despite the shittiness and fuckery of the speeches, it all ended exactly where I'd wanted it to. I twisted out of Alyssa's grip a little before turning over to hover above her. She looked peaceful as she slept soundly with a grin on her face. A slight sheen of sweat coated her naked body—no doubt a result of our hours spent together before falling in an exhausted heap.

God, I could take her again. I was ready, aching for her. It would have been selfish to wake her up and demand more attention. I nuzzled against her side and softly kissed her neck. She murmured in her sleep and rolled closer to me.

I stroked one hand along her side, trailing my fingers over her body. She tilted her hips up to meet mine.

"Lys," I whispered as I moved my kisses down to her chest.

Her hands moved to my hair, drawing my lips closer to her skin. I risked a glance up at her face and caught her smiling sleepily at me.

"Anyone would think you're ready to go again," she said with a chuckle.

Fuck, sometimes being selfish was totally worth it.

Although that didn't mean that I wouldn't make it worth her while.

CHAPTER TWENTY-NINE

EXPECTING

"GOOD MORNING, SLEEPYHEAD." Alyssa greeted me with a cup of coffee in hand, sitting on the couch almost precisely where she'd fucked me for the first time as my wife. She was wearing the bathrobe again and her hair was wet. She'd obviously been up for a while and had showered while I was sleeping in. "I ordered breakfast. It just arrived."

I thanked her as I leaned over to kiss her before helping myself to a plate of bacon and eggs from the room service trolley.

"Sleep well?" she asked, unable to wipe the grin off her face.

I nodded as I chewed my breakfast through a wide smirk of my own.

She watched thoughtfully as I ate.

"What's on the agenda today?" she asked as I finished off the last few mouthfuls. She reached forward to place her cup back onto the trolley, showing off a significant amount of thigh and boobs.

"I suppose staying here and fucking like animals is out of the question?"

She laughed.

I raised my eyebrow at her to let her know that I wasn't joking. Even after our effort last night, I wasn't nearly finished celebrating our marriage.

She stood and walked over to me before placing my plate back onto the tray. She rested her legs on either side of mine and positioned herself onto my lap. "We can't do that *all* day."

"We can try." I kissed her neck slowly, feeling myself growing harder against her.

A knock on the door startled both of us, and we jumped to our feet. Being the most dressed of the two of us, even though I was only wearing shorts, I stood to answer it while Alyssa ducked into the bedroom.

Mum and Phoebe stood waiting outside the door. "Hey, baby!" I said, scooping Phoebe into my arms.

"Morning, Daddy," she said, rubbing her eyes as if she'd not long woken up.

"I'm not interrupting, am I?" Mum asked.

I shook my head. She was, but I wasn't about to let her know that.

"I come bearing news," Mum said. "Where's Alyssa?"

The bedroom door opened again. I looked over and saw Alyssa stepping out wearing a loose-fitting sundress. "I'm here. What is it?"

"It's Ruby," Mum said, her face breaking out into a grin. "She went into labour last night, but we didn't want to disturb you two until we absolutely had to. She's at the hospital as we speak."

"Oh, my God," Alyssa exclaimed. "Oh, my God!" She looked over to me. "Declan—"

"I know," I interrupted. "Go finish getting ready, and then we'll go."

"Do you want me to watch Phoebe a little longer?" Mum asked as Alyssa disappeared back into the room.

I nodded. "That would be great, if you don't mind. It'll be one less thing for Alyssa to stress about. I know this visit isn't going to be easy on her." I was just hoping for a perfect outcome for mother and child, but positive or negative, it wasn't going to be an easy day for Alyssa.

Mum touched my cheek tenderly. "My little boy is well and

truly grown up now, isn't he?"

I shrugged her off. I was doing what I thought Alyssa needed; that's all that mattered to me.

Within ten minutes, Alyssa and I were in a taxi on the way to the Royal Brisbane Hospital. Alyssa was a bundle of nervous energy beside me. Her foot bounced excitedly as we travelled.

"Are you okay?" I asked as the taxi dropped us at the front door. It was our second visit to a hospital in little over a week. At least this was for a much happier occasion than Morgan's accident. I hoped.

Alyssa nodded as she looked up at the building in front of her. She'd spent so much time there in Phoebe's early life that just the sight of the place was bound to cause her some panic. I rubbed my hand gently on the small of her back.

"It's fine," I murmured quietly into her ear. "Everything will be all right."

"How can you know that for sure though?" she asked, turning to me, and I saw all of her fears, and all of the reasons she didn't want to try for more children, written on her face.

"I don't," I admitted. "But sometimes you've got to have a little bit of faith."

With a little nod, she took a deep breath and walked into the hospital with me in tow.

AS SOON as news went out that Alyssa and I had arrived, she was whisked off to join Josh and Ruth, who were already helping Ruby in the birthing suite. I was all for it, until I realised it left me alone in the waiting room with Killer Curtis.

"Didn't expect to see you again so soon," Curtis muttered, looking up over the top of a magazine at me. He seemed surprised to see me there, as if he thought I'd simply drop Alyssa at the hospital and leave her there alone. As if I could.

I didn't know how long we were going to be thrust together, but I figured it was fate or the universe or some shit trying to tell me to play nice and try to patch things up with my father-in-law.

"We came as soon as we heard."

"You may as well sit," he muttered. "We could be here for a while. Ruth was in labour with Lys for almost a whole day."

A day stuck alone with Curtis? I was in some kind of hell. Or maybe I wasn't. Maybe it was just opportunity knocking loudly on the door.

"How about when Alyssa was in here?" I asked. "With the twins?"

He flinched at my mention of Alyssa's hospital trip before looking back at me and meeting my eyes. Something he saw there must have given him encouragement to continue.

"No, her trip was much quicker, because of the emergency. She was taken straight into surgery to have her caesarean. She wasn't even awake when the babies were born."

I sat on the single-seater lounge across from him. "Were you there for her?" I asked.

"Everyone came. Everyone who cared about her was there when she needed them."

"No," I said adamantly. "Not everyone. You have to believe that. I still cared for her. If I had even the slightest inkling of what was going on with her, and if my head wasn't in my own arse at the time, I would have been there for her too."

"If you cared so much, why did you leave? You had to know it would hurt her."

"Of course I did," I snapped, instantly regretting my tone. I buried my head in my hands. "I just thought it would be better for her in the long run," I admitted. "I didn't think I wanted—" I laughed bitterly at the stupidity of my younger self, and of what it had cost me. "Well, everything I've got now actually."

"I'll never understand how you could walk away so callously. Even if you didn't know about the pregnancy and all that other stuff, how could you just leave? How could you not even call?"

I sighed. I didn't think I would be able to adequately describe my thought process from when I'd left Alyssa. I barely understood it myself anymore. I turned the question back on him. "Before I left, would you have said I loved her?"

He regarded me for a few moments. "Yes," he answered somewhat begrudgingly.

"Then you have to understand that I didn't 'just leave.' Leaving was the hardest thing I've ever had to do. That's exactly why I know I'll never do it again. I can't live without her, Curtis."

"I still don't understand how you could do it," he admitted.

I chuckled without mirth. "Neither do I, but it seemed like the only logical solution to my seventeen-year-old self. And then I was too stubborn and hurting too much to fix it."

He hummed then sat in quiet contemplation for a few minutes. I thought the conversation was over until he finally spoke. "So, how do you know you're not going anywhere this time? How do you know that you won't think it's the best thing for her again?"

"I can't do that to her again because I know now that she needs me as much as I need her. And I need her like I need oxygen."

I could see by the softer expression on his face that he at least realised that I wasn't going anywhere, and maybe that walking away hadn't been as easy for me as he'd originally thought. Maybe we still weren't quite back to where we had been before my disappearing act, but we were getting closer.

We sat in silence for another hour before Alyssa came back out from the delivery room.

"It's a little boy," she said. A smile lit her face. "Mum and bub are both doing great. Ruby's just being moved to the ward now, but she's asking for you, Dad."

Curtis's smile matched Alyssa's, and for half a second, I felt like I was intruding on a private moment. He stood and walked past her, giving her a little squeeze as he went.

I waited as Alyssa walked over to me and sat on my lap, sighing softly. I wrapped my arms around her gently, trying to anticipate the different emotions that could overwhelm us both.

"Are you all right?" I whispered, giving her the opportunity to admit it privately if she wasn't. I was worried that seeing Ruby give birth to a healthy baby boy would cause her some grief.

She gave me an odd look, no doubt questioning the reason

behind my gentle probing. I chuckled softly. "Never mind, I just thought . . ."

She nodded quickly, her expression showing she had realised where I was coming from. "Really, I'm all right. In fact, I'm better than all right. It was just so special being in there and seeing how different things can be."

I stroked her hair as she leaned against my chest.

"I guess it's nice to be reminded that not every birth leads to a death."

I kissed her hand, uncertain what else to say.

"Ruby was asking for you too."

"Really?" I asked, somewhat shocked.

She laughed. "Of course, don't sound so surprised. You're family now."

"Whether they like it or not?" I chuckled.

Alyssa laughed in response.

"Shall we give your folks a few moments alone with them?"

She nodded against me.

"How about we go to the gift shop while we wait?"

"You really are a softy, you know?" She laughed before standing and offering her hand to me.

"Just don't tell anyone." I winked at her. "I've still got a reputation to protect."

WE FOUND an extremely overpriced gift basket with a little blue teddy bear and some chocolates in the hospital gift shop. We decided to stop for a quick drink while we waited, to give Ruth and Curtis some extra quality time with the new family. Alyssa told me about the part of the birth she had witnessed—although I suspected that she edited the story heavily. A fact I was thankful for.

After our drinks, we headed back to the maternity ward and found Ruby's room. We quietly made our way through the door, just as Ruth and Curtis were leaving. Ruth touched my shoulder lightly as they passed. Alyssa's hand grabbed on to mine, and she tugged me the last of the distance to Ruby's bed.

Ruby was sitting upright in the bed with a tiny bundle of blankets cradled to her chest. She looked exhausted but thrilled.

"Hey, Mummy," Alyssa murmured, bending down to kiss Ruby's cheek. "How is he?"

"Who? Noah or Josh?" Ruby giggled. I couldn't say when—or if—I had ever seen her so full of joy and peace.

Josh stood up from the side of the bed just then, juggling a pile of clothes, nappies, and a bag.

"Did someone say my—" His eyes fell on me, and he stopped cold.

Alyssa squeezed my hand; I wasn't sure whether it was in support or to tell me to say something.

"Congratulations," I said, smiling in what I hoped was a winning way.

Josh seemed to regard me for a moment before smiling weakly in return. "Thanks."

I felt both Alyssa and Ruby relax as the tension broke a little.

"May I?" Alyssa asked Ruby, who paused for just a second before nodding and passing the bundle across.

Alyssa's well-practised hands cradled the baby in what I assumed were all the right places to ensure nothing happened to him. I watched in amazement as a small face and two clenched fists poked out from the blankets. He was so tiny. I couldn't image Phoebe ever being so small, even though I knew logically that she must have been.

In fact, she'd probably been even smaller.

Alyssa squished in beside Ruby on the bed, bouncing and shushing the baby like a pro.

She was such a natural mother, born to it. I felt the renewed sting of her confession about not wanting more kids. Had she felt a similar pain each time I'd professed the same desire to be childless? If so, I was hurting her long before I left.

Ruby and Alyssa sat side by side on the bed whispering about something or other, and I felt like I didn't belong. I wasn't about to go up and clap Josh on the back for a job well done—awkward congrats were the best Alyssa and Ruby could hope to expect.

Ruby nodded about something and then Alyssa stood and walked closer to me. "Here, why don't you have a hold?"

She held the baby out to me, and I shook my head.

She looked almost amused. "Why not?"

I bit my lip before whispering, "What if I hurt him?"

She smiled in what I was certain was meant to be an assuring way. "You won't hurt him."

I looked at the little bundle again. He seemed so small and fragile, like the slightest breeze would break the bundle of blankets apart.

"If you're worried, sit down," Ruby said, smiling widely. "It makes it easier."

I sat in a vacant armchair in the corner of the room, swallowing nervously. Josh skulked by Ruby, watching intently—as if daring me to make a false move. Once I was seated, Alyssa explained how to hold my arms before placing the baby into them. The bundle felt almost weightless once I was cradling it on my own.

I watched as his little eyes—wide and unfocused—roamed all around the room and his tiny fists clenched and unclenched by his mouth.

"You're a natural," Ruby cooed. "Remember that hold for when you have more of your own."

Alyssa shifted nervously beside me, but I didn't think Ruby or Josh noticed. I kept my mouth shut. If she hadn't told them that she didn't want more kids, I wasn't going to spill her secret. Instead, I just ignored Ruby's statement. Luckily, Noah seemed to have impeccable timing and started crying before the silence had become awkward and questions were asked of either Alyssa or me.

Alyssa lifted the baby out of my arms and passed him back to Ruby before we made our excuses to leave. I knew any tentative peace between Josh and me wouldn't last if I tried to stay while Ruby breastfed.

We had a quiet journey back to the hotel where we went straight to the room that Phoebe shared with Mum. We didn't even really discuss it, but being around one new little family made us both long to be with our own. We got Phoebe ready before heading out to Southbank and the museums together. It wasn't exactly how I'd envisaged spending the day after my wedding, but afterward I couldn't have imagined it any other way.

CHAPTER THIRTY

HONEYMOON

PHOEBE COULDN'T HAVE been more excited with the news about her new little cousin. At least once an hour, while at Southbank, we were asked when we would be going to see little Noah. We wanted to take her to see him, but didn't want to disturb the other mothers in the maternity ward with an excited toddler. We agreed instead to wait for him to go home—Ruby had already indicated, repeatedly, that she wouldn't be staying in hospital long.

We stayed one more night in the hotel and when it was time to check out the following morning, we packed up the Monaro and headed back to see Mum in Browns Plains. Once she'd finished her holiday, she'd moved back into our old house, and when we returned from our day out, she discreetly let me know that she had plenty of space if we wanted to stay. I agreed readily because I could easily see that Alyssa wanted to hang around to help Ruby once she got home from the hospital. We had another week before either of us had to be back home for work.

It was surreal entering my old childhood home knowing that

someone else had lived there for so many months. All of the furniture was still in place, but the personal touches that had made it our home were still packed away in boxes. I didn't know whether Mum would actually pull any of it back out or if she would just begin filling the shelves with new memories.

We settled in quickly to my old room, and almost immediately realised the convenience of having a live-in babysitter—a convenience we were sure to take advantage of during our honeymoon. Mum seemed to appreciate the fact that we were newlyweds, declaring within moments of our arrival that she wanted to buy something for Phoebe, not-so-subtly taking Phoebe out for a few hours, leaving Alyssa and me alone.

Alyssa snuggled close beside me on the couch, and I wrapped my arm around her shoulder. She sighed contentedly as she settled into place.

"It's been a big week," she murmured.

I nodded against the top of her head. "But a good one."

I could feel her grin against my arm. "So, you're not concerned that Noah's arrival overshadowed our wedding?"

I laughed. "Are you kidding? It means I'll never have any problem remembering my nephew's birthday."

"Your nephew," Alyssa breathed. There was so much emotion in those two small words.

"What is it?" I asked, not sure that I understood why she seemed overwhelmed by my choice of words.

She shifted her body weight before climbing onto my lap. "It's just nice hearing you talk about Noah that way. Even though we were getting married, part of me worried that you might never accept my family again after the hard time they gave you," she admitted.

"Our family," I murmured, to ease her concern. I kissed her nose gently to punctuate my point.

"Our family." She grinned, sliding back onto the couch and settling comfortably back against my side.

We sat in silent awe for a few moments, allowing the enormity of the last few days to overtake us.

Alyssa turned to me. "Are you as curious as I am about the presents we got?"

I chuckled. "God, I thought you'd never ask."

We spent the next hour slowly opening each item. It wasn't nearly as much fun as I'd hoped though. In fact, Alyssa suddenly switched to methodical bridezilla mode so fast it was almost comical—except for the fact that I was copping the brunt of a full-frontal assault. Before I even touched the first gift, I was under very strict instruction not to separate the presents from cards, because she needed to make a list of who gave us what so she could write the appropriate thank-you notes.

Near the bottom of the pile, I found a gift from Danny and Hazel. It was an achingly familiar envelope. As I slid it open, my mind was immediately filled with the memory of opening the similar envelope in Danny's office while being reprimanded for my on- and off-track behaviour at Bathurst the previous year. That one had contained the tickets for the trip that had changed my life forever.

At the thought, I made a note to send Danny an extra thank-you card; he had given me the best gift of all. It was through his interference that Alyssa and Phoebe were back in my life.

As I examined the contents of his present, I realised it really was almost identical to the previous one. The only difference was that this time there were *three* tickets to London—premium economy rather than business—leaving Sydney in late January.

"But I thought you didn't meet the requirements?" Alyssa asked quietly when she saw what I held in my hands.

I shook my head. "I didn't."

"Wow. That's really generous of him."

"You're not wrong," I murmured, turning the key to Danny's apartment over in my hand again. I didn't know why he'd chosen to give me the London trip even though I'd failed to earn it, but I appreciated the gift nonetheless. I grinned unthinkingly as I imagined reliving some of the better parts of that trip.

"What are you thinking about?" Alyssa asked quietly, her voice low and husky, making me wonder if she was having similar thoughts.

"I was just remembering the huge stainless-steel island in the kitchen." I grinned and met Alyssa's eyes.

She flushed slightly and looked away, gently biting her lip. "That apartment had a great icemaker," she murmured.

I was impossibly hard as images of Alyssa writhing beneath me while I tortured her with whiskey and ice sprung to my mind. I adjusted myself quickly, but my movement didn't escape Alyssa's keen eye. I slid the key and plane tickets back into the envelope and placed it on top of our little pile of treasures before standing and reaching for Alyssa's hand.

"What?" she asked.

"I think it's time for a break." My hard-on was straining desperately. I needed her.

"And what, *exactly*, did you have in mind for our break?" she asked as I pulled her to her feet and straight into my arms.

"Oh, I think a re-enactment is in order," I whispered against her cheek as I ran one hand along the front of her body.

She shivered lightly beneath my touch, which I took as a sign that I was good to go. I scooped her up into my arms and carried her to my old bedroom, and then dropped her lightly onto the single bed. I quickly turned and ran into the kitchen, grabbed the ice trays from the freezer, and tipped the contents into a glass. I hunted around the pantry for some whiskey, but came up empty. All I could find was some Baileys, but in the end I decided that would have to do. After all, Alyssa was ready and waiting for me. I poured the Baileys over the ice then carried it to the bedroom.

I started to undress as I walked down the hall, shifting the glass from one hand to the other as I yanked my t-shirt off. After I entered the room, I kicked the door shut behind me. My heart began to pound, and I dropped my shirt in surprise when I took in the sight of Alyssa lying down, waiting for me.

She'd taken the time I was in the kitchen to undress down to her bra and panties. She was stretched out along the bed with her legs crossed at the ankles and her hands tucked up behind her head. It meant that I had a great view of . . . well, of almost every part of her.

The cold glass in my hand was all but forgotten as my mouth went dry in anticipation of kissing her all over. I stepped forward to cross the room to get to her, but in my haste I tripped over my discarded t-shirt. I managed to right myself seconds before I toppled onto my arse, but my momentum carried me—or more specifically, the hand holding the cup full of ice and Baileys—into the end of the bed. Before I could stop it, I was covered from neck to groin in the freezing-cold mixture.

"Motherfucker!" I cried as my nipples puckered instantly, and my dick shrank away in shock.

I looked up at Alyssa, expecting her to be at least a little concerned. Instead, it looked like she was struggling to hold in her laughter—struggling and failing. She was suddenly in a fit of hysterics.

"Are you 'right?" I asked, unable to stop the snark in my voice.

She pressed her lips together and actually managed to stifle her laughter.

"Sorry," she murmured as she scooted up the bed to get closer to me. "I shouldn't laugh." Her hands reached out for me, grabbing my waist and pulling me closer to her. She pressed her mouth against my stomach, and I felt her wet tongue swirl gently against me.

"Mmm," she hummed. "Baileys?"

I tipped my head back and pushed my hips toward her. "Uh-huh." I sighed as she continued her ministrations on my stomach.

She ran her tongue from the waistband of my shorts to my abs in one smooth motion.

I moaned with desire as she licked the cool liquid off my body.

She hummed again as her hands came to rest on my waist. She pulled me closer to her, holding me tightly as her mouth moved around my stomach and up to my chest.

I put my arms around her, and my hand tangled into her hair. I pulled her gently upward as I dipped down, desperate to taste the Baileys on her tongue. I held her body closely against mine, and she gasped a little as the liquid soaked into her bra and coated her skin.

I pulled back from the kiss and grinned evilly. "Now you're covered too."

She gaped at me. "You did that deliberately."

"Not initially, but it was too good an opportunity to pass up." I shrugged.

"Ooh, you know that means war, don't you?"

I laughed. "Bring it."

She leapt up from the bed, practically jumping onto me.

I caught her easily and she wrapped her legs around me. I held on to her with one arm, using the other to tickle her.

She squirmed against my arms, fighting me roughly to the point where I worried I might drop her.

I wrapped my arms around her tightly and kissed her, distracting her long enough to move back over to the bed. I lowered her most of the way to the mattress, but let her fall the final distance—wanting to see more of that mock-anger burning in her eyes. As soon as I let her go, gaining the desired reaction, I climbed on my hands and knees to hover over her.

She looked up at me indignantly for a second.

"That's it, buster," she threatened teasingly. She tried to tickle me, but I twisted away and got her first. We wrestled like that for a few more moments until we were both panting from exertion and sticky from the drying Baileys.

When our eyes met, we had one of those perfect moments. We both smiled at each other before I moved the hair away from her face and lowered myself over her. Our lips brushed over each other's gently at first, soft and tender, before building to a crescendo.

Then everything but each other was forgotten and all our remaining clothes were shed. We began to move together as only we could. I was intent to lose myself in her, and held her eyes captive to declare it.

AFTER OUR afternoon delight, Alyssa and I showered then started dinner. The rest of the evening flew by as we showed Mum and Phoebe some of the gifts we'd received, including the trip to London.

As soon as we'd read Phoebe a story and tucked her into bed, we headed to bed ourselves. I would have felt guilty that we weren't spending much time with Mum, but she'd announced that she was going to the movies and would be home late. I knew she was just giving us our space, but I didn't like thinking about her imagining what I was doing to Alyssa.

"Ruby goes home tomorrow," Alyssa murmured as we lay in each other's arms drifting toward sleep.

I hummed, knowing she wanted to say more.

"Maybe we can take Phoebe over there to meet Noah?"

"That sounds like a good idea," I agreed.

"He really is a cute little baby, isn't he?"

I shrugged. How could I do anything more? After all, I had no real basis for comparison. He was the first newborn baby I'd ever really seen up close. He was just tiny and pink, not to mention just a little bit wrinkly.

"You don't think so?" she asked. I felt her head turning to appraise me.

"I honestly don't know. I've never been around a baby before."

I felt her head rest against me while she turned thoughtful. "I forget sometimes."

"Forget what?"

She sighed. "That you missed out on all those early experiences."

I was silent. I knew her well enough to know her tone wasn't accusatory—she wasn't blaming me for not being there—merely stating the fact. I resisted the urge to apologise again. I knew there had to come a time when we were able to move past it and talk about it without apologies and pain. It was a fact that I hadn't been there. An inescapable and horribly shitty one, but a fact nonetheless.

"They're hard work," she said after a few minutes.

"What are?"

"Babies. They're a lot of hard work."

"I don't doubt it," I stated.

"They're worth it though."

I thought of Phoebe. Even though she was no longer a baby, she was proof that it was worth the hard work. I smiled. "I don't doubt it."

We fell back into silence again.

"And you'd want more kids?" she murmured thoughtfully after another couple more minutes had passed. "Even with the hard work?"

I thought before answering. I knew her stance on the issue, and I didn't want to upset her. "I would love to have another child *with you*. But you don't want more kids, right? And I can live with that."

"Yeah. That's right," she whispered before snuggling back against my chest.

ALYSSA CALLED Josh early to arrange our visit. Ruby was expected to leave the hospital around lunchtime, so we organised a dinner date with them. We explained to Phoebe that we would go see her new little cousin Noah at Uncle Josh and Aunt Ruby's later that evening.

We then spent the day with her, taking her around to all her old favourite places. To ensure she knew she had to be gentle around Noah, we explained how delicate babies were.

Despite our misgivings that she might inadvertently hurt him, Phoebe was amazing with her little cousin. She was enthralled by him, making us promise that she could come and play with little Noah when he got bigger. Ruby even set her up on a chair with some cushions and supervised her while Phoebe cradled him.

Phoebe was in heaven, and again I felt my stomach drop with the sensation of knowing she'd never have a little brother or sister of her own to hold. I would happily support Alyssa's decision, but I still felt a pang of loss at times. Alyssa must have seen the look in my eyes, because she nestled into me before guiding my arm around her waist.

EACH NIGHT as we headed to bed, Alyssa seemed thoughtful about something, but each night our lust took over, and we barely spent any time talking. The few times I tried to raise the issue of her distraction, she'd told me it was nothing, and I let it drop because I didn't want to push it. The couples' therapy we'd had played in my mind, Dr. Henrikson's reminders of when to probe and when to back away stabbing at my memory. It wasn't causing us arguments, so it wasn't something I needed to push her about.

Yet.

By the time we got back to Sydney, we'd both spent plenty of time with family. We'd even been able to spend a little time with Ben and Jade.

We soon got back into the usual grind, only now it was different. Rather than being Declan Reede and Alyssa and Phoebe Dawson, we were the Reedes. It probably meant little to a casual observer, but it meant the world to me.

When I went back to work, I was quickly whisked off for a series of physicals and other tests required by the contract I'd signed to be back in the ProV8. I still wasn't sure how Danny was going to arrange it when Morgan was likely going to be out for the rest of the season, but if my dream was still going to be realised I wasn't going to complain. Track days were booked for the end of August to give me the opportunity to test my reflexes back behind the beast before tackling Phillip Island.

Unfortunately though, my wish to see the track from the inside of a V8 hit a snag a few days after getting back to work.

"Do we have a problem?" Danny asked, his voice cautious.

"What do you mean?" I asked, genuinely uncertain what could be concerning him. Aside from the two incidents in Townsville, my behaviour had been exemplary.

"These turned up on my desk this morning." He tossed an envelope across the table at me.

I pulled open the envelope, tilting it and watched as a half-dozen photographs spilled out across Danny's desk. I leafed through them quickly, but immediately realised what they were when I saw a girl pawing at me. Memories of my horrid birthday weekend came flooding to my mind. "This isn't—"

"Isn't what it looks like?" he asked, with one eyebrow raised.

"No! It's not," I said.

"What, pray tell, do you think it looks like?"

"Well, first off that I was actually enjoying myself." I screwed my nose up.

Danny chuckled once. "See, what I think it looks like is that you found yourself in a situation you weren't comfortable in. Maybe even a situation someone else put you into."

I looked up at Danny in shock. Was he actually taking my side on something? I nodded in response to his words. "I guess it is what it looks like then."

"The oddest thing about these photos is the timing of their arrival," he mused.

When did they arrive? The question was on my lips, but died in my throat as Danny shook his head ever so slightly. I got the impression something bigger was happening, something I didn't quite understand. I knew who'd sent the photos—there was no doubt in my mind it was Hunter, because he'd been the one to orchestrate the surprise for my birthday. I debated telling Danny so, but realised it wouldn't be any benefit. Danny obviously wasn't concerned about the photos. I just wasn't sure exactly what his concern was then.

"I have to be honest with you, Declan," he said after a beat, breaking my train of thought by grabbing the photos back and pushing them into his desk drawer. "When I found out about the new rule regarding the endurance racers, you were the first person to spring to mind. I thought it would be a good way to be able to keep your skills up, without risking the loss of any major sponsors."

Still mute with confusion, I nodded.

"Unfortunately though, circumstances have changed since then. There are situations at play now which limit my options."

"Okay?" I couldn't figure out exactly what he was trying to tell me. I wished he would just come out and tell me what he was thinking, but obviously there was some reason he wouldn't. Or couldn't.

"Ideally, I would have run you in Morgan's car. You two have very similar racing styles and complement each other well. You've shown that in many enduros in the past."

I nodded, agreeing completely with him. Morgan and I had a way of communicating which, short of my disastrous showing the previous year, had seen us be very successful.

"Unfortunately, Morgan has been ruled out for the rest of the year."

I'd seen Morgan just a few days earlier. He was healing well and with physio was expected to be back for the following year's race calendar, but the team doctor was taking his lead from the physiotherapist, who was unwilling to sign a release before Phillip Island.

Morgan was desperate to be back, but until he had that clearance, he couldn't race.

"This means we will only have one car running in the endurance races." He paused for a moment, seeming to weigh his words heavily before speaking. "I spoke with Hunter yesterday about the potential for you to co-drive with him at Phillip Island."

I scoffed. "That would have gone down well."

His eyes fell to his desk drawer for less than a fraction of a second.

I trailed the same path before turning back to him. I could have sworn he nodded slightly.

"How would *you* feel about that situation?" he asked after a moment's pause.

"Driving with Hunter?" I clarified. "You're kidding, right?"

"I can't see any other options, I'm afraid," he almost sounded apologetic.

"But with Hunter? He hates me, and believe me, the feeling is more than mutual."

"I just don't know what other option I have." He sighed.

"Put me in Morgan's car then."

"I'm afraid it's not that easy, Declan. I'd need to approve the move with all the sponsors, organise rebranding if any wanted to change. And I'd still need to find two other drivers, one for each car.

It's just not viable."

My dream was slipping further away with every word he spoke.

"With more time. More resources. Maybe a car that wasn't under a sponsorship contract, maybe I could consider it."

I nodded as my hope ebbed to the floor. "So, it's off the cards?"

"Unfortunately, the opportunity for you to drive under the Sinclair Racing banner is off the cards. I've offered the seat to Smythe."

It didn't surprise me that the rookie driver from the Production Series had been tapped. It was a good way for him to cut his teeth in ProV8s. While that thought turned over in my mind, something else struck me. Danny's words were odd, and seemingly chosen with care. There was something he wanted me to read between the lines. I couldn't race under the Sinclair Racing banner . . . but I could still race. How? It didn't make sense. There was no way I could —

I blinked as the thought struck me. There was one way. It was bold. It was fucking *stupid*. It would be hard, but I thought I might be just lucky—and crazy—enough to pull it off. I grinned wickedly before outlining my idea to Danny. A small, knowing grin crossed his lips halfway through my plan. When he actually looked thoughtful and didn't refuse me outright, I guessed it meant I'd read the situation correctly, or at least had suggested something that was actually workable. The task I was suggesting was monumental, but having Danny onside for the plan would make it easier.

Life was all about the small victories.

CHAPTER THIRTY-ONE

JUST MANAGING

IT HADN'T TAKEN long for the enormity of what I'd asked of Danny to hit me. We'd had another meeting just as everyone else was leaving for the afternoon to discuss it further. Having assumed halfway through the day that I'd actually completely misread the situation, I'd expected him to rubbish my plan outright.

But not once did he tell me not to do it.

Of course, he hadn't offered me his outright support either, but I wasn't exactly expecting that, especially when I was effectively talking about leaving Sinclair Racing.

Instead, what he had offered me was a glimmer of hope. He'd sat me down and told me all the negatives of my plan. In doing so, he'd outlined, in detail, everything I needed to achieve in order to pull it off.

Almost as soon as the meeting started, under the pretence of him explaining why it couldn't work, I could see what he was doing—giving me a plan of attack.

Once I'd realised where he was going with it all, I pushed aside the part of me that wanted to tell him to shove it up his arse. I bit my tongue and grabbed a pen and notepad from his desk. While I quickly scribbled notes about all of the work that would be involved to pull it off, he waited patiently then filtered a little more information my way.

I wanted desperately to ask him a few questions and demand some straight answers, but I knew I wouldn't get any—at least not yet. I was going to have to try to read between the lines of what he'd told me for a while. His hands were clearly tied by something—either sponsorship contracts or something else.

My first port of call, after getting Danny's implicit approval, was to see Alyssa. I hoped she would be able to help me somewhat. At the very least, I would rely heavily on her support to get through the difficult times and shitload of work ahead of me. She wouldn't be able to help out too much with the actual legal side of it—like drawing up the contract that I would need—but she could offer her support.

Danny had explained it all to me in our meeting. Apparently, because she worked for Pembletons, the firm that would represent him in the negotiations, she had a conflict of interest and wouldn't be able to help me. I didn't really completely understand what he was talking about, but I hoped that Alyssa would be able to at least point me in the right direction and straighten out some of the confusion I felt over the whole thing. If nothing else, just knowing she was in my corner would do me the world of good.

My mind was in overdrive the whole way home, running through my meeting with Danny and the rest of my day again and again. I kept coming back to the photos. Looking back on it now, I couldn't believe that I hadn't even thought to tell Alyssa about the incident.

It wasn't that I'd withheld the information deliberately; it had been nothing more than an oversight because my entire birthday weekend had been such a shit-fest that the girl Hunter had all but thrown onto my lap had ended up as nothing more than a blip on my radar.

I had to fess up to Alyssa now though, just in case Hunter pushed the envelope even further and tried to send them to her. Not that I thought she'd put any more stock in the situation than

Danny had. One thing was absolutely certain; the photos that had arrived on Danny's desk had come from Hunter. I knew it, and thankfully Danny seemed to know it too.

Obviously, Hunter didn't want me in his car for the upcoming enduros. I actually understood that completely, because I didn't want to race with him either. In fact, I would do anything to avoid the possibility. And shoving two drivers who didn't trust each other into a car was a recipe for disaster.

I wasn't at all surprised he would stoop so low, but I did have to chuckle to myself at the thought of how stupid Hunter had been, showing his hand so early. He'd also clearly demonstrated the key difference between us; if it was honestly in the best interest of the team—and had been my one and only chance to get back in a ProV8 more permanently—I would've sucked that shit up and raced with him. I would've even tried to win, despite the fact that he'd end up on the podium too.

Despite spending the journey home with my head spinning in circles, I was so psyched by the idea I'd had that I was practically leaping out of my skin by the time I arrived. I raced in the front door, intercepting Phoebe as she ran to greet me. I picked her up and spun her around until she squealed excitedly.

"Daddy's got some good news!" I exclaimed, kissing her on the top of the head before I placed her back on the floor.

"What is it?" she asked. Her eyes were wide and full of excitement.

"I'll tell you as soon as we find Mummy."

Phoebe grinned and raced off, leaving me to follow her. I found both of my girls in the kitchen. Alyssa was just pulling out the start of dinner. She welcomed me with a quick kiss and asked me to help her by finding a few items she needed to finish off our meal.

I complied immediately, placing them on the bench before turning to Alyssa and loosely grabbing her hands, bringing them to rest on my chest. My index finger toyed with her wedding band and engagement ring absently as I smirked at her. I couldn't wait to tell her my news, and I knew the perfect way to do it. Phoebe was practically jumping up and down with excitement.

"What is it?" Alyssa asked in response to both my stance and Phoebe's anticipation.

"I'm going to race a ProV8 again." I grinned.

Phoebe started squealing. She was so loud that I barely heard Alyssa's next statement.

"Even with Morgan . . ." Alyssa trailed off.

I knew she'd never be able to finish the sentence. Since our return to Sydney after Townsville, things had become much warmer between the two of them. She felt that she owed him for the thing with Hunter, especially when it had cost him so much. No matter how much Eden, Morgan, and I tried to convince her otherwise, she blamed herself for the accident that cost Morgan the championship and a good portion of the race year.

I nodded excitedly. "Yeah."

"But how?" she asked, looking at me warily. "Not in *his* car?"

She hated the thought of me racing with Hunter even more than I hated the idea. At least I was willing to consider it if I absolutely had to. Which I might not now.

I grinned even wider as I shook my head. "Nope."

"Then *how*?"

"I'm going to be a privateer."

"Huh?"

"I'm going to run my own car."

Alyssa stood blinking at me for a few moments. "But you don't have a car."

"I can rent one for the weekend. And a licence too."

Alyssa stood agape for a moment more before asking, "How much is that going to cost?"

"A lot," I admitted. "But I have a plan."

"Oh, you have a plan, do you?" Despite the scepticism in her voice, I could see excitement dancing just behind the incredulity in her eyes. I'd relied on her support to take things further, and the glimmer of enthusiasm I saw in her fuelled my own exhilaration to dizzying new heights.

I stepped forward and whispered into her neck. "Yes, and it involves spending some quality time with each other after Phoebe's in bed tonight."

She chuckled. "You know I'm almost always up for some quality time, but I don't see how *that* will help you get back in a car."

"Ha ha." I rolled my eyes and turned my attention back to my other girl, the one who wouldn't mock me. "Are you excited that Daddy's going to be back in a ProV8 again, baby?"

Phoebe nodded enthusiastically. "Can I go in one too?"

I turned to see that Alyssa wasn't looking or listening.

I winked at her. "We'll see what we can do."

"THAT'S A big to-do list," Alyssa breathed as I finished my explanation.

"I know. I've got no idea how I'm going to manage it all. I do know I won't be able to get it all done before Phillip Island. So I'm not trying to. Instead, I'm aiming for . . . "

"Bathurst," Alyssa finished for me.

I grinned. I shouldn't have been surprised that Alyssa knew the race calendar so well, especially when it came to *that* race; the anniversary of the crash that had inadvertently led me back to her. I could only imagine the significance of the date in her mind considering how much it meant to me.

"The hardest thing is going to be finding the time to make the calls I need to make," I admitted. "Although in theory Danny is giving me his support, he can't be seen as assisting me. I definitely can't do it at work."

Alyssa bit her lip. "I may be able to help you out there."

I raised my eyebrow at her. Ever since we'd returned from our holiday, Alyssa had been having issues at work. Truthfully, I think she'd been having issues long before then, but hadn't wanted to admit it.

"And just how would you do that?" I asked.

"I need to take some time off work," she started. Her voice was calm and in control. "I . . . " She sighed heavily and something snapped within her. "I just . . . I can't do it," she sobbed. "I can't be there. I can't stand the guilt they give me every day when I have to leave to pick up Phoebe. It's just not fair. I've never been made to feel so *worthless*."

I gathered her up into my arms instantly.

"Shh, Alyssa," I murmured, trying to quell her sobs. I realised she had been holding back so much more than I'd ever imagined, and felt like an arse for not seeing it sooner. For not pushing her a little more. "Tell me about it."

She nuzzled deeper into me. "It's Carmen, she and her *daddy* have been out for me since we were paired up. If she wasn't so incompetent, I'd swear she was trying to make me look bad. Sometimes I think Mr. Kent is the only one on my side."

"Of-fucking-course!" I exclaimed, slapping myself on the forehead for my stupidity. "Kent!"

Alyssa pulled away and gave me a funny look. Probably because she'd poured her heart out and I'd completely changed the subject.

"Sorry, it's just, well, Andrew Kent's son is Dane."

Alyssa's look turned to one of confusion.

"*Dane Kent*," I said, wondering what she didn't understand. "Former ProV8 driver, Dane Kent."

"So?" She sniffed, her tears completely dried up after the sudden shift in the conversation.

"He retired just before I started driving. He was the driver I replaced at Sinclair."

"And?"

I grinned. "Don't you see? He's retired, but he's still in shape. Still able to drive." I paused for a moment, but I realised she wasn't going to see the connection I'd seen in my mind in an instant. "He could be the second driver in my car. That's the biggest piece of the puzzle I've been worrying about."

A smile lit Alyssa's features. It was stunning to watch as her joy started in her eyes and spread rapidly outward across her face.

"Of course," she murmured. "Do you think he would though?"

"I have no idea!" I stood and chuckled a little, feeling a bit like a mad man, but I was too excited about the new plan to care. My sudden realisation made so many things fall into place. It was perfect. "But just think about it if he did. Two ex-Sinclair Racing drivers in the one car staging a stunning comeback together."

"The press would have a field day." She grinned.

"Exactly! Imagine the publicity."

"The sponsors!"

"Fuck, baby," I murmured. Seeing her so excited about me getting back in the car was doing things to me. I swooped back onto the bed, pushing her onto her back as I did. I captured her mouth with mine and kissed her hard. "You and me, we're going to make this work."

Her response was a moan as my erection rubbed against her thigh.

IN THE harsh light of morning, the list seemed so much bigger than it had the day before. The task ahead of me would have been monumental even without having to front up at Sinclair Racing every day for work.

I still had my job in the pits to train for, even though I'd officially been moved from Hunter's pit crew because of our "differences". My boys had all requested the same change so there was a shake-up of the teams, but that didn't mean we weren't required to be at the top of our game. The official word on Morgan was that we were waiting on clearance, but everyone on the team knew the truth; he was definitely out for the season.

While Alyssa negotiated with Phoebe to get her to eat her Weet-Bix, and I packed up everyone's lunch, I suggested to Alyssa that maybe it was time to move on rather than just take time off. I hated the thought of her being unhappy at work. I questioned whether she should hand in her notice and find something else. She looked at me like I'd grown an extra head.

"All I'm saying is that you don't need that fu—stinking job if they can't treat you with respect."

She smiled sadly at me. "But we still have a mortgage to pay, and we still have Phoebe's day care costs."

I crossed my arms. "I don't care."

"But—"

I pressed my finger to her lips to silence her. "We'll manage."

I was quoting the very words she'd used to comfort me after she'd first moved to Sydney what felt like a lifetime ago, but they were as true now as they had been then. As long as the three of us had each other, we had everything we would need.

Since then, we'd saved up a little, even with the cost of the wedding. The small extra allowance I received driving the Mini, plus the few bonuses from my wins, added up to a decent little fallback plan. It wasn't much, and it wouldn't last forever, but it was enough that we could make it work for a while.

She opened her mouth to argue.

"Daddy, can I have apples for school?" Phoebe asked, with her mouth full of mushed Weet-Bix.

"Of course, baby," I answered, turning to throw one into her lunch pack. I glanced back at Alyssa before she could resume her argument. "You have to admit that the bonuses from racing the Mini have helped us get in front. Besides, I'm not pissing away my salary like I used to."

She looked thoughtful for a second.

"And," I continued while I was on my winning streak, "I've still got my cars and a few stocks left that we can sell if we get desperate." I winced as I mentioned selling my babies; we'd managed to avoid losing any so far, but I would willingly sacrifice anything for her happiness.

"And what would I do? Any other law firm would be just as bad. It's the nature of the career."

I shrugged. "Don't work for a law firm then."

"I'm not going to go back to working in a shop."

"I'm not asking you to." I already had an idea forming in my head, but I wasn't sure exactly how she would respond to it.

She sighed. "I worked so hard to get to where I am. To get my degree and be able to use it. I don't want to throw it all away now."

"Then don't." I smirked.

"What are you thinking?"

A splooshing sound told us that Phoebe had taken advantage of our distraction to pour herself a glass of milk; unfortunately, it went all over the floor instead of into the cup.

"Here, let me get that," Alyssa said, grabbing the paper towels from the bench. She poured some of the remaining milk into the cup and began to soak up the mess.

"I have an idea," I said.

Alyssa shook her head slightly. "And that would be?"

"Work for me."

"What?"

"I've never had a manager. Now that I'm on the cusp of a new career as a privateer, I really think I should have one."

"I wouldn't have the first clue about how to be a manager."

"I'm sure it's not hard."

She laughed. "Tell that to all the stressed managers out there."

"What I mean is, the job is all about putting the client's career first and advancing their opportunities. I know you'll have my best interests at heart, so you just need to do whatever needs to be done."

"Like what?"

"Like talking with the sponsors and negotiating contracts for this privateer gig."

She looked thoughtful for a moment until the piece of paper towel in her hands grew wet and attracted her attention anew.

"Besides, managers get a cut of their talent's salary."

She laughed. "And in this scenario you'd be the talent?"

"Of course!"

She stood up and met my eye. "You really think I could do it?"

"Why not?" I asked. "You've got the law degree behind you, so I know you'll be able to read the contracts for me. You're a naturally warm and giving person, and I'm sure the sponsors will respond to that."

"And the fact that it would mean you're able to palm a significant chunk of your to-do list onto me?" She raised her eyebrow.

I chuckled. "Well, that's just an added bonus."

She looked thoughtful. "I don't know, Dec."

"Give me one reason why not."

She bit her lip. "I just don't know if I want everything in my whole life to revolve around your career."

I tried to cover how much her words stung, but I couldn't.

She reached out and stroked my face lovingly, reassuring me silently. "What I mean is that I'm so deliriously happy with the way we are at the moment that I wouldn't want to ruin it by working together."

"It won't ruin anything," I argued. "If anything, it'll make it better, because you'll be less stressed."

She regarded me thoughtfully. "What if . . . something *happened* to you?" She looked at Phoebe, indicating she didn't want to say anything that would worry her, but I realised she was talking about something as in an accident.

I thought about it for a minute. If Alyssa fashioned her career around mine, and then I couldn't drive . . .

The fact that we'd be down from two incomes to none would devastate our finances, but I was certain we'd manage. Somehow.

"Well, maybe you can use me as a test case?" I suggested. "If it works and you like it, then you can try to get a couple of other drivers on board, maybe?"

"I'll think about it."

I smiled. "That's all I can ask. But it would be helpful if you could do it. I mean, God knows I don't exactly read the contracts I'm given. I'd hate to be having to deal with something as important as sponsorship dollars. Especially with the risks I'm facing anyway."

She shook her head with a small, knowing smile on her face. I could tell she was at least partially swayed by my argument. The more I thought about it, the more perfect a solution it seemed, and the more excited I was by it.

CHAPTER THIRTY-TWO

RACING LINE

ONE WEEK.

THAT was all it took for everything to be different.

The first day that I'd planted the seed that maybe she didn't need to work anymore, Alyssa had a deep and meaningful conversation with Andrew Kent and had managed to score his son's phone number, among other things.

She couldn't really explain everything that they'd discussed for confidentiality reasons, but apparently, Danny had called Pembletons as soon as I'd told him my idea. The two men had already discussed the possibility that I would whisk Alyssa away to help me, at least temporarily. Andrew Kent's only suggested alteration to the plan was that Alyssa should take an unpaid leave of absence instead of quitting, stating that her job would be there when she was ready to have it back.

The following day, Alyssa handed in her formal intention for a six-month leave of absence, effective immediately. Not all of the partners were happy, but Alyssa had Andrew Kent's support so she didn't give a shit what the other partners thought.

On the third day, we set up communication central in our home study. We had a fax machine, a two-line phone, a mobile, two laptops, and a desktop computer. We paid for the telephone company to come and install the extra lines we required, even paying double for them to put us as a priority on the list.

By the fourth day, I had a confirmed co-driver, even though I had yet to raise the sponsorship money I would need in order to hire the car from Danny or pay Kent's fees. As expected though, the media went crazy the minute the press release was issued that I was driving as a privateer at Bathurst. Then when we announced that Dane Kent was heading out of retirement to race alongside me a few days later, it went mad again.

By the end of the working week, Alyssa had used the contacts that Danny had unofficially given me to generate some significant sponsorship money. It was more than enough to cover the cost of the car, the signage, the entrant fee, our accommodation, and the insurance. I couldn't have asked for more.

Alyssa had pulled together a minor miracle in much less time than I could have ever imagined, so it wasn't a great surprise to me when she had three clients within the first week. True, one was a driver on hiatus with an injury, one a driver who'd retired almost three years earlier, and the other was me. But nonetheless, for a manager-stroke-publicist just starting out in the game, it was a fan-fucking-tastic start.

Then she used the perseverance and grit that I knew she possessed in spades to find opportunities to promote me that would help to keep the sponsors satisfied. She contacted *Woman's Idea*, the magazine who'd interviewed us months ago, and arranged for them to do an interview with Dane and me. The same photographer arrived on our practise track day and took photos of us in our suits as well as in more casual clothing. Even better, Alyssa had secured a time-for-prints agreement with her, so we got free use of the photos for our promotions.

It was all going so well.

In fact, the only problem with the new arrangement was that I barely saw Alyssa. During the day, she worked her arse off on the phone arranging this, that, or the other, and then at night she would pore over the contracts that came in, reading and rereading any clauses that had the potential to cause us trouble. I honestly couldn't imagine anyone taking better care of me or my career.

"You know, you really shouldn't have signed the first contract thrown at you by Sinclair Racing," she murmured one night over the top of the paperwork she had brought into bed.

"Why's that?" I asked, kissing her shoulder, trying to get her to focus her attention on other things besides the paperwork: namely *me*.

"It really was a stock-standard contract that gave them all the power. I've seen some of the negotiated agreements, and there were *a lot* of clauses they would have been willing to move on."

What she'd said stayed with me as I headed into work the next morning. I wondered whether that was what bound Danny's hands when it came to Hunter, and why he was so seemingly willing to lend his support to my *alternative* venture. Was he unable to do anything to censure Hunter without cause? Was that what he'd meant by needing to wait for hard evidence? Certainly Hunter had been on a tighter leash since Townsville. I would probably never know for sure. One thing I did know was that Danny would never tell me.

THE COUNTDOWN for Bathurst was on.

During the weeks leading up to it, both Dane and I had interviews with morning TV shows, radio, local papers, pretty much anyone that would have us. The words "media slut" were a more than adequate description of us during that time. But it was all worth it for the end goal.

There was, however, one magazine that was champing at the bit to get either, or both, of us, that Alyssa simply refused outright. After all, they'd already made their money off me, through their "star writer" Miss M and her trashy, rumour-filled stories. Each time Tillie or Talia tried to call us, Alyssa was quick to dismiss them.

Of course, that didn't stop them from running the story about my comeback. Only, instead of exclusives, they had to use second-hand information. At first, they made a half-arsed attempt to tar and feather me, but without printing long-dead issues, they had nothing.

It was a crazy time for everyone. I was working on my privateer career in the evenings while still holding down my day job. In the end, I was still signed up to race at Phillip Island, albeit only in the Mini. Because I didn't have to pit for Hunter now, it was set to be a fairly easy weekend. I just worried about Alyssa's safety. I wanted to ban her and Phoebe from attending, but I never could.

In the end, she took the need out of my hands by apologising and telling me she would be too busy to attend—what with Bathurst a little under a month away. Her announcement left me free to concentrate on nothing but my driving. Well, nothing but my driving and avoiding Hunter like the plague.

I finished the weekend at Phillip Island first in the Micro Challenge championship, because I'd managed to claim pole, and then place first, second, and first in the races. It should have been cause for celebration, but there was no time, because the big race was creeping closer and closer.

Somehow there seemed to be more things left to organise each day and nothing ever seemed to get marked off as complete. There were items on the list I'd compiled from Danny's advice that took much longer to arrange. Customised race suits and HANS devices were two items we'd have to order as early as possible because we needed to ensure they had the sponsors' logos on them, but we couldn't order too early or we risked missing a sponsor.

Although Alyssa organised so much other stuff, I was responsible for the design of the car's exterior and the sticker placement. Of course, she helped me a lot with that as well because she knew the sponsor contracts inside and out. She knew who'd been granted major sponsorship and any mandatory placements. It cost a small fortune to have concept designs drawn up of the final car, but it was worth the money because it meant we could get the required sign-offs before spending the money on the vinyl stickers and finding some problem after the car was finished.

Even as everything else fell into place, I was left needing to arrange the team who would support me when I went racing.

For myself.

It was going to be so strange. Sure, I would be using a Sinclair Racing car, and I was racing on their team licence, but I had to pay for that right, a pretty penny in fact. Well, a pretty penny and a fuck-tonne of ugly ones. For all intents and purposes though, it was my car and my team.

On top of the promotion and sponsors, and pit crew, there were the simple logistics of the weekend. We had to get the car to the racetrack, get us into town, and arrange accommodation for the rest of the team. I had a newfound appreciation for all of the office staff at Sinclair Racing. They made it all look so easy. We'd already decided that Alyssa was going to be with me, but because she was going to be there in her official capacity as my manager, Mum was going to be on hand to look after Phoebe for us as well.

Morgan had volunteered to oversee the car on race day, managing the pit crew and race strategy. Thankfully, he'd learned a lot hanging around with Eden over the years and she was teaching him more every day.

My boys had been given the weekend off from Sinclair Racing without even having to ask for it, and they'd already agreed to pit for me. I had to pay them, of course, and I had to get Danny to sign off to allow them to work for me, but it meant I had a crew I trusted to the ends of the earth pitting for me.

The hardest thing to deal with was the doubt in the public mind. I'd heard the rumours circulating ever since the announcement had been made, but each day they seemed to get louder and more persistent.

Two weeks out from Bathurst, I was discussed in depth on the ProV8 show. In a debate featuring current and past drivers, they argued about whether or not I was washed up. They questioned whether I would still be able to handle a V8, especially with no real practice other than my Mini races and two track days that I'd shared with Sinclair Racing.

I'd been asked the same question by almost everyone who had

interviewed me: with such a hex on my career right before my forced retirement, did I feel the pressure to perform? My answer was always the same: yes and no.

I felt the pressure to be successful in the form of putting my nuts on the line with the sponsors. I hadn't started a race for almost twelve months, but I also hadn't successfully finished one in the six months prior to that.

My entire future in a V8 rested on this one race. If I got through the weekend unscathed and managed to finish in a decent position, it would give me the perfect opportunity to renegotiate my position with Sinclair Racing.

Then there was the pressure of the knowledge that every bump, scratch, and dent on the car would come out of my pocket. It was the reason we'd ensured we had contingencies in place, but still . . .

If the car was a write-off, we'd lose everything. That realisation made me appreciate Alyssa's agreement to my wacky plan that much more. I was risking everything we owned, everything we were, on one race, and Alyssa stood behind me 100 percent.

Despite all of the pressure that I faced though, I was actually relatively calm about the upcoming race. There were two reasons for my calm: Alyssa and Phoebe. Just as I'd come to understand at Emmanuel's graveside, I knew no matter what happened on race day, even if I crashed out as spectacularly as I had the last time I drove around Bathurst, they would be there for me. All that mattered to them was that I came home safely.

That meant more than I could imagine.

In addition to working and getting everything ready for the big event, I also had to plan for the race itself. It had been such a long time since I'd properly raced a V8, and my return debut would be in a one-thousand-kilometre race that would last close to eight hours. I spent as much time as I was able to preparing myself physically and mentally as best as I could for the long race.

Part of my preparations included endurance training. I would wake extra early, creep into the gym at home, and spend hours thumping away on the treadmill or the cross-trainer, interval training as best as I could. During those long stretches, I had nothing to occupy my thoughts, so I often found myself recalling the way my life had been just twelve short months ago.

Some days, I tried to envisage what my life would be like if we hadn't met on that plane on the way to London. Would I still be in the dark over my son and daughter? Would I still have my head up my own arse? Would I still be sleeping with random women in a vain attempt to find something that I now realised I would only ever have with Alyssa? One innocent touch from her satisfied me more than a hundred random fucks. The truth was, though, that I couldn't imagine my life without her in it. I hadn't realised how dead I'd been inside until she brought me back to life.

More often than not, the end result of my mornings spent in the gym, and inside my own head, was racing back up to the bedroom and climbing into bed with Alyssa to do our own special stamina training.

It was after one of these "training" sessions that Alyssa turned to me, biting her lip anxiously. She'd been scratching her fingers absent-mindedly across my scalp, but she stilled her hand as she spoke. "I was thinking . . ." She trailed off.

"Yeah," I said, urging her to continue the scratching at least, because it had felt fan-fucking-tastic.

"Well, it's just . . ." She paused again and looked into my eyes, as if trying to assess how I would take whatever she had to say. I tensed a little in preparation, not knowing what it was, but knowing it was obviously important to her. "I've seen the way you're facing this race and everything. You should be scared. Hell, you should be terrified, but you're not. You're cool and calm, and just doing what needs to be done."

"Babe, you know there is a hell of a lot going on down below the surface that no one else gets to see."

She nodded. "Yeah, I know, but you're still willing to face something terrifying in the hope that something good will come out of it."

"I couldn't have done any of it without you by my side."

She smiled sweetly. "I know. It's just that it's made me realise that maybe I need to face some of my own fears in the hope that something good comes of it."

I frowned, utterly thrown by what it was that could be so terrifying for her that would bring something positive.

"So, I was thinking that maybe . . ." She paused again and took a deep breath. "Maybe I should book an appointment to have the Mirena removed? Maybe we should . . . you know, *try*?"

"Try?" I asked stupidly before the impact of her words hit me. I knew much more about the Mirena — the hormone-releasing IUD — than I had when we were in London. I knew the basics of what it was and what it did.

And she . . .

She wanted to remove it.

Which would mean . . .

It would mean . . .

"You want to try for another baby?" I asked almost incredulously as the words sunk in.

She nodded slightly, her eyes showing her raging terror over the idea even as she agreed to it.

"You'd do that for me?" I asked stupidly.

She shook her head. "No, I'd do it for *us*; for all of us. For our family."

I couldn't help the wide, shit-eating grin that spread from ear to ear across my face. I was surprised at the intensity of the warmth that coursed throughout my body at her words. She wanted to try for another baby.

It was more than just the thought. Her agreement meant she truly believed I would be there for her.

She trusted me.

Even though she was scared of what could go wrong, she would do it. For us. It was a momentous fucking decision for her, and I was determined not to fuck it up.

"That would be . . . Wow . . . That would be fucking awesome. Are you sure about this though?"

"Are you?" she asked, throwing my question back at me, and I saw the faintest hint of doubt in her eyes. I realised that her primary fear may have been about what could go wrong, but there was a part of her that was scared of having to face it alone again.

I was the cause of that fear, and it was my responsibility to erase it. Her trust wasn't absolute, but she wanted it to be.

"Absolutely positive. But maybe we should wait until after the race so we have plenty of time to practise." I winked at her. "And then we'll talk about it some more."

CHAPTER THIRTY-THREE

QUALIFIED

BEFORE I KNEW it, it was time.

All of our preparation and all of the stress came down to one event, one weekend, and ultimately to one race.

We travelled to Bathurst on Tuesday, arriving a little after lunch, and set up amongst the other teams. We didn't stand out or draw any excess attention, which was good because it made us feel like we belonged. It felt a little strange arriving so early for a meet, but it was necessary. All the things that Danny and the other office staff had always organised at Sinclair Racing, I now had to do for myself. Things like getting the car scrutineered before the race-meet, having the documents checked, and arranging for Morgan to attend the team managers' briefing.

The other thing I had set up, without Alyssa's knowledge, was that she was never to be left alone. If I wasn't with her, she would be with Mum or Morgan. My boys were keeping an extra eye out for her and Phoebe when they could and even Eden, despite being in the Sinclair Racing shed, had also agreed to watch out for Alyssa. I felt safe in the knowledge that Hunter wouldn't be able to get within one hundred metres of my girls without my knowledge, and that made me feel better about the weekend.

I spent all morning Thursday going over the finer details of the car. It had come to us in pristine condition from Sinclair Racing, but we needed to ensure it was prepped and ready for dealing with the pressure of Bathurst. My boys and I ran through the majority of the checks on the car; we even managed to drag Liam down from the Sinclair Racing sheds to cast his eye over it. We used the excuse that it had to be good for a few extra hours of time against our apprenticeships. He laughed at our cheek, but agreed nonetheless.

Dane and I had already agreed that I would take the first practise session. Not that I needed it any more than him—we were both as fucking rusty as the other—but because I was the one who'd hatched the grand plan; it was my money and reputation on the line, therefore it was only fitting that I was the one to take the V8 out for her first run.

It took me a moment or two to get used to the car. I noticed a few things in my first lap. For example, I had to brake much earlier than I did in the Mini—I realised that very quickly when I took my first corner much too fast and almost ended the weekend long before it had even started.

In exchange, I could accelerate out of the corners faster, which came in handy, although it meant I had to be in the correct racing position that much earlier.

After a lap or two though, I'd found my groove again. My fingers danced across the steering wheel almost as if they'd never been parted from it. My hand jerked through the gears with practised precision. Up. Down. Clutch. Accelerator. Brake. It was a familiar dance with a favourite partner.

Hard to the left, rein in the car with the brakes, and then accelerate hard up Mountain Straight. Hard to the right, roar through the cutting and Reid Park before racing past McPhillamy and into Skyline.

Despite the year that had passed since my last time around this track at this speed, I'd not forgotten the view as I neared the top of the mountain. I took one quick look to calm me, and then I focused back on the car and feeling the way it responded to my touch as I fell through the S bends and into the Dipper. I barely braked for the soft right then jumped down on the pedal before the hard left around Forrest Elbow.

I hit the accelerator hard the moment I was free, and was zooming down Conrod Straight in next to no time.

I couldn't force the smile off my face the whole way around the track. Morgan's voice squawked over my radio regularly, letting me know how the car looked from the outside.

As we got further into the session, I couldn't help having a little fun and ribbing him in reply, telling him that his fiancée's voice was much sweeter in my ears.

When I came in, there was a fifteen-minute window for me to brief Dane about the car, and then I was sitting on the edge of the track watching him drive my money—my family's future—around the track. I finally knew how Danny felt every time I had taken to the track, especially in that last six months.

I probably owed him another apology.

Or six.

"WE'RE GETTING great times," Morgan enthused, reading the in-car telemetry reports together with the official lap times.

"And without getting a single scratch on the car," Alyssa said, winking at me.

I grinned.

"Great job today, everyone!" Dane enthused. It was clear he'd missed being on the track more than he probably ever admitted to himself. After all, he'd retired on his terms—while he was in front. He definitely wasn't past his prime. In fact, some of the current drivers had at least ten years on him. Not to mention he was pumping out lap times that easily matched my own, and were pretty darn close to being on par with the forerunners in the race.

I couldn't help but grin at him too. I considered myself to be lucky to have scored him in my car, despite him being retired.

"Speaking of which," Alyssa murmured before continuing much louder, "whatever result we get in qualifying tomorrow, we're having a team dinner to celebrate. After all, we're here. We're at Bathurst."

A round of cheers broke out among our motley crew.

"Our shout, of course," Alyssa continued. "To say thank you to all of you for the hard work you've put in to get us here."

A little while later, we'd broken up for the night, each heading off to do our own thing, ready to reconvene early Friday morning. Alyssa instructed me that because there was nothing more I could do to organise or plan, I wasn't allowed to stress about anything else. She and Mum had apparently been busy arranging dinner and they'd somehow managed to organise a roast in the shit-arse tiny little caravan oven. The women in my life never ceased to amaze me.

Midway through our meal, Morgan arrived to talk strategy.

"Sure, man." I laughed. "As if you didn't just smell this fuck-awesome meal and want to join in."

Alyssa slapped my arm lightly. "Language," she hissed quietly, shooting a pointed look at Phoebe.

I shot her a smirk in the form of an apology and helped myself to another serve of potatoes. I told myself it was because I needed to carbo-load, but the truth was they were just that fucking delicious that I couldn't get enough of them. I'd forgotten how great Mum's home cooking was.

Alyssa had more manners than I did and invited Morgan to join us. I think he thought about it for all of two seconds before accepting. We ran through our race plan once more, based on the information given in the drivers' briefing, but then the conversation flowed naturally on to other things; like my plans for his bucks' party.

Alyssa and Eden had already vetoed any plans for us to strip at Eden's hen night. Instead, I was planning something special for Morgan, and he was going crazy not knowing what it was. I saw Alyssa giving me a knowing smile, because, well, she did know what it was.

Eden had already roped Alyssa into helping organise the wedding because Alyssa was her closest female friend. I think that made her the matron of honour or some shit, but I tended to go into a bit of a trance when the girls started talking about wedding garbage. I'd been there, done that, and never had to go through it again, so it was all wasted information for me.

After dinner, Eden came in search of Morgan, so we invited her in to stay for a while too.

The conversation was easy and the night held no stress. I wondered whether Alyssa had planned it that way, but I had no way of knowing for sure. All I knew was that by the time Eden and Morgan left and Phoebe was in bed, I'd had no time to panic about what might happen the next day, which was a good thing.

I needed to stay out of my own head in order to stay sane.

Alyssa invited me to go for a walk in the evening air. Never one to miss an opportunity for some alone time with my wife, I agreed readily. We grabbed our jumpers and headed out into the dark.

I wrapped my arm around Alyssa's shoulders as we wandered aimlessly around the campsite. A number of people recognised me, some shouted out in support, others gave a call of gentle ribbing — clearly they were Ford fans — and a few even came up to ask for my autograph.

"I wanna be able to say I was there to witness your triumphant return," one bloke said to me as I signed his shirt.

Just as she had so long ago when I'd been swamped at Dreamworld, Alyssa stood back and took it all in stride. I remembered what she had pointed out to me then — that my messy little pen marks made people happy. It definitely made the idea of autograph hounds seem less predatory and actually made me relax and enjoy the process a little more. These people cared whether I drove or not. It mattered to them, which made it matter all the more to me.

Eventually, our walk took us out of the more crowded areas, and we were able to find some alone time.

"Thank you for everything you've done to get me here," I murmured as I pulled her closer to me.

She rested her head against my chest. "I've actually really enjoyed doing it. More than I ever thought possible. Thank you for giving me the push I needed to do it."

"I'm glad you've enjoyed it. I'm sure getting the opportunity to boss me around helps." I chuckled.

"Oh, definitely." She laughed. "That's the best perk."

I guided her chin up so she was looking at me. "You can order me around some more right now if you like," I murmured, with more than a hint of lust in my voice.

She whimpered softly as I captured her mouth, effectively stopping her from being able to issue any orders. My tongue met hers. Despite having incredibly intimate knowledge of her body and soul, I was always willing to explore some more.

After we'd broken apart for some oxygen, I rested my forehead against hers. "It's a dream come true."

"All this?" She indicated the camping ground and track behind us.

"No, you. Well, you and Phoebe. My life now. Just all of it. This . . ." I grinned at her and inclined my head in the direction she'd indicated. "This is just the icing on the cake."

"I love you, Declan," she said. As if there were any doubt.

"I love you too, baby."

I kissed her again, and she shivered against me. As much as I would have loved to strip her down and fuck her silly while we had time alone and without any other pressing matters, I knew it was too cold for me to do that.

FRIDAY MORNING passed in much the same fashion as Thursday had. A few more tweaks, a little fine-tuning, and driving around the track with the utmost care. Alyssa schmoozed with the sponsors a little and we all had plenty of team photos taken.

Despite not being part of the official Sinclair Racing outfit, there always seemed to be at least one member of their staff hanging around in our pits. More often than not, it was Eden, but once or twice it was Liam or Mia.

Finally, it was Friday afternoon and it was time for the

qualifying laps. During the practise sessions, I'd been relatively easy on the car, testing the waters so to speak, but for qualifying I had to go out as if I were under race conditions. I had to work out what my best was, and then go one better.

I slid the HANS device over my head before placing my helmet on over the top. The butterflies in my stomach were dive-bombing around as I climbed into the car. I closed my eyes for a tiny moment. As much as I had enjoyed wielding a wrench for Liam, it was nothing compared to the feeling of euphoria that was building within me, knowing that I was moments away from changing my life. I put the netting up on the window and gripped the steering wheel tightly. I pulled the straps on the racing harness tight, and was utterly unable to help the fact that I was grinning like a schoolboy.

Once Morgan had called out the all-clear into his mic, I started the car. I hummed contently as I listened to the purr of the engine. My mouth was dry due to my anticipation, so I took a deep drag on my water line. Nothing could beat the feeling of being in control of a V8 — well . . . almost nothing.

I thought back to early that day, to being with my girls as we prepared for the day at the track. Somewhere nearby, in the stands, they were watching, waiting for me to show the crowd that I was still able to do this. That despite rumours to the contrary, I wasn't washed up. I revved the engine and the deep thrum that issued was like the sound of the gods.

I edged forward from my pit before taking my time to get to the end of pit lane. It didn't matter when I hit the track. All that mattered was I had twenty minutes to qualify. Twenty minutes to get my beast around the track as fast as I could. Twenty minutes to justify the faith Danny was putting in me for this meet, and the time and cost Alyssa and I had invested.

I tried not to remind myself that the last time I had driven a ProV8 — really driven, under race conditions and not just for track days or the practice laps the day before — was at last year's Bathurst.

As soon as I hit the end of pit lane, I slammed my foot to the floor and quickly made my way through the gears. I may have been a little rusty compared to how I'd once raced but at that moment, that didn't matter. All that mattered was I was in a car again. I was *racing* again.

I could almost feel Alyssa's eyes burning into me as I pushed the car to the edge. I was trying everything I could to get the best time I could. I was desperate to make the Top 10 Shootout, if only to get the opportunity to have a practise run at the real race.

Morgan's voice issued regularly from my headphones, letting me know my current times. They were good, but they weren't quite good enough. At least they were competitive though. I was showing everyone who was watching that I could still do it; I *did* still have it. There would be no more debates. I was earning my right to be on the track the only way I ever could, lap by lap, second by second.

The end of qualifying was called, and I brought the car back into pit lane.

Morgan raced over to me while I was getting out of my race gear, and I couldn't help but grin widely at him.

"Fuck, I missed that!" I exclaimed when he was near enough to hear me.

"You looked good out there, man." He whistled. "It made me want to be out there with you."

"Next year, we'll both be out there, you just watch."

He grinned wickedly at me.

"So?" I asked.

"So, what?" He feigned innocence.

"Put me out of my misery. How'd I do?"

He winced. "Eleventh."

"Fuck!" I felt a stab of disappointment that I hadn't made it into the Top 10 Shootout, but then I realised I'd qualified eleventh. Out of thirty-one cars, I'd finished eleventh fastest. I was in the top half of the field without big-team backing. "Eleventh!"

"It puts us in decent standing for the race," Morgan said soothingly, obviously not picking up on the change in my tone.

Alyssa, Mum, and Phoebe all arrived a second later. I scooped Phoebe up in my arms and wrapped my arms around Alyssa. "Eleventh!" I whooped excitedly.

"You're silly, Daddy," Phoebe squealed as I spun her around in my arms.

"Nuh-uh," I said. "I'm eleventh!"

She giggled.

Mum came up to me and gave me a gentle squeeze. "I'm so proud of you."

I blushed slightly before shrugging out of her grip. I didn't want to hurt her feelings, but I also didn't want the boys to see. It was bad enough having the reputation of being pussy-whipped, I didn't need to add mama's boy to that as well.

We all spent the next hour celebrating the fact that we'd qualified in what was, for all intents and purposes, a very competitive position. Eventually, I had to go and see to some more of the official business before we were able to leave the track for the team dinner.

When I arrived back in the pit, I hollered out a ten-minute warning for the maxi taxis I'd ordered to take us out.

Everyone was gathered around moments later, including my pit boys who just two seconds earlier had been buried up to their necks under the bonnet of the car. I looked over and saw that the beast was all back together and closed up. It didn't take them long to come running when food was mentioned.

We found a nice little steakhouse close to the track and set up for a good night of fun and friendship. The conversation flowed rapidly around the table, but the booze didn't. Everyone wanted to stay fresh for the weekend.

CHAPTER THIRTY-FOUR

FAITH

SATURDAY WAS A relatively easy day. I basically stayed close to my girls other than when I was needed for another practise session or some media commitment. The autograph hounds were out in force, but I just signed what I could and hid away for a break whenever I desperately needed one.

I watched wistfully from the sidelines as the Top 10 Shootout occurred. I could feel the excitement rolling through the tracks as all of the TVs showed the current leader and how their split times compared with the other competitors out on the track. I imagined being out there next year. Would I be racing under Sinclair Racing colours? They had two drivers, could they handle a third?

Finally, the shootout was finished and the final results were in. We had our leader board ready for racing the next day. The big race. I kept thinking about the thousand kilometres that would change everything.

Could I do it?

Although I was secretly hoping for a surprise win, the realist in me knew it was unlikely. I thought about what I needed from the weekend and I realised it was simple. The only way I could exorcise my demons was to get around the track cleanly. I couldn't crash out of this race, it was just far too important.

I spent a few moments looking over the grid. Hunter Blake's name was listed in third position. I felt the usual glee at Sinclair Racing starting in such a strong position mixed with the grief over it being Hunter who got them there.

Between the anticipation of what was to come on Sunday and the nerves I felt over what I'd achieved so far, I was literally feeling ill.

By the time the final drivers' briefing rolled around, I was a bundle of nerves. I listened as intently as I could to all the information they were giving out, but most of it went in one ear and out the other. I bounced my leg nervously, desperate to be out of the cloying conditions of the tiny room filled with too many bodies.

It wasn't made any better when it ended and Hunter gave me a deathly sneer and whispered, "I'll see you on the track, fucker. If you make it up the mountain."

I paused, realising that maybe he hadn't been as stupid as I had thought. I began to imagine all sorts of scenarios that involved his car smashing into mine. I couldn't help but wonder whether there was a chance he'd sent the pictures to Danny with some other purpose in mind.

His words played over and over in my head, sending me into a dizzying spiral of negative thoughts. I couldn't shake the worry that maybe I would end up like Morgan . . . or worse.

Hunter's words haunted me for all of about two seconds, because Alyssa, Mum, and Phoebe were waiting right outside of the door for me. Alyssa entwined her fingers around mine and told me that I wasn't to worry about a single thing for the rest of the night.

We had another quiet family dinner, low-key and calm. Just me and the women in my life.

After dinner, and after we'd tucked Phoebe into bed, Alyssa whispered that she had a surprise for me. I followed her out of the caravan, and she led me through the camping ground to the same spot we'd stopped at a few nights ago; only there was now a small domed tent erected on the site.

Alyssa gently pulled on my hand to move me forward, and we

continued until we were almost on top of the tent. She bent down and began to undo the zip. "You looked like you wanted to do something more than *talk* when we were here the other night," she murmured. "And, to be honest, so did I."

I quirked my eyebrow at her and licked my lips. There was no need to ask her what she meant, because it was written clearly in her eyes. I watched as she bent down and climbed in through the open tent flap, and then almost leapt in after her. Even with the excitement of racing and spending so much one-on-one—practically uninterrupted—time with her, I was so desperate for *more*. I turned and instantly zipped the tent back up.

I'd barely finished and turned to face her when her lips were on mine. I wrapped my arms around her tightly in response. Our actions were somewhat limited by the space; the tent was so small that my head pushed into the roof even when I was on my knees.

My lips remained practically glued to Alyssa's as we twisted and bent to remove all of our clothes. Within the tiny space, all I could hear was our breathing and the twin beating of our hearts. It was so dark in the canvas, I could barely make out shapes, and yet my hands knew her so intimately that they knew exactly where to go, where they wanted to go, and set out to explore readily.

Once I was certain every shred of our clothing had been shed, I guided Alyssa to the plush blanket on the ground, supporting her head as I kissed her deeply. My mouth only left hers to begin a new exploration of her skin. Her hands scratched my scalp as I planted soft, open-mouthed kisses against her collarbone and onto her chest.

I took one of her sweet nipples between my lips before sliding my tongue softly along the perfect bud. I gently scraped my teeth along the delicate skin of her breast before bringing her nipple into my mouth again and sucking softly to make her mew beneath me.

My hand found her other breast, and I kneaded it softly before lavishing attention on it with my mouth and tongue.

"Fuck, Alyssa, you taste so good," I whispered against her skin.

"Kiss me," she begged as she twisted her fingers into my hair and tugged lightly.

I slid back up her body and claimed her mouth again,

supporting myself with one hand, leaving the other free to run across her beautiful breasts and smooth stomach. I ran it up and down the length of her body a few times while my tongue continued to tangle sweetly with hers.

Our breaths and heartbeats were still the only sound I could hear, but they were now faster and more urgent than they had been.

I slid my hand across her stomach once more before dropping my fingers down gently to slide against her pussy. The instant my skin touched her heat, she bucked her hips and arched her back, exposing the long column of her throat. I twisted slightly to claim her neck, sucking gently on it as I pressed my fingers against her clit.

I shifted my head down and took her nipple into my mouth again, rolling my tongue across it before sucking and nibbling on it as I pushed two fingers into her.

"Oh, my God," she cried out softly.

I drew the two fingers out, running them up to moisten her clit before gently sliding them back into her again. I repeated the process, slowly teasing her as I continued to taste her skin. I was so fucking hard, wanting her so badly, but I needed to use this time to say a silent thank-you for everything she'd done to get me to Bathurst.

I continued my slow torture—mine and hers—licking and caressing her skin with my mouth while my fingers moved deeper inside of her, until she was practically begging me to fuck her. I shifted my body weight so that I was hovering just millimetres above her, then I brought my lips back to her and kissed her delicately.

She fought slightly to break her mouth away from mine, and in the darkness I could see something was troubling her. I sat back on my haunches, trying to ignore the erection that stood out proudly from my waist and the fact that my head smacked into the canvas of the tent and twisted it out of shape momentarily.

"What is it?" I asked.

"I just ... well, I didn't want anything to happen without warning you first."

I tilted my head in confusion. "Warning me about what?"

"I know we talked about it, and were going to wait, but then the opportunity just came up a few days before we left, and I figured that maybe it was time to just do it, you know?"

I chuckled. "No, I can honestly say that I don't know."

I saw a flash of the white of her teeth as they captured the silky, slightly darker skin of her lips. "Mum forwarded a letter from my doctor last week. It was a follow-up to remind me that it was time for my annual Mirena check-up and, well, I figured why not get it removed while I was there." She was whispering by the time she'd finished her sentence.

"Really?" I could barely believe what she was saying. Was she saying . . .?

"Yeah, but if you've changed your mind, I understand. We don't have to . . . We'll just have to use something else for protection."

I smiled brightly, even though I knew she wouldn't be able to see me. I leaned forward over her again, feeling the warmth radiating from her skin. I lined myself up with her entrance before kissing her softly.

"I want to," I murmured against her mouth.

I pushed against her, moaning as I slid deeply into her. With her right below me, I could make out her features better, and I met her eyes. They communicated her feelings to me so clearly: fear, joy, and love. I tried to show the strength I felt in us.

Knowing that we were utterly unprotected and leaving an element of our lives completely up to fate was scary, but as I moved inside of her, it felt so right. I knew the chances made it unlikely that we would conceive that night, but it was a possibility. If we were that lucky, who knew . . . maybe the magic of Bathurst would run in the veins of our child.

ALYSSA AND I had eventually dressed and snuck back into our caravan very late. I probably should have tried to be in bed earlier, but I figured it probably didn't matter, because I would most likely have just lain awake, unable to sleep anyway. Hunter's words might not have been haunting me, but the upcoming race was.

We woke begrudgingly when the alarm went off well before dawn and, after a light breakfast, headed back to the track for the final preparations.

The team messed around in the pits, changing all of the parts for a fresh run, until it was time for Dane and me to go to the final drivers' meeting. Every second that passed, the nerves in my stomach built. Hunter was remarkably silent throughout the meeting, but bailed me up afterwards, just as we were passing the Sinclair Racing pits.

"I see you're still up to your old tricks after all, *squirt*."

I tried to ignore him and continued walking.

"I mean the late-night, pre-race booty call thing didn't work that well for you last year; you still crashed out after all."

I gritted my teeth but kept moving.

"The chick last night was a bit of a fucking screamer though, wasn't she? I swear I heard her from my hotel."

I tried to put his words out of my mind—I knew he was just trying to psych me out—but it was hard when he was talking about Alyssa so disrespectfully. He definitely knew that Alyssa was my weak spot.

"If you've changed your mind, I understand." He had put on a horrid, nasally, whiny voice which sounded absolutely nothing like my Alyssa, but I froze as I recognised her words. "What the hell is a Mirena anyway?"

I turned, ready to swing, but froze when I saw Danny standing a short distance away behind Hunter. I decided to try to shrug it off. I needed to stop letting the fucker get under my skin. I realised that there was only one way he could have possibly heard *that* part of the conversation.

"At least I have a red-hot woman I can have booty calls with rather than having to skulk around in the darkness, living vicariously through others."

He gaped for a moment, and I took the opportunity to stab at him again.

"It must be such a sad, lonely existence you live," I jibed, trying to get him to bite while Danny was watching and listening. As I'd anticipated, he swung at me, and I ducked easily out of the way.

Danny took that moment to announce his presence by clearing his throat, and Hunter whirled around quickly.

I stood triumphant. Danny had finally borne witness to one of Hunter's calculated attacks on me. I realised it wouldn't change much in the short term; whatever had bound Danny's hands about the photos wouldn't change for some time—maybe the end of the season, maybe the duration of the contract.

"Hunter, don't you have a race to prepare for?" he asked, clearly intending it as a dismissal.

Hunter looked like he was going to argue, but wisely, and disappointingly, kept his mouth shut.

"Declan," Danny said, reaching out his hand to shake mine. "Good luck out there today."

I shook his hand, grinning from ear to ear.

"You're going to need it," Hunter muttered under his breath.

Danny had clearly heard and quickly asked, "You don't think Declan can do it?"

Hunter scoffed. "He's a privateer. They never win."

"Yes, he's a privateer, indeed. In a well-sponsored, well-maintained Sinclair Racing car. I think he has as much chance as anyone else."

I couldn't help the way my spine straightened a little as I listened to the faith Danny was showing in me.

"So long as he doesn't crash the car." Hunter snickered. His eyes flicked to me and somehow I just knew he was referring to Morgan's crash rather than my own. His words from the previous day came back to me, and I grew worried again about whether he had some sort of master plan.

"Why don't we make it interesting?" I said, surprising even myself when I spoke.

"What are you suggesting, Declan? Some sort of wager?" Danny asked with his eyebrow raised. "You know putting money on the outcome is illegal."

"I'm not talking about money." I don't know where the idea had come from, but it was snowballing. I could finally see an easy way to be rid of Hunter for good, and all I had to do was what I was planning on doing anyway. "If I crash out of the race, I'll quit Sinclair Racing, and you'll never hear from me again."

Hunter's mouth lifted into a sick smile. He took far too much enjoyment out of the idea, which made me more concerned that I was right in my thinking—he wanted to try to force me to crash, just like he had done to Morgan.

"And if you don't?" Danny asked, egging me on.

"I don't know," I answered, carefully measuring my words. "What's it worth to you, Hunter?"

He shook his head. "I'm not betting on the race."

I could tell he wanted to, but perhaps he didn't want to play his hand just yet. Not in front of Danny.

"Aw, come on, Hunt," I said his name in such a way that it rhymed with the word I really wanted to call him. "It's your chance to get rid of me." I winked at him.

There was a crowd gathering around us. I could see both my and Hunter's crews lining up to watch our exchange. I knew that if we made the bet—which technically had no legal standing—the loser wouldn't be able to welch without facing some serious repercussions and embarrassment around the company. "Or do you want to admit that you know I'm good enough to get around every single lap without incident."

"Fine. If you actually manage to finish the race, then I'll leave Sinclair Racing."

"Looks like we have something extra to race for," Danny said, meeting my eye and letting me know that he meant something extra for *me* to race for.

If everything went to plan, I was going to be back on the Sinclair Racing team as a ProV8 driver, and Hunter would be gone.

For good.

SITTING ON the grid felt eerily similar to the last start I'd had in a V8; except instead of being in pole position, I had ten cars lined up ahead of me. I closed my eyes and allowed myself to get centred in the last few moments before it was time to go.

My team had done everything possible to get the car to where it needed to be. The car was running the best times we could expect. Now, it would all come down to strategy, pit stops, and driving, and there was only one of those things I could control.

With my eyes closed, I reflected on that fateful race just one year ago and how different it was to the one I was about to run, even though it was the same event. Back then, I'd been avoiding Alyssa. I hadn't known about Phoebe and Emmanuel. In fact, children had been so far from my agenda that they hadn't even been a blip on my radar. I'd been miserable and haunted, and completely unable to admit it to anyone—including myself. When I raced back then, it was because it was the only thing I had left in my life, and I hadn't even been able to do it properly.

Now, things were drastically different.

In comparison, I thought back to the little fist-bump Phoebe had given me moments before I climbed into the car. "Good luck, Daddy," she'd practically shouted as I put my HANS device and helmet on. Then she'd blown me a kiss through the netting.

I closed my hand into a fist around the wheel, delighting in the feel of my wedding band pressing into my finger underneath the hard gloves, as it reminded me that I belonged to Alyssa.

Whatever else happened, I had my family now.

Racing wasn't my whole life any longer; it was just something I enjoyed doing. Hopefully, I would be able to kick some arse and show everyone that I was no longer lost. I wasn't just making a comeback, I was stronger than ever.

I opened my eyes and watched as the marshals cleared the track of all personnel.

"It's nearly time," Morgan told me through my headset. "You ready for this, squirt?"

I gave him the thumbs-up.

"The commentators want to talk to you if you're willing."

"That's fine," I murmured into my mic. I would have preferred some more alone time to meditate, but I no longer needed to cling to my old superstitions and rituals. I could forge new ones, like spending the night before every race with Alyssa, Phoebe's little fist bumping against mine, or wearing the custom helmet Alyssa had designed for my birthday.

A moment after I had given my approval, I heard three voices discussing the start of the race and waited patiently to be addressed.

"It's been quite a while since we've seen our guest on the ProV8 circuit. Let's check in and see what he's up to. We've got Declan Reede talking to us from the starting grid now. How are you feeling, Reede?"

"Pumped. I'm just really excited to get out there and do what I can."

"You've had a very tumultuous year and haven't been in a ProV8 since Bathurst last year. Not only that, but you're racing as a privateer so are doing this all without the backing of the Sinclair Racing team. It seems there is a lot going against you. Do you think that's going to hurt your chances today?"

Arseholes. I should've anticipated the negativity in their question as soon as Morgan had said they wanted to talk to me. Way to kill the mojo. "All I can do is go out there and give it everything I have. I've spent a lot of time getting myself and my priorities sorted out so that I don't have a repeat of last year."

I heard them talking about my crash and listened to the crunching of metal in the archive footage—the fucking vultures must have had it keyed up, ready to go, long before they knew I would mention it.

"Well, everyone up here is excited to see you back. We're behind you and Kent all the way. Best of luck to you, Reede."

"Thanks."

The three commentators left me there, because the race was close to starting. They began talking amongst themselves regarding the star power that Dane Kent brought to my car. I heard a few more sentences about how the fans were rooting for my comeback even though I'd had six months of crashes leading up to my disappearance from the ProV8 circuit.

The connection was finally cut, and I was left to the sounds emanating from the car.

I hoped I could live up to their expectations.

I hoped I could live up to *mine*.

CHAPTER THIRTY-FIVE

RACE YOU

I ALLOWED MYSELF one second of solitude and shut my eyes.

I pressed my foot against the pedal, pushing it deep onto the floor, and listened to the angry snarl that issued from the beast that encased me. The perfect roar of the engine blocked out all other sounds and left me momentarily in peace with my thoughts. Memories of Alyssa and Phoebe danced in my mind. Images of a new addition—a tiny bundle swaddled in yellow, lying lovingly in Alyssa's arms—began to tempt me, fitting perfectly into our existing family.

My lips lifted at the picture my mind had offered up. A familiar sound broke me from my reverie and my eyes snapped open; it was time to go.

Ride on instinct.

Don't think.

Don't overthink.

You know what needs to be done. Just do it.

I can do this.

I will do this.

I only needed to make it through one thousand kilometres without crashing. It didn't matter where I finished, just that I did.

Easy.

I got away cleanly from the starting line, and launched quickly to the left. As soon as I spotted the gap, I weaved my way through the cars to instantly claim two places. My radio blared to life almost immediately with Morgan congratulating me but warning of an incident in front of me. The first corner had claimed a casualty or two, just as it did every year, but there was no safety car, so whoever was involved must have been able to keep racing.

My ears pricked up when Morgan mentioned Hunter's name. I wasn't sure if he was the instigator or whether he'd just been caught up, but he'd brushed against the wall. I smiled as I imagined Danny cursing in his trailer.

It didn't take me long to settle back into rhythm with the car. It was just like dancing with a long-lost lover. No matter how long I'd been away from the game, I would never forget how to bend the car to my control.

My fingers danced across the instruments. Up. Down. Clutch. Accelerator. Brake. One, two, three, four. Hard to the left. Up Mountain Straight. Hard to the right. Through the cutting and Reid Park. Past McPhillamy and into Skyline. The road fell away underneath me, and then I was floating through the S bends into the Dipper. A soft right, followed by a hard left around Forrest Elbow, and then I was flying down Conrod Straight grinning like a lunatic.

I knew the racetrack like the back of my hand, and I was using every bit of that knowledge and my newfound confidence to my advantage.

I passed the start/finish line and it flashed away beneath me.

I smiled again, imagining Alyssa's eyes resting on the car as I raced past the pits.

One lap down; 160 to go.

AT LAP thirty-six, a safety car was called so I took the opportunity to pit. After I'd climbed from the car and seen Dane away safely, I grabbed a bottle of water and settled in behind Morgan to watch the race on the monitors we had. There were less of them than in the Sinclair Racing camp, but it was enough for us. I could see what was happening around Dane, and I could see everyone else's track position.

I watched as Dane used the space I'd earned to push the car faster and faster.

"You two make a great team," Morgan murmured.

"Almost as good as you and I would have been if we could've raced together again."

"Aww, you getting all mushy on me there, Deccy-boy?" Morgan made kissing noises until I punched his shoulder to shut him up. A few of the pit crew laughed until I shot them a warning glare.

"Just keep your eye on Kent and make sure he doesn't crash that car, will you?" I chided Morgan, half-jokingly.

Alyssa, Phoebe, and Mum were hanging around behind the pits. I waved them in with a smile before downing another mouthful of water.

"You're going really—" Alyssa started to talk, but I pressed my finger against her lips to silence her.

"Don't jinx me," I warned.

Alyssa laughed and kissed my fingertips lightly. She then clasped my hand, holding it tightly as she stood beside me while we watched Dane complete lap after lap.

He pitted once, and I focused on the crew as they flew around the car, changing tyres, brakes, and adding extra fuel. I saw Dane give me a thumbs-up through the window and stared after him with renewed excitement as he drove away to complete the last laps of his day. I was going to take the reins back for the last fifty or so laps.

He came in just before lap 110 to hand the car over to me. I couldn't have been happier with the way things were going when he patted me on the back as we changed over.

"Go get 'em," he whispered softly just before securing the netting and shutting the door.

I nodded as much as the HANS device on my neck would allow—which wasn't much—and gave him the thumbs-up.

I would beat Hunter, or die trying.

I DRIFTED PAST McPhillamy and headed into Skyline.

For the first time in the race, I was closing in on Hunter. It had taken almost every one of the laps I'd had left. Everyone had made their final compulsory pit stops and all that remained was to battle out to the end.

I wasn't sure what Hunter was doing, or why I was able to finally gain some ground on him, but I was catching glimpses of him more and more often. It was hard not to feel paranoid even though it was entirely possible he was running the car on a lower throttle for fuel conservation. That would have given me that little bit of extra power over him.

Maybe he'd pitted early, hoping for a safety car—a popular strategy at the Mount Panorama track. If that was the case, he was probably concerned about making it around the track for the remaining laps. More than one car had miscalculated their fuel load and ended up stopping midway through the final lap or two as the tank emptied.

I, on the other hand, still had plenty of fuel left and a relatively fresh set of tyres—perfect for an aggressive push. Dane and I had chosen to pit later in the windows, using the emptier tank and hot tyres to push ahead on the track. So far it seemed to have worked for us, because we were in the top five with no compulsory pit stop left. In the last leg, there had been a little bit of jostling between the cars ahead of us, and I kept swapping places with one of the Ford boys.

If I could position myself correctly through the S bends, I had a chance to get the jump on Hunter and overtake him down Conrod Straight. I wasn't sure whether my car would really have enough in it to get around him, but based on Morgan's voice squawking excitedly in my ear, it was possible.

My lap times were a good half a second ahead of Hunter's.

My current push, if successful, would see me jump out of the fourth-fifth-sixth pack and into the second-third pack. I could almost taste a podium finish. We were barely ten laps away from the end. It could all change in an instant though; the track was notorious for last-lap breakdowns and accidents. The mountain was a cruel mistress. Regardless, I was ahead of where I'd finished the previous year.

I put my concerns about what *might* happen out of my mind and concentrated on what *was* happening. My breathing steadied as I pushed the car into a faster rhythm again. Up. Down. Clutch. Accelerator. Brake. One, two, three, four.

I saw Hunter's brake lights ahead, and then I braked late before pushing hard to the left.

Up Mountain Straight. Hard to the right. Through the cutting. Reid Park. Past McPhillamy and into Skyline. Float through the S bends and the Dipper.

Within a few laps, Morgan informed me I'd cut Hunter's lead from just over a second to mere fractions of one. He didn't need to tell me though, because I could see how close Hunter was. I could feel the slipstream coming from his car embracing mine tightly and tucking me neatly behind his arse. If he was working the fuel conservation angle as I suspected, my position had to be driving him crazy.

We were coming up to the straight; there was just a soft right and then a hard left around Forrest Elbow first. Hunter slammed his brakes aggressively before the hard left, and I had to go wide to avoid running into the back of him. I twisted the car around as quickly as I could, feeling the tail get a little loose on the marbles, but I held control of it. I slammed down a gear and then pushed the accelerator hard, using my position to run door to door with Hunter down Conrod Straight.

As much as I could in the HANS, I turned my head to watch as I raced past him on the outside. I felt like waving, but realised that would have been a little bit too obnoxious; especially considering I was stealing third—his chance for a podium finish—from him.

My place on the outside put me in a perfect position for the soft right coming up, but I needed to ensure that I dominated the track to get ahead of him. And I needed to be sure that I had the line for the sharp left that followed or I'd lose the ground as quickly as I gained it. I pushed as hard as I could, but he lost speed rapidly as we approached the corners.

Without warning, he twisted his car toward me, and if I hadn't been paying so much attention to him, I would've missed his next action. The thought that he'd misjudged the corner and understeered would've crossed my mind if it were any other driver, but I knew him too well. He'd glanced in the direction of my car before he'd flicked the wheel toward me once more.

I turned the car away from him as quickly as I could, sending it wide around the corner and flicking the tail out. It had the intended effect, removing myself from the danger of Hunter's car, but also left me scrambling to get back onto a good line on the track.

Because he didn't have my car to stop his turn as readily, Hunter speared off toward the wall before righting and slotting himself directly behind me. I felt his front bumper scrape my rear bar and winced, wondering momentarily how much that little scrape was going to cost me.

That thought speedily left my head when I realised I was in third place.

I was in *third*.

After everything that had happened over the last year—the last four years, in fact—I couldn't believe I was actually in third as a privateer. More than that, I felt completely in control behind the wheel for the first time ever. Even at the height of my career, I'd never felt so in command of every aspect of my life. I was on a high, and not even Hunter swerving from side to side in my rear-view mirror could bring me down.

Just as I was settling in to try to close in on second, my car lurched forward sickeningly. Hunter had leapt forward on the accelerator behind me, giving my arse a love tap. I cut across his nose, boxing him in before slamming on the gas and launching the car as hard as I could down the straight. Hunter came up the inside of me, edging further alongside my car with each second. He gave my car another love tap, this time on my rear quarter panel—at almost the exact spot he'd hit Morgan's car—and the rear of my car spun loose, allowing him to gain even more ground on me.

I wrestled with the steering wheel and dropped off the accelerator to regain control. I reminded myself that I didn't need to beat him to win the bet, just stay on the track. The old me—the hot-headed one who was angry with the world because of the stupid decisions I'd made—would have chased him down and gained ground on him, stupidly throwing away everything that mattered in the race just to settle my own personal vendetta against the fucker.

A part of me still desperately wanted to, but I didn't.

Instead, I concentrated on solidifying my track position and ignored Hunter as best as I could, while still paying enough attention to be certain that I would be ready for any more smart-arse tricks he had up his sleeve.

I followed Hunter's taillights closely through the rest of the lap, never letting him out of my sight and ensuring he didn't gain even a fraction of a second advantage over me. In almost no time, we were back to the lead-in to Forrest Elbow. This time, I didn't let Hunter get the jump on me. I slammed on the accelerator, took a risk, and snuck up the inside.

I had the racing line. According to CAMS guidelines, he should have relinquished the position to me, but instead he pushed his car heavily into mine. I had two choices, push forward and risk getting tangled up with his car because it was obvious he wasn't playing by the rules anymore—if he ever really had—or back off, allow him to gain the position, and then lodge a complaint with the officials.

"Let him have it." Morgan's voice filled my ear just a fraction of a second after I'd tapped the brakes to get myself out of the fray.

A second later, Morgan informed me that Hunter had already been given the white-and-black flag for unsportsmanlike driving. I couldn't help the smile that spread across my face as I heard the news. Hunter was obviously being relayed the same information, because his car suddenly lurched to the side, allowing me plenty of room.

There was no doubt in my mind that he had something more up his sleeve though, so I was cautious as I crept up alongside him, ensuring I left plenty in reserve. I dialled up my throttle a little more to give myself that extra push I might need to get away.

Our cars were side by side, my door was level with his, when he once again tugged sharply on his steering wheel, but I anticipated his movement perfectly, slamming down a gear, ramming my foot flat to the floor, and accelerating away from him easily. Because of his speed and desperation, his move sent him straight into the barrier.

I heard the crunch of metal on concrete behind me and felt bad. Just not for Hunter.

Instead, I felt terrible for Danny, who'd have to pay for the repairs; for the guys in the Sinclair Racing pit, who'd all worked so hard over the weekend to ensure the car was at its best; and for every other person whose hopes and dreams for the weekend were resting on that arsehole's shoulders.

The yellow flags came out along the track and my stomach began to flutter at the possibilities that had just arisen. We were so close to the finish, just a few laps remaining, and the field was about to be bunched up by the safety car. I could almost taste a victory sweeter than any of my entire career to date.

A victory with my wife and little princess watching.

A victory that I'd had a huge role in orchestrating.

When the cars bunched up, I sat impatiently on the arse of second, twisting the wheel from side to side occasionally to keep the tyres warm.

"Relax." Morgan's voice sounded anything but calm as he issued the command.

"That's easy for you to say," I murmured in response.

"Just finish. That's all you need to do now, squirt. You've already proven yourself to everyone watching."

I clenched my fists tightly around the steering wheel as the lights went off on the safety car. My heart was in my chest, and I could barely even breathe. All I could do was concentrate on the bulk of metal and machine surrounding me.

I felt the car as if it was an extension of my own body. The dents and scratches that Hunter had caused were nothing more than bruises and battle scars. For the weeks after last year's Bathurst, I'd battled with injured ribs. I'd managed. This was no different. The scratches and scrapes wouldn't stop me from

334

achieving what I wanted to.

The safety car peeled away and we were racing again. The car in fourth place tried to take me around the outside, but I was too quick. I darted forward, with the car in front of me squarely in my sights. There were only two laps left in the race, mere minutes to stake my claim after hours and hours on the track.

I stuck to the bumper in front of me like glue, refusing to let him shake me and taking advantage of his slipstream. Slowly, the car behind me slipped further away, until there were spots on the track when I couldn't see him in my rear-view mirror at all.

Before I knew it, I was on the final lap. My heart was still thumping wildly somewhere behind my Adam's apple as I came around the final few turns. I pounced on the driver in front of me as we hit the chase, running through it side by side. He had the speed, but I had the racing line. I darted around until we were side by side again on the run up to the start/finish. I watched as the chequered flags waved excitedly just ahead of me, signalling the arrival of first place.

Crossing the line without claiming the ultimate win didn't affect me the way that it would have just one year earlier. I was easily able to concentrate on what I had achieved, rather than what I hadn't. Everything that had happened over the last year led me to where I was and I couldn't have been happier.

I'd finished the race. That alone was huge. It no longer mattered what position I finished in, just that I finished. I had achieved what I had set out to, and I hadn't let Alyssa's hard work be in vain.

That I'd finished on the podium with my pride intact was fan-fucking-tastic.

As I climbed out of the car, I could hear camera shutters whirring all around me, but I only had eyes for two people.

Morgan and Dane raced out, followed closely by the boys from the pits. I was slapped on the back and congratulated repeatedly, but I walked past them all in a daze. At the back of the rabble, Alyssa stood, wearing a small, triumphant smile and a look in her eyes that told me she hadn't doubted my ability for a second.

Phoebe was perched on her hip, shouting loudly to be heard over the din around them.

The sounds and people around me faded to white noise, a slight humming with only a few key words standing out. *Third place. Terrific achievement. Rare accomplishment for a privateer.*

Instead, I heard Phoebe's words as if she were shouting them to me across an empty room. "Yay! Daddy won!"

I took another step forward and it felt like time stood still. It was like a dream where no matter how fast I could run, it wasn't fast enough. I wanted to already be by Alyssa's side, but instead I had to cover a great distance. Another step through the crowd and slowly my boys began to realise what I was after—or more specifically *who*.

My path cleared gradually and the faces whirled past me in a blur as I broke into a run toward the two people who meant the most to me.

As soon as I was close enough, I hugged the two of them tightly. I gave them each a kiss on the cheek. I wanted to say something meaningful or poignant, or just . . . anything.

But I couldn't.

I was completely lost for words. When I met Alyssa's eyes though, I realised there was nothing more that needed to be said.

Everything was exactly as it was supposed to be.

And the rest of our lives were only just beginning.

EPILOGUE: SWEET VICTORY

I RAN MY finger over the photo on the wall across from Phoebe's room—a picture of me on the podium as champagne flowed freely. It was my permanent reminder of the sweetest victory I'd ever experienced, and she'd insisted I hang it where she'd see it every day. I could never have guessed my placing third would mean so much to her.

Even now, almost six years later and heading toward her tenth birthday, she wouldn't let me move it. Honestly, I couldn't think of a win or placing in the rest of my career as a driver that meant more to me than that one either.

The days, weeks, and months that followed that meeting were some of the most interesting I'd ever lived through.

WHEN I'D returned to Sinclair Racing after placing third at Bathurst, I didn't think I'd ever seen happier faces. Everyone had congratulated me and slapped my back. I didn't think a single person was upset that Hunter had crashed or that I had beaten him in our little bet.

Surprisingly—or maybe not so surprisingly, given his personality—Hunter arrived at work shortly after me. He laughed off our bet and refused to acknowledge the fact that he'd lost or that he was effectively welching on the deal.

It had taken him a little over an hour to confront me. There was little doubt that he wanted to approach me sooner, but didn't want to do it around anyone else. He was up to his old tricks again, but somehow they didn't bother me anymore. They couldn't. It was like

I was impervious to his bullshit. In fact, I even had a plan to deal with him. Well, a plan that Danny and I had hatched together.

It started with the new security cameras Danny had included in the sheds, and ended with ensuring I was down there alone. When Hunter appeared around the corner, ready to strike, I slipped my hand into my pocket and leaned against the conference table, waiting for him to act.

"You think you're so fucking clever, don't you?" Hunter hissed.

"I don't know what you are talking about."

"Ducking and weaving like that on the track," he seethed.

I shrugged, smirking at the very idea of him being kicked out of Sinclair. "I was just driving to the conditions you created."

"Like fuck, you little shit! You knew exactly what you were doing. You made me crash." He was trying to stay quiet, but I knew he could lose it at any time.

I laughed and crossed my arms over my chest. "Oh no, Hunter, you did that all on your own."

"The marshals investigated me because of your stunts."

"My stunts? The marshals investigated you because you were driving like a fucking lunatic. It was nothing less than you deserved." In fact, he'd received much less than he should have in my opinion. The officials couldn't do more than issue a warning, because he hadn't caused any damage to any other vehicle. To top it off, there was no evidence that his erratic driving was malicious.

"Why didn't you just stay the fuck off the track?"

I smirked. "I thought you wanted me there."

He narrowed his eyes at me.

"What? Are you afraid of a little competition?"

"I'm going to fuck you up the first chance I get," he threatened.

I looked around, dropped my wrench back into my toolbox, and held my arms out. Then I took a couple of steps to the right. I wanted to ensure his best angle was captured on the cameras. "We're alone now."

He laughed. "I'm going to fuck you up good and proper." He didn't move toward me though. He obviously realised I wasn't going to bite, so he changed tack and began to talk about Alyssa.

"Or maybe I should just fuck your wife instead?"

I tilted my head to one side and regarded him. He had a certain menace about him, there was no denying that, but I was done letting it get to me. There was nothing he could do to hurt me or my girls; I had too many people watching out for me now. How I had ever let him under my skin before was beyond me. He was all bluster and bullshit, and I found myself laughing at the ridiculousness of it.

My laughter seemed to be the catalyst for Hunter, who drew his arm back and swung at me. It connected with my cheek, just below my eye. It didn't hurt, but the shock sent me staggering back half a step until I could right myself. People who'd been congregating nearby heard the scuffle and in an instant, the room flooded with people. Before I could fully comprehend what was happening, Hunter was being escorted from the premises by security and Danny had his evidence in the form of a video of Hunter's attack on the company CCTV.

Danny was on hand almost immediately to ensure that I filed a police report about Hunter's actions, no doubt to ensure there was a justifiable reason to break the contract. In turn, Hunter threatened to press charges against me for Bathurst, but nothing more came of it before he disappeared. I could only assume someone warned him that the situation would be worse for him than for me if the reason behind my fury came to light.

It would have been nice to say that Hunter got everything he deserved in the years since, but I honestly didn't know if he did. As far as the media was concerned, there was a whirl of controversy over his sudden departure from the Sinclair Racing camp. Alyssa and I organised an AVO against him, ensuring he would keep his distance from us.

The last we'd heard of him, he was in the United States, racing trucks or some shit.

After Hunter's departure, Danny had been in need of a new driver. Morgan's doctors were still unwilling to sign off on his injuries, which meant he was unable to drive for a little while longer—at least until the new season. Finding himself driverless,

Danny did the only logical thing he could. He recruited a driver who'd come back from hiatus to race, and place, at Bathurst.

Dane Kent accepted the offer impossibly fast; probably because the time away from the track, followed by such a successful run at Bathurst, had rekindled his love of racing.

Even though I'd spent the better part of the year desperate to be back in the main seat, I wasn't upset that Dane had been offered Hunter's place. In fact, I'd been the one who'd suggested the placement. I'd been more than happy to continue my apprenticeship and complete the Micro Challenge to see out my year.

The main reason I was okay with it was that I had my own ideas for what the new racing year would bring for me. My small taste at team ownership had changed my entire perspective. On top of that, the persistent rumours that Wood Racing was struggling because Paige had been unable to secure a decent driver, and therefore the almighty sponsorship dollar, hadn't escaped my attention. After consulting with Alyssa, and getting her agreement, we came up with a plan.

When I'd approached Danny with my idea, around the same time I'd suggested Dane as a replacement for Hunter, he'd been more than supportive. Between the two of us, we were able to knock out a deal with Paige that would see the end of an era for her, but the start of a new one for me. Emmanuel Racing, a subsidiary of Sinclair, was to be raised from the ashes of Wood Racing. Based in Brisbane, my team would operate out of the former Wood premises.

I'd ridden the high of my Bathurst result and the contract on Wood Racing for a long time. The euphoria of my career highs took me right through to Christmas of that year. That was when Morgan and Eden had used the staff Christmas party to announce a little surprise. They had wanted to wait for Morgan to make a full recovery before getting married, but had used that time for their own form of physical therapy. All that therapy earned them something else. They were expecting. Alyssa and I had given each other a secret smile, hoping that we might have our own announcement before too long.

It was only later that week, when Christmas day rolled around, that I discovered Alyssa's smile had held a few more secrets than my own, and every career achievement took a back seat to the knowledge that I was going to be a daddy again—and this time, I'd have the opportunity to do it right from the beginning.

I threw myself into researching pregnancy and childbirth. I didn't care if she'd been there and done that; I hadn't, and I wanted to make sure I was prepared now that it was real and happening. Phoebe was beyond excited when we told her we'd have a new little brother or sister for her, due near her birthday.

The new year brought our belated honeymoon to London, where I'd fussed over everything Alyssa ate, touched, and did. Whenever she couldn't get a seat on the tube or a bus, I would growl and complain until people vacated theirs. There was nothing I wouldn't do to make her pregnancy as comfortable and safe as possible. Truthfully, I probably pissed her off to no end. It was testament to her love for me that she didn't snap at me for being over the top. Of course, that didn't mean I escaped the hormones scot-free.

To facilitate the start of the new team, my little family had moved back to Brisbane soon after returning from our overseas trip. By March, we were settled in a new house in Ormeau, and Phoebe had started her prep year at school. Even though Alyssa never said it in so many words, I think she loved the fact that we were close to her family again. It was probably one of the main reasons she'd agreed to take the risk of team ownership.

As per our deal, Paige stayed on as team manager during the transitional year, but I was secure in the knowledge that I was ultimately her boss.

Initially, we'd run just the one car, but after three years of running a successful team, an opportunity had come up to purchase an additional CAMS licence from another dying company. We'd jumped at the chance to run two main cars, plus one in the production series. The business may have been a success, but neither Alyssa nor I were willing to overlook a new avenue for expansion. I was savvier with contracts than I had ever been before, and I had Alyssa to thank for that.

Even now, so many years later, Danny was still a silent partner. I'd offered to buy him out a couple of times, but he wasn't silly. He liked the return on investment he received, without having to be hands-on running two teams. Ultimately though, he caused me no stress so I was content with the partnership. In fact, without the heavy mentoring he'd given during the first few years, Emmanuel Racing might never have been the success it was.

The only sad thing for me was that the current season was my final year racing. I needed to spend more time nurturing new talent and ensuring we were competitive year after year, well into the future and long after my own retirement.

"Sweetie, it's time," Alyssa murmured from behind me, startling me away from my memories.

"Yeah?" I asked, placing my hand over her swollen belly. It wasn't my first rodeo, but somehow the moment managed to make me nervous every time.

She nodded. "They're very close together now. Just a couple of minutes."

It would be easy to assume that having been through the whole baby thing before, it would get easier, but no. I was as unsure as I had been the other times, first with Brock five years ago, and then with Beth a little over a year after that.

My palms were sweaty as I grabbed Alyssa's hospital bag and the car keys.

"Remember, you're not racing now." Alyssa grinned to let me know she was joking, right before biting her lip and folding in half as the pain of another contraction hit.

I placed my hand on the small of her back and massaged tiny circles until she stood again and shuffled forward a little more.

"Mum, Dad, we're going now!" I called out, ensuring the babysitters knew they were up to the plate.

Curtis stepped out and helped me guide Alyssa into the car.

"You take care of my baby now," he warned after she was safely in, pointing his index finger at me and giving me a stern look.

"I always do."

He nodded and smiled. "I know."

It had been a hard road, getting Curtis onside, but eventually we'd found common ground—Alyssa and his grandkids—and it was almost impossible to imagine how much I used to fear him or how much animosity had been between us.

"Stop daydreaming and let's go," Alyssa demanded, leaning across the car to shout through the driver-side window.

"Yes, boss."

ALYSSA'S FACE was flushed and sweat made her hair cling to her. She was exhausted and showed the obvious signs of being awake for almost twenty-four hours straight. I didn't care about any of that though, because in her arms she held yet another tiny miracle.

Each time I'd witnessed one of our perfect children come into the world, I longed to get right on to creating another. I couldn't believe that I'd ever *not* wanted kids. I didn't think I'd ever get sick of having more.

Alyssa, however, tended to disagree. In fact, I was certain she would declare that this time was her last, just like she had after each of the others.

As I plucked our son from Alyssa's hold so she could go freshen up, I knew I had, at most, half an hour alone with them both before the horde showed up. It was times like those that I was glad we'd made the shift back to Brisbane. I thought about how lucky I was to be so close to family and friends.

I was contemplating how lucky I was and had become lost in the eyes of my third-born son when I heard Josh's voice.

"Is he daydreaming again?" Josh's laughter filled the air.

"He does it a lot." Alyssa was smiling, the signs of fatigue washed away by the shower she'd had while I'd grown acquainted with little Parker.

"Is this the little one who's caused you so much trouble?" Ruby asked, reaching out to take Parker from my arms.

Alyssa grimaced at the memory of what had been a terrible

pregnancy; one that had included morning sickness, fainting, fatigue, and two stays in hospital. "That's the one. The last one," she added, shooting me a pointed glance.

"Maybe," I said as I sat on Alyssa's bed, pulling her in to my side as she cuddled up against me. Noah gave me a shy smile as he waved from behind Ruby's legs. It was hard to believe that the boisterous and outspoken parents that were Ruby and Josh could have produced such a quiet little man.

"When are Mum and Dad getting here?" Alyssa asked.

"As soon as they can get Beth into her car seat, no doubt." Ruby laughed.

"Yeah, they were struggling with that when they rang me earlier," Josh said.

I laughed. Besides Phoebe, Beth was certainly the one most like me. At two, she was a major handful. Surprisingly though, Curtis and Ruth turned up minutes later with the rest of our family. Beth ran over to sit between Alyssa and me on the bed, and Phoebe held Brock's hand. I gave her a smile that I reserved just for her. Although I loved all my kids the same, I'd always feel guilty about not being there for the first few years of her life, and tried everything I could to make it up to her.

Glancing around the room, I wondered vaguely when my own mother would come. As if on cue, she knocked on the door before entering the room.

"Flynn's out in the waiting room," she said as she came in.

"Tell him to sneak in. I'm sure the nurses won't mind." I'd already managed to get most of them onside about the growing number of visitors to our room, with a few smiles and an autograph or two.

Moments later, Mum came back in with Flynn and his boyfriend, Luke. Luke placed a vase of flowers on the side table, giving me a little wink as he did so.

Once, only seven years earlier, I'd thought I had everything figured out. I'd thought I was better off without Alyssa, without kids, without anything or anyone that currently filled the hospital room.

Looking around at all the faces, and feeling the warmth of love surrounding me, I couldn't help but think what a fucking dickhead I'd been.

THE END

Read more about the Reede family in:

ABOUT THE AUTHOR

Michelle Irwin has been many things in her life: a hobbit taking a precious item to a fiery mountain; a young child stepping through the back of a wardrobe into another land; the last human stranded not-quite-alone in space three million years in the future; a young girl willing to fight for the love of a vampire; and a time-travelling madman in a box. She achieved all of these feats and many more through her voracious reading habit. Eventually, so much reading had to have an effect and the cast of characters inside her mind took over and spilled out onto the page.

Michelle lives in sunny Queensland in the land down under with her surprisingly patient husband and ever-intriguing daughter, carving out precious moments of writing and reading time around her accounts-based day job. A lover of love and overcoming the odds, she primarily writes paranormal and fantasy romance.

Comments, questions, and suggestions for improvements are always welcome. You can reach me at writeonshell@outlook.com or through my website www.michelle-irwin.com. Thanks in advance for your correspondence.

You can also connect with me online via
Facebook: **www.facebook.com/MichelleIrwinAuthor**
Twitter: **www.twitter.com/writeonshell**

Printed in Great Britain
by Amazon